Labyrinth

by

Helen R. Hull

Double 9 BOOKS

Labyrinth

by Helen R. Hull

ISBN: 978-93-71818-97-1

Published by

DOUBLE 9 BOOKS
2/13-B, Ansari Road
Daryaganj, New Delhi – 110002
info@double9books.com
www.double9books.com
Tel. 011-40042856

ABOUT THE AUTHOR

Helen Rose Hull was born on March 28, 1888, in Albion, Michigan, as the eldest child of Warren C. Hull and Minnie Louise McGill Hull. Her father worked as a teacher, school superintendent, and real estate agent, while her mother was a schoolteacher before marriage. Encouraged early by her grandfather Levi T. Hull, who published her stories in his local newspaper, she took on family financial responsibilities with her brother after her father became unemployed following World War I. Hull attended Lansing High School and Michigan State University before becoming an elementary school teacher. Beginning her writing career in 1914, she published seventeen novels and sixty-five short stories over more than fifty years. Her work often focused on family relationships, gender issues, race, and women's economic status, addressing social concerns through character-driven stories. She taught creative writing for four decades at Columbia University alongside her lifelong partner, Mabel Louise Robinson. Hull also taught at Wellesley and Barnard Colleges. She passed away in 1971 at age 83. Notable works include Quest and Islanders, both reflecting on women's roles and social questions of their times.

CONTENTS

PART I AN IDYLL—FROM THE INSIDE

CHAPTER I....................9

CHAPTER II....................14

CHAPTER III....................20

CHAPTER IV....................23

CHAPTER V....................32

CHAPTER VI....................36

CHAPTER VII....................40

CHAPTER VIII....................43

CHAPTER IX....................48

CHAPTER X....................55

CHAPTER XI....................64

PART II BOTH ENDS OF THE CANDLE

CHAPTER I....................69

CHAPTER II....................76

CHAPTER III....................84

CHAPTER IV....................88

CHAPTER V....................93

CHAPTER VI....................103

CHAPTER VII....................110

PART IIIBLIND ALLEYS

CHAPTER I....................112

CHAPTER II 121
CHAPTER III 126
CHAPTER IV 131
CHAPTER V 134
CHAPTER VI 137
CHAPTER VII 144
CHAPTER VIII 148
CHAPTER IX 151
CHAPTER X 156
PART IV ENCOUNTER
CHAPTER I 159
CHAPTER II 164
CHAPTER III 169
CHAPTER IV 175
CHAPTER V 179
CHAPTER VI 184
CHAPTER VII 186
CHAPTER VIII 194
PART V IMPASSE
CHAPTER I 198
CHAPTER II 205
CHAPTER III 207
CHAPTER V 215
CHAPTER VI 219
CHAPTER VII 222
CHAPTER VIII 229
CHAPTER IX 237
CHAPTER X 238

CHAPTER XI 240
CHAPTER XII 246
CHAPTER XIII 250

PART I
AN IDYLL—FROM THE INSIDE

CHAPTER I

"Tell Letty, Muvver. Tell Letty."

"Again? Oh, Letty!" Catherine opened her eyes. Letty, on her stomach, was pointing at a black ant slipping along a grass blade.

"'Nother ant. Tell Letty."

"Don't squirm off the rug, or the ant will crawl up your rompers and take a nip." Catherine looked up through the motionless leaves of the birch trees under which she had spread the rug. "Once there was a busy ant," she began, "and he went out for a walk to find a grain of sand to build his house. His brother went out for a walk, too—" Her thoughts drifted through the story: how close the sky looks, as if the heat had changed its shape, and it rested there just above the tree— "The busy ant found a grain of sand and ran back to his hill to lay it on his house." The haze seems thicker; the forest fires must be worse, no rain forever—

"Uh-h," Letty grunted, and held up her small brown hand, the ant a black smear on her palm.

"Why, Letty!" Catherine pulled herself up on one elbow. "You squashed him!"

"Bad ant. Nip Letty."

Catherine reached for Letty's fist just as a pink tongue touched it.

"Going to eat him, are you? Little anteater." She brushed the ant away and rolled her daughter over into her arm. "You might wait until you are nipped."

Letty chuckled and lay quietly for a minute, while Catherine looked at her. Brown legs and arms, yellow rompers, yellow hair with sun streaks of palest gold, blue eyes squinted in mirth, a round and sturdy chin.

Catherine closed her eyes again. Out from the woods behind them came with the lengthening shadows the odor of sun-warmed firs and dried needles. Quiet—release from heat—from thought.

Suddenly Letty squirmed, pounded her heels vigorously against her mother's knee, rolled over, and began her own method of standing up. Her process consisted of a slow elevation of her rear, until she had made a rounded pyramid of herself. She stood thus, looking gravely around, her hands flat on the rug, her sandaled feet wide apart.

"Hurry up, anteater," jeered Catherine. "You'll have vertigo."

But Letty took her time. Finally erect, she started off across the meadow.

"Here, you!" Catherine sat up. "Where you going?"

"Get Daddy." Letty's voice, surprisingly deep, bounced behind her.

"Wait for me." Catherine stretched to her feet, reluctantly.

Letty would not have waited, except that she stumbled into an ant hill hidden in the long grass, and went down plump on her stomach. So she lay there calmly, turning her head turtle-wise to watch her mother.

Catherine had borne three children without adding a touch of the matron to her slender, long body. In knickers and green smock, her smooth brown hair dragging its heavy coil low down her slim neck, she looked young and strong and like the birch tree under which she stood. There was even the same suggestion of quiet which a breath might dispel, of poise which might at a moment tremble into agitation. The suggestion lay in her long gray eyes, with eagerness half veiled by thin lids and dark lashes, or perhaps in the long, straight lips, too firmly closed.

A shout came up the path between the alders, and Letty scrambled to her feet.

"Daddy!" she shrieked, and headed down the path, Catherine loping easily after her.

There they were, Charles and the two older children, Spencer carrying a string of flounders, Marian with the fish lines hugged under her arm, and Charles between them, each of his hands caught in one of theirs. They stopped as Letty pelted toward them.

"Fishy! Sweet fishy!" Letty reached for the string. Spencer drew it sternly away, and Letty reached again, patting the flat cold flounder on the end.

"Letty, you'll get all dirty and fish smelly." Spencer disapproved.

“Sweet fishy—” Letty’s howl broke off as her father swung her up to his shoulder.

“Fine supper we got, Mother,” said Charles, grinning.

“And I caught two,” cried Spencer, “and Marian caught one—”

“It was bigger’n yours,” said Marian, sadly, “if it was just one.”

“Well, but Marian hollered so when a fish picked at her line and so she scared him off.”

Marian peered up under her shock of dark bobbed hair, and finding a twinkle in Catherine’s eyes, giggled.

“I did holler,” she said. “I like to holler, and fish haven’t any ears and couldn’t hear me—”

“This being the ninth time this discussion has been carried on,” said Charles, “I move we change the subject. Anything will do—”

Spencer sighed. The procession moved up the lane, Father at the head, with Letty making loud “Glumph! Glumphs!” as his rubber boots talked, Spencer next, trying to space his smaller boots just in his father’s footsteps, and Marian with Catherine at the rear.

“Who’s going to clean those fish?” Catherine wrinkled her nose.

“Well, we caught them. Division of labor, eh, Spencer?”

“The male has the sport, and the female the disgusting task of removing the vitals, I suppose.”

“Amelia won’t,” announced Marian. “She said she couldn’t clean fish, it turned her stomach.”

“I wouldn’t keep a maid that wouldn’t clean fish.” Charles dropped Letty on the broad granite step of the farmhouse, and settled beside her. “Who’ll get me some shoes?” He hauled at his red rubber boot, and the clam mud flew off in a shower.

Letty grabbed again at the string of fish as Spencer stood incautiously near her.

“Take them into the sink, Spen,” said Catherine. “Marian, can you find Daddy’s sneakers? You’ll all need a scrub, I’ll say.”

She looked at them a moment. Marian, dark; irregular small features, tanned to an olive brown; slim as witch grass. Spencer, stocky, with fair cropped head and long gray eyes like her own. Charles—he looked heavier, and certainly well; the sun had left a white streak under the brim of his battered hat and behind his spectacles, but the rest of his face was fiery.

"Cold cream for you, old man," she said. "You aren't used to our Maine sun and sea burn."

"I think I'll be a captain," said Spencer, seriously, turning from his opening of the door. "And fight. Like father." He gazed admiringly at the old service hat on the step.

Catherine's mouth shut grimly and her lids drooped over her eyes.

"Plan some other career, my son. Your father didn't fight, anyway. Did he say he did?"

"Now, Catherine, I just told them about the camp at Brest."

Catherine looked at her husband, a long, quiet glance. Then she followed Spencer into the kitchen.

"Oh, 'Melia!" The heat from the stove rushed at her. "You built a fire to-night!"

"Yes, I did." Amelia, a small, wiry, faded Maine woman, turned from the table. "That oil stove's acting queer, and anyways, it don't seem as if you could fry fish on it."

"We might eat them raw, then, instead of sweltering." Catherine pushed her sleeves above her elbows, and reached for a knife.

"Now that's a real pretty ketch, ain't it?" Amelia nodded at Spencer, who watched while the flounders were slipped from the cord into the sink.

Catherine cleaned the fish. She left Amelia to fry them while she set the table. The heat from the kitchen crept into the long, low dining room. Then Catherine drew Letty, protesting shrilly, into the bedroom, where she undressed and bathed her. When she had slipped the nightie over the small yellow head, she kissed her. "Now you find Daddy, and I'll have Amelia bring your milk out to the porch."

She called Marian, who came on a run, peeling her jumper over her head.

"Can I put on my white sailor suit to show Daddy, Muvver?" She dragged it from the clothes-press. "Oooh! That's cold water!" She wriggled under Catherine's swift fingers.

"There, little eel." Catherine knotted the blue tie. "Run along. Where's Spencer?"

"He's washing hisself, I think." Marian smoothed up her blue sock with a little preening motion, and vanished.

"Mis' Hammond!" came Amelia's thin call, and Catherine went back to the kitchen.

Letty was in bed on the porch, her smeary white duck sitting on the pillow beside her, her deep little voice running on in an unintelligible story of the day.

"Supper ready, Catherine?" Father stood in the doorway of the dining room, Marian and Spencer at his heels. "We fishermen are starved. Oh, you aren't dressed yet."

"I'm as dressed as I shall be." Catherine pushed her hair back from a moist forehead. "Let's eat."

"Well, we like to see you dressed up like a lady once a day, don't we?" Charles grinned at her as he pulled up his chair.

Catherine felt her hands twitch in her lap. "Steady," she warned herself. "He's just joking. I've been busy—I should have dressed this afternoon—"

"Some flounder!" Charles bit into the golden brown fish. "What you been doing all the time, Catherine, while we went provender hunting?"

"Thinking," said Catherine slowly. "That is, I thought in between Letty's demands for more story."

"What did you think about, Mother?" Spencer's face lighted with quick curiosity.

"Some about you, Spencer, and some about Marian and Letty, and some about Daddy, and mostly about—me." Catherine was serving the salad. She had deft, slim hands with long fingers, and her movements were slow and beautifully exact.

"What about us?" asked Marian.

"I have to think some more, first." Catherine looked up at Charles. "A lot more."

CHAPTER II

The house was a gray mass in the evening, with one pale yellow window where the kitchen lamp shone. Catherine lay motionless in the wicker lounge on the low front veranda. Amelia had gone home. Spencer and Marian were asleep. Charles had gone to the village store for tobacco. Down below the house the smoke and heat mist veiled the transparency of the sea. So still was the night that Catherine heard the faint "mrrr" of wings of a huge gray moth that flew against her cheek and then away.

"Queer," she thought. "If the house were empty, it would have many sounds, rustles and squeaks and stirrings. But because children sleep there, it is quiet. As if the old ghosts and spirits stood on tiptoe, peeking at the intruders."

She stretched lazily, and relaxed again. The loudest sound in the night was her own soft breathing. Then, faintly, the gravel in the path slipped. Charles was coming back.

Catherine dropped her feet over the edge of the couch and clasped her arms about her knees. When he comes, she thought, I will tell him. If I go on thinking in the dark, I'll fly to bits.

She could see him, darker than the bushes, moving toward her. Then she could smell his pipe.

"Hello!" she called softly, and he crossed the grass to the steps.

"Say, what a night! And what a place!" He slapped his hat beside him, and sat down at Catherine's feet, backed against the pillar. "It's been fierce in town to-day, I'll bet. You're lucky to be able to stay here." He puffed, and the smoke moved in a cloud about the indistinct outline of his face. "Wish I could!"

"When are you going?"

"To-morrow night." Charles sounded aggrieved. "I wrote you I had just the week-end."

"I hoped you might manage a little longer—"

"Can't manage that conference on Monday without being there."

"What conference is that?" Catherine swung one knee over the other; as she watched the face there in the dark, she could feel its expression, although the features were so vague.

"The committee on psychological work in the schools. You remember? Planning it all through the East. It's a big thing."

"Oh, that new committee." Catherine was apathetic.

"That woman I spoke of, Stella Partridge, is mighty keen. She's working out an organization scheme that beats any plan I've seen. I tell you what, old girl, it's great to see the world wake up and swing around to asking for what you want to give it!" Charles cuffed at her foot. "Remember that first year down here? With Spencer a baby, and buying this old house a tremendous undertaking, and me writing a book that I didn't dare hope would sell? Things are different now, aren't they?"

"They are different." Catherine's voice hardened subtly. "I helped with that book, didn't I?"

"Jove! I should say you did. All that typing, and correcting, and then the proof reading."

"And now—" Catherine hesitated.

"Well, now my work has broadened out so much, and there are the three children. I can afford to hire the typing done now, eh what?"

"Yes."

"What's the matter with you, Catherine? You've had a kind of chip about you somewhere ever since I came this time. I can't help it if I can't spend all my time playing in the country with you and the children, can I? After all, I have to see to my work, and it's increasingly demanding."

"I haven't any chip on my shoulder, Charles?" Catherine caught her breath. "I do want to talk to you."

"Fire ahead." Charles tapped out the ashes from his pipe and reached up for her hand. "What's eating you?"

"Oh, Charles!" Catherine's slender fingers shut inside his warm palm. "Help me out! You ought to understand." Her laugh shivered off abruptly. "You know I'm proud of you, just puffed up. Do you know I'm jealous, too? Jealous as—as nettles!"

"Huh? Jealous? What about? Come down here, where I can hug you."

"No. I don't want to be loved. I want to talk. I'm not jealous about your love. I guess you love me, when you think of it—"

"Now, Cathy, you aren't turning into a foolish woman."

"I'm turning into something awful! That's why I've got to do something. It's your work, I'm jealous of."

"Why, my work doesn't touch my feeling about you."

"That's not what I mean. I mean I'm proud of you, every one is, and you aren't proud of me. No one is. No one could be. I'm—"

"Why, Cathy! I am! You're a wonder with the children. And the way you've stood back of me. What are you talking about?"

"I don't want to get emotional. I want to make you see what I've been thinking about. All the nights this summer while I've sat here at the end of the day. I've tried to think—my mind is coated with fat, my thoughts creak. Charles"—her voice trembled—"can you imagine yourself in my place, all summer, or all last year, or the year before? Planning meals or clothes—instead of conferences? Telling stories to Letty. Holding yourself down on the level of children, to meet them, or answer them, or understand them, until you scarcely have a grown-up thought? Before Letty was born, and the year after, of course I wasn't very well. That makes a difference. But now I am. What am I going to do? Could you stand it?"

"But, Catherine, a man—"

"If you tell me a man is different, I'll stop talking!" Catherine cried out.

"I was going to make a scientific statement." Charles stopped, the tolerant good nature of his voice touching Catherine like salt in a cut finger. "To the effect," he went on, "that usually a man's ego is stronger, and a woman's maternal instinct drowns her ego, so that she can live in a situation which would be intolerable to a man."

"Well, then, I'm egoistic to the root." Catherine jerked her hand away from his grasp. "At any rate, the situation is intolerable."

"Poor old girl!" Charles patted her knee. "The summer has been dull, hasn't it?"

"It's not just that. Do you know, I was almost happier while you were in France and I was working—than I am now!"

"Didn't care if I did get hit by a shell, eh? Didn't miss me at all?"

"I did, and you know it." Catherine was silent, her eyes straining toward him in the darkness.

"That was part of the war excitement, wasn't it?"

"No. But something happened in me when you told me you were going. I had been living just in you, you and the two children. I thought that was all I ever wanted. And I thought you felt toward me the same way. Then—you could throw it over—because you wanted something else."

"Catherine, we've had that out dozens of times. You know it was a chance for the experience of a lifetime, psychological work in those hospitals. And then—well, I had to get in it."

"I know. I didn't say a word, did I? But I went to work and I liked it. Then you came back—"

"Well?" His word hung tenderly between them.

"Yes." Catherine sighed. "Like falling in love again, wasn't it? Only deeper. And we wanted Letty." Her voice quavered again. "That's it! I love you so much. But you don't sit down in your love—and devour it—and let it devour you. It isn't right, Charles, help me! I"—she laughed faintly—"I'm like your shell-shocked soldiers. You couldn't really cure them until peace came. Then they weren't shell-shocked any more. I'm shell-shocked too, and I can't cure myself, and I see no armistice. I'm growing worse. I know why women have hysterics and all sorts of silly diseases. I'll have 'em too in a day or so!"

"Funny, isn't it, when I'd like nothing better than a chance to loaf here with the kids. But you'll get back to town soon and see people, theaters, club—"

"And hear about the whooping cough the Thomases had—and—oh, damn!" Catherine was crying suddenly, broken, stifled sobs.

Charles pulled her down into his arms, holding her firmly against his chest.

"There, old girl! Stop it! What do you want?"

Catherine pushed herself away from him, her hands braced against him.

"I won't be silly." She flung her hand across her eyes. "I'm sorry. But I've tried to figure it out, and I just drop into a great black gulf, and drown!"

"What are you figuring on?" Charles let his fingers travel slowly along the curve of her cheek until they shut softly about her throat.

Catherine held herself sternly away from the comfort of touch.

"I can't endure it, day after day, the same things. Petty manual jobs. And I'm older every day. And soon the children will be grown up, and I'll be flat on the dump heap."

"In a few more years, Cathy, I'll have more money. Now you know we can't afford more servants, I'm sorry."

"I don't want more from you!" Catherine cried out. "I want to do something myself!"

"You know how much you do." Charles scoffed at her, but she caught the hint of scratched pride in his voice. "In the middle-class family the wife is the largest economic factor."

"Charles, if I work out a scheme which puts no more burden on you"—Catherine's breath quickened—"would you mind my going back to work? I've figured it out. How much I'd have to earn to fill my place—"

"You mean—take a job?"

"Yes."

Charles reached for his pipe.

"What would you do about the children?" He cleared his throat. "They seem to need a mother."

"Well, they need a father, too, but not to be a door-mat."

"Everything I think of saying, Catherine, sounds awfully mid-Victorian."

"I know what it all is! You needn't think I don't. But I know the answer to it all, too, so you needn't bother saying it."

"I suppose I better consider myself lucky you aren't expecting me to stay home and take care of Letty. You aren't, are you?"

Catherine laughed. She knew Charles wanted to laugh; he was tired of this serious talk.

"You won't mind, then?" she added, tensely. "You see, if you aren't willing, and interested, I can't do it."

"Try it. Go ahead. I'll bet you'll get sick of it soon enough. After all, you women forget the nuisance of being tied to appointments, rain or shine, toothache or stomachache—"

"Ah-h"—Catherine relaxed in his arms, one hand moving up around his neck. "It has seemed so awful, so serious, thinking it out alone. You are an old dear!"

"All right. Have it your own way." Charles struck his match and held it above the pipe bowl. The light showed his eyes a little amused, a little tender, a little skeptical. It flared out, leaving dancing triangles of orange in the darkness. Catherine shivered. Was he just humoring her, like a child? Not really caring? But she shut her eyes upon the mocking flecks of light and slipped off to the step below him, her head comfortably against his arm.

She was tired, as if she had cut through ropes which had held her erect and taut. She could feel the slight movement of muscles in the arm under her cheek, as Charles sucked away at his pipe. The soft darkness seemed to move up close and sweet about them, with faint rustles in the grass at her feet. Queer that just loving couldn't be enough, when it had such sweetness. Her thoughts drifted off in a warm, tranquil flood of emotion; her self was gone, washed out in this nearness, this quiet. Charles stirred, and unconsciously she waited for a sign from him out of the perfect, enclosed moment.

He spoke.

"I want you to meet Miss Partridge when you come back to town. Great head she's got. We're using her plan of organization in the small towns."

Catherine sat very still. After an instant she lifted her head from his shoulder and yawned audibly.

"I'm sleepy. The day has been so warm," she said, and rose. She kicked against something metallic and stooped to pick up Letty's red pail and shovel, as she passed into the house.

CHAPTER III

"Dark o' the moon! Dark o' the moon! Dark—Mother, see what I found!" Spencer broke his slow chant with a squeal, and dangled above his head the great purple starfish. Sure-footed, like a lithe brown sea animal, he darted over the slippery golden seaweed toward Catherine, who looked up from the shallow green pool over which she had been stooping.

"Lemme see too!" Marian's dark head rose from behind a rock and she stumbled after her brother. Plump! she was down in the treacherous kelp, her serious face scarcely disconcerted. Marian always slipped on the seaweed.

"Isn't he 'normous? He's the 'normousest yet." Spencer laid the star on the rock, bending over to straighten one of the curling arms.

"I found one almost as big," declared Marian, "only pink. And pink's a nicer color. Isn't it, Muvver?"

"If you like it." Catherine took Spencer's sea-chilled fingers in hers and drew them down to the under side of the ledge over the pool. "Feel that?"

"What is it?" Spencer's gray eyes darkened with excitement.

"Lemme feel too!" Marian sat down on the seaweed and slid along to the ledge. "Where?"

Catherine guided her fingers. How like sea things those cold little hands felt! "What does it feel like?"

"Kinda soft and kinda hard and—Oh, it's got a mouth!" Marian squirmed away. "Tell us, Muvver! What is it?"

"Can you guess, Spen?"

"May I look, Mother? I think it's—snail eggs."

Catherine laughed.

"Lean over and look. I'll hold you." She seized his belt, while he craned his neck over the bit of rock.

"Purple, too!" He came back, flushed. "I know!"

"Lemme see!" Marian plunged downward, her legs waving. "It's full of holes. What is it?"

"Sponges," said Spencer, importantly.

"Sponges is brown and bigger," cried Marian.

"These are alive and not the same kind as your bath sponge."

Catherine straightened her back and looked out over the sea. Opal, immobile, so clear that the flat pink ledges beyond the lowest tide mark were like blocks of pigment in the water. Something strange in this dark of the moon tide, dragging the water away from hidden places, uncovering secret pools. Once every summer Catherine rowed across to the small rocky point that marked the entrance to the cove, to see what the tide disclosed. There was a thrill about the hour when the water seemed to hang motionless, below the denuded rocks. Spencer felt it; Catherine had touched the sensitive vibration of his fingers as he searched. Marian found the expedition interesting, like clam digging! Catherine remembered the year the fog had come in as the tide swung back, suddenly terrifyingly thick and gray about them, so that she had wondered whether they ever would find their own mooring; she could see the ghostly shore, with unfamiliar rocks looming darkly out of the grayness, as she rowed slowly around the cove, trying to keep the shore line as guide. Charles had come out to meet them; his "Hullo!" had been a whisper first, moving through the mist and seeming to recede. Then he had come alongside them, the fog drops thick on his worried face. Spencer had liked that, too, although Marian had crouched on her bow seat, shivering.

No fog to-day. The horizon line was pale and clear. She should go back for Letty. They had left her behind them on a sandy stretch of beach, with a pile of whitened sea-urchin shells.

"Mother!" Spencer repeated his summons. "What is dark o' the moon?"

Catherine explained vaguely as they scrambled up the rounded, slippery rocks to the patch of coarse grass at the top of the small point. Where was Letty? She had been visible from there. Catherine began to run, down to the muddy flats that separated the point from the mainland. Only a few minutes since she had last seen her head, like a bit of bright seaweed. The water was so far out, surely— Panic nipped at her heels as she flew. "Letty! Let-ty!" There was the pile of shells. "Letty!" A spasm of fear choked her breathing. Then a call, deep and contented.

"Letty here." Around the clump of beach peas and driftwood— The yellow head nodded out of a mud hole left by a clam digger on the beach. "Letty swim."

Catherine picked up her daughter.

"Letty, darling! You little imp—" The gray mud dripped from rompers and sandals.

"Oh, she's all wet." Marian puffed up. "And dirty!"

"Now how are we going to get you home without a cold, young woman!" Catherine stood her on the beach, and sighed. Letty, her fingers full of the soft mud, looked up with bright, unremorseful eyes.

"My sweater's in the dory, Mother." Spencer frowned at his sister. "You haven't any sense, Letty."

Letty's rompers served as a bath towel, and the sweater made a cocoon. She sat beside Marian, while Catherine and Spencer rowed the old dory across the half mile of quiet water. The children chattered about their discoveries, and Catherine listened while her thoughts moved quickly beneath the surface of the talk. Fear like that—it's terrific, unreasoning, overwhelming. How would you bear it if anything happened! You have to be all eyes, and be with them every instant. How can you plan, thinking of anything else? And yet, things happen to children, of any mothers—

"Dark o' the moon—pulls the ole water—away from the earth—" Spencer chanted as he rowed. "Dark o' the moon—"

"What makes you say that all the time, Spencer?" demanded Marian.

"I like to say it. Pulls the ole water—away from the earth—"

"Not so deep, Spencer. You drag your oar. See—" Catherine pulled the blades smoothly along, just beneath the surface.

"I know. I meant to." Spencer was intent on his oars again.

CHAPTER IV

The mail bag hung on the post. Catherine drew out its contents. A letter from Charles. The paper. Her fingers gripped over an envelope. From the Bureau, in answer to hers. A piece of fate, in that square white thing. She thrust it into her pocket. Later, when the children were asleep. She could think then.

Now the air was full of the children. Letty's deep squeals of mirth, a strange noise from Spencer, meant to be whinnying, as he pranced up the path dragging Letty's cart, protests from Marian, "You are silly, I think!" Would Marian always be so serious? And Spencer—he was always exhausting himself by the very exuberance of his fancy. Catherine followed them slowly. Suddenly the sounds broke off for an instant of surprised silence; Catherine lifted her head. The children were out of sight around the bend, and she could not see the house yet. Other voices, and a shriek from Letty. She hurried past the alder growth. There was a car by the side door, and people. Marian flew toward her.

"Muvver! Mr. Bill and Dr. Henrietta! They've come to see us!"

"Good gracious! What can I feed them?" thought Catherine. Then, as she came nearer and saw them, she thought, "I'm getting to be the meanest kind of domestic animal."

Dr. Henrietta Gilbert, fair, plump, serene, immaculately tailored, looked up from her seat on the step, one arm around Letty, who was gleaming brown and sleek from the carelessly draped red sweater. Spencer hovered at her shoulder, his face lighted with pleasure.

"Hello, Catherine!" she held up one hand.

William Gilbert stood behind them, his dark, tired face smiling a little, his long, lean body sagging lazily. Catherine reached for his hand.

"Well, you two!" she cried. "How'd you find this place?"

"Charles gave us minute directions." Dr. Henrietta rose neatly. "He wouldn't come. He's too important for trips. What's happened to Letty? She seems to be clothed for a prize fight."

"Letty swim!" shouted Letty proudly.

"You drove from New York?" Catherine lifted Letty into her arms, and enveloped her in the sweater. "I didn't know you could get away."

"Labor Day," said Bill. He was gazing at the children, his eyes half shut behind his thick glasses.

"If you can't put us up, Catherine, we'll hunt for a boarding house. But we wanted to see you."

"Of course I can. Do you think I'd let you escape, when I'm starving for human beings?"

"With all of these?" Bill nodded at the group.

"They are animals, not human beings, aren't you, Marian?" Dr. Henrietta laughed at Marian's distressed face. "Your woman in the kitchen"—she dropped her voice mysteriously—"thought we were bandits and didn't ask us in."

Amelia was pleased to meet them, when Catherine ushered them properly into the house.

"Don't that beat all!" she said, loudly, as they followed Spencer to the guest room. "I thought they was peddlars. Drove all the ways from New York! Don't that beat all!" She made flurried rushes about the kitchen, pulling open the cupboard doors. "Now don't you fuss, Mis' Hammond. If baked beans is good enough I can make out a meal, I guess. She's a doctor, eh?"

After a fleet half hour Catherine had Letty bathed, fed, and tucked into her cot. She had slipped out of her knickerbockers and smock into a soft green dress. No time to brush her hair; she adjusted a pin in the heavy brown knot, and glanced at her reflection. Letty's voice rose in deep inarticulate demand from the porch. Catherine stepped to the door. Bill stood outside.

"She wants you to say good night to Ducky Wobbles." Catherine smiled at him; she had, at times, a lovely smile, unreserved in its warm friendliness. She was fond of Bill; his dark silence piqued her, but she felt that it was a silence of steady, quiet wisdom, which couldn't break itself up into tiny words.

"Can't I say good night to Letty instead?"

"No! Nice Ducky!" Letty wobbled her duck at him. "Goo'ni' to my Ducky!"

"Well, then, good night to Ducky and to his Letty."

Letty dropped back into her pillow, content.

"Now you go to sleep, old lady." Catherine closed the door, and stopped for a moment to supervise Marian's preparations.

Spencer had filled the wood basket with shining pink-white birch logs. Catherine drew out the crane with the kettle and laid a fire on the andirons in the huge old fireplace. Dr. Henrietta came out, dangling her eyeglasses on a long black ribbon over her sturdy white finger.

"This is a charming old place, Catherine. You all look well, too. A summer in the country certainly sets the children up."

Catherine glanced at her, as the flame crept around the logs.

"You ought to try it, if you want to know what it does to you—" she paused. "Moss in every cranny of your brain—" Bill was coming in. "After supper I'll tell you!"

Supper was over. Spencer had piloted Bill and the car safely into the barn, running back to tell Catherine, "Moth-er! Mr. Bill thinks his car scared all the old cow ghosts in the stalls." When he and Marian were in bed, Catherine came back to the living room, the square envelope from the Bureau in her hand.

"It's queer you two should come to-night," she said. "I need you to talk to."

Bill had settled in the old fiddle-back walnut chair, the smoke from his pipe turning his lined face into a dim gargoyle. Dr. Henrietta was fitting a cigarette into her long amber holder.

"Charles hasn't been here much this summer, has he?" she asked.

"Only occasional week-ends." Catherine sat down on the footstool on the hearth. The light shone through the loosened brown hair about her face and turned her throat to pale ivory. "He was here a week ago."

"Your sister? Has she been here?"

"No. She decided to spend her vacation in the mountains with that friend of hers. Nobody's been here! I haven't seen anyone since last May, except for flying shots at Charles. If I begin to spout a Mother Goose rhyme at you, you might understand why."

"Well, you haven't the mossy look I connect with mothers," said Henrietta, as she smoked in quick little spurts. "Have a cigarette?" She tossed her silver case into Catherine's lap.

"Sworn off." Catherine ran her finger over the monogram. "Amelia would know I was a fallen woman—haven't lighted one since—oh, since Charles came back from France."

"Didn't he care for those home fires?" Bill took his pipe out of his teeth, drawled his question, and went on with his inspection of the flames.

Catherine laughed.

"Tell me what you two have been doing since I saw you."

Henrietta retrieved her case and extracted a second cigarette.

"Same things. Babies, clinics, babies. Bill's had a bridge over in Jersey. The *Journal's* taken a series of articles I did on that gland work last year. Public school on the East Side is going to let me run sort of a laboratory clinic on malnutrition. Mother instinct down there feeds its infants on cabbage, fried cakes, and boiled tea."

"You're a wonder, Henry." Catherine sighed. "Putting over what you want."

"It's only these last few years, you know, that I've had any recognition."

"You're a wonder, just the same. Isn't she, Bill?"

"Um." Bill's grunt gave complete assent.

Catherine looked steadily at her friend. Even in the soft firelight Dr. Henrietta Gilbert retained her smooth, competent neatness. A smoothness like porcelain, thought Catherine. Porcelain with warmth in it, she added hastily to herself, as if she had made an unfair accusation. Firm, kindly lips; contented, straightforward blue eyes; plump, ungraceful body; Dr. Henrietta had a compact, assured personality, matter of fact, intelligent, enduring. Catherine wondered: do I give, as she looks at me, as complete an impression of me? I feel hidden away. Then she thought, quickly, of the grim days when Spencer lay so piteously still except when he struggled for breath, when he had so nearly died—pneumonia—and Henrietta had seemed to hold herself between the child and death itself, calm, untroubled. She was a wonder!

"You couldn't have done it, could you," she said suddenly, "if you had had children?" Then she stopped, aghast at her heedlessness. She had never said that when Bill was there to hear her. But Henrietta's response was cheerful and prompt.

"Certainly not. That's why we haven't any."

Catherine glanced shyly toward Bill. His eyes, inscrutable as ever, did not lift from the fire.

"That's"—Catherine hesitated—"that's what I want to talk about."

"What?" Henrietta was on her guard.

"Oh, I don't mean you. I mean me?" She balanced the letter on her knee and pointed at it. "That letter. I haven't opened it, but it's an omen."

"Don't be mysterious," Henrietta jibed at her.

"I want to go to work. I wrote to the Bureau, where I had that job while Charles was in France. This is their answer."

Bill leaned forward to tap his pipe out on the fire tongs. Catherine felt his eyes on her face.

"Catherine! Bully for you!" Henrietta clapped her hand on Catherine's shoulder. "Have you told Charles? Can you manage it?"

"I told him." Catherine drank eagerly of the bluff encouragement in Henrietta's voice. "He calls it my 'unsatisfied trend.' But he wouldn't object, of course."

"I thought you didn't care much for that work. Statistics, wasn't it?" Bill put his question quietly.

"Part of it I didn't." Catherine admitted that reluctantly. "But a new investigation is being started, on teaching. I am interested in that. I taught, you know, before I married, and I think that is as important as anything in the world."

"Read the letter, woman!" Henrietta shook Catherine's shoulder.

Catherine ran her finger under the flap and unfolded the square page. As she bent near the firelight, a log rolled off the burning pile, sending a yellow flame high into the chimney, touching into relief the wistful, tremulous lines of her mouth.

"They want me." Her voice was hushed, as she looked up at Henrietta. "At once. Dr. Roberts says he had been looking for someone. He thought I was unavailable."

A shrill, frightened cry darted into the room, sharp as a flame. Catherine leaped to her feet.

"Spencer. He has nightmares." She went hastily out to the sleeping porch.

He was moaning in his sleep, one hand brushing frantically over his blanket. Catherine's hand closed over his. "There, Spencer," she said, softly, "it's all right, dear." He did not wake, but the moaning dropped into regular, quiet breathing, and his hand relaxed warmly in hers. She stood a moment, listening. Then she stole to the other two beds, bending over each. Letty's breathing was so soft that her heart stood still an instant as she listened. At the door of the porch she clasped her hands over her breast.

"Am I wicked?" she thought. "When I have them—to care about—" A passion of tenderness for them shook her; she felt as if the three of them lay at the very core of her being, and she enclosed them, crouching above them, fiercely maternal.

Slowly she went back to the living room. She heard Bill's low voice, and then Henrietta's,

"Catherine can do it. She has brains and strength—"

Her entrance broke off the sentence.

"I'll light a lamp," she said briefly. "This firelight's too sentimental. I want hard common sense."

"Here, let me." Bill flicked a match with his thumb nail, and Catherine fitted the heavy orange globe down over the lamp.

She seated herself in the straight chair near the desk.

"Well," said Henrietta, "I don't see any more clearly than I did in the dark. If you have the nerve to try this, Catherine, go ahead. I'm all for you."

"You think, professionally, that it won't harm the children?"

"You can hire some woman, can't you, to take your place as slave? I suppose you still can look at them occasionally."

"Yes. I suppose"—Catherine twisted her fingers together—"I suppose I am as conceited as most mothers, wondering whether they can get along eight hours a day without me."

"You aren't happy, are you?" Henrietta flung at her, abruptly. "You have the blues, black as ink. You have to hang on to yourself about trifles. You—"

"Oh, yes, yes!" Catherine's laugh shrilled a little. "Don't go on with my disgraceful disposition. I admit it. But don't women have to put up with that?"

"My Lord, no. No longer than they are willing to. Most of them find it easier to lie down. You've got too much brains to be sentimental, Catherine Hammond."

"What do you think, Bill?" Catherine appealed to him suddenly. She felt him, in his motionless silence, probing, inspecting, and never saying what he saw.

"It is for you to decide," he answered.

"You know you can't get advice out of Bill! It's a wonder he ever can serve on an engineering commission." Henrietta laughed at him, in friendly, appreciative amusement. "He has to offer technical advice there. He won't give any other kind."

"You won't consider my specifications?" Catherine was a trifle piteous, under her light tone. "Even if I need—well, it is rebuilding, isn't it?" She wondered why his opinion seemed so necessary. She had Henrietta's, and Henrietta was a woman. But she wanted to reach across, to pull at those passive, restrained hands, to beg him to speak.

"I really think that you have to decide yourself." He paused. "You realize, probably, that it will be like handling a double job. Charles would find it difficult to take over a new share of your present job. Most men would."

"I don't want him to. I couldn't bear to do the slightest thing to interfere with him. His career is just starting—and brilliantly. It wouldn't be right to bother him."

"Why not?" Henrietta sat up, hostility bristling in her manner. "Why not a fair sharing of this responsibility? He wanted the children, didn't he? You're as bad as some of my clinic mothers. They go out to work by the day, and they come home to work by the night. I asked one of them why she didn't let her man help with the dishes and the wash, and she said, 'Him? He's too tired after supper.' And she was earning more scrubbing than the man!"

"You wouldn't make Bill sit up with your patients, would you?" cried Catherine, hotly, "or typewrite your articles?"

"Of course Henrietta has only one job," said Bill.

"Charles has expected the children to be my job." Catherine spoke slowly. "He is in competition with other men whose wives have no other thought. Like Mrs. Thomas, for instance. You met her?"

"I've met scores of them. Most of them haven't brains enough to think with," said Henrietta, crisply. "You have. That's the trouble with you. Now think straight about this, too."

"I am trying to." Catherine's cry hung in the pleasant room, a sharp note of distress.

"It is true, as Catherine sees"—Bill leaned forward—"that the average man grows best in nurture furnished by the old pattern of wife. But you can't generalize. This is Catherine's own problem." He rose. "I wish you luck, you know. Good night." He went slowly across the hall, and closed the door of the guest room.

"You can't drag Bill into an argument," said Henrietta. "Now he's gone." She pulled her chair around to face Catherine. "I want to see you make a go of this. To see if it can be done. It's got to be, some day. I wouldn't take the chance, you see."

"But it was children I most wanted." Catherine groped among her familiar thoughts. "I didn't know I wouldn't be contented. I'm not sure I shouldn't be."

"You aren't. The signs are on you, plain as day. And you've hit straight at the roots of your trouble. I've seen it, longer than you have, and I've just been waiting. When Charles went off for his adventure, he left you space to see in!"

"Are you—happy?"

"Me? Of course. Reasonably."

"You don't want any children?"

"Good heavens, no! I see enough of children."

"But you like them. You couldn't handle them as you do—"

"I take out my well-known maternal instinct that way, if you like."

"You're hard as nails, Henry."

"Catherine"—Henrietta's face was grim under its fair placidity—"when I was sixteen, I saw my mother die in childbirth. She had eight children. Two of them are alive now. She was only thirty-three when she died. She died on a farm in Michigan, and my father thought she picked a poor time, because he was haying. I swore then I'd be something besides a female animal. William knew what I wanted. It's a fair deal to him. He knew he was getting a wife, but not a mother. That's all there is to that. I like you. When you fell for Charles so hard, I was afraid you were ended. Now I have hopes!" Her hand, firm and hard, shut about Catherine's. "Only, don't handicap yourself with this clutter of feelings."

Something in the clutch of the firm fingers gave Catherine a quick insight. Henrietta wasn't hard! Not porcelain. A shell, over a warm, soft creature—a barnacle, hiding from injury as deep as that her childhood had shown her.

"You're a nice old thing." Catherine laid her other hand over Henrietta's. "And"—she came back to her own maelstrom—"you think it will be fair to the children? I ought to be more decent—better for them—if I can get some self-respect."

"That's talking. You write and take that job, instanter! I'll look around for a woman for you. When can you come down?" Henrietta withdrew her hand.

"That's another thing." Catherine frowned. "Dr. Roberts says as soon as possible. School doesn't open, though, for two weeks. I don't like to drag the children back."

"You see?" Henrietta made an impatient lunge with her foot.

"I'll have to think that out."

They sat in silence for a few moments. Then Henrietta rose.

"I'm glad we blew in," she said. "But we have to start off early."

"You've helped." Catherine stood in front of her friend, her hands clasped loosely. "I'll hunt you up in town, when I need an injection of common sense."

She went through the quiet house, setting the screen in front of the crimson ash of the fire, turning down the lamp, hanging away the red sweater Letty had worn home, placing a row of damp little sandals on the kitchen steps where the morning sun would dry them. She stood there for a moment, looking off across the water. A huge crimson star hung low in the east; she thought she caught a flicker of reflection in the dark stretch of water. Perhaps it was only a late firefly.

For hours she lay awake, staring out at the great birch tree, watching the faint motion of its leaves, and the slipping through them of the Big Dipper as it wheeled slowly down its arc.

CHAPTER V

They all stood in the sunshine in front of the house, watching the tan top of the Gilberts' car disappear into the alders.

Spencer sighed ostentatiously.

"Wisht we had a nottomobul," he said. "Mr. Bill let me help him squirt oil and I filled a grease cup and put it back."

"Should say you did!" scoffed Marian. "Look at your sleeve! You're awful dirty."

"Aw, shut up," growled Spencer.

"Shut up! Shut up!" shrieked Letty, dancing on her toes, and pulling at Catherine's hand. "Shut up!"

Catherine, who had been caught in a tight knot of confused thought by Henrietta's final mockery, "You won't come down for weeks, I know. And here's your job, waiting for you! You can't break through!" came back with a little start.

Spencer was staring dolefully down the lane; Marian hovered at his smeared elbow, ready to taunt him again if he stayed silent; Letty pranced as if she wanted to say, "Sic 'em!"

Catherine smiled. She knew how they felt. The arrival of the Gilberts was a large stone dropped into the smooth evenness of their days. Their departure—she couldn't carry on that figure, but she knew the emptiness it left, a funny little sickish feeling, almost a fear lest the days would stay empty.

"Well, isn't he a dirty pig, Muvver?"

"You hush up!" Spencer flushed as Catherine's grave eyes rested on his.

"Amelia says she wants some peas picked. The basket is in the woodshed."

"I picked 'em last," said Marian.

"You never did!" Spencer's anger bubbled up. "You—"

"And some potatoes," continued Catherine, calmly. "If you aren't too cantankerous, Spencer might dig those, and Marian might pick the peas."

Spencer dug his toe into the turf.

"Letty dig!" Letty pulled at Catherine's hand, her lower lip piteously imploring. "Letty dig, Muddie!"

"I have some letters to write." Catherine picked up Letty and started for the house. "I hope you two can see to the vegetables."

With a brief glance as she opened the door, she saw Spencer with a gruff "Aw, come along!" heading for the woodshed.

Letty twisted and squirmed in her arms. "Dig!" she declared.

"You can dig in your sand pile." Catherine set her down. "Where is your red pail? You find that, while I find my pen."

She couldn't go back to town before school opened. Her pen made tiny involved triangles at the edge of the blotter. Charles wouldn't like it if she brought the children down so early. Still, that would give her a few days to set the house in order, to find a woman to take her place. What a queer thought! Henrietta had one in mind, she had said, a sort of practical nurse and housekeeper. There were the children's clothes to see to. When could she do that? She wouldn't have time for sewing. She dropped her head down on the table, her hands clasped under her forehead. I can't do it, she thought. Too many things. *Things!* That's it. Clothes, and laundry, and dirt in the corners. One hand groped out for the letter from Dr. Roberts, and she lifted her head. Her mouth set in a hard, thin line; the smears under her gray eyes made them larger, weary with a kind of desperation.

"I remember so well your admirable work," he had written. "I can think of no one with whom I should prefer to entrust this new piece of work."

If I don't do it now, I never will, she thought. Never. Perhaps I haven't the courage, or the endurance.

"Mis' Hammond!" came Amelia's nasal call. "D'you want a fish? Earle's here and wants to know."

"Yes." Catherine drew her paper near.

"Huh? D'you want one?"

Catherine rose abruptly and hurried into the kitchen.

"Buy one, Amelia," she said. "Good morning, Earle."

"Well, he's got cod and haddock and hake." Amelia was stern.

"Haddock," said Catherine. "There's change there in my purse."

When she came back to the porch, Letty was not in sight, nor did she answer Catherine's call. Her red pail lay beside the sand pile.

"Oh, damn!" thought Catherine, as she flung her pen on to the table and started in quest of Letty. "If I don't find her, I'll regret it. Letty! Mother wants you!"

Incredible that those small legs could travel so fast. Catherine peeked into the poultry yard. Last week she had found Letty there, trying to catch an indignant rooster. But Letty seldom repeated.

As she rounded the corner of the house, she saw the child, and her own heart contracted terribly. Letty was lying on her stomach on a broad stone, part of the well curb, her small yellow head out of sight, her heels in the air.

"Who left that cover off! If I call her, I may startle her—"

Amelia appeared at the door, a water pail in her hand, her pale eyes popping out in her tight face.

"Sh-h!" Catherine laid a finger on her lips, as she stole softly toward Letty, with knees that trembled. Her hand closed firmly over a kicking foot, and she dragged the child suddenly back. Then she sat down on the grass.

Letty wriggled violently to be free.

"Letty fish!" she waved a bit of string. "Fish!"

"Well, don't that beat all!" Amelia stood over them. "Who left that well cover off?"

"You didn't?" asked Catherine wearily.

"My land, no. I was just coming out to draw a bucket. I'll bet that Earle done it."

"Letty, be still!" Catherine's tone hushed the child. "I have told you never to go near that well, haven't I?"

Letty smiled, beguilingly.

"Pretty Muddie. Letty fish." Her small face wrinkled into the most ingratiating smile she possessed.

"You are a naughty Letty." Catherine rose. "Come along and be tied up, like a bad little dog."

Letty's wrinkled nose smoothed instantly, and her eyes closed for a scream. Catherine lifted her firmly into her arms, one hand over the open mouth.

She sat in her room, waiting for Letty's shrieks to subside. They did, soon, and she heard her chirrup. "Get ap! Get ap!" and knew the rope which tied her had become a horse.

Fiercely she seized her pen and wrote. If she stopped to think again—Anything might happen, anyway! She stopped long enough to see clearly that if anything happened while she, the mother, was away, she might have a load of self-reproach heavier than she could endure. It's part of the struggle, she thought. Someone else can play watchdog, surely. There! She had committed herself. A note to Charles. She was glad his conference had been so interesting. She had just accepted a position at the Bureau, like her old job there. She might come down a few days early. With love—

CHAPTER VI

The porter dropped the bags on the platform beside them, and held out his pink palm. Then he swung up to the step, as the long train began to move. Until the train was out of sight down the curving track, Catherine knew it was useless to start her procession. A fine drizzle filled the air under the shed, and the roofs of the street below them gleamed dull and sordid.

"Spencer, will you take that bag? And Marian, this one—" Catherine pulled Letty up into her arm and with a suitcase dragging at her shoulder, piloted the children toward the stairs. "Daddy may be downstairs. Careful, Marian, on those wet steps."

There he was, at the bottom of the narrow, dark stairs. Catherine's heart gave its customary little jump—always, when she saw Charles again, even after the briefest separation.

Marian clung to his arm, Spencer let himself be hugged, Letty squealed with delight. Catherine looked at him, her eyes bright. He did look well! And he had a new suit, in all this rain!

"Here's a taxi, right here. Jump in. Where are your checks?" he bundled them in and handed the checks to the driver.

"This is a crowded street, Mother, and awful loud!" said Spencer, his nose against the glass.

"I like the big station better," said Marian, adjusting herself with interest on the little folding seat. "Why can't we get out there?"

"This is nearer home, dear."

Daddy sat next to Mother, and the taxi rattled off, spurting slimy mud.

"Hard trip, old girl?" Charles put his arm around Catherine's shoulders.

"Fair." Catherine shone at him softly. "Sort of a job, putting the family to bed on a sleeper. But it's over."

"An awful homely street," muttered Spencer, his face doleful.

"It's got lots of things in it," said Marian, wiggling down from her seat, and thrusting her face against the door. "See the folks and the stores and the street cars."

"It's dirty." Spencer turned from the window and looked darkly at Catherine. "I want to be back home," he said.

Catherine smiled at him. Poor boy! The little quiver of his nostrils was eloquent of nostalgia, of the rude necessity of adjustment.

"Our street isn't like this, Spencer," she assured him. "You will like that better."

"Turned into a country kid, have you?" Charles reached for the boy's arm. "Fine muscle! You'll have to try some handball with me this winter."

Spencer lost his forlornness at once. "In the court? Oh, gee!"

"I've got muscle too, Daddy." Marian bounced across to her father's knees. "Feel me! Can't I play ball with you?"

"Letty play!" wailed Letty.

The taxi jolted to a standstill in the traffic, and Letty was diverted by a large and black mammy descending from the street car close to the cab.

"Girls can't play," said Spencer conclusively.

"They can, too, can't they, Muvver!"

"Your mother agrees with you, Marian," said Charles. "But not on our handball courts, eh, Spencer?"

Catherine flushed at the submerged note in Charles's words.

"Don't you give my daughter an inferiority complex!" she said, lightly.

But Charles went on, the note rising to the surface.

"You won't find the house in very good shape. I wasn't expecting you so early."

The glow of the meeting was disappearing under the faint, secret friction. Catherine thought quickly, "He didn't like it—the job, or my coming down. But he isn't admitting it." Aloud she said, "Did Flora desert you?"

"Oh, no. She's there, her mouth larger than ever. I meant the finishing touches."

"We can give those."

"There's Morningside Park!" Spencer's shout was full of delight. "Rocks and trees an' everything!" The taxi had left One Hundred and Twenty-fifth Street and was bumping along the side street which bordered the park. The rocks shouldered up gray and wet through brown, worn shrubbery.

"There's where we had the cave," cried Marian. "I remember it."

Up to the Drive, a few blocks south, and just around the corner the taxi halted.

"Here we are!" Out they all scrambled, to stare up at the gray front, tessellated with windows, while Charles maneuvered the luggage. Catherine felt Spencer's cold hand creep into hers; she held it firmly, knowing that he, too, had the sinking depression with which that monotonous dingy structure filled her.

But Sam, the elevator boy, came out, all white grin and shiny eyes, to greet them and carry in the bags. Letty, as of old, clasped her hands over her stomach as the elevator shot up. The key clicked in the lock and the door opened on the familiar long hall. They were home again.

"When we have breakfast," declared Catherine, "we won't feel so much like lost cats!"

Flora, her gold tooth gleaming in her dark face, was loudly and cheerfully glad to see them. Catherine scurried for towels, and left the children scrubbing their hands, while she walked back through the hall with Charles, who had said he must go to his office immediately.

They faced each other in the dim light. Catherine struggled to throw off the constraint which had settled upon her.

"That's a grand suit," she said, laying her hand on his sleeve. "You better take your rain coat."

"It's at the office. I am afraid I can't come in for luncheon. I made this engagement downtown before I knew you were coming to-day."

"That's good." Catherine smiled at him. "Leaves me more time—there are endless things to do."

He looked at her, a curious reserve in his eyes.

"You are really going to do it, take that job?"

"I wrote you—"

"When do you start?"

"Monday. That's why I'm here." She couldn't help that air of defense! "I had to have a few days to shop for the children, and get the house running."

"Hard on them, isn't it?"

"I thought a few days couldn't matter so much to them as to me."

"No." Charles turned the doorknob.

"Charles!" Catherine seized his hand. "Are you—cross?"

"Of course not." He sounded impatient. "But I have to get over to college sometime to-day."

"Have you changed your mind about my trying this?"

"No." He pursed his under lip, hesitatingly. "I didn't know you were going to jump in so immediately. But it's quite all right."

Catherine released his hand, and he pulled open the door. He stood a moment on the threshold, and then wheeled.

"I—I'm glad you're home." Catherine was in his arms, her lips quivering as he kissed her.

"There, run along!" She patted his shoulder, her eyes misty.

But when he had gone, she leaned against the door, brushing hot tears from her lashes. She could hear the children, their voices raised in jangling. It was going to be hard, harder than she had thought. Bill was right; she would have a double job. She might have more than that, if Charles really carried a secret antagonism to her plan. Perhaps he was only gruffy; perhaps this was only a flicker of his unadmitted dislike of anything which threatened change, anything at least which he had not originated. But she saw, clearly, what she had felt as a possibility, that she had, for a time, his attitude as further weight to carry. That he wouldn't admit his attitude made the weight heavier, if anything. As she went slowly towards the sounds of squabbling, she saw her attempt as a monstrous undertaking, like unknown darkness into which she ventured, fearing at every step some unseen danger; and heaviness pressed down physically upon her.

CHAPTER VII

Breakfast restored the temper of the children, and lifted part of her own heaviness. The day then stretched into long hours. The children couldn't go out into the park, as the drizzle of the morning increased to cold rain. Toward noon Dr. Henrietta telephoned, and Catherine found her voice like a wind blowing into flame her almost smothered intentions. Henrietta was sending over that evening the woman she had mentioned: Miss Kelly. She could come at once, if Catherine liked her. She would have to come by the day, as she had an invalid mother. "We'll run in soon, Catherine, Bill and I. Don't you weaken!"

Lucky Miss Kelly wouldn't want a place to sleep, thought Catherine, as she went about the business of unpacking and reordering the apartment. With New York rents where they were it was all they could do to shelter the family decently. Was it really decent, she wondered, as she laid the piles of Spencer's clothes away in the white dresser, and looked about the little court room where he slept. She went to the window. A hollow square, full of rain and damp odors; windows with drab curtains blowing out into the rain; window sills with milk bottles, paper bags—the signs of poor students, struggling to wrest education out of the jaws of hunger! And yet, when she and Charles had found this apartment, they had thought it fine. A large, wide, airy court; none of your air shafts. She glanced up where the roof lines cut angles against the sodden sky. Spencer did watch the stars there, on clear nights. She picked up the laundry bag, stuffed with soiled clothes, and left the room. Marian's room was next, a little larger. She had planned to have Letty's bed moved in there this fall, opposite Marian's. Flora was on her knees, her yellowed silk blouse dangling from her tight belt, as her arm rotated the mop over the floor.

"Had a pleasant summer, Flora?" asked Catherine, as she opened Marian's bag.

"Land, yes, Mis' Hammond." Flora whisked her cloth. "I'm gonna get married to a puhfessional man. He's been showing me tenshions all summer. He ain't committed hisself till last week."

"You are!" Catherine looked at her in dismay. "When?"

"Oh, I ain't gonna give up my work, Mis' Hammond. Not till I sees how he pans out. I tried that once, and my las' husband, he couldn't maintain me as I was accustomed to be. So I says to my intended, I'll get married to you for pleasure, but I keeps my job. He don't care."

Catherine laughed. She knew that Flora had made earlier experiments in marriage, once to the extent of going back to Porto Rico. But she had, through all her changes of name, kept her good humor, her cleverness, and her apparent devotion to Catherine.

She rose swiftly from her knees, her long string of green beads clinking against her pail of water.

"I believes in keeping men in his place," she said, with an expanding grin. "If you don't, they keeps you in yours."

Catherine, adding the pile of Marian's dirty clothes to the jammed laundry bag, laughed again.

"I suppose so," she said. "What am I going to do with all this laundry! You'd think we hadn't washed all summer, the way things pile up."

"I'll take that right home to-night, Mis' Hammond. My sister can do it for you. My gentleman friend is stopping by for me in his car."

Catherine smoothed the cretonne scarf on the dressing table, adjusted the bright curtains, moved the little wicker chair to make room for Letty's bed, and with a grimace at the glimpse of the court even through the curtains, went on to the living room. Letty was asleep in Catherine's room. Spencer and Marian had scorned her hint that a nap might be good for them, and were sitting disconsolately in chairs drawn near the windows. Here, at least, was something beside too intimate suggestion of neighboring lives, even if the rain held it to-day in somber dullness. Beneath the windows the tops of trees pricked through the mist, as if one looked down into a forest; they were only the poplars and Balm of Gilead that grew on the steep slope of Morningside, but as Spencer had said, they were *trees*. And beyond them, extending far off into the dim gray horizon, the city—flat roofs, with strange shapes of chimneys, water tanks, or elevator sheds, merged to-day into dark solidity. On clear days, there was a hint of water in the distance, and the balanced curve of a great bridge. After all, thought Catherine, there was air in the bedrooms—you couldn't expect birch trees and stars in the city—and they did have distance and sometimes the enchantment of the varying city from these windows. But it was queer—she smiled as Spencer eyed her over his book—queer that beauty, sunlight, air, should be things for which you paid money; that you had to think yourself fortunate if you could afford one window which did not open upon sordidness.

"Moth-er, do you think I'd get too wet if I just went outdoors for five minutes?" Spencer was dolorous. "My throat is all stuffed up, and I'll lose my muscle, just sitting still."

"No fun going out here," grumped Marian.

"In a little while I am going out shopping for dinner. Would you like to go?"

CHAPTER VIII

In raincoats and rubbers, each with a bobbing umbrella, Catherine sighing at the lost summer comfort of knickerbockers and boots, the three went out into the rain. The children sparkled as if they had escaped from jail. Spencer peered from under his umbrella at the heavy sky.

"Mebbe when the tide turns the wind'll change," he said.

"Huh!" Marian giggled. "In the city? That's only in the country."

"I guess there is wind in town, too, and tides, aren't there, Moth-er?"

"Wind, all right!" The gust at the corner of Amsterdam Avenue caught their umbrellas like chips. They ducked into the wet wind, rounded the corner, and bent against it down the avenue.

"Isn't there any tide?" insisted Spencer.

"Yes, of course," Catherine answered, absently. Too far such a day, she supposed, to go down to her old market. That restaurant had changed hands again; a man behind the large window was even then drawing outlines for new gilt letters. The same hairdresser, the same idle manicure girl, intent on her own fingers, the drug store. They crossed the street, their feet wobbling over the cobblestones, slipping through the guttered water. There they were, at the market.

"Where's the kitty?" demanded Marian, her eyes bright in her rose-tanned face.

"Kitty?" Catherine weighed the oranges in her fingers, and looked about for a clerk.

"Why, yes, Muvver. That little gray kitty—"

"He'd probably be grown into an old gray alley cat by this time."

Catherine frowned a little over her list. She should have come out earlier; everything looked wilted, picked over. Vitamins, calories, and the budget. The old dreary business of managing decently, reasonably. The country and a garden of your own did spoil you for these dejected pyramids.

"There's another thing," she thought, as she watched the clerk hunt for a satisfying head of lettuce, stripping off brownish, slimy leaves. "When can I market, if I am downtown at nine? Perhaps this Miss Kelly can do it, with Letty, as I always have done." A swift picture of Letty in her go-cart, herself with the basket hanging from the handle. Marketing had been her most intellectual pursuit.

Back to the meat counter, with its rows of purplish fowls, their feathered heads languishing on their trussed wings, and the butcher, wiping his hands on the apron spotted and taut over his paunch.

Marian, her eyes round and black, watched him sharpen his knife, while Spencer lingered near the door. Spencer didn't, as he said, like dead things. Neither did Catherine, shivering as the butcher shoved aside the quivering lump of purplish-black liver. Queer, the forms that the demands of ordinary living took; forms you never dreamed of, when you entered living.

"We should have brought two baskets!" Catherine looked at the bundles.

"Send 'em over, lady?"

"It's so late."

"I can carry some, Moth-er." Spencer came back from his post at the door.

Marian had the bag of oranges under her arm, Spencer the basket, Catherine a huge bag of varied contents. A scramble at the door to open the three umbrellas, and they started up the street, the wind gusty at their heels.

"Be careful crossing the street," warned Catherine. Marian, darting ahead, reached the curb, slipped, and sat down plump in a puddle, the oranges rolling off, bright spots on the wet cobblestones. Marian, dismayed, sat still, her mouth puckered.

Catherine pulled her to her feet with a hand abrupt, almost harsh. The throbbing behind her temples which had begun the day before, in the steady drive of closing the house and getting off, had increased to a heavy drum. "Pick them up," she said. "Don't stand there like a ninny!"

Spencer's grin faded at the tone of her voice, and her flare of weary temper subsided as she watched them scurry after the fruit. They stowed the oranges into pockets, and corners of the basket.

Finally they were home again. Flora's loud "Glory, glory, halleleuia," swept down the hall as they opened the door, and Letty's accompaniment.

"She's found my drum!" Spencer fled to the kitchen, and a wail followed as Letty was reft of her instrument.

Catherine pressed her lips firmly together as she hung her dripping coat on the rack. "Steady," she said. "They are as tired as I am." Then she thought: that's the great trouble with being a mother. You never get away for a chance to sulk and indulge your bad temper.

Charles came in, with his blandest air of preoccupation. Flora had prepared the dinner, and then gone home when her gentleman friend called for her, to cook her own evening meal, leaving Catherine to broil the steak and set things on the table. Since Letty had slept so long, she was permitted to sit in her high-chair during dinner, where she conducted an insuppressible and very little intelligible conversation.

"She certainly needs training," declared Charles.

"She isn't often on hand for dinner," said Catherine, wearily.

Spencer and Marian cleared away the table, while Catherine bathed Letty, deafening herself to the crash which came from the kitchen. What had Marian dropped this time?

Then she heard them, chattering away to their father, with the occasional interruption of Charles's deep laugh. She hung away Letty's towels and garments, and let the water run for Marian's bath. Wasn't that Kelly person coming in? Would she, Catherine wondered, give the children their baths? Could she let anyone else do that? Those slender, rounded bodies, firm, ineffably young and sweet, changing so subtly from the soft baby curves of Letty into young strength. Oh, at every second there waited for her some coil of sentiment, of devotion, to hold her there, solid, unmoving, in the round of the past few years.

She was too tired to-night to think straight. She called Marian from the door, and was answered by a demonstrating wail.

"Not yet, Muvver. I have to see my Daddy."

But at last both she and Spencer were bathed and in bed. As Catherine turned out Spencer's light, she heard the doorbell.

"Who is it, Moth-er?" Spencer's head came up from his pillow.

"I don't know, son. But you go to sleep."

"Mother—" His voice was low, half ashamed. "Mother, what makes me ache in here?"

"Where?" Catherine hung over his bed. He drew her hand to his chest.

"When I think about my porch—an' everything."

"You better think about something here, Spencer." Catherine's words were tender. "Something you like here. That will cure your ache."

"But I can't think up anything to think about! You tell me something nice—"

"'F you talk to Spencer, you'd ought to talk to me, too," came Marian's sleepy protest from the adjoining room.

"Sh-h! You'll wake Letty." Catherine's mind moved numbly over Spencer's city likes. "Spencer, you might think about Walter Thomas. You can see him soon—"

"Well." Spencer sounded very doubtful. But Charles called her, and Catherine said good night to him and to Marian.

It was Miss Kelly who had rung. Catherine sat down in the living room, brushing her hair away from her face, to which weariness had given a creamy pallor under the summer tan, and wished furiously that she was not so tired, that she could see into this rather plump, sandy, stubby person who sat opposite her, with calm, light blue eyes meeting her gaze. She looked efficient, if not imaginative. Well, the children had imagination enough, and if Henrietta thought Miss Kelly would do, surely she would. Charles had retired into his study. Miss Kelly folded her plump hands in her lap and looked down at her round, sensible shoes as Catherine spoke of Dr. Gilbert's high recommendation.

She couldn't come before Monday. She liked nursing better, but the hours were so uncertain, and her mother needed her. Yes, she had cared for children before. She had always, for several years, had twenty-five dollars a week, when she lived in her own home.

H-m, thought Catherine, that will make one large dent in my wages! But I must have someone, and I can't fill my place for nothing. So Monday morning, about eight. Too bad the children were in bed, but then on Monday Miss Kelly could see them.

When Catherine had closed the door on the last descending glimpse of Miss Kelly's round face behind the elevator grill, she hurried back to the study. Charles looked up from his book.

"Did you like her, Charles? You do think she looks capable?"

"She has an air of honest worth." Charles laid aside his book. "Did you hire her?"

Catherine nodded.

"I shouldn't care to have you supplanted by that face, if I were Letty—or Spencer—or—"

Catherine moved around to the desk to the side of his chair, her fingers twisting together in a nervous little gesture.

"She looks sensible and good natured, and Henrietta says she is fine. I've got to try someone."

"I suppose you must."

Catherine, balancing on the edge of the desk, looked steadily at her husband. He was holding his thoughts away from her, out of his eyes.

"It's mostly Letty, of course," she said. "The others will be in school." She sighed. "She can come Monday, the day I start."

Then they were silent. Charles rubbed his thumb along the edge of his book, and Catherine watched him, her gray eyes heavy.

No use talking about it to-night, when she was so tired. She pushed the affair away.

"Poor Spencer is homesick for Maine," she said. "He wanted to know why he ached—"

"He needs to get out with boys more," said Charles sharply. "He's too notional for a boy his age."

Catherine felt a quick flicker of heat under her eyelids. Charles had said that before this summer.

"I want him to be a man," he continued, "not a sentimental little fool."

"I think you needn't worry about that." Catherine was icy. Then suddenly she slipped forward to the arm of his chair, her head down on his shoulder, one hand up to his cheek. "Good Lord, I'm tired! Don't talk about anything, or I'll fight!"

Charles pulled her down into his lap and held her close.

"That's more like it." His mouth was close to her ear. "Sitting off and staring at me! Silly old girl—"

Catherine laughed, just a weak flutter of sound.

"Call me names! But hug me, tighter!" She laughed again. Words, she thought—you can't get a person with words. They stand between you like a wall.

"You'd better go to bed. You feel limp as a dead leaf."

"Yes." She stretched comfortably. "In a minute—"

CHAPTER IX

Catherine sat at one of the living room windows, the floor about her chair littered with packages, the result of her shopping for the children. She unwrapped them methodically, clipped a name from the rolls of tape in her basket, and sewed the label in place. Spencer Hammond; Marian Hammond; Letitia Hammond. She was thankful that none of them had a longer name! After three gloomy days the sun shone again, pricking out spots of red in the roofs of the distance, falling in splotches of brilliance on the white stuff Catherine handled. The children were playing in the dining room, where the east windows admitted the broad shafts of sunlight. Poor kids! They had begged her to go outdoors with them, but her mother had telephoned that she was coming in.

Catherine had not known she was in town. She had been visiting her son in Wisconsin, George Spencer. Catherine had seen little of that brother since her own departure for college; he had married and gone west, sending back, at astonishingly frequent intervals, photographs of his increasing family. Mrs. Spencer visited him at least once each year, returning always with delighted accounts of the children, of George's business, of his wife.

Catherine folded the striped pajamas and laid them on the pile at her right. Her thoughts drifted around her mother and the small apartment in the Fifties where she kept house for Margaret, the youngest of the family. Letty came in a little rush toward her.

"Letty draw." She spread the paper on Catherine's knee. "For Gram." Her yellow head bent over it intently.

"What is it, Letty?" Catherine laid a finger softly on the little hollow just at the base of Letty's neck, an adorable hollow with a twist of pale hair above it.

"She says it's a picture of her fishing," called Marian. "Catching cunners. But I'm painting a good picture of our house for Grandma—"

"Letty paint?" Letty looked up, her eyes crinkled.

"Grandma will like a drawing just as well." Catherine picked up a set of rompers. "Mother's going to sew your name right on the band." Letty watched a moment and then trudged back to her corner on the dining room floor.

What would her mother think when Catherine told her of her plan? Catherine's hands dropped into her lap. She wouldn't say much. She never did. But that little crinkle of Letty's eyes was like hers! You saw her laughing at you. Since her own marriage Catherine had wondered about her mother, and the last few months, while she had struggled with her moods and desires, she had found that the admiration she had always felt had gathered a tinge of curiosity, or speculative wonder. How had her mother attained the lively serenity, the animated poise, the quiet, humorous tranquillity with which she bore herself? Catherine remembered her father only as a somewhat irritable invalid; the accident which had injured him and finally killed him had happened when she was young, and Margaret a mere baby. And yet, somehow, her mother had seemed to keep a whimsical invulnerability. She had sent them all to college, however she had managed even before the cost of living gained its ominous present-day sound. Only for the last few years, since Margaret, the last of them, had grown into a youthfully serious welfare worker, had Mrs. Spencer's income been adequate to the uses for it. And yet—Astonishing adjustment, thought Catherine. As if she had found what she most wanted in life. As if things outside herself couldn't scratch her skin.

There was a scramble of children to the door at the ring of the bell, and Catherine rose, her work sliding to the floor. They loved her, the children. Was that the answer to her curiosity? That her mother was essentially maternal? Catherine smiled as the delighted shouts of greeting moved down the hall toward her. No, that wasn't the answer. They had never felt, Catherine, or George, or Margaret, that they were the core of her life; what was?

"Cathy, dear!" How pretty she was, thought Catherine, as she bent to kiss her. A moment of encounter while she gazed at her; always Catherine had to pause that moment to regather all the outward details which during absence merged into her feeling of the person as a whole. She hadn't remembered how dark the blue of her mother's eyes was. Or was it only the small blue hat with the liberty scarf, and the new blue cape?

"How smart you look!" she said. "And a new dress, too!"

Mrs. Spencer slipped off her cape with a little twirl. "Paris model, reduced." She handed the cape to Spencer.

"It's pretty, Grandma." Marian touched the blue silk. "Little beads all over the front."

"You certainly look well!" Mrs. Spencer settled herself in a rocker, unpinned her veil, let Marian take her hat, and upon insistence from Letty, allowed her to hold the silk handbag. "Now please put my things all together, won't you?" She ran her fingers through her soft gray hair. Catherine watched her with tender eyes. Something valiant about those small hands, white and soft, with enlarged knuckles and fingers a little crooked, marked by hard earlier years.

Not until after luncheon did Catherine talk with her mother. The children had to show her their pictures; Charles came in, and Mrs. Spencer wanted to know about his new work; dinner had to be planned. Finally Letty was stowed away for her nap, and Spencer and Marian, with the promise of a walk when she woke, went off to read.

"I'll help you with that sewing." Mrs. Spencer threaded her needle. "You've done your shopping in a lump, haven't you? I thought you usually made some of these things."

"I won't have time this year."

Catherine was half afraid to tell her. Her proposition sounded absurd, as if she heard it through her mother's ears. But Mrs. Spencer listened quietly.

"That's what Charles meant, then," she said.

"He spoke of it?" Catherine looked up.

"He asked if I had heard how modern you had suddenly become."

Catherine snapped her thread. She wondered why she had felt this desperate need to make her mother approve of her scheme, and Charles, too. Wouldn't approval come after she had carried it through, if she could?

"Do you think me foolish—or wicked?"

Mrs. Spencer patted the tape into place on the blouse she held.

"Not at all, Cathy," she said.

"But you don't think I ought to do it?"

"That is for you to decide. You say you have found a nurse?"

"Yes."

"Did Dr. Henrietta Gilbert suggest this to you?"

Catherine's head came up at that, but her irritation scurried off into amusement; her mother looked so guileless, stitching with busy fingers.

"You don't see, then, that I can't help it? That I must try something? Oh, Mother, I've thought and thought—"

"Yes, that's just it. You think too much. You always thought, Cathy. That's why I was relieved when you met Charles. You didn't think much for a while, at least, and I hoped"—Mrs. Spencer was looking at her, her head on one side, her eyes bright, her mouth turning up in a funny little smile—"I hoped your thinking days were over. But it's in the air so. Women seem to take pride in being restless, unhappy. We were taught to consider that a sin."

"Is that why you're so nice?"

"No." Mrs. Spencer smiled. "Maybe my children were smarter than yours. I didn't find them such bad company."

"Oh, that's not it!" Catherine cried out. Then she laughed. "Mother, you're outrageous. You're making fun of me, just as if—"

"As if you wanted to be a missionary again."

"But I was only a child then. That was amusing."

"Yes. You didn't think so, then." Mrs. Spencer folded the blouse neatly. "Hasn't Spencer grown tall! I see you're buying eleven-year-old clothes for him."

"Well"—Catherine's mouth was stubborn—"I'll just have to show you! And Charles, too. He thinks it's a whim, I know."

"He hasn't objected?"

"Oh, no. Not in words. He wouldn't."

"Poor Charles. These modern women in your own home!" Mrs. Spencer's eyes crinkled almost shut. "Do you know why I came back early? Your sister Margaret has a modern turn, too."

"But she's not in town yet."

"No. She wrote, asking if I wouldn't like to stay with George this winter."

"Why?"

"I suppose she thinks a mother is a sort of nuisance. She wants to set up housekeeping with her friend."

"The little wretch!"

"Not exactly. But I did want that apartment myself, as I am fond of it. I think I'll take a roomer."

"Mother!" Catherine stared at her.

"She's been reading something a German wrote. What is his name? Freud. She's been thinking, too, I am afraid."

Catherine was silent; she recognized her instinctive protest as a flourish of habit, of righteousness for someone else. After all—

"She needn't be so apologetic," said Mrs. Spencer deliberately. "If she doesn't need me, I shall be glad to find someone nearer my own age."

Letty's deep voice announced her awakening. Mrs. Spencer decided to walk over to Riverside with Catherine and the children, as she could go on downtown from there by bus. After several minutes of agitated preparation, a frantic search for roller skates, they were in the hall, Letty rolling noisily along on her wooden "Go-Duck," her busy legs waving like plump antennæ. Catherine held the strap of Marian's skates firmly; Marian was all for skating right down the hall. Then, just as the elevator came, Catherine remembered that she hadn't paid Flora for the week.

Flora's gold tooth flashed as Catherine handed her the money.

"I certainly is obliged," she said. "My frien' and I, we're going on the Hudson River boat to-morrow, and I suspicions he's short of cash."

"You'll be in early on Monday, Flora? Miss Kelly is coming, and she'll need you to show her about things."

"Sakes, yes. You can go about your business, Mis' Hammond, with a light soul."

Flora was delighted at this venture of Catherine's. Catherine thought, a little grimly, as she hurried after the family, that Flora was the only one in the house who was pleased. It's her dramatic sense, she speculated, waiting for the elevator. I wish I had more of it myself, and Charles, too.

The sharp blue clarity of the air was like a sudden check rein, pulling Catherine's head up from doubtful thoughts. As they waited at Amsterdam Avenue for the car to rumble past, she glanced up the street; in the foreground the few blocks of sharp descent, and then the steady climb for miles, off to the distance where street and marginal buildings seemed as blue as the sky. It was like a mountain, with blue-gray shadows across the canyon of the street, and jagged cliffs of buildings merging into solid rock up the slope. She reached for the head of Letty's red duck. "You better walk across the street, Letty."

"No! Ducky go!" and bumping over the cobblestones it went, propelled vigorously, while Spencer and Marian stumbled along on their skates.

The walk through the half block of park behind the University buildings was smooth sailing. Catherine and her mother followed the children. "Wait for us at the gate!" warned Catherine.

At last they were across the Drive and safe on the lower walk of the park.

"Here's my old bench." Catherine sat down with her mother. "I can see clear to those steps from here."

Spencer was off with a whoop, his figure balancing surely as he sped. Marian chased him, a determined erectness in her body. Letty paddled after them, chanting loudly to her duck.

"When school opens," Catherine sighed, "they'll have some exercise, poor chickens. City life isn't easy for them."

"It's no place for children." Mrs. Spencer watched a passing group, a beruffled little girl yanking fretfully at the hand of her nurse, a small, fat boy howling in tearless monotony. "Not even a yard."

"We talked about a suburb last year. But Charles hates the idea of commuting, and he is so busy with his additional work that he'd never be home at all."

"Won't you miss these little expeditions with your children?"

Catherine looked hastily at her mother. But the bright blue eyes were apparently intent on a tug steaming along the river. The tide was running swiftly down, swirling off into the quiet water near shore bits of refuse, boxes, sticks, which caught the sun in dazzling sham before they drifted into ugly lack of movement.

"They don't need me when they are playing here," said Catherine. "Anyone would do, just to watch them."

"I wonder," said her mother. "I see some of these nurses do outlandish things."

"Miss Kelly looks intelligent and kind." Again stubbornness in Catherine's mouth, in her lowered eyelids. "And I might as well admit, I'm reaching the place where I won't be either of those things. You'd be ashamed of your daughter if you knew how peevish she can get!"

"Catherine, dear"—Mrs. Spencer laid her hand softly on Catherine's—"you know I don't mean to interfere. But are you sure you haven't just caught the general unrest, in the air and everywhere?"

"Where did it come from?" The children were coasting toward them, down the little hill. "Why do I feel it?"

"Oh, the war, no doubt."

"The war! Blame that for my hatred of this dreadful monotony, my lack of self-respect, my—my grubby, dingy, hopeless feeling!"

"I can see you have your mind made up." Mrs. Spencer caught Marian as she tumbled, laughing, against the seat.

"I beat Spencer back!"

"Come on and I'll beat up the hill!" Spencer wiggled to a standstill.

A wail went up. Letty and her duck were upside down, a jumble of legs and red wheels. Spencer clattered away to rescue her, Marian after him.

Mrs. Spencer began with a little chuckle a story of George's two youngest children. Catherine relaxed, content to leave her own problem. Her mother had said all she meant to say. The sun dropped lower and lower, until it seemed to catch on the sharp margin of the New Jersey shore and hang there, red, for long minutes. The tide had slackened and the water caught a metallic white luster. The park was almost deserted now. Finally Catherine called the children. They came; she smiled at their scarlet cheeks and clear eyes, their smudged hands and knees.

"Home now, and dinner."

"See the gold windows!" Spencer pointed to the massed gray buildings above the park.

"That's the sun," explained Marian, panting up the steps.

They waited with Grandmother until a bus lumbered to a halt, and they could wave her off down the Drive.

CHAPTER X

Charles came into the hall as they entered, clattering skates and duck.

"Hello!" He pinched Letty's cheek. "Where you been?" He moved close to Catherine and continued, in a confidential undertone, "I thought you'd be here. I brought Miss Partridge in. Don't you want her to stay to dinner?"

Catherine, with a swift glance at the disheveled group, and a swifter consideration of food—what had she told Flora to prepare?—shrugged.

"Of course," she said. She concealed a secret grin at the relief which ran over Charles's nonchalance. In the old days—how long ago!—one of her most sacred lares had been just that, that Charles should feel free as air about bringing any one in at any time. What was home for? But with three children, perhaps she burned less incense at that altar. She was moving toward the door of the living room as she thought.

"Here's my wife and family, Miss Partridge."

"I am glad you waited for us." Catherine disengaged herself from Letty's fingers and went to meet the woman who was rising from the window. "I have wished to meet you." Catherine smiled as she spoke; her smile touched her face with a subtle irradiance, charming, completely personal. She's younger than I had supposed, Catherine was thinking, and quite different.

"Dr. Hammond urged me to wait." Her voice was clear and hard, like a highly polished instrument. Her manner was as cool and detached as the long white hand she extended. "And this is the family?"

"Letitia, Marian, and Spencer," announced Charles. Catherine watched them make their decorous greetings with a little flicker of pride. Sometimes Marian had ridiculous fits of shyness and wouldn't curtsey. "You'll have to test them, Miss Partridge," Charles went on. "See if my paternal bias misled me in my tests. Their I.Q.'s seem satisfactory."

"Of course they would!" Miss Partridge's smile lifted her short upper lip from a row of even teeth so shining that they looked transparent. "Such a handful must keep you busy, Mrs. Hammond. You've just come in from the country, haven't you?"

"Good Lord!" thought Catherine. "I'm to be treated like an adoring mother." Her level glance met the dark brown eyes for an instant; she felt a queer clatter, as if she had struck metal. Aloud she said, "Won't you have dinner with us, Miss Partridge? I should enjoy hearing your side of all these new schemes."

"That's it." Charles was hearty, insistent. "Let me take your wraps."

Elegant, slim, in soft taupe tailor-made, close-fitting velour hat. She gets herself up well; Catherine was aware suddenly of her own appearance in rough tweed coat and last year's hat with its bow of ribbon rather wilted. Not so hasty, she warned herself; look out, or you'll have a rooted dislike out of this feeling. Queer, how some women heighten their femininity by tailored clothes. Miss Partridge, without a demur, had stripped off her jacket and removed her hat. Her blouse of dull gleaming silk fitted closely about her throat, her dark hair was wound in a heavy braid about her smooth, small head; lovely skin, with a pale luster. Catherine noted in a flash the heavy jade cuff links, the small bar of jade that fastened the collar, the chain of dull silver and jade which looped into the belt. She's the sort that affects the masculine for more subtle results, was the swift conclusion, as she ushered the children out of the room.

It was a nuisance, having a maid who couldn't stay to serve dinner. But in other ways Flora couldn't be touched, and they did like not having to house her. Catherine heard the tone of that clear, hard voice as she moved from bathroom to kitchen, lighting the gas under the vegetables, supervising Letty's supper and bath. Is she brilliant, or shrewd, she wondered, as she directed Spencer in his grave attempt to lay another place at the table. She is young to have achieved her reputation. Has she one, or has she made Charles think she has? Don't be a cat!

At last Letty was in bed, the children were clean, the chops were broiled, the corn steamed on the platter, and with a last glance at the table, Catherine went to the living room door.

"Dinner is ready," she said. "We have a maid by the day, who goes home at six," she explained, and then stopped. She wouldn't apologize!

As they seated themselves, Letty's shout broke across the hall.

"Lady kiss duck! Lady kiss Ducky goo' ni'."

"Spencer, please tell Letty we are at dinner."

But Letty's shout gained energy.

"That's one of her rites," said Charles. "Miss Partridge might as well be initiated at once. Come along!"

Catherine laughed at Marian's distressed face.

"Muvver, isn't Letty *awful*! A strange lady—"

Charles and Miss Partridge were back, and Marian sank into embarrassed silence.

"Isn't she an amusing baby, Mrs. Hammond!" Miss Partridge unfolded her napkin with a lazy gesture; her smile disclosed her teeth, without touching her large dark eyes.

"She's the most stubborn one of the family," said Charles.

It was difficult to play a continuous part in the conversation when you had to leave half your mind free for food and drink, thought Catherine, as dinner moved along under her guidance. She didn't, she discovered, know half that Charles had been doing all summer. Miss Partridge had assisted in the summer-school work, to begin with. Time for salad, now. Spencer helped clear the first course away, breathing heavily as he pondered over his movements with the plates and silver. Catherine brought in the huge green bowl, filled with crisp, curling leaves, and Spencer followed with the plates of cheese and crackers. As Catherine poured the dressing over the leaves and stirred them, her hands moving with slow grace, she picked up the threads of the talk. Miss Partridge thought a family must be illuminating; you could watch instincts unfold. And Charles—"I tried Spencer, to see if he had that prehistoric monkey grip, and Catherine thought I was endangering his life. But you're so busy keeping them fed and happy that you haven't time to experiment."

When dinner was over, Catherine stood in the living room door.

"If I may be excused for a few minutes," she said.

"Is it dishes, Mrs. Hammond?" Miss Partridge turned from the window, where Charles had been pointing out the view. "I'm not a bit domestic, but I think I could wipe them."

"Oh, no, thank you." Catherine smiled. "Just the children."

They were in Spencer's room, arguing in low tones about which chair Marian was to have. Catherine adjusted the reading lamp, suggested that Spencer curl up on the end of his bed. "Now you may read for a whole hour," she said. "Then Marian must bathe. If you will call me, I'll rub your back for you." She started toward the door. "You will be quiet, won't you," she asked, "since we have a guest?"

"Of course, Muvver," said Marian. "Isn't she a handsome lady?"

"No, she isn't," said Spencer, loudly.

"Remember Letty's asleep just next door."

Catherine stopped outside their closed door. They were quiet, dropping at once into their stories. Good children. She brushed her hair from her forehead with an impatient hand. "I feel like—like a nonentity!" she raged. "Almost as if I were invisible. Not there to be even looked at. Perhaps I am jealous, but it doesn't feel like that. She's not the vamp type. Too smooth and egoistic. It's what Charles can do for her, not Charles that she is after. O, well—"

But before she had returned to the living room the bell rang. Henrietta and Bill!

Catherine held out her hands, one to each, and drew them into the hall.

"You dears!" she cried. "I am glad to see you. Come in."

She stepped back into visibility with their entrance. Henrietta had met Miss Partridge at Bellevue one day. William bowed with his usual courtly silence.

"Did you like Miss Kelly?" demanded Henrietta, as she settled into the wing chair before Miss Partridge had it again. "She came in, didn't she?"

"She's coming Monday."

"Is Monday the great day?" Bill was looking at her, and Catherine smiled swiftly at the warm, quiet friendliness of his eyes.

"Monday!" she declared. "I telephoned Dr. Roberts this morning."

"Isn't it fine, Miss Partridge"—Henrietta turned briskly to her—"this move of Mrs. Hammond's."

"I haven't heard about it." Miss Partridge's dark, smooth brows lifted.

Did Charles look uneasy, almost guilty, as he stretched out in his armchair and fumbled in the box of cigars?

"You haven't?" Henrietta grinned slyly at Catherine. "Haven't you heard that Mrs. Hammond is renouncing the quiet, domestic life for a real job?"

"Why not say exchanging jobs?" Charles was intent on the end of his cigar.

"Or annexing a second job?" That was Bill's quiet voice.

"I am going to work at the Lynch Bureau," explained Catherine, "as investigator." She felt a flash of delight in the astonishment which rippled briefly over Miss Partridge's smooth face. Knocked down her first impression, she thought maliciously.

"Really? How interesting!" Miss Partridge smiled. "But what will your sweet children do?"

"They'll go to school and have an efficient nurse," said Henrietta abruptly, "and they'll be vastly better off when they aren't having the sole attention of an intelligent woman like their mother. And that's that!" She dangled her glasses over her forefinger. "Did you decide that girl was malingering, Miss Partridge? She certainly had no physical symptoms. Just a case we ran into the other day," she added, to Catherine.

Charles, in answer to a query from Bill, had started a long and eager explanation of an industrial test he had been working up.

Catherine noticed that even as Miss Partridge answered Henrietta's question, her eyes had turned to Charles and Bill. "Is your husband a doctor, too?" she finished.

"Heavens, no! Bill couldn't be anything so personal as a doctor." Henrietta laughed. "Could he, Catherine? He's an engineer."

And presently, maneuvering cleverly, Miss Partridge was talking industrial tests with Charles, while Bill, puffing on his old pipe, let his half-shut eyes rest on her face, and then move across to Catherine. Was he smiling?

Marian's call came just then, and Catherine rose.

"May I come along, Catherine? I haven't seen the kids since that night in Maine." Henrietta stopped at Spencer's door, and as Catherine draped Marian's slim body in the huge bath towel, she heard Spencer's eager voice and Dr. Henrietta's bluff tone. Marian, her face rosy and her dark hair rumpled, threw herself into Henrietta's arms. "Hello, my Doctor!" she cried.

They had a moment in the hall, when Henrietta looked firmly into Catherine's eyes.

"You stop your worrying," she said. "You won't swing your job unless you are clear of doubts. Brace up!" Her hand clasped Catherine's. "If I can help you any way, be sure you let me know."

"Oh, you are a brick!" Catherine's fingers were convulsive. "I do need you!"

The three in the living room looked up at their entrance.

"Spencer sent you his regards, Bill. He wished me to tell you that he thought the cows recovered from the alarm your car caused them."

Bill removed his pipe, a slow smile on his gaunt face.

"What cows?" demanded Charles.

"Ghost cows, Charles. Not in your lexicon. But we felt them in that old barn, behind those stanchions."

When they had gone, Charles followed Catherine into the dining room, gathered a handful of coffee cups, and walked after her into the disorderly kitchen.

"What'd you think of her?" he asked, casually.

"Her being the cat?" Catherine grinned at him. She was at ease again, confident, the sense of nonentity gone.

"Oh, Stella Partridge, of course. Fine person, isn't she! No nonsense about her. Mind like a man's."

"Is it?" Catherine stacked the dishes in the sink.

"Has the qualities which are conventionally labeled masculine. Like that better?"

The clatter of the garbage pail cover served for Catherine's answer.

"Bill's a queer duck, now, isn't he?" Charles lolled against the table, his long body making a hazardous oblique angle. "Never can make up my mind whether it's shyness or laziness."

"I don't think it's either of those things, if you mean his lack of loquaciousness."

"Loquaciousness!" Charles threw back his head in a laugh. "That's some word to use about Bill!"

"I suppose I might as well wash these confounded dishes to-night." Catherine turned the faucet and the water splashed into the sink.

"Where's your dusky maiden?"

"To-morrow's Sunday."

"Oh, say, it's too bad I brought a guest in to-night, eh?" Charles waited comfortably for her assurance that it wasn't too bad.

"We'd hate the mess in the morning," was Catherine's dry retort.

Charles was in extraordinary humor, the purring kind, thought Catherine, as her hands moved deftly among the dishes. And I'm not. I feel as if I should like to yell! She bent more swiftly to her task. Charles straightened his long angle and reached for a dish towel. He needn't be magnanimous about wiping dishes! As he rubbed the towel round and round a plate, he began to sing. Somewhere—rub—the sun—rub—is shi-i-ining—rub! And Catherine had, suddenly, a flash of a picture, smarting in her throat. The shabby little flat where they had first lived, before Spencer was born; Charles wiping the dishes, singing, and Catherine singing with him, ridiculous old hymns and sentimental tunes. And always after the occasional guests had gone, the "gossip party," as they labeled it, speculation, analysis, discussion of the people who had gone, friendly, shrewd, amusing, ending when the dish towel was flapped out and the dish-pan stowed under the sink with the ritualistic but none the less thrilling, "There's no one can touch my girl for looks or charm or brains!" and Catherine's, "I'm sorry for everyone else—because they can't have you!"

Charles was echoing that old custom. But he didn't realize it. And Catherine thought, with a stabbing bitterness, "He has this feeling of comfort, not because we are here together, but because the evening has pleased him."

"What do you think is Bill's secret, then?" Charles broke out.

"He's thinking of something else, not of that; he's keeping me off his real center," hurried Catherine's thoughts. "I won't be horrid and cross."

"Isn't it lack of conceit?" She reached for the heavy frying pan. "Most of us have to talk to assert ourselves, to make folks listen to us. Bill hasn't any ego—"

"Oh, he's got one, all right." Charles balanced the pile of dishes precariously near the edge of the table. "Looks more conceited just to sit around with that cryptic expression—"

"I don't think so!" Catherine scrubbed vigorously at the sink. "He never looks critical."

"Couldn't get a harsh word out of you about Bill, could I?" Charles jested a little heavily. "He's always been that way, ever since he was a kid."

"Now when Miss Partridge"—Catherine resisted the impulse to say "your Miss Partridge"—"when she is silent, she looks too superior for words."

"Nonsense! I felt you were misjudging her. Now, she's awake, ready to talk—"

"About herself."

"Meow!" Charles grinned. "Though we did talk a good deal about the work. But, of course, that's only natural."

"She didn't even see me until Henrietta pointed at me and yanked me out of the pigeon-hole where she had me stuck."

"I hope you aren't going to dislike her, Catherine." Charles was serious. "Since I have to see her in connection with the clinic, it might be awkward—"

"Thank the Lord, those are done!" Catherine turned from the sink. "Don't worry, old thing," she said, lightly. "I don't hate her. We never have insisted on love me, love all my dogs, you know."

"I thought you'd appreciate her." Charles was sulky.

"She's extremely handsome."

"She's as warm hearted as she is brilliant, too."

"Like a frog, she is!" thought Catherine. But she reached for the button and snapped out the light.

"I'll hurry with my shower," she said, preceding him up the hall. "Then you can have the tub. It's late."

The bathroom was littered with the children's discarded clothes. Little sluts! thought Catherine, gathering socks and shirts and bloomers. My fault, I suppose. I can't make 'em neat! Like a nice warm tub myself, she growled, but Charles is waiting. Someone's always waiting.

She sat in the dark by the window in their room, while Charles splashed and hummed. Yellow cracks edged a few of the windows of the opposite wall, not many, as it was so late. Above the rim of the building she could see one great blue-white star with a zigzag of pale stars after it. Vega, she thought. Smiting its—what is it? Wonder if you could see stars at noon from the bottom of this court? It's like a well. She drew her dressing gown close over her throat. It feels nasturtium colored, even in the dark, she thought, running her fingers over the heavy silk. Her one extravagance last spring, lovely flame-orange thing. Why, she hadn't braided her hair. Her fingers were tired. They moved idly through the heavy softness.

Her elbows on the window sill, she stared up at the star. Monday, she thought. Monday I shall have something else to think about. Just as Charles does. This dreadful mulling over words and looks, hanging on the wave of an eyelash. That's what women do, poor fools, trying to keep all the first glamor. Love. She heard the water gulping out of the tub. Love needs to be back of your days, *there,* but not the thing you feed on every second. Terrible indigestion, eating your heart out forever. Ugh, the sill was gritty with dust. She rubbed her elbows resentfully. That song Charles had hummed in the kitchen had sent her back through the years. She hadn't wanted anything else in those days. Passion, its strange, erratic light making everything else seem tinsel. Tenderness, making all else in life seem cold. And quarrels—the still, white silence, swift product of some unexpected moment, so that you felt yourself imprisoned in an iceberg, from which you never could escape—that was part of the struggle of admitting another person, your lover, into yourself. And child-bearing. Peculiar, ecstatic, difficult; commonplace physical preoccupation for long stretches of your life. Catherine shrugged. Perhaps, if you weren't husky—she twisted from her cramped position—perhaps some women never got over childbirth. It did eat you up. Her mother would say she was thinking too much. She rose, stretching her arms above her head, the silk slipping away from them. Then, as she heard Charles scuffling along the hall—he did need some new slippers—suddenly her heart opened and poured a golden flood over her being. Why, now, this instant, she loved him, and all the earlier passion was a thin tinkle against this sound—sunlight in the wide branches of a tree, and cold earth deep about the roots, and liquid sap flowing.

Her fingers closed about the crisp curtain edge as Charles pushed open the door.

"You in bed?" His whisper was cautious. "Oh, no." He snapped on the light, while Catherine gazed at him, waiting. His pink pajama coat flopped open.

"There isn't a damned button on the thing. Got a pin?" He shuffled across to the dressing table. "My wife's been to the country."

"Poor boy." Catherine rushed to the sewing table in the corner. "I'll sew 'em on if your wife won't." Ridiculous, enchanting. She pulled him down beside her on the bed, seized the coat, burying her knuckles against the hard warmth of his chest. "Don't wriggle, or you'll have it sewed to your diaphragm."

Charles was silent. Catherine's wrist flexed slowly with the drawing of the thread. It's like weaving a spell, she thought, with secret passes of my hand, to melt that hard resentment he won't admit. She broke the thread and glanced up. Charles, with a quick motion, laid his cheek against the sweet darkness of her hair.

"First time you've so much as seen me since you came back," he said.

"Too bad about you!" Catherine jeered softly.

CHAPTER XI

"It's the Thomases on the 'phone." Charles came out of the study. "They want us to come out this afternoon to see their house."

"Out where?" Catherine looked up from her book, while Spencer and Marian fidgeted for the reading to continue.

"Croton. They've moved, you know. Bought a farm."

"Walter Thomas?" asked Spencer. "Has he got a farm?"

"Thomas says there are trains every hour, and we can stay for Sunday-night supper."

"But the children—"

"I thought your mother was coming in."

"She may not wish to stay late."

"Well, you'll have to decide. Thomas is waiting. It would be rather nice to get out of town for a few hours."

Catherine's brows drew together.

"We're all right," said Marian. "Go on away!"

"Yes, you are." Catherine sighed briefly. Charles had his air of "Are you going to deprive me of a pleasant hour?"

"You wouldn't go without me?" she asked. "Tell Mr. Thomas that if mother wishes to stay, we'll come. We can telephone him."

Mrs. Spencer said she would like nothing better than a chance at the children without their interfering parents, and in the late afternoon Catherine and Charles set forth. The cross-town car was jammed; Catherine, from an uncomfortable seat just under the conductor's fare box, watched the people about her with remote eyes. She hated these humid, odorous jams. She always crawled off into a dark corner of herself, away from the jostling and pushing of her body. Heavy, dull faces—she lifted her head until her eyes could rest on the firm solidity of Charles's shoulder and head. Nothing professorial about that erect head, the edge of carefully shaved neck between collar and clipped fair hair that showed under the soft gray hat. But even the back of his head looked intelligent, alive. He turned suddenly, and over the crowd their eyes met in a mysteriously moving flare of acknowledgment. He grinned at her—he knew her hatred of such crowds; and turned away again. Catherine shivered a little. That was what she wanted to keep, that awareness of each other, that intimate self-recognition. She couldn't keep it if she was worn down into dullness and drabness and stupidity. She had, she knew, stirred Charles out of his easy acceptance of her as an established custom, and for the day, at least, she had submerged his resentment. As the car stopped under the tracks she was thinking, if I can win him over to believe in what I am, what I want, inwardly, in his feeling, not in words,—then I can do anything!

They sat together on the train and talked. Charles had spent one Sunday during the summer with the Thomases; they had a tennis court and chickens. Thomas had been promoted to Assistant Professor, but he kept his extension classes still, as the oldest boy was entering college this fall.

"He was crazy about some old French verse forms that day. Couldn't talk about anything else. Mrs. Thomas wanted to talk about the refinishing of the walls."

"I'll wager she did. Verse forms interest her only as a means to the salary end."

"But she's a fine type of woman, don't you think?"

Catherine shrugged.

"She's about as intellectual as a—a jellyfish. She's not a jellyfish, though."

"Thomas gets enough enjoyment from his own mind."

They walked from the station through the crowded, dingy houses near the river, climbed a long hill, and at the top found the country, soft and lovely in the hazy September sunlight. As they climbed, the river dropped beneath them, opal-blue and calm, the hollows of the wooded Westchester hills gathered purple shadows, and on the slopes toward which they climbed a branch of maple flamed at times like a shrill, sweet note in the mellow silence.

"It must be good for their children, living out here." Charles sniffed at the air. "Smell that wood smoke! Bonfires, and nuts—"

"How'd you like to climb that hill every night?"

"Thomas has a flivver. There, you can see the house through those poplars."

The Thomases were on the porch, rising to meet them with a flurry of innumerable children and dogs and cats. Mrs. Thomas, small, pink, worried, with curly gray hair and a high voice; Mr. Thomas, of indifferent stature, with an astonishingly large head, smooth dark hair, nearsighted eyes behind heavy glasses, and a large, gentle mouth; the children—there were only five, after all, from Theodore, the eldest, who was curly and pink like Mrs. Thomas, down to Dorothy, the youngest, who already wore glasses as thick as her father's.

"I wanted Theodore to drive down for you, but you said you wanted to walk." Mrs. Thomas jerked the chairs into companionable nearness. "Quite a climb up our hill."

"Mrs. Thomas can't imagine any one liking to walk," said her husband.

"Not a mother and wife, at least. Men don't know what being on their feet means, do they, Mrs. Hammond?"

Inquiries about the children, mutually. Admiration expressed for the view, for the house, room by room, for the poultry run which Theodore had constructed, for the tennis court, for the asparagus bed.

"Now that the Cook's Tour is ended, what about something to eat, Mother?"

The dining room was small, and warm from the sunning of the afternoon; the Thomas children chattered in high voices; Catherine sighed in secret as she looked at the elaborate salad, the laborious tiny sandwiches, the whipped-cream dessert in the fragile stemmed sherbet glasses, the frosted cake. But Mrs. Thomas, the lines in her pink cheeks a trifle more distinct, hovered in anxious delight over each step in the progress of this evidence of her skill and labor.

"No, Dorothy, no cake. She has to be very careful of sweets, they upset her so easily. Do your children hanker for everything they shouldn't have?"

Theodore broke in with an account of the psychological tests he had taken for college entrance; there was a suggestion of pimples on his round, pink chin. Walter wanted to know when Spencer could come out; Walter was Spencer's age, a chubby, choleric boy who kept rabbits and sold them to the neighbors for stews. Clara, just older, had reached an age of gloomy suspicion; her hair, which her mother was allowing to grow, now that Clara was older, fell about her thin shoulders in lank concavity. Catherine wondered whether the contention between Marian and Spencer sounded to outsiders like the bickering which ran so strongly here. Dorothy was a year older than Letty, but she did not talk so plainly. And that other boy,

Percy—why name him that!—was being sent away from the table because he had pinched Clara.

Inevitably the talk stayed on the level of the children, in spite of attempted detours on the part of Charles. Mr. Thomas ate with an absent myopic eye on Dorothy and the next older boy.

But when at length they left the dining room, he was saying to Charles, "You recall those songs I spoke of? Thirteenth century? I've found a girl who does beautiful translations. A graduate student. She has an astonishing sense for the form." He had come alive, suddenly, the blank, gentle mask of his face breaking into sharp, vivid animation. Catherine watched him, peering at his wife, glancing back at him. She didn't care about the old verse forms, neither did his wife; but his wife didn't care that he could come alive like that, apart from her. Perhaps when they are alone, thought Catherine, he has some feeling for her that compares with this—but I doubt it!

"He's as keen about those musty old papers as if they were worth huge sums." Mrs. Thomas laid her hand on Catherine's arm, as they stood on the edge of the porch, looking far down the valley. Mrs. Thomas had a way of offering nervous little caresses. "Men are queer, aren't they?" Her forehead puckered.

Catherine endured the hand, light, with an insinuating effect of a bond between them, the bond of their sex. We women understand, those fingers tapped softly.

Later, half defiantly, in answer to a suggestion of Mrs. Thomas that Catherine take her place on the faculty women's committee for teas, Catherine explained that she would be much too busy. She saw in the quick pursing of Mrs. Thomas's little mouth the contraction of her eyelids, the rapid twists her announcement made as it entered Mrs. Thomas's mind. Disapproval, hearty and determined; a small fear, quickly over, lest some discredit reflect on her position; a chilly covering of those emotions with her words, "Why, Mrs. Hammond, you've seemed so devoted to your children!"

"Naturally." Catherine was curt. "I am. But they needn't suffer, any more than they did before while Charles was in France and I worked. I can't see any loss to them."

"I hope you won't regret it." Mrs. Thomas drew her own brood into a symbolic shelter, as she flung her arm around Dorothy, who was at her knee with a picture book, clamoring unintelligibly to be read to.

"Fine for you, Hammond. A family needs several wage earners, in these postwar days."

Charles laughed, but Catherine saw the flicker of uneasiness in his face.

"But I'd hate to have to find a cook to supplant Mrs. Thomas."

"Ah, but you see, I can't cook that way." Catherine's lightness covered the glance she sped at Charles. She hadn't, then, touched his real feeling about this. Just a scratch, and she could see it.

"I don't know what's to become of us poor men"—he rose lazily—"unless we turn into housewives."

"You better take a turn at it, just to see what it's like." That was Mrs. Thomas, vigorously exalting her ability.

"It was called husbandry once, wasn't it?" Mr. Thomas smiled in enjoyment of his joke. "Must you go? It's very early. Let us drive you down."

"The walk will be just what we need—"

The evening was soft and black, with faint rustle in the autumn-crisped leaves of the trees that massed against the blue-black sky. Below them the river gleamed silver-dark. They went in silence down the hill, the gravel slipping under their heels. Then Catherine felt Charles groping for her hand, the warm pressure of his fingers.

"Rummy bunch of kids," he said. And then, "That woman can cook, but that's about all. She can't impart gentle manners." Catherine relaxed in content. He wasn't huffy. "Too bad you have to tell people like that what you're going to do. Let 'em see after you've succeeded, I say!"

"Oh!" Catherine's voice was sharp with delight. "You think I will!"

"Lord, yes. Of course. You've got the stuff."

Their clasped hands swinging like children's, they came to the foot of the hill.

PART II
BOTH ENDS OF THE CANDLE

CHAPTER I

Catherine clicked the telephone into place on her desk and sat for a moment with her hands folded on the piles of paper before her. Her cheeks felt uncomfortably warm. Ridiculous, that Dr. Roberts should have come to the door just as she told Charles where to find the shirts he wanted! He might have found them if he had tried. She wondered whether her voice had conveyed her embarrassment; Charles had said good-by abruptly. He was sorry not to see her, but he had to catch the one o'clock for Washington. No, he couldn't stop for luncheon with her. He might be back Sunday night. She had a vivid picture of him, plowing through drawers and closets in frantic search for things right under his nose.

Her hand reached for the telephone. She would call him for a moment, just for a good-by not so hasty. But Dr. Roberts, in the doorway, clearing his throat, said, "Can you let me have those tables now, Mrs. Hammond?" He pulled a chair to the opposite side of the desk and sat down. Charles and the messy packing of his handbag disappeared from Catherine's thoughts. She spread several sheets of figures between them, the flustered shadow in her eyes gone, and hard clarity in its place. Dr. Roberts, head of the educational section of the Lynch Bureau of Social Welfare, was a dapper little man with a pointed beard, whose fussy, henlike manner obscured the intelligent orderliness of his mind.

"The state laws of requirements for teachers." Catherine pointed to one table. "County requirements, country schools. I made a separate table for each. Now I'll work out a comparative table."

"Excellent. Clear, graphic. May I take those?" He rose. "If you aren't working with them now?"

"No. I'm going through these catalogues now." The dusty pile was at her elbow. "If I may have those sheets this afternoon, I'll try some graphs."

When he had gone, Catherine's eyes rested briefly on the telephone. Oh, well, Charles wouldn't want the interruption anyway. He would be home again on Sunday. She opened the catalogue on top of the pile and glanced through its pages, making swift notes on the pad under her hand.

Finally she leaned back in her chair, twisting her wrist for a glimpse of her watch. Whew! Half past twelve, and she was to meet her sister Margaret for luncheon. She stood a moment at the window. Beyond the neighboring buildings the spires of the Cathedral splintered the sunlight; a flock of pigeons whirled into view, their wings flashing in the light, then darkening as they swirled and vanished—like the cadence of a verse, thought Catherine. Far beneath her lay an angle of the Avenue, with patches of shining automobile tops crawling in opposing streams.

She gave a great sigh as she turned back to the office. A long, narrow room, scarcely wider than the window, lined with shelves ceiling-high, between them the flat desk piled with her work. Her work! Almost a week of it, now, and already she had won back her old ability to draw that thin, sliding wall of steel across her personal life, to hold herself contained within this room and its contents.

She hadn't seen Margaret since her return from Maine. She was to meet her at the St. Francis Luncheon Club for Working Women. As she stepped into the sunlight of the street, the slow flowing of the emulsion of which she was suddenly another particle, she had a sharp flash of unreality. Was it she, walking there in her old blue suit, her rubber heels padding with the other sounds, her eyes refocusing on distance and color after the long morning? She loved the long, narrow channel of the Avenue, hard, kaleidoscopic; the white clouds above the line of buildings, the background of vivid window displays. She laughed softly as she recalled the early days of the week. Rainy, to begin with. She had thought, despairingly, that she couldn't swing the job. The children stood between her and the sheets of paper. She had flown out at noon to telephone Miss Kelly, to demand assurance that life in the apartment hadn't gone awry in the four hours since she had left. Queer. You seized your own bootstraps and lugged, apparently in vain, to lift yourself from your habits of life, of thought, of constant concern, and then, suddenly, you had done it, just when you most despaired. She walked with a graceful, long stride, her head high. An excellent scheme, Dr. Roberts had said. He had really entrusted her with the entire plan for this investigation. And she could do it!

Margaret was waiting at the elevator entrance, a vivid figure in the milling groups of befurbished stenographers and shoddier older women.

She came toward Catherine, and their hands clung for a moment. How young she is, and invincible, thought Catherine, as they waited for the elevator to empty its load. Margaret had Catherine's slimness and erect height; her bright hair curled under the brim of her soft green hat; there was something inimitably swagger about the lines of her sage-green wool dress and loose coat, with flashes of orange in embroidery and lining. In place of the sensitive poise of Catherine's eyes and mouth, Margaret had a downright steadiness, an untroubled intensity.

"How's it feel to be a wage-earner?" She hugged Catherine's arm as they backed out of the pushing crowd into a corner of the car. "You look elegant!"

"Scarcely that." Catherine smiled at her. "Now you do! Did you design that color scheme?"

"I matched my best points, eyes and high lights of hair." Margaret grinned. Her eyes were green in the shadow. "Ever lunched here? I thought you might find it convenient. Lots of my girls come here."

They emerged at the entrance of a large room full of the clatter of dishes and tongues.

"I'll take you in on my card to-day. If you like it, you can get one." Margaret ushered Catherine into the tail of the line which filed slowly ahead of them. "This is one of the gracious ladies—" Margaret shot the half whisper over her shoulder, as she extended her green card. "A guest, please." Catherine looked curiously at the woman behind the small table; her nod in response to the professionally sweet smile was curt.

"The patronesses take turns presiding," explained Margaret, as she manipulated trays and silver. "That's the sweetest and worst. Notice her dimonts!"

They found a table under a rear window, where they could unload their dishes of soup and salad around the glass vase with its dusty crêpe-paper rose.

"It's really good food," said Margaret, shooting the trays across the table toward the maid. "And reasonable. It's not charity, though, and the dames that run it needn't act so loving."

Two girls saw the vacant chairs at the table, and rushed for them. One slipped her tweed coat back from shoulders amazingly conspicuous in a beaded pink georgette blouse; the other opened her handbag for a preliminary devotional exercise on her complexion.

Margaret hitched her chair closer to Catherine.

"Now tell me all about it." She tore the oiled paper from the package of crackers; her hand had the likeness to Catherine's, and the difference, which her face suggested. Fingers deft and agile, but shorter, firmer, competent rather than graceful. "Mother says you've hired a wet-nurse and abandoned your family. I didn't think you had it in you!"

"I know. You thought I was old and shelved."

"Just a tinge of mid-Victorian habit, old dear."

"You young things need to open your eyes."

"I have opened 'em. See me stare!"

Were those girls listening? The georgette one was eying Margaret. The other, her retouching finished, snapped her handbag shut and began a story about the movies last night. Catherine was hungry; good soup—why, it was fun to gather an unplanned luncheon on a tray in this way.

"Your old job?" proceeded Margaret.

"A new study—teaching conditions in some middle-western states. I am to organize the work."

Margaret's questions were direct, inclusive. She did have a clear mind. Her business training has rubbed off all the blurry sentiment she used to have, thought Catherine.

"And you can manage the family as well?"

"This woman Henrietta sent me is fine. It's a rush in the morning, baths and breakfast. Flora can't come in until eight, and I have to get away by half past eight. No dawdling."

"And the King doesn't mind?"

Catherine flushed. Margaret had dubbed Charles the King years ago, but the nickname had an irritating flavor. "He's almost enthusiastic this week," she said. "Now tell me about yourself. What's this about your leaving Mother?"

"Oh, I thought she might like to stay with George. Instead of that, she's turned me out, neck and crop, and taken on a lady friend. I'm house-hunting." Margaret laughed. "Trust Mother! You can't dispose of her."

"But I thought you were so comfortable—"

"Too soft. You don't know—" Margaret was serious. "I can't be babied all my life. All sorts of infantile traits sticking to me. You got away."

"Mother said you'd been reading a foreigner named Freud."

"Well!" Margaret was vigorously defensive. "What of it?"

Catherine dug her fork into the triangle of cake.

"I thought Freud was going out. Glands are the latest."

"I bet Charles said that." Margaret grinned impishly as she saw her thrust strike home. "Well, tell him I'm still on Freud. Anyway, I want to try this. Amy and I want to live together. When you wanted to live with Charles, you went and did it, didn't you?"

"I'm not criticizing you, Marge. Go ahead! Don't bristle so, or I'll suspect you feel guilty."

"I do." Margaret had a funny little smile which recognized herself as ludicrous. "That's just the vestige of my conflict."

"There's another influx"—Catherine looked at the moving line—"we'd better give up these seats."

"There are chairs yonder." They wound between the tables to the other end of the room, where wicker chairs and chaise longues, screens, tables, and a mirror suggested the good intentions of the patronesses of the St. Francis Club.

"You can lie down behind the screen if you're dead, or read"—Margaret flipped a magazine—"read old copies of respectable periodicals. Here." She motioned to a chaise longue. "Stretch out. I'll sit at your feet. I have a few seconds left."

"How's the job?"

"All right. I spent the morning hunting for a girl. She's been rousing my suspicions for a time. Going to have an infant soon. That's the third case in two months." Margaret clasped her hands about her knees; her short skirt slipped up to the roll of her gray silk stocking. "But I've got a woman who'll take her in. She can do housework for a month or so before she'll have to go to the lying-in home."

Catherine watched her curiously. There was something amazing about the calm, matter-of-fact attitude Margaret held.

"Do you hunt for the father?"

"Oh, the girl won't tell. Maybe she doesn't know."

"If I had your job, I'd waste away from anger and rage and hopelessness about the world."

"No use." Margaret shrugged. "Wish I could smoke here. Too pious. No." She turned her face toward her sister, her eyes and mouth dispassionate. "Patch up what can be patched, and scrap the rest. I'm sick of feelings."

Catherine was silent. Margaret, as the only woman in a responsible position in a chain of small manufacturing plants, occasionally dropped threads which suggested fabrics too dreadful to unravel.

"Time's up." Margaret rose. "Directors' meeting this afternoon, and I want to bully that bunch of stiff-necked males into accepting a few of the suggestions I've made. I have a fine scheme." She laughed. "I make a list pages long, full of things, well, not exactly preposterous. Women would see them all. But they sound preposterous. And buried somewhere I have the one thing I'm hammering on just then. Sometimes I get it, out of their dismay at the length of the list."

"Here, I may as well go along." Catherine slid out of the chair.

"Will you be home Sunday?" Margaret stopped at the corner. Catherine had a fresh impression of her invincible quality, there in the sunlight with the passing crowds.

"Charles is in Washington. Come in and see the children."

"The King's away, eh?" Margaret waved her hand in farewell. "I'll drop in."

At five Catherine was again on the Avenue, walking steadily north, an eye on the occasional buses. If she could get a seat! As the traffic halted, she saw a hint of movement at the rear of a bus ahead of her. Someone was just getting out. She rushed for it, and clambered to the top just as the jam moved stickily ahead. Just one seat, at the front. This was luck. She relaxed, lazily conscious only of small details her eyes seized upon. When the bus finally swung onto the Drive, she straightened, drawing a deep breath of the fresh wind across the river. A taste of salt in it. She liked the sweep and curving dips of the Drive; the ride gave her a breathing space, a chance to shut off the hours behind her and to take on the aspect of the other life that awaited her. I'll patch up that old fur coat, she thought, and ride all winter. Perhaps I may even afford a new one. Twenty-five a week for Miss Kelly. Another five for my luncheons and bus rides. If Flora will do the marketing, I'll have to pay her more. I ought to help with the food bills, if we feed Miss Kelly, and pay for the clothes I buy for the children, since I would otherwise be making them. Oh! This domestic mental arithmetic sandpapered away the shine of the two hundred and fifty a month which was her salary. But Charles couldn't have additional expenses this year. It wasn't fair, when he had just reached a point at which they found a tiny margin for insurance and saving. Catherine rubbed her hand across her forehead; foolish to do this reckoning in her head; it always left her with that sense of hopeless friction, like fitting a dress pattern on too small a piece of cloth—turning, twisting, trying. Charles had said, "Well, you know *my* income. We can't manage any more outgo there. Not this year." And at that, she didn't see where she was going to get the first three twenty-five dollars for Miss Kelly. Next month, after she had her own first check—but now! She'd saved the first twenty-five on her own fall clothes. If Charles hadn't had that heavy insurance premium this month, she might have borrowed. It would be fine, some day, to reach a place where their budget was large enough to turn around in without this fear of falling over the edges. Dr. Roberts had said, "Three thousand is the best we can do for you now, but later—"

CHAPTER II

Sunday was a curious day. Miss Kelly, who was to have alternate Sundays off, had this one on, and had taken the children out. Catherine caught a lingering, backward glance from Spencer as they all went down the hall, a silent, wondering stare. He had said nothing about Miss Kelly, nothing about the new order of things; Catherine felt that he held a sort of baffled judgment in reserve. Letty, as always, was cheerfully intent on her own small schemes. Marian had confided last night that Miss Kelly was nice, but her stories sounded all the same, not like Muvver's. Next Sunday, thought Catherine, I'll have them. It's absurd to feel pleased that Spencer doesn't adjust himself at once. I want him happy.

She sat at the breakfast table, too listless to bestir herself about the endless things that waited for her. The morning sun was sharp and hard on the stretch of city beneath the window, picking out slate roofs and chimneys. Alone in the empty apartment, its silence enclosed and emphasized by the constant sounds outside—the click of the elevator, the staccato of voices in the well of the court, the rumble of a car climbing the Amsterdam hill—Catherine relaxed into complete lethargy, her hands idle in her lap.

The week had been drawn too taut. Surely coming weeks would be less difficult, once she had herself and the rest of the family broken into the new harness. She wished that Charles were sitting across from her, the Sunday paper littering the floor about his feet. She would say, "One week is over." And he—what would he say? "How do you like it, old dear?" And she, "You know, I think I am making a go of it." Then if he said, "Of course! I knew you would," then she could hug his shoulder in passing, and go quite peacefully about the tasks that waited. She sighed. If I have to be bolstered at every step, I might as well stop, she thought.

She would like to sit still all day, not even thinking. Instead, she pulled herself to her feet and cleared the breakfast dishes away methodically. Then she opened the bundles of laundry, sorted the clothes and laid them away, found fresh linen for the beds, laid aside one sheet with a jagged tear to be mended later, investigated Flora's preparations for dinner, and, finally, with a basket of mending, sat down at the living room window. Perhaps Flora could see to the laundry, although Catherine always had done that;

she must plan, in some way, to have Sunday reasonably free. Miss Kelly had offered to take care of the children's mending; but—Catherine's fingers pushed out at the heel of the black sock—Charles had to be sewn up!

How still and empty the house lay about her! Perhaps Charles was even then on his way home—she had a swift picture of him at the window of the train, hurling toward her.

Ridiculous to feel so tired. She stretched her arms above her head, and then reached for the darning ball. Henrietta had said, "Don't weaken. You'll find the first stages of adjustment the most difficult." True, all right. The texture of her days rose before her, a series of sharp images. Morning, an incredible packing of the two hours: breakfast, the three children to bathe and help dress, Miss Kelly arriving like clockwork to supervise the final departure for school, Catherine's hasty glimpse at her face, flushed under the brim of her hat, before she hurried out for the elevator. Then the bus ride; herself a highly conscious part of the downward flood of workers, the fluster of the morning dropping away before the steady rise of that inner self, calm, clear, deliberate. The office—deference in the manner of the stenographers—she was the only woman there with her own office, with a man-size job. Occasional prickings of her other life through that life—eggs she had forgotten to order. The ride home again, the warm cheeks and soft hands of the children, and their voices, eager to tell her a thousand things at once. Dinner, and Charles. What about Charles? Her fingers paused over the crossing threads of the darn. He had been busy with crowds of new students and opening classes. Under that, what? She fumbled in her mist of images. She had scarcely seen him, except at dinner. Usually he had a string of stories about the day. He had gone back to the office two evenings, and to Washington on Friday. She didn't know much about his week. Had he withheld it? Had she been too engrossed?

The telephone in the study rang. Catherine hurried. Perhaps it was Charles.

"Is Dr. Hammond in?"

"This is Mrs. Hammond." That clear, metallic voice! "Dr. Hammond is out of town."

"Oh, yes. I thought he might be back. Would you give him a message for me? Miss Partridge. Please ask him to call me as soon as he comes in."

"Certainly." Catherine waited, but the only sound was the click of the telephone, terminating the call.

"Well!" Catherine sat down at the desk. Now, there's nothing to be irritated about, she told herself. Her eyes traveled over the bookshelves, low, crowded, piled with monographs and reviews. That curtness is part of her pose—manlike. But she certainly hits my negative pole!

Miss Kelly came in with the children, noisy and hungry, and the five had dinner together. Catherine tried to talk with Miss Kelly. Her round, light eyes met Catherine's solemnly, and she replied with calm politeness to Catherine's ventures.

"No, Marian, dear," she said suddenly. "One helping of chicken is enough for a little girl your age."

"Spencer had two!" Marian turned to her mother. "Why can't I?"

Catherine smiled a little wryly. She thrust under the sudden flash of resentment. Of course, Miss Kelly had them in charge. What was the matter with her to-day! She seemed to react with irritation to everything.

"Marian's stomach seemed a little upset yesterday," confided Miss Kelly.

"We'll have our salad now." Catherine dismissed the question.

But after dinner, when Letty had been led protestingly away for her nap, and Miss Kelly, armed with a volume of Andersen's "Fairy Tales," reappeared in the living room, Catherine couldn't resist the swift entreaty of Spencer's eyes.

"Miss Kelly," she said, placatingly, "if you would like to go home now, I can read to the children. I am quite free this afternoon."

Miss Kelly agreed placidly. When she had gone, Spencer stood a moment beside Catherine, his eyes intent on her face; Catherine saw a wavering tenseness in his look. He wanted to hurl himself at her, and he didn't want to. She couldn't reach out for him, if he felt too grown-up for such expression. She smiled at him, and with a huge sigh he settled into the wicker chair, one foot curled beneath him.

"She was glad to go home, wasn't she?" he said.

"I'm glad she went," announced Marian. "She bosses me."

"Good for you," said Spencer. "Mother, read us 'Treasure Island.' I'm sick of old fairies."

Margaret came in, her ring waking Letty. Catherine laughed at the unconcealed expectancy with which the children welcomed their aunt.

"You've ruined them," she said, as Marian danced up the hall, her eyes wide with anticipation for the packages Margaret carried.

"Well, they are delighted to see their old aunt, anyway!" Margaret dropped to the floor, scattering the bundles, her hands held over them in teasing delay.

"Your dress, Marg! On the floor in that?"

"Just a rag. Here, Letitia, your turn first."

Catherine went back to her chair to watch the orgy. Margaret was extravagant as water.

"It isn't really a rag, Aunt Margie, is it?" Spencer had his head on one side, deliberating. "It looks like—like pigeons."

"If I could find a gentleman of your discrimination, Spen, I'd grab him in a jiffy!"

"It is like pigeons, isn't it, Mother?" Spencer looked perplexed.

"Yes." Catherine wished Margaret wouldn't tease him. She was lovely, her gray-silver draperies floating around her slim, curving figure, the purple glinting through. It was like a pigeon's breast, that dress.

Letty had a doll, soft and round and almost as large as Letty herself.

"Company for you, when your mother's off at work."

Letty's arms were fast about it, and her deep voice intoned a constant, "Pretty doll! pretty doll!" until Marian's present appeared from its wrappings.

"You stand on it and jump, this way." Margaret was on her feet, her suède toes balancing on the crosspiece.

"Letty jump!"

"Not in here!" Catherine reached for the stick. "You idiots! You'll knock the plaster off."

"Letty jump!" Catherine bundled Letty and the doll into her lap.

"Let's see what Spencer draws."

"Spencer was a difficult proposition." Margaret smiled at him. "I thought of a rubber ball, and then I remembered he had one. So I got this." She poked the box into his hands.

"It's as good as Christmas, isn't it, Muvver?" Marian was on tiptoe, her Pogo stick clasped to her side, her head close to Spencer's as he tore off the papers.

"Thought I'd help make him practical, to please the King."

"What is it?" Spencer knelt beside the box full of pieces of steel.

"You stick them together, and make skyscrapers and bridges and water towers and elevators. The clerk said you could build a city."

"Let me help, Spencer?" Marian flung herself on the floor beside Spencer.

"Me help!" Letty squirmed down from Catherine's lap.

"You might take the things into the dining room," suggested Catherine.

Spencer gathered up the box.

"I'm much obliged, Aunt Margie," he said, and Marian and Letty echoed him as they followed into the next room.

Margaret settled herself in a chair at the window.

"I thought your nurse would be in charge." Her eyes wandered out to the distant glint of water. "Thought you'd given up the heavy domestic act."

"I sent her home." Catherine smiled. "Weak minded, wasn't it?"

Margaret nodded.

"Certainly. You look fagged. You ought to be out horseback riding or something. You know"—she turned, her face serious—"if you're going to do a real job, you have to look out. You have to relax sometime."

"I have to read the d'rections first, don't I?" came Spencer's firm tones. "You can sit still and watch."

"Now I didn't budge from my bed until noon," went on Margaret, "and then Amy had breakfast ready for me, and then I jumped in a taxi and came up here. I have to run along in a minute, high tea down in the Village. But you've been at work since early dawn, haven't you?"

"Oh, there were a few things—"

"Why don't you find a real h ousekeeper in Flora's place?"

"I can't afford to pay more, yet. And Flora is too good to throw out. I can manage."

"You know"—Margaret's eyes were bright with curiosity—"I should like to know what started this, your leaving your happy home, I mean. I thought you were the devoted mother till eternity."

"I am," said Catherine, calmly. Then she leaned forward. "Do you realize that the loneliest person in the world is a devoted mother? This summer, Margaret, I thought I'd really go crazy. I was so sorry for myself it was ludicrous. I'm trying to find out if I am a person, with anything to use except a pair of hands—on monotonous, silly tasks."

"Of course, the trouble is just that. You are a person. I'm glad you've waked up, Catherine. You know, there isn't a man in the world that I'd give up my job for."

"I want a man, too." Catherine's mouth was stubborn. "And my children. I want everything. Perhaps I want too much."

"Oh, children." Margaret glanced through the wide doors. "Maybe I'll want some, some day. Nice little ducks. Now I've got Amy—and love enough to keep from growing stale. I want you to meet Amy some day." She rose, adjusting the brim of her wide purple hat. "Amy's waiting now. Tell Charles I'm longing for a glimpse of him." She made a humorous little grimace. "Want to see how he likes this new arrangement."

Margaret telephoned for a taxi, and then hung over the children, offering impossible suggestions, until the hall boy announced her cab.

Marian wanted to go down to the Drive, to jump. Catherine waved good-by to Margaret, her other hand restrainingly on Marian's shoulder.

"Not Sunday afternoon, Marian. There are so many people down there, you'd jump right on their toes. You watch Spencer."

The children played in reasonable quiet. Catherine finished her darning, her mind playing with the idea of the graphs she was working on. As she rolled up the last stocking, she wondered what she used to think about, as she sat darning or sewing. Nothing, she decided. Plain nothing. I could let my hands work, and my ears listen for the children, and the rest of me just stagnate.

She delayed supper a little, hoping that Charles might come. She wasn't sure about the Sunday trains. Finally she gave the children their supper and put Letty to bed.

Spencer was still engrossed in the construction of a building when Bill Gilbert came in.

"Henrietta isn't here?"

"No, but do come in." Catherine led him into the living room. "Is Henry coming?"

"She had a call, and said she'd stop here on her way home."

"Charles hasn't come yet. He's been in Washington since Friday."

"Friday? I thought I saw him downtown, with Miss Partridge. He probably went later."

"He went at one."

"This couldn't have been Charles, then. It was about four. I thought their committee had been meeting. Hello, Spencer. What you doing?"

Spencer had come in, his hands full of steel girders.

"Mr. Bill, you're a nengineer, aren't you? Well, could you show me about this bridge?"

More than an hour later, when Henrietta did come, Bill was stretched full length, his feet under the dining room table, his eyes on the level of the completed bridge, a marvelous thing of spans and girders, struts and tie-beams.

"I'm too weary to stay, Cathy." Henrietta set her case on the table; her fair skin looked dusted over with fatigue. "Convulsions. One of those mothers who won't believe in diet or doctors for her child. The father sent for me. The child is alive in spite of her."

"Do sit down and rest, at least."

"No. I'm too ugly. Do you want to come, Bill, or are you staying?"

Bill pulled himself awkwardly to his feet, one hand reaching for his pipe.

"This piece of work is done," he said, smiling down at Spencer's engrossed head. "I've had a fine evening, Catherine."

He had. When they had gone, and Catherine was supervising the children's preparations for bed, she still had the feeling of the evening; she had pulled her chair into the dining room, to watch them; Bill had looked up at her at long intervals, with a faint, queer smile in his eyes; he had said nothing, except to offer solemn, technical advice, simplified to meet Spencer's eagerness.

"I'm going to be a nengineer," said Spencer sleepily, as she bent over him. "An' build things."

"I want to be one, too," called Marian.

"You can't! You're only a girl."

"Mr. Bill said I could if I wanted to. He said I could be anything."

"So you can." Catherine tucked her in gently. "But you have to go to sleep first."

At eleven Catherine telephoned to the station, to ask about trains from Washington. No express before morning. Charles wouldn't take a local; he must have decided to take a sleeper. She set the sandwiches she had made for him away in the ice chest. No use worrying. She had to have some sleep, for to-morrow. Had Bill seen him, Friday afternoon? She hated the queer way waiting held you too tight, as if you were hung up by your thumbs. Charles might have wired her. But he knew she never meant to worry.

She was half conscious, all through the night, of the emptiness of his bed, opposite hers. Once she woke, thinking she heard the door click. She sprang up in bed to listen. Nothing but the constant, faint cacophony of city sounds. It must be almost morning—that was the rattle of ash cans.

CHAPTER III

Astonishing how much less hurried the morning seemed, with no Charles shaving in the bathroom, shouting out inquiries about his striped shirt, his bay rum—he had a blind spot for the thing he wanted at the moment. We need two bathrooms, thought Catherine. I've spoiled Charles. Breakfast, too, was more leisurely; none of the last-minute scramble, no sudden longing for crisp bacon, after the toast was made and the eggs were boiled. There was time, actually, for a manicure. Flora appeared promptly at eight, her Monday face lugubrious.

"Sunday's fearful exhausting, Mis' Hammond," she said, as Catherine finished the consultation about dinner. "It's the most exhaustin'est day us working women has, I thinks."

"And when Mr. Hammond comes, be sure to ask him if he wishes breakfast, Flora. He may have had it on the train."

"Sure, I'll ask him. You run along and quit your worry, Mis' Hammond."

Catherine, hurrying across the Drive for the bus, was worried. She felt almost guilty: first, because the morning rush had been so lightened; and then, because she was going off, downtown, just as if Charles scarcely existed. She had laid out fresh clothes for him, on his bed, but she knew how he would rush in, full of pleasant importance from the trip, wanting to shout bits of it to her while he splashed and shaved and dressed, wanting her to sit down for a late cup of coffee while he talked. If only he had come home yesterday! Well, to-night would have to serve, although by evening there would be the film of the day over that first sharpness of communication.

At the door of her office she paused, her fingers on the key. She must leave, outside the door, this faint guilt which tugged at her. She had wasted that hour on the bus. The order and quiet within were like a rebuke. She crossed to the window and raised the heavy sash. The cool bright morning air rushed in with a little flutter of the papers on the desk. Across the street and a story lower, behind great plate-glass windows, she could see busy little men hurrying about, lifting the white dust covers from piles of dark goods: that was an elaborate tailoring establishment, just waking into activity. Her desk had a fresh green blotter, a pile of neatly sharpened pencils, and her mail—C.S. Hammond. Extraordinary, this having things set in order without your own direction! She might call up the house, to see if Charles had come. But surely he would telephone.

Dr. Roberts came briskly in. She was to have a new filing cabinet, he wanted her to meet the stenographer she was to share with him; the President of the Bureau would be in that morning, and wished to talk with her for a few minutes.

President Waterbury was a large and pompous gentleman who used his increasing deafness as a form of reproach to his subordinates. Catherine, sitting calmly near his massive mahogany desk, nodded at intervals in response to his grave, deliberate remarks. Her work during the war had convinced Dr. Roberts of her ability, hem, hem, although that had been on a social study, and this was, hem, educational. Since Mrs. Lynch, one of the founders of the Bureau, was a woman, it was peculiarly fitting to place a competent woman in charge of one of their many investigations. Ah, hem. A pleasure to welcome her there. Serious concern, this administering of responsibility. He was dismissing her with an elegant gesture of his old white hand, its blue veins so abruptly naked between the little tufts of hair.

Catherine went back to her office.

"Oh, Mrs. Hammond!" The bobbed-haired office stenographer rose, with a shake of her abbreviated skirt. "You were wanted on the wire. Said you were in conference with the President. Here's the number."

"Thank you. No, I don't need you now." Catherine waited until the door closed. She still hesitated. It must be Charles. Better to call him outside, at noon. The telephone operator in the main office had a furtive, watchful eye which probably matched her ear! But noon was an hour away.

"Charles? Hello."

"That you, Catherine? I've been trying to get you for a solid hour!"

"I'm sorry." Was that girl listening! "When did you get in?"

"Early. Catherine, where have you put my lecture notes? The seminar, you know. That class meets to-day. I can't find a damned shred of them."

His voice seemed to stand him at her shoulder, with the funny, distracted flush, and rumpled hair of one of his fruitless searches.

"I haven't seen them this fall." She was moving rapidly about the house, almost in kinæsthetic images. Where would she look? "Didn't you file those in your office last spring? With the manuscript of your book?"

"Um. Perhaps. I'll look there. Good-by."

Catherine hung the instrument slowly in place. Not a word of greeting. But he had probably thrown his study into bedlam—and his disposition. She smiled, faintly, and refusing to admit the little barbed regret, turned to her work.

At noon, in the stuffy telephone booth at the elevator entrance of the St. Francis Club she tried to reach him. But Miss Kelly said he wasn't coming in for luncheon, and no one answered the call for his office.

The afternoon closed around her with steady concentration. Dr. Roberts had said that on Friday there would be a conference: a head of a normal college and a state commissioner of education would be on hand from the West. She wanted this preliminary classification ready.

As she approached the house that evening, she discovered, ironically, that her mind was revolving schemes for propitiation. Steak and onions for dinner, and cream pie, and tactful inquiries about the trip.

There was no rush of children at the sound of her key. She heard Marian's voice, and then Charles's. She hurried down the hall. Letty sat on her father's knee, a crisscross of adhesive plaster on her forehead, from which her hair was smoothed wetly back.

"She would jump on my Pogo stick, Muvver," protested Marian, "and I told her not to, and—"

Catherine was on her knees beside the chair, and Letty's mouth began to quiver again at a fresh spectator of her injury.

"It isn't a bad cut," said Charles, distantly. "Fortunately I came in."

"But where's Miss Kelly?"

"She left at six. I supposed you had instructed her to stay here until you came."

"I told her to run along." Flora stopped at the doorway, her red flowers bobbing over the brim of her hat. "I says I'd stay. An' those chillun was all right one minute and the next they wasn't."

"Where's Spencer?" Catherine rose. She had waited a long time for a bus, but it was just past six.

"In the bathroom, washing off the blood," said Charles, severely. "He was wiping Letty's face when I came in."

"She fell on the radiator," went on Marian, "an' I told her not to—"

"It's all right now." Charles set Letty on her feet, and patted her damp head. "But you surely ought to insist on that woman's filling your place, since you aren't here."

"I shall." Catherine's eyes sought his with a defiant entreaty. "It isn't very serious, after all," she finished, in white quiet. As she went into her room to leave her wraps and brush up her hair, she found her hands trembling, and her knees. She sat down at the window for a moment. Of course, she thought, they are my responsibility. That's only just. But he needn't hurry so to hold me up to blame. As if they planned it—a staged rebuke for my entrance. Spencer was at the door, his eyes large and serious.

"Hello, son!" Catherine shoved aside the tight bitterness, and smiled.

"Oh, Moth-er!" He ran across to her, burying his head for a brief instant on her shoulder. "I thought—I thought she was dead. Only she hollered too loud."

"I'm sorry, dear." Catherine hugged him. "But it's all right."

"And"—Spencer's lower lip quivered—"Daddy said why didn't I watch her if she didn't have a mother. She's got a mother, and I was just sitting there reading."

"Letty's all right now. Come, we must broil that steak! Aren't you hungry?"

Dinner was ready, all but the steak. Catherine felt that she thrust her hands violently into a patch of nettles and yanked them away, as she cajoled her family back into calm humor. Charles, carving the steak, suddenly lost his air of grave reproach, and began a story about a family with two sets of twins that he had seen on the train. With a sigh, Catherine relaxed her grip on the nettles. She might run into them, later!

"We looked for you all day yesterday," she said, finally.

"Several of the men stayed over, and I had a fine chance to talk with them. Brown of Cornell, and Davitts."

"Mr. Bill came in, Daddy, and showed me how to build a bridge."

"He thought he'd seen you Friday," said Catherine idly, "but I told him you went at one."

"Oh, yes." Charles was casual. "I missed that train. So I went around to the clinic."

His voice was too casual! And the swift glance he shot at Catherine as she rose.

CHAPTER IV

"I've got to run over those lecture notes." Charles stretched lazily up from the table. "They need freshening a bit."

"You found them, then?" Catherine had Letty in her arms, soft and sweetly heavy with drowsiness.

"Yes. I'd forgotten about carrying them over to the office."

"I was in the sacred sanctum of the President's office when you called."

"Oh, that's all right. I found them in time." Charles strolled out of the room.

"Daddy!" Spencer followed him. "Couldn't I show you my bridges and things? I can make anything."

"Not to-night, Spencer. Daddy's got to work."

Catherine's query about home work for school relieved Spencer's gloom. While she undressed Letty, smiling at the sleepy protests, Spencer and Marian cleared the table. When she reappeared they were trying to fold the long cloth, one at each end, Marian arguing heatedly about the proper method. Charles banged his study door in loud remonstrance. Catherine showed them the creases. Then they spread their books on the bare table.

"You sit here with us, Mother," Spencer begged. "I can do my sums much quicker. Marian doesn't have to do home work. She's just—"

"I do, too, have to do home work. The teacher said so."

"There, you shall, if you like." Catherine ruffled Spencer's hair. "Try not to disturb Father."

She sat there with them for an hour and more. Marian snuggled against her, showing her the pictures in her "suppulment'ry reading." Spencer bent over his work in a concentration directed toward the impressing of his sister, his cheeks growing pink, his hand clutched over his pencil. Although she sat so quietly, her outer attention given to the children, her deeper thoughts went scurrying and creeping up to the closed study door, away from it. He needn't have worked to-night. Don't be absurd. If he has a lecture to-morrow—he wants to shut himself away. Slowly her thoughts circled, like gulls above the water, concealing in their whirls the object which drew them.

"Muvver, does Spencer have to whisper his sums aloud?"

"Perhaps that helps him." Catherine smiled at Spencer's indignant face. "You may whisper your story, if you like."

What were they swooping over, those gull-thoughts? Better to scatter them and see. Not that he had missed the train; not even that he had not troubled to run in for a moment that afternoon; nor that he had chosen to see Miss Partridge. That might so easily be explained. No. Just that queer, investigating glance, that deliberate offhand manner, when he had told her. It set a wall between them.

The telephone rang distantly, behind the closed door. The children lifted their heads to listen. A rumble of Charles's voice. Then silence again.

When Spencer and Marian had laid away their books and gone to bed, Catherine returned to her seat at the empty table. I want him, she thought. But if I open his door and go in, then I become, in some way, a propitiator. Perhaps I only imagine all this. I am tired. She drew the pins from her hair and let the heavy coil slip over her shoulder. Elbows on the table, fingers cool and firm against her forehead, as if she might press order into her thoughts, she waited.

Suddenly she rose, shaking her hair back from her face. That is grotesque, she thought, sitting here, and hastily she went through the hall to the study door, flinging it open.

"Oh, hello." Charles looked up alertly from his book. He, too, had been waiting. "Kids in bed?"

"Aren't you through?" Catherine yawned gently, drawing her fingers across her lips. "I'm sleepy, and lonesome."

But under her lightness sounded a plunk, as of a stone dropping, a confirmation of a fear, as she saw the wary alertness on Charles's face vanish in quick relief.

"Just through," he announced. "Come on in. It's curious, how stale these lectures seem, after a year. Have to refurbish them entirely." He slipped the sheets into a manila cover. "That one's ready, at least."

Catherine sat on the corner of his desk, her fingers sliding through a strand of her hair.

"Did you have a good trip?" she asked. Anything, to banish this separateness. "I haven't heard a word about it."

"You weren't home. I was bursting with news this morning."

"Can't you remember a little of it?"

"I might try." Charles leaned back, his thumbs caught in his belt. As he talked, Catherine listened for the under-tones, so much more significant than the events. It had been a good trip. The men had received him rather flatteringly, praised his latest monograph, shown interest in the new psychological clinic. He had a comfortable, well-nourished look; around his eyes, with the prominent jutting of socket above, the lines were quite smoothed away. Catherine looked at him, at the strong, slightly projecting chin, at the smooth hard throat above the neat collar.

"Davitts hinted at an opening in a middle-western college," he said, finally. "Head of the department. I told him I was in line for promotion here, if I got this next book done this year. He seemed to think he had something better up his sleeve."

"Away from New York?"

"Ye-up." Charles was blandly indifferent. "Nothing definite, you know. Just hints."

"Would you even consider it?" Catherine's hands, even her hair against her fingers, felt cold.

"It never does any harm to let people offer you things. And I don't know—" He was drawing idle triangles on the manila covers of his lecture. "Sometimes a position like that means much more power, prominence, reputation, than anything here could. Would you mind?" He was eying her carefully. "Be better for the children." And after a pause. "Or would you have to stay here—for your job?"

"Have you just made this up—for a joke?" Catherine slipped to her feet. "Are you just teasing me?"

"Not a bit. That's what Davitts said."

"Charles!" Her fingers doubled into a fist at the edge of the desk. "Don't lurk around! Let's talk it out. You don't like it, my working? You"—she stared at him—"you don't mean you'd hunt for a job somewhere, in a little town, where I couldn't work, just to—"

"Good Lord! Now why go off at that tangent, just because I gave you a bit of news. Didn't I say I wanted you to have what you wanted?"

"But you don't like it, do you?"

"Damn it, give me time to get used to it. It's all fired queer to go off without any one caring, and come back to a deserted house. I'll probably get used to it, but give me time."

"Do you want me to give it up?"

"Are you tired of it already?"

"Do you really care to know how I feel about it?" Catherine's voice was low and tense. "I feel as if I'd escaped from solitary confinement. At hard labor, too! I feel as if I could hold up my head and breathe. And then, underneath, I feel you pulling at me, wresting me back. Oh, you say you don't mind, but—"

"Catherine, see here." Charles stood up and leaned toward her. "I—I haven't meant to be a hog. But a man has a kind of knock-out, to find he isn't enough, with his home and all. Here, let's forget it. I've had a hard week-end, and last week was a fright. That's all."

"It's not that you aren't enough." Catherine flung herself at that phrase. "You know about that! Any more than I'm not enough, for you. There's more to you than love, isn't there? Why isn't there more to me? If you'd only see—"

"The only thing that bothers me is the children. Now, take Letty—"

"But I have left them with Flora many times. I've had to. And they bump their heads when I'm home. That's not the point. It's your blaming me."

"All right!" Charles threw up his hands in a sweep of mocking surrender. "I won't say a word."

"I want you to say it, not hint it."

"Anything you like." His hands closed on her shoulders. "Here, you haven't kissed me since I came home."

There were sudden wild tears under Catherine's lids, and she thought desperately, oh, not that! Not kisses as the only way—to touch, to reach each other!

"Didn't even kiss me good-by. Nice kind of wife." Charles pushed her chin up with a firm finger. "There now—"

"You didn't give me a chance." Catherine was quiet, thrusting under her rebellion. Suddenly, through her misted lashes, she saw just for a flash, an echo of that wary, investigatory glance. She swung out over a great abyss.

Bill had seen him, with Miss Partridge. Nothing to that, surely, except this feeling, which was not jealousy, but fear of what he was defending himself against.

"I wanted to find you, but I didn't like to come up to the Bureau," he was saying. "So I went down to the clinic and talked over things with Stella Partridge." The brisk, matter-of-course words drew her back sharply from the abyss. "It took the edge off, not finding you here, this morning." He was threading his fingers through her hair.

"You're spoiled rotten!" Catherine could laugh at him now. He meant that for his apology, and she would let it lift her out of fear and hurt.

CHAPTER V

The week settled into a steady march. Flora had taken on the marketing, Miss Kelly had agreed never to leave the house until Catherine arrived, Charles was amiably preoccupied with the rush of the opening semester. It hadn't been so hard to adjust things, thought Catherine. Takes a little planning—I was too impatient.

Her work at the office was focussed on the Saturday conference. She wanted her preliminary analysis in tables and graphs clear and adequate enough to present to the men; there would be discrepancies between the apparent system and the actual practice in the state which the commissioner could point out. She hadn't time to complete the study of the normal schools; they were astonishingly numerous and varied.

"It's just hit or miss, this whole educational business," she said to Dr. Roberts, on Friday afternoon, as they talked over the material. "No central direction or purpose."

"Too much imitation and tradition." Dr. Roberts had his pointed beard between the pages of a catalogue. He lifted it toward her, his bright blue eyes and sharp nose eager on the scent of an idea. "Too little conscious plan. People are afraid of thought. Trial-and-error is the working basis. But that's slow, and you have this heavy crust of tradition."

"I'd like to scrap it all and make a fresh beginning!"

"There never is such a thing as a fresh beginning. You have to work from what exists."

Catherine pushed aside a pile of catalogues, her face alight with scorn.

"But why, if it's stale and wrong? Take these normal schools. Young people, girls mostly, go there, because they have to have a diploma to teach. What do they get? Things out of books. They learn to teach paragraphs of geography, not to teach children. It would be ridiculous, except that it is terrible. Perhaps it's because men run them."

"Women"—Dr. Roberts smoothed his beard—"are popularly supposed to submit more docilely to tradition."

"Supposed by whom?" Catherine's hand sent a catalogue banging to the floor. "That's been a convenient way of holding their wildness under, I think." She felt her mind throw up swift thoughts that burst and scattered like Roman candles. She couldn't gather the splintering brightness. "We've had, as women, too small an orbit."

The stenographer thrust her bobbed head into the door, to say that Dr. Roberts was wanted on the telephone. Should she connect his party here?

"No, I'll take him on my own 'phone." He rose, smiling. "We'll have to thrash this out to-morrow," he said, "or some day. Don't frighten our committee to-morrow, though, by announcing that you are wild, will you?"

Catherine, erect in her seat on the bus top, the golden October air fresh on her cheeks, went on coruscating. It was true, that about women. They felt that children were the most important part of life. So they stayed with them, cared for them, held under all their own—was it wildness?—bending it to food and clothes and order—and then? They threw their children out into the nets laid by men, not viciously, not deliberately, but with all that pompous weight of tradition. The way things should be done, learned, thought. If you could scrap it all and begin—where? With something, a kernel of intelligence, what children are, and what you wish them to grow into, what will nourish that growth. Charles was on that track, with his new clinic, and all his work.

As she climbed down from the bus and started up the hill toward Broadway, her thoughts still sparkled, spreading out in great circles of light about her, vague projects, shadowy schemes, beautiful structures of clarity and sanity for the world, for the children.

"What a stride!"

The circles contracted swiftly, and she turned.

"Bill! Hello." She emerged slowly, shreds of the dream still shining. They fell into step.

"How goes it?" His glance veered to her face. "You look as if you'd had your salary raised."

"Better than that." Catherine wanted to break into his dark, withdrawn glance; she wanted, suddenly, to draw him into this glittering mood. "Bill, it's wonderful. I feel my mind budding! It wasn't dead. Like a seed potato—shoots in every direction, out of every wrinkle!"

"You look it." Bill nodded. "I saw that you walked on air."

"I've been recasting the universe." She laughed, as they waited a moment for passing traffic. "That's better than building bridges, isn't it?"

"It is less confining."

They went quickly past the subway kiosk, dodging the home-pouring workers, past the peanut stand panting warm and odorous at the corner, to the wide hill of steps in front of the University library. A flower vender thrust his bunches of roses at them.

"I want some!" Catherine dug into her purse.

"Aren't they stale?" Bill watched her fasten the creamy, buff-pink buds to her coat.

"Probably. But they look fresh now." Catherine swung into step again. Queer, how that occasional little side glance of Bill's gave assent to her mood, dipped into it, recognized it, without a word.

"I suppose," she said, as they rounded the corner of Amsterdam, "that I can't stay on this level. It's too high. But I've just reached it to-day. Assurance, and a long sight into what I can do."

"There's always, unfortunately, another day." Bill frowned slightly. "Another mood. But you seem to have hit a fair wind. Henrietta told me that Miss Kelly was panning out well."

"Yes." The view ahead, of the dipping, climbing avenue, with its familiar shops, its familiar clatter of the cobblestones, was sharp as a background of relief against which to-day stood out. "I know what I feel like, Bill. If you want to know."

"I do. Always."

Simple words, but Catherine heard them with faint wonder. Bill was never personal. His profile, with its long nose and lean cheeks, like a horse, was reassuring.

"Well, then. Did you ever watch a treadmill? Round and round, all your effort taking you nowhere but around? That's where I've been. That's what I've done. The same circle, day after day. And now I'm out of it, on a long, straight road. Going somewhere!"

"I hope it's straight." They had reached the apartment entrance, and Bill shook his head at Catherine's suggestion that he come in.

"No road is really straight. But as long as it goes somewhere!"

Bill looked at her; Catherine thought he started to speak, and then refused the words.

"Spencer is longing for your next call," she said.

"I'll drop in some evening. Henry's been busy."

"Don't wait for her, then. Just come."

At the door Miss Kelly met Catherine.

"Letty hasn't seemed quite well," she said. "I put her to bed."

"What's wrong?" Catherine stared at Miss Kelly's bland, pink face. "She isn't really sick?"

"It's hard to tell, with a child." Miss Kelly followed Catherine down the hall. "It may be just indigestion."

Letty, her small face flushed and scowling, wrinkled her eyes at her mother.

"Don't want to go to bed. Want to see my Muvver."

"Here I am, Letty." Catherine touched her cheek, felt for her wrist.

"She has scarcely any temperature," announced Miss Kelly. "Just a degree. But I thought—"

"Surely, she's better in bed. Did she have any supper?"

"Broth."

"Don't wait, Miss Kelly. I know you wish to go."

"Well, since you are here."

Catherine removed her coat and hat. The roses dropped to the floor.

"Pretty!" Letty reached for them.

"I'll put them in water." Catherine came back with a vase. "Do you feel sick anywhere, chick?"

"Letty not sick. Get up." Catherine caught the wiggling child, and pulled the blanket into place.

"You lie still, and mother'll be back presently. I must see to dinner for Daddy."

She hurried into the kitchen. Spencer and Marian were under the dining room table, playing menagerie, and unable to answer her except in fierce growls. Charles hadn't come in. Probably Letty wasn't really sick. She had little flurries of indisposition; perhaps she had eaten something.

Charles came in, with a jovial bang of the door, and a shout, "Ship ahoy! Who's at the helm?"

"Don't tell him, Muvver." Marian's head butted the tablecloth aside. "Sh!"

"'Lo, Cath!" He swung her up to tiptoe in his exuberant hug. "Where are the kids?"

"Grrrr!" and "Woof!" The table cloth waggled.

"Ah, wild animals under foot!" Charles gave an elaborate imitation of a big game hunter, creeping toward the table, sighting along his thumbs. "Biff, bang!" He reached under, seized a leg, and drew out Marian, giggling and rolling. "Bagged one! Bang, bang! Got the panther!" He had Spencer by the collar. "Teddy, the great hunter!" He straddled them, his arms folded, while they shrieked in delight.

A wail from the doorway, "Letty play! Shoot Letty!"

Catherine ran past them, gathering the child into her arms. Her hand, closing over the small feet, found them dry, hot, and the weight of the child seemed to scorch through her blouse against her shoulder.

"What's the matter with my baby?" Charles followed them. "Let me have her, Catherine."

"She's supposed to be in bed." Catherine covered her with the blanket. "Now you stay there, young lady! Mother will come in soon."

She touched the scarlet cheek, her fingers feather soft. Letty's eyelids, heavy and dark, drooped, and her protest broke off.

Catherine drew Charles into the hall.

"Would you call up Dr. Henrietta? I think her fever is coming up."

"Is she sick?" Charles looked aggrieved at this intrusion upon his mood.

"I hope not." Catherine gave him a little push. "Call her up, and see when she can come in. I'll have dinner on directly."

The wild animals were washed and combed, and dinner served when Charles came out of the study.

"She's not in. Probably at dinner. I left word with the clerk. But I say, Catherine. I got tickets for 'Liliom' to-night." He looked blankly disappointed. "You said you wanted to see it, and I was downtown. Good seats, too."

"Oh, Charles!"

"And I even called up that girl we had last year, to stay with the children. That graduate student, you know."

"Well." Catherine lifted her hands in a little gesture of resignation. "If Letty's sick— But 'Liliom'! I do want to go."

"Maybe she'll be all right when she's asleep."

But she wasn't. Eight o'clock came, with Charles fidgeting like a lamprey eel on a hook, and no word from Henrietta. Letty was asleep, her hands twitching restlessly. Catherine shook her head, as she read the thermometer.

"I can't go, Charles. Almost a hundred and one."

"What ails her? Has that woman you've got been feeding her pickles?"

The door bell rang. Charles, with a mutter of "Dr. Henry, perhaps," rushed to the door. He came back.

"It's Miss Brown, come to stay the evening. What shall I tell her?"

"Tell her I can't go." Catherine was abrupt. She was disappointed and she was fighting off a sturdily growing fear about the next day,—and she resented Charles's air of injury.

"I hate to, after I begged her to come in."

Catherine brushed hastily past him and went to the door. Miss Brown, a plump, pale, garrulous woman of middle age, a southerner, waited.

"Letty, the baby, isn't very well," explained Catherine. "Nice of you to come in so promptly. Some other night, perhaps." And presently the door could be closed upon Miss Brown's profuseness of pity.

Charles was glooming about his study.

"When you leave them all day for your job," he said, "I should think you might—"

"No, you shouldn't think!" Catherine laughed at him. "You're as bad as Spencer, little boy!"

The bell rang again.

"That's Henry!" Catherine hurried to the door, and opened it to Stella Partridge's little squirrel smile and extended hand.

"Good evening, Mrs. Hammond. I told Dr. Hammond I'd let him have this outline when it was finished."

"Won't you come in, Miss Partridge?" Catherine heard Charles coming. He lounged beside her, hands in pockets.

"No, thank you. I just brought this outline, Dr. Hammond." She handed him the envelope.

There was a moment of silence, in which Catherine felt a tugging at her will, as if Charles tried to bend her to some thought of his. She glanced at him, still sulky.

"I have it," she said. "Why don't you take Miss Partridge to your show, Charles? If she would like it. Have you seen 'Liliom,' Miss Partridge?"

"Letty is indisposed," said Charles, "thus interfering, after the fashion of children, with her parents' plans."

"Can't I stay with her?" Miss Partridge opened her dark eyes very wide.

"Mrs. Hammond is punctilious."

Catherine withdrew a step. If Charles added another word—she could hear the rest of his sentence, about her leaving them all day! But he merely added, "Would you care to go, Miss Partridge?"

"Ought you to leave Mrs. Hammond, if the baby is ill?"

"It's always a relief to be rid of a disappointed man, Miss Partridge." Catherine was thinking: how disdainful that cold, hard voice makes her words sound! "Letty isn't seriously ill, but I want the doctor to look at her. I shall be happier here."

Miss Partridge seated herself in the living room, and Catherine, after a glance at Letty, and a moment of search for the tie Charles wished, sat down opposite her. She was charming to look at, Catherine realized; a soft, fawn colored suit, exquisitely tailored over her slender, sloping shoulders; a long brown wing across the smart fawn hat, a knot of orange at her throat. She drew off her wrinkled long gloves, and revealed a heavy topaz on her little finger.

"Your work, Mrs. Hammond? You are finding it interesting?"

"Very." Catherine felt as expansive as an exposed clam.

"Mr. Hammond was saying you had some kind of educational research in hand."

"Yes." Was that Letty, crying? Charles came in, rubbing his sleeve over his hat.

"I don't need glad rags, do I, since you aren't in evening dress?"

"No gladder than those." Miss Partridge rose.

Catherine stood at the living room door, listening for the sound of the elevator. Charles came rushing back.

"You're sure you'll be all right?" That was his little flicker of contrition. "I don't like to leave you this way, but the tickets might as well be used."

"Have a good time." Catherine kissed him lightly.

"Wish it was you, going!" He was in fine fettle again, offering a small oblation before his departure.

Letty woke, complaining that she wanted a drink. Catherine sat beside her, smoothing the silky fair hair, until she slept again. Her forehead didn't feel so parched. But Catherine went to the telephone and called Henrietta. Bill answered.

"Oh, Catherine! Henry got your message. She had to stop at the hospital first. She'll be in. Is Letty really sick?"

"I hope not. But I need Henrietta's assurance."

"She'll be along."

Spencer looked up from his books.

"I think Daddy ought to stay home if you have to," he said, frowning.

"Daddy isn't any use if the children are sick," announced Marian, with dignity. "Is he, Muvver?"

"Not as a nurse," said Catherine. "But he's a great comfort to me, you know."

"How?" Spencer was still accusing.

"Just being." Catherine smiled at him. Spencer had a curious way of reaching out, thrusting fine feelers about him, investigating subtleties of relationship. He was staring at her intently, as if he pondered her last words. Then with a sigh, postponing judgment, he closed his book.

"My home work's all done, and I did it alone, because Letty is sick. Is that a comfort to you, Mother?"

"It is." Catherine was grave.

When they had gone to bed, Marian in Catherine's room, so that Letty would not disturb her, Catherine moved restlessly about the apartment. She was thinking about them, her children. What they needed. More than food and shelter, more than physical safety. They needed a safety in the *feeling* around them. A warm, clear sea, in which they could float, unaware that the sea existed. Tension, ugly monsters, frighten them, disturb them out of their own little affairs. Spencer especially, but Marian, too. Letty was such a baby, still, but she was growing; she was still turned inward. Catherine wandered to the door and listened. She was breathing too rapidly. If Henry would only come!

She sat down at the window, staring out at the dull yellow glow which held the city as a mass and dimmed the stars. You can't pretend for them, she thought. They catch the reality under the surface. But that perfect safety of feeling—who has it! She felt herself opposed to Charles, struggling with him, toward that intense calm that might hold the children free and unaware. Perhaps some women could attain that—she was abject, despairing—women who could lose their own struggling selves. But what then? The children grew up, and made their own circles, never reaching anything but this going-on. Surely somewhere, along the way, there should be something beside immolation for the future, otherwise why the future? Marian, Letty—I can't do it, she thought. Drown myself to make that quiet, white peace. I won't drown. I keep bobbing up, trying to be rescued. Something in me, shrieking. If I can rescue that shrieking something, and silence it, then surely there's more in me, more poise, more love, to wrap them—no, not wrap them, to float them in. If Charles will help!

She had a sharp vision of Charles and Stella Partridge, sitting side by side in the darkened theater, their eyes focussed on the brilliant fantasy of the stage. Charles had been delighted to go. He didn't have play enough, these last years. I wish I were beside him,—her hand reached out emptily, as if to grasp his. Good for him, seeing other people, other women. They stimulate him, even if I don't like them. She caught, like a reflection in a mirror, the tone of that short walk from the bus with Bill. Something exciting about that—an encounter with another person.

A ring of the bell; Dr. Henrietta at last.

Catherine stood behind her, as she examined Letty, drowsily fretful at the disturbance. What strong, white, competent fingers Henry had! They went into the living room.

"She's not very sick." Henrietta sank into a chair and snapped open her cigarette case. "I'm not sure—tell better to-morrow. I'll come in early. You better keep the other children away from her. It might be something contagious."

"She's had measles." Catherine was openly dismayed, as the bugbear of contagion rose. "Good land, if she has, it means they all get it, just like a row of dominoes. Henry! What shall I do?"

"Oh, get a nurse and quarantine them. You don't need to stay in. Charles doesn't."

"I couldn't."

"Well, wait until to-morrow. May be just indigestion. I've given her a dose for that." Dr. Henrietta stretched in her chair, crossing her ankles, slim and neat in heavy black silk above small, dull pumps. "We don't want your career busted up yet. How's it going? And where's friend husband?"

"I sent him off to the theater with Miss Partridge." Catherine grinned. "He had the tickets, and was sure' I needn't stay with Letty."

"I never yet saw a man who was worried about his child when he had something he wanted to do." Henry puffed busily. "They regard children as pleasant little amusements, but put them away if they bother."

"Charles isn't quite like that—"

"No defense necessary. I'm just offering an observation. Sorry I had to be late. I stopped to watch Lasker do a Cæsarian on a case of mine. Beautiful job. But how's your work? Bill said he ran into you, spoke of your looking well."

"My job is fine." Catherine saw, at a great distance, the mood in which she had come home. "Henrietta, I must go down to-morrow. There's a conference. I've been getting ready for it all the week."

"Miss Kelly will be here, won't she?"

"It's Saturday. She'll have to take Spencer and Marian—although I suppose Letty has exposed them already."

"She may have nothing at all, you know. I'll come in as early as possible. What time is this conference?"

"Ten."

"Um. I'll try to make it. I promised to stop in at the hospital. Charles can stay, can't he, if I should be detained?"

"Don't you let her have anything that will quarantine me! If I am thrown out now, I'll never get back."

"All righty." Henrietta rose, shaking down her skirt. "I won't." She ground out her cigarette in the ash tray, with a shrewd upward glance at Catherine. "You go to bed. You look too frayed. This is just a first hurdle, you know. I'll come in before nine to-morrow. But you make Charles stay, if I should be later."

CHAPTER VI

Catherine woke into complete alertness. Charles had come in. She heard his cautious step in the hall. Letty was sleeping easily, her breathing soft and regular again. Catherine slipped noiselessly out of the room.

"Hello!" She brushed into Charles at the door. "Marian's in my bed," she whispered. "Have a good time?"

"Oh, fair." Charles yawned. "How's Letty?"

"Asleep. Tell me about it in the morning. We might wake her."

In the morning Catherine was fagged. All night the awareness of Letty had kept her at the thin edge of sleep, drawn out by the faintest stirring. The child was sitting up in bed, now, clamoring for her doll, her bwekkust, and her go-duck; her cheeks were pink, but they seemed flower-cool to Catherine's fingers.

"Let's see if you have any speckles, Letty." She peeled the night dress down; one round red spot in the shell hollow of her knee. "Is that a speckle, Letty Hammond, or a mosquito bite!" Letty gurgled deliciously as Catherine's fingers tickled. "Let's see your throat. No, wider? Does it hurt?"

"Uh huh. Hurt Letty." Letty's arms were tight around her neck, and she bounced vigorously up and down on her pillow.

"Here, stop it." Catherine pinioned her firmly. "Where does it hurt?"

"Hurt Letty. Here." Letty sat down with a plump, and pointed at her toe.

"Well, you don't look sick, I must say. But that spot—" Catherine imprisoned her in the night dress again, and tucked her firmly under the blanket. "I'll bring Matilda, and you can put her to bed with you. Dr. Henrietta's coming to see you soon."

Marian appeared at the door.

"Daddy's asleep and I didn't know he was in his bed." She giggled. "I most woke him up jumping on him."

"Hurry and wash, dear. And don't come in with Letty, please."

Catherine sighed a little as she hurried to thrust herself into the shafts of the morning.

Letty's frequent interruptions, and Charles's reluctance to wake; the discovery that there were no oranges; the demoniac speed of the clock—it was after eight when they sat down to breakfast. Catherine drank her coffee, and hurried off to dress.

Flora came in. Catherine heard her, with relief, offering to make fresh toast for Charles. Miss Kelly appeared. She was calmly solicitous as Catherine explained Dr. Henrietta's visit. "Of course, I couldn't go into quarantine," she said, "on account of my mother."

"I understand. If you'll just take the other children outdoors for the morning—"

They had gone. It was nine, and no Dr. Henrietta. Catherine fastened a net carefully over her coiled hair, brushed her hat, poking at the limp bow of ribbon, and then went slowly to the study, where Charles was rummaging through a drawer of his desk.

"You have no classes this morning, have you?" she began.

"No, I haven't. Do you know where I put that outline Miss Partridge left?"

"Here it is." Catherine lifted it from beneath the evening paper. "Charles, Henry is coming in. She said as early as possible. I can't wait for her. Would you mind?"

"What's she coming for? Isn't Letty all right?"

"I don't know. She has a red spot. Henry thought she might have something—scarlatina—"

"I thought they'd had 'em all, those red diseases."

"Her fever is down. I think she's not sick. But Henrietta wanted to be sure. Would you mind—waiting till she comes?"

"Stay here this morning?" Charles looked up, an abrupt frown between his eyes. "I can't, Catherine. I can't play baby tender. I've got a meeting."

"So have I." Catherine stood immobile in the doorway. "A very important one. Those men from the West are here. At ten. I am to present the work I've been doing."

"Can't Flora keep an eye on Letty till Henry comes?"

"I think one of us ought to be here."

"Good Lord, Catherine! I have to meet the committee on choice of dissertation subjects. Do you want me to telephone them that I have to stay home with the baby?"

"You couldn't stay just an hour?"

"Be reasonable, Catherine. I can't make myself ridiculous."

"No?" Catherine stared at him an instant. Then she turned and left him.

He followed her into the living room, where she stood at the window.

"Call up your mother," he suggested. "She can probably drop in."

"Why," said Catherine evenly, "does it make you more ridiculous than me? That dissertation committee meets a dozen times this fall. Letty is your child, isn't she? Don't tell me I'm her mother!"

"I expected something of this sort, when you announced that you had to have a career." Charles walked briskly in front of her, stern and determined. "We might as well fight it out now. Do you want me to take your place? You said not. Do be reasonable."

"I'm so reasonable it hurts." Catherine's laugh was brittle. "Go on, to your meeting. I'll stay, of course."

"Well, really, I'm afraid you'll have to." Charles hesitated, and then added, gruffly, "It's unfortunate it happened just this way." His gesture washed his hands of the affair.

As he strolled importantly out of the room, Catherine's hand doubled in a cold fist against her mouth. He can't see, she thought. There's no use talking.

When he had gone, Catherine hovered a moment at the telephone. No use calling her mother; she wouldn't be able to come up from Fiftieth Street in time to do any good. She sat down at the desk, her hands spread before her, her eyes on her wrist watch. Henrietta might still come. The minutes were thick, cold liquid, dripping, dripping. Letty's loud call summoned her, and she hunted up the dingy cotton duck, while that slow, cold drip, drip continued. Half past nine. The minutes split into seconds, heavy, cold, dripping seconds. Time could drive you mad, thought Catherine, while the seconds dripped upon her, if you waited for it long enough.

It was almost ten when she telephoned the Bureau.

Dr. Roberts' neat accents vibrated at her ear.

"I am sorry," she said, "but I cannot get away. One of the children is ill. I've been waiting for the doctor. You have the final sheets and graphs I made, haven't you? There's a list of questions and notes in the left drawer of my desk. I regret this. If you wish any explanation of the graphs, please call me."

He sounded abrupt, irritated, under his perfunctory regret. As Catherine hung away her hat and coat, she felt a cold, heavy weight back of her eyes, deep in her throat. Time had lodged there! I can't sit down and cry, she thought. No wonder he is angry. It's my business to be on hand. She had once, swimming at low tide, found herself in a growth of kelp, the strong wet masses tangling about her frightened struggles. Charles had dragged her out, to clear green water and safety. She laughed, and pressed her fist again against her mouth. He wouldn't drag her out of this tangle, not he!

She sat beside Letty, reading to her, when Dr. Henrietta finally came.

"Catherine! You stayed!" Her round face set in dismay. "I tried once to call you. That baby died, the one we delivered last night. I've been working there."

"I knew you'd come when you could." Catherine pushed her chair away from the bed. Henrietta pulled off her coat, pushed up her cuffs from her firm wrists, and bent over Letty.

"She's all right," she said, presently. "Just a touch of stomach upset last night. That's good."

"Ducky sick." Letty waved her limp bird at Henrietta.

"Keep him very quiet, then." Henrietta poked the duck down beside Letty, and shook herself briskly into her coat.

Catherine followed her into the hall.

"I might as well have gone down to the office." She was ironic.

"Exactly. I'm awfully sorry, Catherine, that I am so late. It's almost noon, isn't it? I thought I could keep life in that little rag." Her eyes looked hot and tired. "But I couldn't. Just keep Letty from tearing around too much to-day. She'll be sound as a whistle to-morrow again."

"Well, at least we escaped a plague." Catherine leaned against the wall, inert, dull.

"Wouldn't Charles stay?" Henrietta peered at her. "Too busy, eh? Well, Monday you'll be free as air again."

"I wonder."

"Now, Catherine, don't be so serious. A year from now you won't know you weren't there!"

"It's not just that, Henry. It's the whole thing." Catherine flung open her hands. "Am I all wrong, to try it?"

"You know what I think. Here, put on your hat and come out in the sunshine. Haven't you some marketing to do?"

"No. Flora does it. But I will go to the corner with you."

Flora could keep an eye on Letty. Catherine hurried for her wraps, and joined Henrietta at the elevator.

"You've had a horrid morning, haven't you?" she said, swinging up from her inner concentration. "The poor baby—"

"If we can pull the mother through. She's been scared for months. She doesn't know, yet."

They stood at the corner, the clatter of the street bright about them.

"I've another call at Ninetieth. I'll ride down." Henrietta signaled the car. "Buck up, Cathy. It's all part of life, anyway. Death—" She shrugged. "That's the queer thing." Her placid mask had slipped a little. "Pleasant words to leave with you, eh?" She jeered at herself. "So long!"

As Catherine recrossed the street, she hesitated, glancing back into the shade behind the iron palings of the little park. Was that Charles, just within the gate, and that slim, elegant, tan figure beside him? She turned and fled. She wouldn't see them, not now. Not until she had fought through this thicket of resentment. After all, she had known, all the time, that what fight there was to make she must make unaided. The sun was warm and golden, and there came Spencer and Marian, shouting out, "Moth-er!" as they chased ahead of Miss Kelly.

"Oh, we had a nice time." Marian danced at her side, clinging to her arm. "Miss Kelly told us a new game."

How well they looked, and Miss Kelly, trudging to catch up with them, was serene and smiling. Letty wasn't sick. It was all a part of life. She could manage it, everything, someway!

Miss Kelly, puffing and warm, was delighted with the news about Letty.

"I was trying," she said, "to figure out some way about mother, so I wouldn't have to desert you." Catherine's quick smile saw Miss Kelly as a sunlit rock, equable, sustaining.

Flora shooed the children out of the kitchen. She was engrossed in the ceremonial preparation of stuffed peppers with Spanish sauce. Catherine, preparing orange juice for Letty, was secretly amused at the elaborate rites.

Not until Flora had closed the oven door on the pan did she look up at Catherine. Then—

"Gen'man called you up, Mis' Hammond. I plumb forgot to tell you. He pestered me 'bout where you was, and I told him you was out for the air."

"Who?" Catherine poured the clear juice in to a tumbler. "Did he—" She turned quickly. "Who was it?"

"Lef' his number. I put it on the pad."

Catherine flew into the study, deaf to Letty's shrill call. It was the Bureau. Her voice, repeating the number, was imperative. She had forgotten that Dr. Roberts might call. The whir of the unanswered instrument pounded on her ear drum. After one. The Bureau was deserted. What *would* he think! Why, it looked—she pushed the telephone away, dull color sweeping up to her hair. It looked as if she had lied. But it had been so late when Henrietta had come that any thought of the conference had been worn down. She would have to explain, Monday, as if she had been caught malingering.

"Hello." Charles stood at the door, uncertainty in his greeting. "What's the verdict? Pest house?"

"No." Catherine was jamming the whole dreadful morning out of sight, stamping on the cover—"Henry says it was just indigestion. She's all right."

"Did you get down to your meeting?"

Catherine shook her head.

"Now that's a shame," Charles advanced tentatively. "I hoped Henry would come in time."

Easy to say that now, thought Catherine. Then—I won't be ugly. I can't endure it.

"I felt an awful brute." Charles threw his arm over her shoulders. "But you saw how it was."

"Oh, I saw!" An ironic gleam in Catherine's eyes.

"And here Letty didn't need you, anyway. You might even have gone last night."

"I must see to her lunch." Catherine twisted out of his arm, adding with a touch of malice—"You know you had a good time."

"Oh, fair." Charles was indifferent. "Left me sort of done this morning. Miss Partridge wanted me to thank you for her pleasant evening."

"I thought I saw you at the gate just now," said Catherine.

"Yes. I just ran into her on my way home."

"Don't look at me that way!" Catherine cried out sharply.

"What way?" Charles expanded his chest, bristling.

"As if you expected to see me—*suspecting* you!"

"Well, good Lord, you sounded as if you thought I'd spent the morning with Stel—Miss Partridge."

"I hadn't thought so. Did you?"

"Of course not." Charles began, with elaborate patience. "I told you that dissertation committee—" Catherine's laugh interrupted him, and he stared at her. "I don't know what you're trying to do," he said slowly. "I'm sick of this guilty feeling that's fastened on me. Last night because I wanted you to go to the theater, this morning because I had to go to a legitimate meeting. You don't act natural any more."

Catherine went quickly back to him, her finger tips resting lightly against his shoulders.

"And so he deposited the blame where it wouldn't bother him—on her frail shoulders!" Her eyes, mocking, brilliant in her pale face, met his sulky defiance. "Philander if you must, but don't act as if you'd stolen the jam!"

"I'm not philandering."

"No, of course he isn't." Catherine brushed her fingers across his cheek. "Not for an instant. Now come, luncheon must be ready."

"But I may!" His voice came determinedly after her, as she went into Letty's room, "if I don't have more attention paid to me at home!"

CHAPTER VII

Saturday, Sunday, Monday morning again. Catherine, shivering a little in the wind from the gray river, as the bus lumbered down the Drive, tried to escape the clutter of thoughts left from the week-end. She had borrowed twenty-five dollars from Charles that morning, for Miss Kelly. She had pretended not to see his eyebrows when she laid the market bills in front of him. Flora had said, when Catherine suggested more discretion in shopping: "Yes'm, I'll make a 'tempt. But charging things in a grocery store jest stimulates my cooking ideas."

Perhaps I'll have to take back the shopping. A gust caught her hat, wheeled it half around. And clothes! I've got to have some. How? I won't have a cent left out of that first check. It's like an elephant balancing on a ball, or a tight-rope walker without his umbrella, this whole business.

Last night, when her mother had come in, and Bill and Dr. Henrietta, her mother with several amusing little stories about the friend who had come from Peoria, Illinois, to spend the winter with her—too plump to fit easily into the kitchenette—Charles, with his affectionate raillery of Mrs. Spencer—her mother was fond of Charles. But he needn't have made a jest of Saturday morning, and his refusal to give up his job to stay home with Letty. "That's what poor men are coming to, I'm afraid," her mother had told him. Henrietta had jibed openly at him, so openly that only Mrs. Spencer's gentle and fantastic mockery had smoothed his feathers. And Bill had said nothing. Catherine drew her collar closely about her throat. She had found him looking at her, and in his glance almost a challenge, a recall of that brief walk on Friday. "I hope it's straight, your road," he had said then. She shrugged more deeply into her coat. Straight! Was it a road? Or merely a blind alley? Or a tight-rope, and she had to poise herself and juggle a hundred balls as she crossed; the house, the children, the bills, Charles, always Charles, and her work. She came back to the thought of Dr. Roberts and the explanation she must offer.

Dr. Roberts, however, seemed miraculously to need no explanation. He had called to tell her that the committee was to stay over Monday, and that she could meet the two men after all. With sudden release from the tension of the past days, Catherine moved freely into this other world, and her road seemed again straight. She was quietly proud of the conservative response her suggestions met; her mind was agile, cool, untroubled. There grew up a plan for a first-hand study of several of the normal schools. Someone from the Bureau might go west. Catherine brushed aside her sudden picture of herself, walking among the bricks and stone, the people, for which these dust-grimed catalogues stood.

As she went home that evening, little phrases from the day ran like refrains. "A masterly analysis, Mrs. Hammond. Your point of view is interesting." And Dr. Roberts, after the men had gone—"I call this a most encouraging meeting, Mrs. Hammond. Sometimes the personal equation is, well, let us say, difficult. But you have tact."

Oh, it's worth any amount of struggle, she thought. Any amount! I'll walk my tight-rope, even over Niagara. And keep my balls all flying in the air!

PART III
BLIND ALLEYS

CHAPTER I

Margaret and Catherine were lunching together in a new tea room, a discovery of Margaret's. The Acadian, Acadia being indicated in the potted box at the windows, the imitation fir trees on the bare tables, and the Dresden shepherdess costume of the waitresses.

"It's a relief, after St. Francis every day," said Catherine. "The soup of the working girl grows monotonous."

"Hundreds of places like this." Margaret beckoned to a waitress. "Our coffee, please, and cakes." The shepherdess hurried away. "Isn't she a scream," added Margaret, "with that sharp, gamin face, and those ear muffs, above that dress! Why don't you hunt up new places to eat?"

Catherine glanced about; sleek furs draped over backs of chairs, plump, smug shoulders, careful coiffures, elaborately done faces.

"The home of the idle rich," she said. "I can't afford it. I'm not a kept woman. Fifty cents is my limit, except when I go with you."

"You draw a decent salary." Margaret pulled the collar of her heavy raccoon coat up against a snow-laden draft from the opened door. "What do you spend it for? You haven't bought a single dud. Why, you don't slip off your coat because the lining is patched. Does Charles make you give him your salary envelope?"

Catherine was silent and the shepherdess set the coffee service in front of Margaret.

"Well?" Margaret poured. "I'm curious."

"Only a rich man can afford a self-supporting wife," said Catherine lightly. "I was figuring it up last night. I've got to make at least a hundred a week."

"What for?" insisted Margaret.

"Everything. There's not a bill that isn't larger, in spite of anything that I can do. Food, laundry, clothes. You have no idea how much I was worth! As a labor device, I mean."

"Um." Margaret glinted over her mouthful of cake. "I always thought the invention of wives was a clever stunt."

"They can save money, anyway. I tried doing some of the things evenings, ironing and mending, but I can't."

"I should hope not!"

"Well, then, I have to pay for them. Charles can't. It wouldn't be fair."

"You look as if you were doing housework all night, anyway." Margaret's eyes gleamed with hostility. "Why can't the King take his share? You're as thin as a bean pole."

"Wait till you get your own husband, you! Then you can talk."

"Husband!" Margaret hooted. "Me? I'm fixed for life right now."

"They have their good points." Catherine rose, drawing on her gloves. Margaret paid the bill and tipped with the nonchalance of an unattached male.

"That's all right." Margaret thrust her hands deep into her pockets and followed her sister. She turned her nose up to sniff at the sharp wind, eddying fine snow flakes down the side street. "I know lots of women who prefer to set up an establishment with another woman. Then you go fifty-fifty on everything. Work and feeling and all the rest, and no King waiting around for his humble servant."

Catherine laughed.

"I'll try to bring up Spencer to be a help to his wife," she said.

"Oh, Spencer!" Margaret glowed. "He's a darling! Tell him I'm coming up some day to see him."

They walked swiftly down the Avenue; Catherine felt drab, almost haggard, worn down, by the side of Margaret's swinging, bright figure.

"How's your job?" she asked. "You haven't said a word about it."

"Grand." Margaret's smile had reminiscent malice. "You know, I've persuaded them to order new work benches for the main shop. I told you how devilish they were? Wrong height? Well, I cornered Hubbard last week. It was funny! I told him I'd found a terrible leak in his efficiency system. He's hipped on scientific efficiency. I tethered him and led him to a bench." She giggled. "I had him sitting there cutting tin before he knew where he was, and I kept him till he had a twinge of the awful cramp my girls have had. Result, new benches."

"You won't have half so much fun when you accomplish everything you want to, will you?"

"That's a hundred years from now, with me in the cool tombs." They stepped into the shelter of the elevator entrance to the Bureau. "I'm working now on some kind of promotion system. Of course, most of the girls are morons or straight f.m.'s, but there are a few who are better."

"What are 'f.m.'s'?"

"Feeble-mindeds. Like to do the same thing, simple thing, day after day. It takes intelligence to need something ahead." She grinned at Catherine. "They make excellent wives," she added. "Now if you didn't have brains, you'd be happy as an oyster in your little nest."

The splutter of motors protesting at the cold, the scurry of people, heads down into the wind, gray buildings pointing rigidly into a gray, low sky—Catherine caught all that as background for Margaret, fitting background. Margaret was like the city, young, hard, flashing.

"Of course, f.m.'s make rotten mothers," she was finishing. "In spite of the ease with which, as they say, they get into trouble."

"You know," Catherine's smile echoed the faint malice in her sister's as they stood aside for a puffing, red-nosed little man who bustled in for shelter—"I think you take your maternal instinct out on your job. Creating—"

"Maternal instinct! Holy snakes!" Margaret yanked her gloves out of her pockets and drew them on in scornful jerks. "You certainly have a sentimental imagination at times."

"That's why you don't need children," insisted Catherine. "Just as Henrietta Gilbert takes it out on other people's children."

"You make me sick! Drivel!" Margaret glowered, gave her soft green hat a quick poke, and stepped out of the lobby. "Good-by! You'll lose your job, maundering so!"

"Good-by. Nice lunch." Catherine laughed as she hurried for the waiting elevator.

She stood for a few minutes at the window of her office, before she settled down to the afternoon of work. There was snow enough in the air to veil the crawl of traffic far below, to blur the spires of the Cathedral. The clouds hung just above the buildings, heavy with storm. She would have to go home on the subway; no fun on the bus such an evening. Dim gold patches in distant windows—office workers needed light this afternoon. Her eyes dropped to the opposite windows. Revolving fussily before the great mirrors—how dull and white this snow-light made them—was a plump little man; the shade cut off his head, but his gestures were eloquent of concern about the fit of his shoulders.

Her window, looking out on the honeycombing of many windows, and down on the crawling traffic, and off across the piling roofs, had come to be a sort of watch tower. For more than two months now, she had looked out at the city. She had come to know the city's hints of changing seasons, hints more subtle, far less frank than the bold statements of growing things in the country. A different color in the air, altering the sky line; a different massing of clouds; a new angle for the sun through her window in the morning; a gradual stretching of the shadows on the roof tops. She stood there, gazing out at the terrific, impersonal whirl. If she could see the atoms, separately, each would be as fussy, as intimately concerned in some detail as little Mr. Plump opposite, pulling up his knee to twist at his trouser leg. And yet, out of that tiny squirming could grow this enormous, intricate whole.

The stenographer at the door drew her abruptly from the window.

"Oh, yes, Miss Betts. I wanted you to take these letters." She bent swiftly to her work.

She grimaced wryly as she was jammed and pushed through the door into the crowded local. Shoving feet, jostling bodies, wrists at the level of her eyes. Hairy wrists, chapped thin wrists, fat wrists, grubby, reaching up for straps; and the horrid odor of dirty wool, damp from the snow. A wrench, a grinding, and the terrific, clattering roar of the homeward propulsion began. She longed for the quiet isolation of the hour on top of the bus, in which she could swing into fresh adjustment. Lucky that heads were smaller than shoulders and set in the middle. The figure against her began to squirm, and her swift indignant glance found a folded newspaper worming up before her eyes. Friday, December 9. She stared at the date, its irking association just eluding her. The 9th. She set her lips in dismay as she caught her dodging thought. That reception, to-night! She had meant to buy fresh net for her dress, her one black evening dress—and Margaret's appearance had driven it out of her head. No room for her abortive shrug. Well, probably fresh net would have fooled no one.

At the sound of her key in the door, Marian rushed through the hall. Catherine, shivering a little at the sudden warmth after the windy blocks from the subway, bent to kiss her.

"Muvver!" Marian's eyes were roundly horrified. "Spencer's run away. We can't find him anywhere!" Her voice quavered. "He's lost himself!"

"What do you mean!" Catherine thrust her aside and ran through the hall. Letty was clattering busily around the edge of the living room rug on her go-duck. "Where's Miss Kelly?"

"Kelly gone. Spennie gone. Daddy gone." Chanted Letty, urging her steed more violently.

"Flora!" Catherine went toward the kitchen, to meet Flora, her mouth wide and dolorous.

"He's done eluded 'em, Mis' Hammond," she said. "They been hunting hours an' hours."

"What happened?" Catherine was cold in earnest now, a gasping cold that settled starkly about her heart.

"He ain't come home after school. Miss Kelly, she took Marian and went over there, but they wasn't no one lef' there. Chillun all gone."

"Yes, Muvver, we went over three times, Miss Kelly and me, and he wasn't there, and the janitor said no children were there."

"But he always comes straight home." Catherine's hand was at her throat, as if it could melt the constriction there. "You didn't see him, Marian?"

"No." Marian flopped her hair wildly. "Miss Kelly was waiting for me, and Letty, and we had a walk, and he wasn't here—"

"Has Mr. Hammond been in?"

"Yessum, he's been in, and out, chasing around wild like."

"He knows, then?"

"He come home sort of early," explained Flora. Catherine shrank from the dramatic intensity of Flora's words. "Came home, and foun' his child wasn't here. He's gone for the police."

The telephone rang, and Catherine hurried herself into the study.

"Yes?" Her voice was faint. "Yes? Who is it?"

"That you, Catherine?"

"Have you found him?" she cried.

"No." The wire hummed, dragging his voice off to remoteness. "Has Miss Kelly come back?"

"Where have you looked? I'll go hunt—"

"You stay there." Then, suddenly loud, "You might call up the hospitals. I've notified the police station. They are flashing the description all over town."

"Where are you now?" begged Catherine, but there was only silence, and the terminating click.

Flora was at her elbow.

"Ain't found him?" She clucked her tongue.

"You better go on home, Flora." Catherine couldn't look at her. She felt a ghoulish contamination, setting her mind afire with horrible pictures. Spencer, run down in the snowy street. Spencer—"I must stay here anyway."

Flora wavered. She wanted, Catherine knew, to see the end of this melodrama.

"Your own family will need you," she urged. "Go on."

Then, swiftly, to Marian, "Please keep Letty quiet. Mother wants to telephone."

She closed the door and pulled the telephone directory to the desk. How many hospitals there were! Hundreds—Has a little boy been brought in, injured? He is lost. Unless he were terribly hurt, he could have told you who he is. Has a little boy been brought in—yes? He's nine—no, not red hair. The wind yelled down the well outside the window. Surely he wouldn't be hurt, and not be found. Still and unmoving, in some dark street—oh, no! No! She clutched her arm against her breast, as her finger ran down the dancing column of numbers. Someone at the door. She listened, unable to stand up.

Miss Kelly came in, her face mottled with the cold, her hair in draggled wisps on her cheeks.

"I don't know where to look next," she said. "I hunted up the addresses of some of the boys he plays with, but they are all home, and haven't seen him since school, not one of them."

"When did you begin to hunt?"

"Immediately." Miss Kelly was dignified, sure of her lack of blame. "We waited here for him, just as we always do. I thought it was too cold for Marian and Letty to wait at the corner."

"He—he's always come straight home, hasn't he?" said Catherine, piteously.

"Always. That's why—" she stopped.

That's why, that's why—Catherine's mind picked up the words. That's why he must be hurt, unconscious somewhere, kidnaped—that little Italian boy who was found floating in the river—Spencer's face, white on black water—stop it! Not that!

"Can you stay to see that Letty goes to bed?" Catherine turned to her endless task. "I haven't called all the hospitals yet."

His gray eyes, long, with the wide space between, and the small, fine nose; fair boy's brows; mobile, eager lips. If I had been here, she thought, as she waited for the curt official voice to answer,—Has a little boy been brought in? If I had been here—oh, if—if—

Finally she sat, staring at the ridiculous gaping mouthpiece. Where would they take him, if he were—dead. Wasn't there a morgue? The word twisted and plunged in her, a slimy thing. She would call the morgue. She heard Miss Kelly's firm voice, "No, you mustn't bother your mother, not now. Come and have your supper, Marian."

He couldn't be dead. That warm, hard, slender body—how absurd! Morbid. He was somewhere, just around the corner. Death, that's the queer thing. Who had said that? Henrietta. She would call her—and ask her.

Before she had given the number, the front door clattered, opened. Catherine pushed herself erect; she was stiff, rigid. She found herself in the hall. Charles, glowering, and in front of him, propelled by his father's hand on his shoulder, Spencer! She couldn't move, or speak.

"Well, here's the fine young man," said Charles.

Spencer wriggled under his hand. His eyes smoldered with resentment, and his mouth was sullen.

Catherine's hands yearned toward him. She mustn't frighten him, but just to touch him, to feel him!

"A great note!" Charles came down the hall, righteous anger on his face. "I called up the police and had them send out their signals."

"Where was he?" Catherine had him now; she lifted Charles's hand away and touched the boy. He was trembling—Charles had been rough!

"I was just playing," Spencer cried out, gruffly. "I didn't know you'd tell the police."

"You've been told to come straight home, haven't you? Tell your mother what you told me, sir!"

"Charles!" Catherine's flash at him was unpremeditated. "You needn't bully him!"

"Tell her!" roared Charles.

"I just said"—Spencer's words tumbled out, full of impotent fury and indistinct with tears—"I said—I said—I didn't want to come home to that old Kelly. I didn't want—"

"He said," remarked Charles coldly, "that he saw no use of coming home when his mother wasn't here."

"But where was he?" Catherine had her arm over his shoulder, in a protective gesture. "Where did you find him?"

"I heard his voice. As I came along Broadway, past that vacant lot. He was down behind the bill boards there, with some street gamins, doing the Lord knows what."

"We just built a fire, Moth-er." Spencer pressed against her. "I didn't know it was so late. We were bandits."

"Go on into your room, Spencer. You know you should come straight home."

"He ought to be punished," declared Charles, as the boy vanished in relieved haste.

"I judge you have been punishing him." Catherine stood between Charles and Spencer's closing door. "He was trembling, and almost crying, and he never cries."

"Did you want me to kiss him when I found him, after the way I've spent the afternoon?"

"You want to make him feel as bad as you have!" Catherine leaned against the wall. She was exhausted; her heart was beating in short, spasmodic jerks, as if she had run for miles.

"I suppose I was mad, clear through." Charles grinned, abashed. Then he stiffened again. "Devilish thing to do. I came home after some lecture notes, for a meeting, and I couldn't even go to the meeting."

Miss Kelly came into the hall. She had smoothed her hair into its usual neatness, and her face was roundly pink again.

"I am afraid I must go," she said. Her eyes inspected them, gravely. Catherine flushed; Miss Kelly had heard them squabbling and she was reproaching Catherine.

"I'm sorry you've been detained. I'll see that Spencer realizes how serious this is," she said.

When the door had closed on her sturdy back, Charles broke out, "If you'd been here, this wouldn't have happened. You heard what he said, didn't you?"

"Don't say that!" Catherine's exhaustion sent hot tears into her eyes.

But Charles had to unload his overcharged feelings somewhere.

"You might as well face the truth. If you care more for a paltry job than for your children—" He shrugged. "But you won't see it. I've got to have my dinner. We'll be late to that reception now. If I miss all my appointments because my wife works, I'll have a fine reputation."

Incredible! Catherine watched him clump down to the living room. He wanted to hurt her. She pressed her fingers, ice-cold, against her eyeballs. She wouldn't cry. He felt that way. Not just because he had been worried about Spencer. There was a heavy coil of resentment from which those words had leaped. And she had thought, for weeks now, that she had learned to balance on her tight-rope, and keep the balls smoothly in air. While under the surface, this!

"Can't we have dinner?" he called to her. "We really must hurry a little, Catherine."

She set the dinner silently on the table, avoiding the defiant glance she knew she would meet.

"Don't wait for me." She paused, a tumbler of milk in her hand. "I want to talk to Spencer."

Charles pulled out his watch and gazed at it impressively.

CHAPTER II

Catherine, sitting on the edge of her bed, drew on one silk stocking and gartered it. She lifted her head; when she bent over like that, faint nausea, like a green smear, rose through her body behind her eyelids. She shouldn't have eaten any dinner. Or was it just Charles, and his restrained disapproval—or Spencer. She sighed, thinking through her talk with Spencer. With insistent cunning he had offered as excuse, his dislike of Miss Kelly, his distaste for the house without Catherine. "I didn't think it was bad," he said. "I didn't do anything bad."

"Inconsiderate," suggested Catherine, looking at the stubborn head on the pillow. Safe! She couldn't scold him, and yet—"You didn't think how we would feel."

"Oh, I thought," said Spencer. "I thought you wouldn't know. And my father wasn't very con-sid-'rate." He thrust his head up indignantly. "He yanked me right away, and the fellows all *saw* him."

Then Charles had called sharply, "Catherine! Are you dressing?" and she had, under pressure, resorted to a threat. She was ashamed of it. She drew on the other stocking, smoothing it regretfully. She had said, "If you won't promise to come home directly, I shall ask Miss Kelly to call for you at school."

Charles came in, bay rum and powder wafted with him, his face pink and solemn.

"Oh, I haven't put in your studs—" She made a little rush for his dresser, but he brushed her away.

"Please don't bother. You're not ready yourself."

Catherine stifled an hysterical giggle. Emotion in these costumes—Charles in barred muslin underwear, his calves bulging above his garters, and she in silk chemise—was funny! She lifted her black dress from its hanger and slipped it over her head. Well, it had dignity, of a dowdy sort, if it wasn't fresh. She stood in front of the long mirror, trying to crisp the crumpled net of the long draped sleeves. Her fingers caught; she had pumiced too hard at the ink on their tips—hollows at the base of her throat—try to drink more milk. Her skin had pale luster, against the black, but her face lacked color. "If this weren't a faculty party," she said, lightly, "I'd try rouge."

"Why doesn't that girl come?" asked Charles, his voice muffled by the elevation of his chin as he struggled with his tie. "Time, I should think."

"What girl?" Catherine turned from the mirror. "Oh—" her shoulders sagged in complete dismay.

"Miss Brown. You got her, didn't you?"

Catherine, a whirl of black net, was at the telephone. How could she have forgotten! "No, Morningside!" She waited. She had called once, that morning, and Miss Brown was out. She had meant—"Is Miss Brown in?" Charles was at the door, an image of funereal, handsome dignity. Miss Brown was not in. No, the voice had no idea when she would be in.

"Oh, say it!" Catherine's fingers pushed recklessly through her hair. "Say it, Charles!" He swung on his heel and disappeared.

Perhaps her mother—but no one answered that call, and Catherine remembered that Friday was the night for opera.

A voice in the hall, although she hadn't heard the doorbell. It was Bill.

"Going out, eh?"

"Apparently not." Charles was elaborately, fiendishly jovial. "I thought we were, but Catherine neglected to provide a chaperone for the children."

Catherine pressed her fingers against her warm cheeks. Her quick thought was: just Bill's entrance scatters this murky, ridiculous tension. This ought to be a joke, not a tragedy.

"Here, run along, you two." She lifted her head and looked at Bill, smiling at her. "I've nothing to do. Let me sit here and read."

"We can't impose on you that way—" began Charles.

"Of course we can!" Catherine tinkled, hundreds of tiny bells at all her nerve ends. "Of course! Come on, Charles."

As Charles stamped into his overshoes, Catherine ran back to the living room. Bill stood at the table, poking among the magazines.

"Thank Heaven you came just then!" she said, softly. "Oh, Bill!"

"What is this momentous occasion, anyway?"

"A faculty reception. It's not that. I'm an erring wife and mother." His glance steadied her, stopped that silly tinkling. "Spencer ran away and I forgot to send word for Miss Brown to come in, and—" That wordless quiet of his enveloped her, like a deep pool in which she relaxed, set free from the turmoil of the past hours. "If I could stay here with you!"

"Are you about ready?" Charles asked crisply.

Had Bill lifted his hand in a heartening gesture, or had she imagined it?

The elevator was slow. Charles laid a vindictive thumb on the button; below them the signal snarled.

"Sam's probably at the switchboard," said Catherine, coldly.

"He won't be, long!" Charles pressed harder.

Catherine turned away, her fingers busy with the snaps of her gloves. The tips were powdery and worn; another cleaning would finish this pair. If Charles wanted to be childish, venting spite on anything— A clatter and a creaking of cables behind the iron grill.

"If you prefer to stay with Bill, why come?"

Catherine's jerk rent the soft kid. The snap dangled by a shred. The door slammed open and they stepped into the car.

Sam was explaining to Charles. In the narrow corner mirror Catherine could see the line of Charles's cheek bone, the corner of his mouth. Poor man! He was in a humor. Well, he could stay there! She wouldn't cajole him out of it; he could wait till she did! It was always she who had to make the overture. Charles sat sulkily down in the swamp of ill feeling and wouldn't budge.

"It's stopped snowing." She lifted her face to the steel plate of sky overhead.

"Temporarily." Charles strode along with great steps. "Here, take my arm." He stopped at the corner.

"Have to keep my gloves fresh." Catherine hurried across the slippery cobblestones. As they climbed up past the dark chapel, she squirmed inside her coat. How ridiculous they were, going along in a pet, like children. Bill would laugh, if he knew. The long windows of the law library dropped their panels of light across the thin snow. When we reach the library steps, thought Catherine, I'll say, let's be good. Only—why must I always be abject, and ingratiating? Again that streak of hard, ribald mockery: let him sulk if he likes. I'm tired of being humble. Below them the wide sweep of steps, the bronze figure aproned with snow; the dignified weight of the building rising above them, the recessed lights glowing behind the columns. How many times they had walked together across these steps!

"Charles." She spoke impetuously. "Don't be cross. What's the use?"

"If you chose to project your own mood upon me—" Charles jerked his chin away from the folds of silk muffler.

"Oh, Lord!" sighed Catherine. "Don't we sound married!"

She could see the building now, with shadowy figures moving past the lighted windows. I can't be humble enough in that distance to do any good. What an evening!

It was like a nightmare, through which she moved as two people, one a cool, impersonal, outer self, given to chatter rather more than usual; the other a mocking, irreverent, twisting inner self, mewed up in confusion and injury. Empty, meaningless chatter. What fools people were, dragging themselves together in an enormous room, moving around, busy little infusoria. Charles liked it. He felt himself erect and important, with the crowding people a tangible evidence of his success, the decorum, the polished surfaces clinking out assurance that here was his group, here he was admitted, recognized. Catherine, bowing, smiling, listening to his voice, offering bright little conventional remarks, was conscious of his feeling. He's feeding on it, she thought. Growing smug. How far away from him I am—far enough to see him smug, and hate it. They had drifted away from the formal receiving line. She twisted at her glove, to hide the torn snap.

"Well, Mrs. Hammond!" Mr. Thomas was at her elbow, his thick glasses catching the light blankly, his head enormous above the rather pinched shoulders of his dress suit. "This is a pleasure." He shook her hand nervously, oppressed by his social obligation. "A pleasure."

Mrs. Thomas bustled up, crisp in rose taffeta, a black velvet ribbon around her pinkish, wrinkled throat.

"So long since we've seen you. We were just saying we must have you out for Sunday night supper. Walter does miss Spencer so much."

"That would be fine!" declared Charles, heartily. "I haven't forgotten that cake."

"We heard such a funny thing." Were the lines in her pink cheeks dented in malice? She bobbed her curly gray head sidewise at Charles. "Someone told Mr. Thomas that your wife had left you, Mr. Hammond."

Catherine saw the ominous twitching under Charles's eyes, but Mr. Thomas put in, hastily.

"I think it was intended for a jest, you know." He turned to Catherine, his large, gentle mouth agitated, as if in distress at his wife's poor taste. "I met Dr. Roberts last week. I know him quite well, you know. He was speaking about your work, Mrs. Hammond. He was extraordinarily enthusiastic."

Catherine took that gratefully, as something in which she was at least not culpable. There was a little eddy of people around them, throwing off several to stop for casual greetings; when they had gone on, Catherine heard Mrs. Thomas's high voice. "The poor boy! I suppose the house seems empty with no mother in it." Her outer self looked across at Charles, calm enough, but her inner self had an instant of rage, a hurling, devastating instant.

"Mr. Hammond was just telling me about Spencer's running away." Mrs. Thomas had a peculiarly self-righteous air in her pursed lips and bright eyes. "How worried you must have been!"

"Oh, Mr. Hammond found him so promptly."

"But just a minute can seem a long time. I remember one day—"

"Pardon me, please." Charles moved away, restrained eagerness in the forward thrust of his head above his broad, black shoulders.

Catherine saw him edge past a group, saw a pearl-smooth shoulder above a jade-green velvet sheath. The Partridge, of course! What was she doing at a faculty reception? She had a glimpse of the squirrel smile, before she picked up the thread of Mrs. Thomas's domestic lyric.

The Thomases wanted refreshments. Catherine's throat was sticky-dry at the thought of food. She had a sharp longing for her own living room and Bill. He could ease her of these innumerable prickings. She made her way to Charles, and then stood, unnoted, at his elbow. Miss Partridge saw her, and her hand swam up in a leisurely arc. Catherine nodded pleasantly.

"I think I'll run along, Charles. You aren't to hurry." She drifted away before his hesitancy reached action.

CHAPTER III

Snow again in the air, wet on her cheeks. I am going home, to see Bill, in search of ballast. She hurried across the campus. The library windows were dark; two cleaning women, aprons bundled about their heads, clattered ahead of her with their pails.

As she pushed open the apartment door, she saw Bill, standing at the doorway of Marian's room, indistinct in the shadow. He moved violently away.

"Have the children been bothering you?" Catherine listened an instant at the door. Nothing but the faintest possible rhythm of breathing.

"I thought I heard Letty call." Bill retreated into the living room. "Where's Charles? The party over?"

"I ran away." Catherine slipped out of her coat. "Leaving him with Miss Partridge." She drew down her long gloves, laughing, and looked at Bill. Something curiously disturbed in his heavy-lidded glance. How tired and gaunt he looked. "What is it, Bill?"

He waited until she had settled into the wing chair.

"Nice dress, that," he said, as he sat down.

"This?" She smiled at him. Her hands lay idly along folds of the black stuff. "Are you bored, sitting here alone? The children haven't really been awake, have they?"

"No. I eavesdropped on them." Again that heavy, troubled look. "I heard them—breathe."

What in that phrase had such poignancy? What in the silence swung a light close to the dark, unruffled surface of this man, illuminating, far down in deep water, that struggling, twisting something?

He rose, brushing aside the curtain, to gaze out at the dim city.

"Better run along," he said, slowly. "You must be weary."

"Oh, no." Catherine's hand entreated him.

At that he turned slightly, to face her. She had a queer fancy that she saw his forehead gleam, his hair shine damp, as if he came swinging up, up to the surface. But he spoke calmly enough.

"I've been thinking over one of Henrietta's truisms, as I eavesdropped on your children. Wondering about it, and you."

Catherine was still; breathing might blur the glass, this glass through which she might have a clear glimpse of Bill.

"It is this." His smile, briefly sardonic, mocked at himself. "That children are the world's greatest illusion. The largest catch-penny life offers."

"Sometimes," Catherine hesitated, "I think Henry says a clever thing to fool herself."

"Isn't it more than clever? Don't you feel, when you are confronted with a black wall of futility, in yourself, that at least there are your children, three of them, and that they may jack life up to some level of significance, and that they are you?"

"Is that an illusion?"

"Isn't it? Our puny little minds, scratching at the edges of whatever it is that drives us along, pick up bits of sand." Bill laid his hand on the back of the chair, dragged it around, and dropped into it, his gaunt profile toward the window, his hands gripped on his knees. "After all, a merry-go-round doesn't go anywhere but around. Isn't that what this feeling amounts to? You don't find yourself convinced that you are the vehicle for your parents, do you? And yet"—the words lagged—"I am sure I have that illusion as strongly as any fool, that I have the need for that consolation."

"Surely"—Catherine spoke softly; she mustn't drive him back—"you, of all people, Bill, are least futile."

He turned his face toward her, a haggard little grin under his somber eyes.

"What could be more futile? Builder of bridges and buildings, which a hundred other men can make better than I. I had a maudlin way, when I was younger, of expecting that to-morrow would give me the thing I wished. To-morrow! Another catch-penny. And this, too, puerile as it sounds. For a time Henrietta needed me, while she fought to get her toes in. But she's past that now."

"Bill"—Catherine strained toward him, her eyes darkly brilliant—"I came home to-night, because I wanted you. Because when I am frantic and silly, you can pull me up. You have, countless times."

"That is your generous imagination." Catherine flung out her hand impatiently. "And you see, I have, instead, spewed out this sentimental maundering."

"Don't talk that way!" cried Catherine.

"No." He rose abruptly, to stand above her, so that she tipped her head back, and one hand crept up to press against the pulse beating in her throat. His glance buffeted hers, entreating something, inarticulate, baffling. Then, suddenly, the old quiet mask was on again, and the water closed over his plunge within.

"Don't ever be frantic, Catherine," he said. "Good night."

She sat motionless when he had gone. Bill, in the dark, listening to the children. Bill, at the window, sending that heavy stare out into the night. Bill, stripped of his concealment. There was a slow brewing of exultation within her. He had come out, to her!

The great illusion. She crept silently to the door where Letty and Marian slept. Spencer moaned softly in his sleep, and she stood for moments beside his bed. They weren't illusory, except as you tried to substitute them for everything. They were part of you, to go on when you stopped. But they were separate, individual, cut off, *themselves*. What had Bill said? You don't feel yourself the vehicle for your parents, do you? You wanted your children, part of you, extenuation for your own shortcomings. Wasn't it an illusion, a flimsy drapery of words over a huge, blind, instinctive drive? Bill wanted children, then, and Henrietta—crisp, efficient—

Catherine undressed hastily and crept into bed. Charles was late. Resentment, like a small sharp bone, still rankled. He's like a little boy. If I could be patient—Bill never takes things out on Henrietta. She doesn't know his feeling. Perhaps it is always that way; one person out of two is not quite happy, never an equal balance. Charles was content until I broke loose. Henrietta is content. You have to offer up a human sacrifice. She stared at the ceiling, where a broken rectangle of saffron light from some court window sprawled. If I could think about Charles, without this jangle of feelings, perhaps I could see what to do. Could you ever think straight? Did emotion always enter, refracting?

Charles *says* he doesn't mind my working, that he's glad if I like it. That's what he thinks; no, what he thinks he thinks! But underneath, he's outraged, and any tiny thing is a jerk of the thin cover over that feeling. Never till this winter has he been so—so touchy. Silly little things. Perhaps—she waited an instant—was that his key? Perhaps I notice it more, because I want approval. But he makes a personal grievance if I forget his laundry. In a way, it is personal. I forget, because I don't think of him every second. I try to remember everything. She twisted over on one side, an arm curled under her head. I haven't asked him to take any share of the house job, or the children. She shivered, as if a cold draft from that hour before dinner blew across her; Spencer, lost, because she wasn't at home. Charles, intimating that he was justified. But she was at home—

The door clicked softly open, and cautious feet moved down the hall.

Catherine smiled. Charles was like an elephant when he attempted silence.

"I'm not asleep," she said, and blinked as he flashed on the light. "You must have had a good time, to stay so late."

"It's a pity you bothered to go at all," he said briefly, as he vanished behind the closet door.

Catherine turned away from the light, her hand closing into a fist under her cheek. She wouldn't wrangle, even if he was still out of sorts. She heard him padding about in stocking feet. He snapped off the light and scuffed down the hall. She heard him whistling. He would wake the children, if he weren't more careful.

He was back again, a stocky figure against the pale square of window as he shoved it open. He was scurrying for bed.

"Charles!" Catherine's cry leaped out. "Come here!"

"Well?" He stood above her. "Brr! It's chilly."

She reached up for his hands, dragged him down beside her, her arms slipping up to his shoulders, clasping behind his neck. He resisted her; she felt stubborn hardness in his muscles.

"Charles," she begged, "what's happening to us! Don't—"

"I'm all right," he said. "I thought you were off color."

Catherine let her hands drop forlornly away.

"You've been sort of touchy." He cleared his throat. "I'm not perfect. But I hate this feeling—that you're standing off, waiting to be critical of me."

"Oh, I'm not!" Catherine sighed.

"All right, then." Charles bent down, brushed his lips against her cheek, and stood up. "Go to sleep. You're tired, I guess."

Catherine lay motionless, listening to the creak of his bed, the soft pulling and adjusting of blankets. The wind was cold on her eyelids, on the tears that crept down. She was humiliated, shamed. She had dropped her pride and evoked touch—passion—only to find him—her hands flung open, to escape the lingering sensation of that obdurate, resisting column of his throat.

Unbidden, racking, a swift visual image of Stella Partridge, smooth ivory and jade. She fled away from it. Not that! She wouldn't add jealousy to her torment. But that eager, forward thrust of his head as he made his way across the room toward her, and that secret, honey-mouthed deference in the casual talk of the woman. Oh, no!

Then, rudely, as if she turned to face some monstrous shape that pursued her, she looked at the image. Perhaps, if Charles was injured, outraged, under his reasoning surface, he might turn to Stella. She wanted something of him, that woman. Perhaps it was love she wanted, although the hard metallic gleam under the softness of her eyes seemed passionless, egocentric.

"Charles," she whispered. What else she might have said, she didn't know. But Charles was asleep.

CHAPTER IV

The next morning, in the accustomed flurry of baths, breakfast, dressing, Catherine jeered at her nightmares of the dark. She would not be a fool, at least. The children were ecstatic about the snow, which lay in caps and mounds and blankets on the roof tops below the windows. Marian made snowballs from the window ledge, and tried, giggling, to wash her father's face. Charles was jovial, amusing himself with the rôle of good-natured father. Yes, he might go coasting with them that afternoon. He'd see if he couldn't get away from the office early. Miss Kelly could telephone him at noon.

Miss Kelly came in; Flora was belated.

"Probably the trolley cars are stuck," said Spencer, full of delight at possible catastrophes the snow might bring.

Catherine left a note for Flora, with the day's instructions, and hurried off. She had swung free of the night in a long arc of release.

The Drive had a dramatic beauty; white morning sunlight piercing the gaps made by cross streets, long blue shadows stretching from the buildings, the river gray blue under the clearing sky, the clean, soft lines of snow turned back by the plows, snow caught in the branches of trees and shrubbery, like strange fruit; gulls wheeling like winged bits of snow. By nightfall all the beauty might be trampled and turned dingy; now—Catherine sat erect, drawing long breaths.

That noon she would squeeze out a few minutes for some Christmas shopping. Saturday wasn't a good day, but if she found a doll for Marian, she could begin to dress it. She thrust her foot into the aisle and peered down at it. Those shoes wouldn't last until January. Well, she would have her third check on the twenty-third, and she had repaid Charles. Funny, how much more it cost to dress herself as working woman than as mother and wife. Perhaps with the first of the year that increase would gain material shape. Dr. Roberts had hinted at it again.

The bus left the Drive and rattled through the city; one note everywhere, the squeak of shovels against the sidewalks, piles of grime-edged snow, files of carts heaped and dripping.

She shivered, hugging her arms close; the last few blocks were always chilly. Wonderful colors in the great shop windows, exotic, luxurious, and bevies of shop girls, stepping gingerly over dirty puddles in their cheap, high-heeled slippers.

Just a half day of work to-day. She could finish the chapter she had been writing. As she waited for the elevator, she had a sharp renewal of herself as a part of this great, downward flood. The morning ride was a symbol, a bridge across which she passed. She nodded to the elevator boy; his grin made her part of the intimate life of this huge building. You'd expect to shrink, she thought, as the elevator shot upwards—swallowed up, and instead you swell, as if you swallowed it all yourself.

Dr. Roberts hadn't come in. Dropping into her work was like entering a quiet, clean place of solitude. She reread the pages she had written, the beginning of her full report, and then wrote slowly, finding pleasure in the search for a phrase which should be clear glass through which the idea, the hard, definite fact, might be visible. The jangle of the telephone bell broke into a sentence.

It was Miss Kelly. Flora hadn't shown up. What did Mrs. Hammond wish done about luncheon?

"Hasn't she sent any word?" The picture of her kitchen, empty, and confused, rose threateningly in the quiet office. "Well, you can find something for the children. I'll be home early."

If something was wrong with Flora! Catherine pushed away the image of disaster, finished her sentence, and glanced at her watch. Almost one. Lucky it was Saturday. She would have time—vaguely—to see to this. Better not stop for any shopping.

When she reached home, the children rushed to the door, accoutered in leggings and mufflers for coasting.

"Mother! Come with us. Daddy's coming!" Spencer and Marian tugged at her arms, and Letty pulled at her skirt.

"I can't, chickens." Catherine hugged them, each one. She loved the exuberance of their greeting, the sharp delight of contrast after the hours away. "Miss Kelly is all ready." She glanced at Miss Kelly's serene face. "Flora hasn't shown up? Nor sent word? I'll have to look her up. To-morrow perhaps I can go."

"I gave the children their lunch," explained Miss Kelly, "but of course I had no time to set the kitchen to rights."

She certainly hadn't. Catherine gave one dismayed look at the disorder, and decided to hunt for Flora first. She must be sick.

CHAPTER V

Catherine tried to pick a firm way through the slush of the sidewalk. Flora must live in this block. She peered at the numbers over dark doorways, under the sagging zigzags of fire escapes. The snow had been thrown up in a dirty barricade along the edge of the walk, and over the upset garbage and ash cans, down the short mounds, shrieked and wailed and coasted innumerable children. It was like a diminutive and distorted minstrel show, thought Catherine, stepping hastily out of the path of a small black baby spinning down into the slush on a battered tin tray. Snow on the East Side, and on the Drive—she had a wry picture of the beauty of the morning.

There. 91-A. She stood at the entrance, with a hesitant glance into the dim hall. Absurd to be nervous about entering. She had never seen where Flora lived, although she had heard the dirge of rising rent and lack of repairs which Flora occasionally intoned. She walked to the first door and knocked boldly.

"Who dar?" The voice bellowed through the door.

"Does Mrs. Flora Lopez live in this house?" Catherine had a notion that the dim house gave a flutter of curiosity, as if doors moved cautiously ajar. "I'm Mrs. Hammond," she added sharply to the closed door. "She works for me."

The door swung open a crack, and a fat dusky face appeared, one white eye gleaming.

"You wants Mis' Flora Lopez?"

"Do you know her? Which is her flat?"

"Sure I knows her." The round eye held her in hostile inspection. "Is you f'om the police station, too?"

"No. She works for me. Is she sick?" Queer, how that sense of listening enmity flowed down the crooked stairway. "Which is her flat?"

"She ain't sick, exac'ly. Ain't she come to wuk to-day?"

"Who zat, want Flora?" The voice came richly down the stairway.

"Which is her flat?" insisted Catherine.

The door opened wider, disclosing a ponderous figure with great soft hips and bosom, a small child in a torn red sweater clinging to her skirts and looking up with round frightened eyes.

"She lives on the top flo' rear. I donno as she's home."

Catherine climbed the stairs. There's nothing to be afraid of, she told herself stubbornly. The sweetish odor of leaking gas, the cold, damp smell of broken plaster and torn linoleum in the unheated halls choked her as she climbed. She was sure doors opened and closed as she passed. She felt herself an intruder, with profound racial antipathy, fear, stirring within her and around her. I won't go back, she thought. She tried to step boldly across the hall, but her rubbers made a muffled, sucking note. At last the top floor. She knocked at the rear door. No sound; merely the strained sense of someone listening.

"Flora!" she called sharply. "Are you there? It's Mrs. Hammond."

Silence. Feet shuffled on bare boards behind that door.

"Flora!" she called again, and the door crept slowly open.

"Why, Flora! What *is* the matter?" Catherine gazed at her. Short hair raying like twisted wires about her face, one eye an awful purple-green lump, the wide mouth cut and swollen, the broad nostrils distended—a dumb-show, a gargoyle of miserable agony. "What has happened to you?"

Flora stepped back, pushing ajar a door.

"Come in, Mis' Hammond." Her voice had the exhausted echo of riotous weeping. "Come in and set down. I was goin' to write you a message."

Catherine followed her into the living room, immaculate, laboriously furnished. The table, purple plush arm-chairs—Flora had told her when she ordered those from the installment house; lace curtains draped on a view of tenements and dangling clothes.

"What has happened, Flora?" Catherine had lost her uneasiness. Flora had a vestige of the familiar, at least; her gray bathrobe was an old one Catherine had given her.

Flora sat down in a purple chair and began to rock back and forth, moaning. Tears ran down her cheeks, gleaming on the bruises.

At a sound behind the door Catherine turned, to find the solemn round eyes of a little boy fixed upon her. He scuttled over to Flora, burying his face on her knees.

"Is he yours?"

"Yes'm." Flora cradled one arm about him. "Yes'm. He's my baby." Her voice rose suddenly into a wail. "An' my li'l girl, where's she! They took her off to shut her up—all 'count of that"—she shook one fist in air—"that man!"

Gradually, in broken and violent bits, Catherine gathered the story. Flora had married her professional gentleman. He hadn't wanted her to keep the children. They were hers, she had worked for them always, and dressed them nice, and left them with a neighbor when she went off to work. She wanted them to grow up nice. She even put little socks on her girl, and the teacher at school said why should she dress her up that way, picking on her because she was black. She was twelve. Then Flora found out her professional gentleman had another wife down south. She let him stay, anyway, "so long as we'd been married, and he was handsome." Then she had to put him on bail to leave the little girl alone, always fooling with her. "I told her to stay with Mis' Jones till I got home." And finally—Catherine was cold with pity and horror—Flora had discovered that he hadn't let Malviny alone, that he had ruined her, and stolen the money she had saved to pay the rent, and was packing his suitcase to leave. "I started out to kill him," she said briefly, "but he knocked me down." Then the police had come.

"They said I let Malviny run the streets. She's awful pretty, Mis' Hammond, most white, she is. Her pa was pale. I was working for her, wasn't I?" Flora's gesture was wide with despair. "Providin' for her and him—" she rocked the boy against her breast. "I done the best I could. She wanted things, and he give her money. She's only twelve."

At last Catherine fled down the stairs, feeling that perversion and horror and the failure of honest, respectable effort barked at her heels. Flora couldn't come back to her, not at once. She had to testify. She won't ever come back, thought Catherine. She'll be ashamed, because I know all this. She had, when Catherine had tried to offer sympathy, shrunk away, into the collapse of the structure of herself as competent, self-respecting working woman. "I done my bes'!" Her pitiful wail dogged Catherine's feet through the brittle, freezing slush of the street.

CHAPTER VI

Catherine, in an old house dress, waded determinedly through the mash of the disordered apartment. Dishes, sweeping, dinner—Miss Kelly had straightened the children's rooms. She was too well paid for general utility. I suppose I am inefficient, thought Catherine. Just to be caught in this mess. But what else can I do? What would a man do in my place? She pulled a chair near the kitchen table and sat down to the task of shelling lima beans, while she speculated as to Charles's procedure. He wouldn't plunge himself into the mess, at least. He would leave it, until someone else stepped in. That's one trouble with women, she decided. They have all these habits of responsibility. Now I should be off playing somewhere, after this week, and here I am!

Charles came in with the children. Miss Kelly, discreetly, had left them at the steps. She's got the right idea, thought Catherine grimly. She's not going to be roped in for something she's not paid for. Letty's cheeks were peonies, her eyes bright stars, and her leggings were soaked with melted snow.

"We had one grand time, didn't we, chicks!" Charles stamped out of his rubbers and shook off his snow-spattered coat. "Had a snow fight and Letty and I beat."

"We landed some hum-dingers right in your neck, anyways," said Spencer.

"Hum-dings in neck!" shrieked Letty. "Hum-gings in neck!"

"You all look as if you'd landed snow everywhere." Catherine shooed Marian and Spencer into their rooms in quest of dry clothing, ran back to the kitchen to lower the gas under the potatoes, and returned to strip Letty of her damp outer layers.

"Even my shirt is wet." Marian giggled, shaking her bloomers until bits of snow flew over the rug. "It was awful fun, Muvver. And we coasted belly-bump. Is that a nice word to say?"

"And now we are starved, like any army after a fight," came a sturdy bellow from Charles.

Bedraggled and glowing, warmly fragrant—Catherine laughed at them as she tugged the pink flannel pajamas onto Letty's animated legs.

"There!" she kissed her, gave the tousled yellow floss a swift brush, and carried her into the dining room to set her safely behind the bar of her high-chair. "Supper and then to bed you go, after this exciting day."

"What's this about the dusky Flora?" Charles came into the kitchen.

"I'll tell you about it later." Catherine spoke hastily. Tired as she was, their home-coming had given her the old sweet rush of pleasure, of safety, of possession. She wanted to keep it untouched, free of that horror and pity.

Much later, when the children were in bed, Charles strolled into the kitchen and reached for a dish towel. Catherine looked up at him as he rubbed a tumbler with slow care.

"Like old times, isn't it, eh?" He set the glass on the shelf.

Catherine swallowed her sigh.

"Me wiping dishes, and telling you about what I've been doing—" Was he deliberately wistful?

"You needn't wait for dishes, need you, to talk?" Catherine's smile blunted the slight edge in her words.

"Somehow, nowadays, there never seems any chance. Nights you have to go to sleep, and day times you aren't here."

"Last night you went to sleep."

"Oh, last night!" Charles with a wave of his towel sent last night into the limbo of things best forgotten.

"Well, tell me. What have you been doing? To-day, for instance."

"I had two interviews this morning." Charles paused. "With two different publishers' representatives. They are keen about this new book on tests. Ready to make me an offer right now, without even seeing an outline. Pretty good, eh?"

"Fine! That's proof of your standing, isn't it?"

"Partly. Partly just the current fad for anything psychological, and then the clinic behind the book is a factor."

"And you have the book—is it half done?"

"It's getting along." Charles had drawn in his lower lip and was chewing it thoughtfully. "The clinic is furnishing material. I've been wondering. Of course Miss Partridge did the organizing there, and she's done most of the tabulating of results. She suggested that we collaborate on a book. What would you think of such a scheme?"

"I'd think," cried Catherine in a flash of irritation, "that it was pure silk for Miss Partridge! That clinic was your scheme, not hers, and—"

"I haven't committed myself." Charles busied himself with a pile of dishes on the shelf, rearranging them critically. His expansiveness contracted visibly. "You needn't be so sure I'd agree with her. I might give her a chapter to do."

"Why doesn't she write her own books?"

"She isn't that type, the type that seeks expression, I mean. She is the competent, executive type. It seems a pity for her not to assemble her results."

In silence Catherine hung away the dish-pan and scrubbed the sink. Be careful, she warned herself. Don't be cattish; this may be entirely reasonable.

"I'm sorry you don't like her." Charles was solemn. "She thinks you are an unusually sweet—"

"She does! She little knows." Catherine grasped desperately for the fraying thread of control. After all, why shouldn't they write a book together? She turned quickly, to find Charles eying her with a cautious, investigatory stare.

"You know—" she grinned at him. "I may write a book with Dr. Roberts. He was looking over my notes yesterday, and he thinks we can find a firm to publish the report, as a marketable book. Of course, the Bureau puts out a report, too."

A thin veil of blankness drew itself over the curiosity in Charles's face. Before he spoke, however, the bell in the hall sounded.

"Company to-night!" Catherine drooped. "I'm worn to a frazzle."

It was Margaret; her gay, "Hello, King Charles!" floated reassuringly to Catherine, dabbing powder hastily on her nose, brushing back her hair from her forehead.

"I brought my partner in to meet you two. Amy, this is the King, and my sister, Catherine—Amy Spurgeon."

Margaret, clear, sparkling, watching them with her humorous grin, as if she had staged a vaudeville act. Amy Spurgeon, slight, dark, her lean, high-cheekboned face sallow and taciturn over the collar of her squirrel coat, a flange of stiff hair black under the soft brim of her gray fur hat. Catherine nibbled at her in swift glances as they sat down in the living room. Margaret had talked about her. "Amy has to have a passion for something." She looked it, with the criss-crosses of fine lines at the corners of her black eyes, and the deep straight lines from nostrils past her mouth. Militant suffragist, pacifist—"She had a passion for the Hindus last winter. Now she has one for me. I can't be a cause, exactly, but she finds plenty of causes on the side." She looks like an Indian, decided Catherine, a temperamental, rather worn and fiery Indian.

Margaret and Charles were sparring; they couldn't even telephone each other without crossing points.

"If they are feeble-minded, why bother with them? You can't change them. Sentimental bosh, this coddling of idiots."

"But they work better, I tell you! Is that sentimental? They make more money for their bosses. That should appeal to your male sense of what is sensible."

"Even if they didn't work better"—Amy's voice shot in, a deep throaty tone, flexible with emotion—"Every human being has a right to happiness and comfort."

"Even human beings with brains have some difficulty cashing in on that right," said Catherine. If Amy and Charles started in on society with the *vox populi* stop out, they would fight all night! Amy stared at her with deliberate inspection.

Presently Catherine told them about Flora. Flora had, since the afternoon, pressed so closely to the surface of her thoughts that she was bound to come out.

"You shouldn't have gone into a nigger tenement alone!" said Charles.

"Why not?" demanded Amy. "Aren't negroes people?"

"I did feel queer, with the house oozing excitement along with smells." Catherine smiled at Charles. "But it wasn't dangerous. Only unpleasant."

"Poor Flora." Margaret was grave. "I didn't know she had any children."

"I knew she was always pleased to have clothes given her." Catherine shivered. "The socks were pitiful! A symbol of her effort."

"Well"—Charles drew at his pipe and paused, impressively—"you can see what happens to a family when the mother isn't at home."

"Listen to the King!" Margaret flared indignantly. "What about the man? Living on her, and—"

"If she'd made him support her, he might have had more steadiness."

"I suppose"—Amy drawled—"you go on the theory that men are so unstable that they can't stand freedom."

Charles had a dangerous little twitch under one eye. Catherine flung herself into the whirl of antagonism.

"Will you tell me, some of you, what I am to do now? Flora won't come back. She'll be drawn into trials and all that for a while, and then she'll hunt up a new place, where no one knows about her. And meantime—"

"Telephone an agency," said Amy.

"I'll send you one of my girls." Margaret's glance at Charles devilled him. "I have one who can work about three months before she has to go to a lying-in hospital, and she's just weak-minded enough to make a good domestic."

"I can't," said Catherine, "haul in a stranger from an agency to leave here all day."

"Well, then," Margaret was briskly matter of fact, "there's just one thing to do. Give up this foolish notion of a career, and step into Flora's empty place."

Charles made a little leap at that idea, and then sank away from it, with a faint suggestion in his mouth of a disappointed fish watching a baited hook yanked out of reach.

"Or," went on Margaret gravely, "Charles can stay at home. So much of your work could be done here anyway, Charles. One eye on the stew and the other on some learned tome."

"Why not?" Amy's tense question knocked the drollery out of the picture. "Why wouldn't that be possible? After all, Mrs. Hammond, you have spent years doing that very thing."

"The King would burn the stew, of course." Margaret rose, sending a light curtsey toward Charles. "Come along, Amy. If we're to walk home. Why don't you ask Sam, if that's the elevator boy's name, if he hasn't a lady friend out of work? That's what we do."

When Catherine returned from the door, her eyes crinkled at the sight of Charles sunk behind the pages of his evening paper.

"Poor old thing!" she said. "Did they rumple his fur the wrong way?"

He crashed the sheets down on his knee, and lifted his face, the tips of his ears red.

"Whatever does Margaret want to lug that thing around with her for."

"I guess she's all right." Catherine was at the window, looking at the pale glowing bowl of the city sky before she drew the shade. "Devoted to Margaret."

"Ugh! I'd like that devoted to me!"

"Don't worry!" Catherine drew the shade, and turned laughing. "She won't be. She seems violently anti-man."

"Wasn't she one of the females they had to feed through the nose down there at Washington?"

"That's rather to her credit, isn't it?"

"She's that fanatic type, all right. All emotion, unbalanced, no brain. Now Margaret has some intelligence. But she's being influenced by this woman. I can see a difference in her. To think that she chose herself to leave your mother for that!"

"I think few people influence Margaret." Catherine moved quietly about the room, picking up books left by Spencer, a toy of Letty's, Marian's doll. "She's hard headed, you know."

"Well," said Charles with great finality, "she won't ever capture any man while she has that female attached to her. Great mistake for a nice girl like Margaret to tie herself up with that woman. She seems the real paranoia type."

"Now you've finished her," Catherine rumpled his hair gently as she passed his chair, "tell me what on earth to do. About a maid, I mean."

"Don't know, I'm sure." Charles frowned briefly and picked up his paper again. "Advertise, perhaps," he added.

Catherine's eyes, pondering on the crisp russet crown of his head, bent intently over the paper, hardened. He didn't know, and he didn't mean to concern himself. Her problem, not his. It wasn't his fault if she had no time to hunt up a new maid. On the contrary, Flora's defection was in a way her fault, a failure of judgment in choice.

"I'm going to bed," she said. "I'm tired to death."

"Right-o," said Charles.

Her serge dress lay in a heap across a chair, where she had dropped it that afternoon. Careless of her. She shook it out, regarding it critically. She should have another dress; perhaps a fresh set of vest and cuffs would carry this one along for a time. As she hung it away she brushed down a coat of Charles. She held it at arm's length, her mouth puckered. She had forgotten to leave that suit at the tailor's that morning, as Charles had asked.

She sat down before the mirror to brush her hair. What had he said last night—that she deliberately neglected the little things he asked, that she stood off, being critical. Was it true? Her hair drooped in two long dark wings over her shoulders as she sat idle, thinking. She did feel separate, no longer held in close bondage to the irking, petty things, like darned socks or suits that must be cleaned, or studs in shirt fronts, or favorite desserts. They used to be momentous, those things. It's true! She flung her brush onto the dresser, where it slid along, clattering against the tray. Now I do stand off, a little disdainful, when he makes a fuss, because I'm not a faithful valet. Well! She stood up hastily, braiding her hair with quick fingers. What of it? If I spoiled him, all these years, then I must take the consequences. But it's not—less love, is it? Or did he love me more as his body servant? Are men like that?

She heard Bill's voice, "Don't ever be frantic, Catherine." Bill wasn't like that. She had almost forgotten Bill and last night. What a muddle of feeling in yesterday and to-day! Bill,—and Charles. Ah, she was critical. Charles was right. Critical of the very quality she had always seen and loved. His—yes, his childishness. Bill had dignity, maturity, that was it. Even in his moment of disclosure. He didn't take it out on Henrietta. Didn't smear her even faintly with blame.

She listened an instant as she went down the hall. Charles hadn't moved. In the bathroom she hung away the towels and threw discarded small stockings into the hamper. Then, with a little rush, grinning at herself, she filled the tub. Charles could wait.

Later, drowsily warm and relaxed, she heard Charles tiptoe into the room. She heard his "brr!" at the chill wind through the opened window. Still later she felt him bending cautiously above her. She heard herself breathing slowly, evenly, until his feet scuffed across the floor and his bed groaned softly. I can't wake up, she thought,—buried deep under soft, warm sand—heavy—even if he—wants me.

CHAPTER VII

Sam, the elevator boy, didn't know a single lady as was out of work. Catherine went on down to the basement. Perhaps the janitor would know. He called his wife. Catherine, in the door, glimpsed the rooms with their short, high windows, full of white iron beds and innumerable tidies. Mrs. O'Lay filled the door, her bulk flowing unrestrictedly above and below her narrow apron strings.

She had a mind to try the job herself. Her daughter had come home with a baby, and could mind the telephone when Sam was off, and all. Her double chins quivered violently at little Mr. O'Lay's protest. Right in the same house, an' all. "If I try it, he won't be all the time leaving the fires for me to tend, and I'll turn an honest penny myself."

She's a fat straw to grasp at, thought Catherine. If she can get between the stove and the sink—

"Sure, I been cooking all these years, and himself ain't dead yet. Nor one of the eleven children. It'd be a fine change for me."

They decided finally that Mrs. O'Lay should come up that afternoon to "learn the ropes." "I'd come up right now, but himself asked in his folks for dinner."

What luck! Catherine hurried back to her own apartment. Her own rooms look neat, and she is at least a pair of hands.

The children were waiting impetuously for Catherine to take them coasting. Marian had suggested Sunday School. Miss Kelly thought they should go, she explained.

"Miss Kelly may take you, then, on her Sunday," said Catherine. "I can't, to-day. And I'm afraid the snow is almost gone."

Spencer and Marian, their leggings already on, wiped the breakfast dishes, while Letty dragged a battered train up and down the hall.

"You come too, Daddy." Marian tugged at Charles's arm.

"No. I'm going to have a nice, quiet morning with my book." He stepped hastily out of the path of Letty's assault.

"I've left the potatoes and roast on the shelf." Catherine looked in at his study door. "Could you think to light the oven and stick them in, at twelve, if we aren't back? Mother's coming in for dinner."

"I'll remember." Marian giggled at her father's grimace, and they were off, the four of them.

On the slope Catherine chose as safe, the snow had been worn thin by countless runners. Spencer and Marian had one Flyer, and Catherine drew Letty on the small sled up and down the walk, to the loud tune of "Gid-ap! horsey! Gid-ap!" until she was breathless and flushed. Then she coaxed Letty into the construction of a snow house, while she sat on the bench beside her. The river was gray under a lead sky; the steep shores of New Jersey were mottled tawny and white. Spencer and Marian puffed up the hill, to sit solemnly beside her, their legs dangling. Letty, a small scarlet ball in her knit bloomers and sweater, an aureole of yellow fluff about her round, pink face, crooned delightedly as she patted her lumps of snow.

"An', Muvver," went on Marian, "the little boy made his dog drag the sled up the hill, and the doggie cried."

"He had snow in his toes," insisted Spencer. "He didn't cry because he had to drag the sled."

"Yes, he did. It was a very heavy sled."

Some one stopped at the end of the bench, and Catherine glanced up.

"Why, Bill!" She moved along, but Marian danced up.

"Oh, Mr. Bill! Come take a belly-bump with us, Mr. Bill. *Can* you go belly-bump?"

"I think so." Bill smiled across her head at Catherine.

"Don't let her bully you, if you don't want to." But they were off, Bill flat on the sled, Spencer clinging to his shoulders, and Marian sprawled on top of Spencer. Letty poked herself erect and opened her mouth for a shriek.

"Here, Letty!" Catherine pulled her, stiff and unbending, onto her knee. "If you don't yell, perhaps Bill will take you down. Don't scare him." Ridiculous and amusing, those flying legs. Like a scooting centipede.

"You come try it, Catherine." They had climbed up the slope to her again.

"Take Letty first." And then Catherine tried it, while the children stood in a row, shrieking with delight. "Go belly-bump, Muvver!" How Marian loved that word! But Catherine insisted on sitting up, while Bill knelt behind her to steer. A swift, flying moment, the air shrill in her ears, and laughing, they grated to a standstill on bare ground at the foot of the hill.

"If we had a real hill, now." Bill dragged the sled up, one hand firm under Catherine's arm. "I remember a hill we used to coast down when I was little. It seemed miles long, on the way up, at least."

Lucky he came along, thought Catherine, contentedly. Or he might have hated to see me, after Friday night.

"Who is that with the children?" she asked. A figure at the crest of the slope, coppery brown fur gleaming in the dull light. Miss Partridge!

"Mr. Bill!" called Marian, as the two plodded nearer. "Take Miss Partridge down just once."

Catherine felt, indignantly, the flush deepen in her cheeks. Why should she mind—

"Good morning," she called. "Won't you try it?"

"So sorry," came the neat, clipped accents. "I must run along to dinner. It looks like great sport." Her cold brown eyes moved from Catherine to Bill. A flash of small teeth. "Great sport. Good-by." A wave of a small, gloved hand, and she was off, swinging smartly along.

"What time is it?" Catherine avoided Bill's smile. "One! My gracious! Come along, you children."

Bill drew Letty up to the street. "Have to walk here. Snow's all gone," and when Letty sat obdurately on the sled, crying "Gid-ap!" he swung her up to his shoulder. She rode home in state, while Spencer and Marian argued about snow in the handball court, about what the carts did with the snow that was shoveled away; and Catherine walked rather silently at Bill's side.

Bill deposited Letty on the steps at the apartment entrance, where she amused herself by bouncing' her stomach against the low railing and gug-gugging at Spencer and Marian, who clattered down the area stairs with their sleds.

"I'm glad you were out for a walk this morning." Catherine wanted to break through the thin ice of constraint—or was it better to pretend that she did not see it? "I was afraid you might stay away from—us," she said quickly.

"That's very good of you." Bill spoke formally, his eyes on the children pelting up the steps.

"Mr. Bill, would you go coasting again?" Spencer stuck his elbow up to ward off a snowball from Marian. "You stop that, Marian. I'm not playing now. Would you?" He frowned at his sister.

"I'm playing." Catherine pinioned Marian's snowy mittens in her own hands. "An' anyway, the snow'll be gone, won't it, Muvver?"

"It'll snow again this winter, won't it?" snorted Spencer.

"When it does, we'll have a coast," Bill said gravely.

For a moment he met Catherine's glance, and suddenly the ice was gone, so suddenly that Catherine almost laughed out in delight. "Will you come, too?" he asked.

"Don't wait for the next snow." Catherine gave Marian a soft push toward the door. "Run along. Take Letty's hand, please." Her smile at Bill was grateful; having admitted her past his barriers, he was unresentful. "Come sooner!" She extended her hand, felt the quick pressure of his fingers.

Like a secret pact—she wondered a little, as she went into the hall. Words are clumsy, with Bill, as if he dwelt so far beneath ordinary surfaces that words didn't reach him.

"You like Mr. Bill, too, don't you, Mother?" Spencer pressed against her confidentially as the elevator creaked up to their floor.

"Yes, I do."

"He's a nice man," Marian agreed. "I'd like to marry him."

"He's got a wife, silly," objected Spencer. "And you're only a little girl and little girls don't get married."

"Pretty soon I can." Marian turned her back on Spencer and darted out of the elevator door, dragging Letty briskly after her.

Spencer's eyes were wide with disapproval, but Catherine laughed at him, and opened the apartment door.

Charles sat at his desk. He looked up ruefully.

"Home again! Say, I forgot all about your potatoes."

"Oh, well." Catherine was undisturbed. "You'll just have to wait longer for your dinner, then." As she hurried to the kitchen she heard Marian, "An' Mr. Bill came and coasted, and Muvver coasted with him, only not belly-bump," and Charles, "So that's why you're so late, is it?"

CHAPTER VIII

Mrs. Spencer came presently. Catherine rose from the oven, blowing wryly on a burnt thumb.

"Take Gram's coat and hat, please, Spencer." She kissed her mother's cool pink cheek. "How well you look!"

"What a pretty chain!" Marian touched the wrought silver and dull blue stones. "Isn't it, Muvver?"

"Margaret gave it to me yesterday, to match my new dress." Mrs. Spencer crinkled her eyes shrewdly. "Propitiation. She can't get over her surprise that I stand her absence so well."

"I suppose that freak woman put her up to it," said Charles, from the doorway.

"Um." Mrs. Spencer tucked her hand under his arm. "Changes are good for us. But Margaret must have had an ill conscience. She's overthoughtful."

"You see"—Catherine stirred the thickening briskly—"you aren't behaving as a Freudian mother should. You are always unexpected."

"Freud!" Mrs. Spencer made a grotesque little grimace. "What does he know about mothers! But I did think"—she glanced sidewise at Charles—"that Margaret might find things less convenient."

"She will!" Charles patted her hand. "Don't you worry, Mother Spencer. These violent crazes for—for freedom—or people—or causes—wear themselves out."

Catherine lifted her head quickly, to find her mother's eyes quizzically upon her. They meant her, too!

"Want to see my book?" Charles steered Mrs. Spencer out of the kitchen. "Catherine's too busy to talk."

Dinner went smoothly; the children told their grandmother about coasting, and she asked about school, about Miss Kelly. She wanted to take them to the Metropolitan that afternoon, to hear a lecture for children.

"Aren't there awful jams?" Catherine sighed. Piles of mending, her serge dress to freshen,—she couldn't take the afternoon off, too.

"Not too jammed for pleasure. But you needn't go." Mrs. Spencer's eyes narrowed. "I suppose you use your Sunday for a scrap-bag of odd jobs, like all other working women?"

"I certainly do." Catherine was abrupt. "But you know you prefer the children without me as mentor."

She caught a quick exchange of glances between Charles and her mother. They've been talking about me—she simmered with resentment—and Charles has won her over to his side, whatever it is.

She had proof of that later. Mrs. Spencer and the children had come home from their sojourn, and after they had given Catherine an excited and strange account of the habits of a tribe of Indians, Spencer and Marian had gone to bed.

"What did you do this afternoon?" Mrs. Spencer laid aside her magazine as Catherine came wearily back to the living room.

"I showed Mrs. O'Lay where to find the various tools for her new job"—Catherine had explained Flora's absence earlier—"conducted her initiation ceremony. And washed out a collar, and darned."

Mrs. Spencer nodded.

"When you might have been with your children. Are you sure, Cathy"—she paused—"sure that you aren't losing the best of your life?"

"But I'm not!" Catherine sat erect in her chair, her cheeks flushed. "On the contrary, I am with the children, and love it, and they enjoy me far more than when I was their constant bodyguard."

"Charles was telling me about Spencer." Mrs. Spencer drew the gray silk of her skirt into tiny folds. "It seemed pitiful."

Catherine was silent a moment, fighting against the swift recurrence of that frightful hour, and against a wrathful sense of injustice.

"Children run away, often," she said. "I think Spencer just happened to catch at that excuse—of my not being here."

Mrs. Spencer shook her head.

"Charles seemed to feel—"

"He told me just how he felt." Catherine flung up her head.

Mrs. Spencer's inspection of her daughter was reflective.

"I don't like to interfere. You know that. But—Charles doesn't seem happy."

"He has no right to—"

"He didn't say that." Mrs. Spencer was stern. "I gathered it. His work isn't going very well. He thinks you aren't interested in it."

Catherine turned her head quickly. Had she heard the door of his study squeak?

"I am. He knows it. Far more than he cares about what I do."

"That's all." Mrs. Spencer rose, preening her skirts like a small bird. "I won't say another word. But think it over, Cathy. There's so much that's crooked and wrenched in the air these days. I don't want you led astray by it. I must run along. Alethea will be expecting me."

In the turmoil of her feelings, Catherine had a sharp sense of the bright, valiant spirit of her mother. She didn't really like to interfere. Charles had coerced her into this! Something wistful and picturesque about the two elderly women, Mrs. Alethea Bragg and her mother, moving serenely about in the great city, nibbling at music, at theaters, at Fifth Avenue shops, taking quiet amusement out of days free from the hectic confusion of trying to live.

"Please don't be concerned about me, Mother." She threw her arm around the firm, neat shoulders. "I'm honestly trying to hunt for a scheme of things that will work for everybody. Not just me. Come in oftener. The children adore it."

CHAPTER IX

Miss Kelly had brought the children down for a visit to the Christmas toy-land in some of the large stores, and at noon Catherine met them for luncheon. Letty had shared the expedition for the first time, and the kaleidoscopic displays had goaded her into a frenzy of noisy delight.

"She's just roared the whole morning, Muvver." Marian was uneasy at the scrutiny of amused neighbors in the tea room. But Miss Kelly diverted Letty into contemplation of an enormous baked potato.

"I want you to come with us, Mother." Spencer felt under his chair for his cap; he hadn't been quite sure where he should put that cap. "You always did—"

"You see, I have to stay in the office, except at noon," Catherine explained. She was conscious of admiration for the deftness with which Miss Kelly had subdued Letty, had arranged the luncheon for the children and herself. "I don't have a vacation until Christmas day. Tell me what you saw."

A recital in duo. Letty had tried to hug every Santa Claus they had seen, even the Salvation Army Santa on the corner. Extraordinary and delectable toys. They couldn't decide what they wanted themselves.

"It is lucky we came down early," said Miss Kelly. "The crowds began to come before we left."

"Did you buy your gifts?"

"I think Spencer bought me one," cried Marian. "He made me turn my back—"

"You shouldn't think about that," said Spencer, earnestly. "If it's Christmas, you shouldn't even think you've got a present."

"You did buy me one!" Marian wriggled ecstatically in her chair. "I know you did!"

Catherine waited with them for a home-bound bus. Spencer pulled her head down and whispered in her ear, "Mother, couldn't I go to the office and wait till you come home? I don't want to go with them."

"It's too many hours, Spencer. You wouldn't know what to do with yourself."

"Well, I don't know, anyway." His eyes darkened. "Staying home and no school and—"

"Here comes our bus." Miss Kelly marshalled them before her, maneuvered them neatly up the steps. Catherine waved to them, watched their bus disappear in the mélêe of cars. Then she edged through the crowd to the windows, and walked slowly toward the office. The cold sunshine veneered the intent faces, the displays of gauds and kickshaws.

Being downtown makes Christmas quite different, she thought. An enormous advertising scheme. That's it. Five more shopping days before Christmas. Look at that window! She strolled past it, her eyes bright with derision. Extraordinary, useless, expensive things, good for gifts, and nothing else on earth. Christmas belonged in the country, in the delicate mystery and secrecy with which children could invest it. Not in these glaring windows. A saturnalia of selling, that's Christmas in New York, she thought, darting across the street as the traffic officer's signal released the flood of pedestrians. Something strained, feverish, in the crowds. Probably half of them with empty purses. Like her own.

Dr. Roberts stood at her window, waiting for her.

"I've been talking with President Waterbury, Mrs. Hammond, and I wished to see you at once." He pulled reflectively at his pointed beard. "There are various ins and outs here. I don't know that you've been here long enough to discover them."

Catherine wondered, with faint discomfort, whether President Waterbury had disapproved of something she had done.

"A deplorable jealousy, for example, between departments." He cleared his throat.

Catherine sat down. She had learned to wait until Dr. Roberts had sent off preliminary sputtering fireworks before he uncovered his serious purpose.

"I happened to learn that Smithson, in the local social department, was interviewing Dr. Waterbury. Had seen him twice. So I was at once suspicious. Smithson, you've met him? Well, he's the type of parasite this kind of organization attracts, unfortunately. We haven't many here, but they exist. Afraid to finish up a job, because then another may not turn up. He's nursed along his study of sanitation, I should blush to say how long. No doubt the buildings in his original investigation have crumbled into decay. And he hasn't published a word. But he can't put off publication much longer, you see. And so he hit upon this other scheme. He doesn't belong in our field." Dr. Roberts's bright little eyes snapped, his beard waggled in a fury. "But he had the audacity to go to Waterbury with this suggestion. He wants to make the field study for me! He—he—" Dr. Roberts stuttered tripping furiously over his consonants. "H-he of-ff-fered to go out west, to gather field mat-t-terial for us. Told Waterbury that I couldn't go, as I was in charge of things here at headquarters. He had almost convinced the President. He's smooth. Smooth!"

"But why on earth does he want to go?" Catherine's voice placated the irate little man. "It certainly isn't his kind of work."

"Not at all. Not at all. But he sets himself up for a dexterous investigator. And Waterbury likes him. The point is this. I can't very well go myself. But you can! I pointed out to Dr. Waterbury that logically you were the person to go."

"To go where, Dr. Roberts?" Catherine sat very still, but back in her head she heard a clear little bell of excitement begin its clanging.

"You have personality and tact. You've already met two of the chief educators of the state. You have the work at the tips of your fingers. Who could be better? Dr. Waterbury agreed with me. It would be an agreeable diversion, no doubt, and of course," he added with proud finality, "then I can obtain for you the raise in salary you deserve."

"You mean that you would like me to make the personal inspection of all these schools?" Catherine's hand moved vaguely toward the shelves of catalogues.

"Just that. It is time now to have that done. Smithson has—yes, he has snooped around, discovering that. He wants the amusement of such a trip, and the glory. For it is an excellent thing. For your reputation. Your expenses are paid, too."

"Why don't you go yourself?"

"It's not precisely convenient. There are several meetings in January. I am to speak at one of them."

I can't go, thought Catherine. Ridiculous to consider it.

"Don't decide immediately. Think it over. Let me know—why, after Christmas. Late in January would do to start. You can no doubt arrange matters at home. You'd like to talk it over with Dr. Hammond, of course."

"How long a trip would it be?" Catherine was vibrating under the clanging of that bell. No, it wasn't a bell, it was a pulse beating just back of her ears.

"You can decide that yourself, practically. Perhaps a month. Depends upon your arrangement of your route. I say, that's fine!" He rose, slapping his hands against his pockets. "You'll think it out! It's by far the best way to convince Waterbury you are serious, and worth a real salary."

Think it out! Catherine let the idea play with her. Trains, new cities, new people, herself as dignified representative of the Bureau. But the children! She couldn't leave them—and Charles. Her clothes weren't up to such a position. She could buy more! Her salary would grow to cover—anything!

When she went home in the cold winter twilight, she had coiled the project into a tight spring, held firmly down below thought. She couldn't go. How could she? But she had a week before she must reject it openly. The pressure of that coiled spring was terrific. At any instant it might tear up through thought and feeling.

Mrs. O'Lay had been persuaded to divide her day so that she spent part of the afternoon in her own basement, and then stayed to serve dinner and clear up the kitchen for Catherine. Charles said he felt as if an Irish hippopotamus hovered at his elbow at the table, but Catherine stretched luxuriously into freedom from dinner responsibility. If Mrs. O'Lay had a sketchy art as a cook, Catherine found dinner more palatable than when she had flown into domestic harness at the end of the day.

The children were full of whispering excitement; the house was made up of restricted zones. Marian wasn't to put her head inside Spencer's door, and mother shouldn't look into his closet. Charles had brought home a tree as tall as Spencer, which spread its branches drooping and green in front of the living room windows. Miss Kelly, calmly methodical as ever, helped the children string cranberries and popcorn to wind through the needles.

"Saturday we will trim it," Catherine promised them, "and Saturday night you can each wrap your presents in red paper and label them."

"Then you'll see them when we are in bed," protested Marian.

"I won't take a single peek!"

Saturday afternoon Catherine stood on a chair, hunting on the top shelf of the hall closet for the box of tinsel and small tree lights. Surely she had left it there on that shelf. She smiled a little, at her own warm content. The shimmering joy of the children had thrown its glow over her, too, and the sardonic Christmas of the streets seemed remote, unreal.

"Hurry up, Muvver dear!" called Marian. "Isn't it there?"

Catherine felt the corner of a pasteboard box, tugged at it, caught it as it slipped over the edge of the shelf, the cover whirling past her hand.

She stared at the contents—a handbag of soft, tooled leather, with carved fastenings of dull gold. Guiltily she reached for the cover at her feet. She had stumbled upon Charles's hiding place. He shouldn't have been so extravagant. Her fingers brushed the soft brown surface in a swift caress as she pushed on the cover, and rose to tiptoe to replace the box.

There, the other box was in the corner.

"What are you after up there?" Charles spoke sharply from the door.

Catherine, her cheeks flushing, dragged out the box of trimmings.

"This!" she called gaily, "for our tree!" She mustn't let him guess that she had seen that bag. She slipped one hand under his arm, laughing to herself at his perturbed eyes. He was in Spencer's class, with that serious fear lest his secret be unearthed before the exact moment. "Come help trim it. You can arrange the lights."

And as they worked, Catherine turned tentatively to that coiled spring of her desire, and found the resilience had vanished. She did not wish to go. She couldn't leave them. Going off to work each day was different. She needed that. But to go away, for days and nights—

"Moth-er!" Spencer's horrified accents came from the other side of the tree. "Letty's chewing the cranberry string!"

"Here, you!" Catherine swung her up to her shoulder. How heavy she was growing! "You fasten Spencer's star to the top branch."

CHAPTER X

Catherine woke. What was that old crone crouched inquisitively at the foot of her bed? She lifted her head cautiously; nothing but her bathrobe over a chair, indistinct in the vague light. It must be very early. She caught the steady rhythm of Charles's breathing. She curled down again under the blankets, full of the relaxed ecstasy in which she had slept so dreamlessly. Dearest—she flowed out toward him in a great, windless tide. I've found him again, she thought. We're out of the thickets.

Dimly she heard the clatter of horses' hoofs, the clinking of milk bottles. It is morning, then. She listened unconsciously for the shrill "Merry Christmas!" of the children. They would wake soon.

As she lay, waiting, effortless, relaxed, a strange phantasy drifted over her, like morning fog in low places. She couldn't, drowsily, quite grasp it. Charles had not known about that plan, tugging, tempting her this last week. How could he have known when she rejected it, completely? And yet, as if he had felt that rejection, fed upon it, sacrificial offering to him, he had been grandly magnanimous, lavish, taking her submission.

Perhaps—she stirred slowly out of the mists—perhaps it was only her own knowledge of the rejection, the sacrifice, binding her more closely to the roots of love, sloughing off that critical, offish self.

She was wide awake now, thinking clearly. Why had she so suddenly decided? What, after all, had wiped out the vigor, the great drive in that desire? She knew just what it meant, her going or her refusal to go. Refusal marked her forever as half-hearted, as temporizing, so far as her work went. That she had recognized from the beginning.

Just the glimpse of that bag, the soft leather under her fingers, had settled matters. Without a conscious thought. An extravagant, lovely trifle, but a symbol of the old tender awareness she had so loved in him. Ridiculous, that a thing could have the power to touch you so. Behind it, shadowy, serried, other things—trifles, evidence that Charles gave her sensitive perception, that he loved her, not himself reflected in her. Just that he knew her purse was serviceable and shabby.

Foolish, and adorable. She sighed, happily. He would hate my going away. He would be outraged.

A faint sound outside the door, a scuffle of bare feet, and then a burst into chorus, "Merry Christmas! Merry—" The door flew open, and in they rushed, the three of them. Catherine shot upright, reaching for her bathrobe.

"Merry Christmas, but hurry back where it's warm."

Marian flung her arms around Charles's sleepy head. "Merry Christmas, my Daddy!"

"It's only the middle of the night, isn't it?" Charles groaned.

"It's Christmas morning, and you hurry and get up!"

When the arduous business of dressing was over, Charles turned the switch, and the colored lights starred the little tree. No one was to unwrap a present until after breakfast. Too much excitement on empty stomachs, insisted Catherine. The children dragged the table nearer the door and ranged themselves along the side, so that they could gaze as they ate.

Presently the room was a gay litter of tissue paper, colored ribbons, toys, books. Letty sat in the middle of her pile, revolving like a yellow top among the exciting things. Spencer had waited tensely while Catherine unwrapped a large bundle, and then turned a little pale with delight at her surprise. Yes, he had made it himself, at school. It was a stand for a fern. He had carved it, too. Book ends for his father. Then he had immersed himself in his own possessions.

Charles admired the platinum cuff links in the little purple box with Catherine's card. Catherine grinned at him. "Nice to give you a present," she said, "without having to ask you for the money for it." She regretted her words; his smile seemed forced.

"What did Daddy give you, Muvver?" Marian, hugging her doll, pressed against Catherine's knee.

"Well, this." Catherine held up a box of chocolates.

"That's not all," said Charles promptly.

"Here's another." Spencer wiggled along on his knees to hand her another box.

Long and thin—that wasn't the same box. Catherine unwrapped the paper, and long black silk stockings dangled from her fingers.

"Fine," she said. "Just what I wanted." She waited for a repetition of "That's not all," but Charles said only, "I didn't know what you would like."

She glanced up quickly. He was teasing her—they had joked about useful gifts. But he had picked up a book. The red cover blurred before Catherine's eyes. He was pulling his chair up to the table light.

The stockings clung to her finger tips, as if her bewilderment electrified them. Mrs. O'Lay, lumbering through the hall to the kitchen, stopped at the door in loud admiration of the tree.

Margaret and Mrs. Spencer were coming in for early dinner. Catherine flung herself into a numbing round of preparations. Whatever it meant, the day shouldn't be spoiled for the children. Whatever it meant—he couldn't have forgotten the bag. She had seen it there. She remembered his sharp inquiry, as she reached to the shelf. Perhaps her mother had hidden it, or Margaret. No, he knew about it. A sickening wave of suspicion curled through her, so that she straightened from her odorous dish of onions, browning for the dressing. It's his gift, to some one else. The wave subsided, leaving a line of wreckage—and certainty.

Funny, how you catch a second wind, when you are knocked out, thought Catherine, as the day wound along. No one even guessed. The children were amazingly good. Even Letty went peacefully to her nap, after a few moments of wracking indecision as to which new toy should accompany her. Margaret left early, for a Christmas party somewhere. Catherine and her mother stood in her room, Mrs. Spencer adjusting her veil at the mirror. They were going out for a Christmas walk with Spencer and Marian, leaving Mrs. O'Lay in charge. Catherine heard a cautious step in the hall. She did not move. But she knew when the feet stopped at the closet door; she heard the faint scrape of pasteboard on the shelf.

"I'm going over to the office." Charles stopped at the door. "I'll probably be home before you are."

"Poor fellow!" Mrs. Spencer cajoled him, her hands patting her sleek gloves into place. "Must you work even on Christmas Day?"

"Just a few odds and ends of work." Charles looked uneasy. But he nodded, and presently the hall door closed after him.

PART IV
ENCOUNTER

CHAPTER I

"Dr. Gilbert will be in immediately." The neat little office nurse ushered Catherine into the living room. "She left word for tea at five."

Catherine said she would wait. The nurse bent down to touch a match to the gas log, and tiny blue flames leaped in mechanical imitation of a hearth fire. Catherine stood at the window, drawing off her gloves. The buildings between the hotel and the corner of the Avenue had been demolished since her last visit; beneath the windows gaped a huge chasm, rocky, pitted with pools of dark water, angled with cranes and derricks,—like a fairy tale, thought Catherine, and the old witch froze them into immobility with her stick, her stick being a holiday.

The room was Henrietta, unimaginative, practical, disinterested. Expensive, department store furniture, overstuffed chairs and davenport, floor lamp, mahogany. Henrietta had ordered the furnishings, the maid had set them in place, and there they stayed, unworn, impersonal. A maid wheeled in the tea wagon, and Henrietta's firm heels sounded in the hall.

"Catherine! Good for you." Henrietta clapped her shoulder as she passed. "Afraid something might detain you." She shook off her heavy English coat, and went briskly to pouring tea. Her close hat had flattened her fine light hair above her temples, giving additional plump serenity to her face.

"That's all, Susie," she told the maid. "If there are any calls for me, take them. I am undisturbed for one hour now."

"Ah, this is great!" She stretched her feet toward the humming gas log; shining toes, ankles slim even in the gray spats. "I suppose you have a mission, since you take the time to come down here to-day. But whatever it is, I am glad to see you."

Catherine sipped at the tea. The hot, clear fragrance was an auger, releasing words.

"Shrewd guess, Henry." She smiled. "I want advice."

"Help yourself." Henrietta's teeth closed in her sandwich with relish.

"And I wanted it from you," Catherine spoke slowly, "because I want advice that goes in my direction."

"Kind we always want. Only kind we take."

"Here it is." Catherine placed her tea cup on the wagon. "Just before Christmas Dr. Roberts asked me to go west, to make the first-hand study of the schools, you know. He gave me until to-morrow to decide." Henrietta's eyes, alert, sharp, over the edge of her cup, waited. "More money, for one thing. Reputation. Chance to show what I can do. But I have to be gone almost a month, I think. I decided at once that it was out of the question."

"Why?"

"That was a week ago." Catherine leaned forward. "In a fit of sentiment. And egoism. I thought they couldn't get along without me, of course. Then—no use to explain the particular eye-opener—I changed my mind. I began to wonder whether this wasn't a sort of test. To see how serious I am. About a job, I mean. Now! Advise me to go."

"Of course, no one is really indispensable." Henrietta grinned. "No one. And what's a month?"

"It seems a long time to leave the children."

"Be good for them as well as you. Isn't Miss Kelly capable of handling them?"

"I suppose so."

"Most families would be improved by enforced separations," declared Henrietta. "They're too tight. Break 'em up. What does Charles say to this?"

"He hasn't heard of it yet."

"Decide first and then tell him, eh?" Henrietta drew out her eyeglasses, running her fingers absently along the black ribbon. "He won't approve, at first. But it is a test. You're right. Your first opportunity to enlarge your position. You'd be a fool not to go, Catherine."

"That's just what I wanted to hear." Catherine's eyes were somber, harassed. "I've thought it out, backwards and forwards. Mother's friend wants to visit some one in New Jersey. If Mother will spend the night at the house—but she won't approve, either."

"Get your approval out of the job, Catherine." Henrietta squinted through her eyeglass. "You want it on every hand, don't you?"

Catherine lowered her eyelids.

"I did, once. I think I do less, now."

"That's right!"

They were silent a moment.

"That's ripping!" Henrietta broke out. "That the Bureau offered it to you. You can't turn it down. I'll drop in occasionally on the kids, if that will calm your anxiety."

"You really think it's not a preposterous scheme, then?"

"The only preposterousness would be in refusing it. It's ripping!"

"What is ripping?"

Catherine turned, a quick stir of pleasure at the low voice. Bill was at the door.

"Come in and hear about it." Henrietta waved toward a chair. "Tea?"

Bill shook his head and sat down near Catherine. He sagged in his chair, a suggestion of unkempt, wrinkled weariness in his face and clothes.

Henrietta explained in hard, glowing phrases, that Catherine had the opportunity of a lifetime. As Catherine listened and watched, she had a renewal of the strange feeling which had haunted her since Christmas morning. We are so lonely—so shut off—so absolutely isolated, she thought. Each of us speaks only his own language. We think we reach another human being, that he knows our tongue, and we discover that we have fooled ourselves. Grotesquely. Charles—remote, unreachable. I imagined that contact. Bill, and Henrietta—she is content, thinking she communicates with Bill.

"Are you going?" Bill glanced at her under his heavy lids.

"I think I am," she said. She wished she could find his thought which reached toward her.

"Perhaps I'll see you. I have to go to Chicago the end of the month on that Dexter contract," he added, to Henrietta.

He left them presently, and when Catherine rose to go, Henrietta's hand lingered, fumbling—queerly for her—over Catherine's fingers.

"I hope you and Bill make connections," she said. "He's not well. I don't know—listless, needs a change, I guess."

Catherine stared at the anxiety, the puzzled bewilderment in Henrietta's round blue eyes.

"I've been worrying at him to see a specialist here, and he won't. Can't budge him, stubborn old Bill. He enjoys you, Cathy. Have dinner or something with him."

"If we do make connections, of course I shall." Catherine felt a little prickling of guilt, as if in some way Bill's confidence violated complete loyalty to Henrietta. "I'm fond of Bill," she added.

"There's nothing seriously wrong with him. But—there's a gland specialist here in town. I told Bill his cynicism would vanish like the dew if he'd let himself be gone over." Henrietta frowned. "He said if his philosophy was located in his liver, he preferred to keep his illusions about it."

"Oh, you doctors! Thinking every feeling has its roots in some gland, and that you can diagnose any unhappiness."

"Jeer all you like." Henrietta's moment of perplexity had passed. "We're animals, Cathy, and a reasonably healthy animal is reasonably happy."

Catherine reached for purse and gloves; as she dangled the shabby black bag over a finger, she felt the stealthy, restless feet of her obsession begin their pacing. Charles, and Stella Partridge. Charles, with all his tenderness, his love—

With diabolic abruptness Henrietta said:

"Oh, by the way, I ran into that Miss Partridge last week, at the hospital. Do you see much of her?"

Catherine flinched. The stealthy feet were running.

"What made you think of her?" she asked.

"Oh—" Henrietta hesitated. "Thinking about you and Charles. I had a little talk with her, while we waited. She's an interesting type, I think."

"What do you make of her? Charles seems to admire her immensely."

"So do several of the staff. She's the kind of modern woman men do like. Unoriginal, useful, wonderful assistant. Cold as a frog—they don't guess that. She's clever. Her line is that men are so generous and fine, give her every opportunity to advance."

"What is she after, do you think?"

"Money. Position. But she's parasitical. Not in the old sense. She's sidetracked all her sex into her ambition, but she uses it as skillfully as if she wanted a lover or a husband."

"I have seen very little of her." Catherine was busy with her gloves. She wanted to escape before those shrewd blue eyes caught a glimpse of her caged, uneasy, obsessive fear.

"She'll get on," said Henrietta. "Wish you could stay for dinner, Catherine. No? Let me know if I can help you out. Tell Charles I think he should be immensely proud of you, being offered this trip, will you? I'll run in some evening soon and tell him myself."

CHAPTER II

Dinner was ready when Catherine reached home. She went in to bid Letty good night; Miss Kelly had put her to bed, a doll on each side of her yellow head. As the small arms flew about Catherine's throat, choking her, and she caught the sweet fragrance of the drowsy, warm skin her lips brushed, a panic of negation seized her. Go away, for days and days, without that soft ecstasy of touch, of assurance? She was mad to think of it. "There, Letty, that's a lovely hug." She drew the blanket close to the small chin.

"An' tuck in Tilda and li'l' Pet," murmured Letty. "My Muv-ver dear."

What was sentimental and what was sane? Catherine, smoothing into place the heavy coil of her hair, washing her hands, delaying her entrance to the living room, where she heard, vaguely, the voices of Charles and the children, struggled slowly to lift her head above the maelstrom. It was only for a few weeks out of a lifetime. The children would not suffer. And I want to go, she thought. Something leaped within her, vigorous, hungry, clamorous. It's not loving them less, to need something outside them, beyond them, something worth the temporary price of absence. Charles loved them, and yet he could go freely, without any of these qualms, into danger, for months.

She marched into the living room, her resolution firm. She would tell Charles about it, after dinner. Perhaps he would be indifferent. Perhaps—her obsession bared its teeth behind the flimsy bars—he might be relieved, at freedom to follow other desires.

Marian, perched on the arm of her father's chair, one arm tight about his neck, squirmed to look up at Catherine, expectant brightness in her eyes. Spencer stood in front of them, hands in his pockets, his face puckered intensely.

"Couldn't it be managed some way, Daddy?" he begged.

"Where's your allowance?" Charles stretched lazily, one hand enclosing Marian's slippered feet, dancing them slowly up and down.

"It's all in hock, for three weeks." Spencer was dolorous. "For Christmas presents, and they're all over."

"It's where?" Catherine laughed, and Spencer spun around, hope smoothing some of his puckers.

"Hock. That's what Tom says. But he says when he needs more money he asks his mother and she tells his father and he gets it."

"And who is Tom?" Charles stood up. Swinging Marian to her feet. "Let's have dinner."

It was Tom Wilcox on the floor below. Spencer had spent the afternoon there; his story came out in excited fragments. He had helped set up a radio apparatus, and he wanted one, to rig up on his bed, like Tom's. Then he could wake up in the night and listen to a concert, or a man telling about the weather.

"He lent me a book about it, Mother." He poised his fork in mid-air, and down splashed his bit of mashed potato.

"Watch what you are doing, sir," said Charles.

Spencer flushed, but hurried on, "And I know I could set one up alone, and it's wonderful, Mother, you can listen to things thousands of miles away, an'—"

"If Spencer has one, I want one on my bed, too," declared Marian, with a demure, sidewise glance at her father. "Couldn't I have one, Daddy?"

"Spencer hasn't one yet." Charles teased him.

"How much do they cost?" asked Catherine, gently. Marian's glance bothered her. The child couldn't—how could she?—feel that thicket which had sprung up this last week, enough to range herself deliberately with her father.

"Well, quite a lot of dollars. Four or five or mebbe six." Spencer was doubtful. "But they last forever, Tom says, an'—"

"What would you do with it?"

Spencer caught the tantalizing undertone in his father's voice.

"Listen!" he cried, "of course, listen!"

"Careful, Spencer." Catherine's eyes steadied him; poor kid! She knew that irritating helplessness. "I'm sure it is interesting."

Mrs. O'Lay heaved herself around the table. "That roast ain't so good as it might be," she observed confidentially to Catherine. "Butchers is snides, that's all."

"It was all right." Catherine ignored Charles's lifted eyebrows. The salad did look a little messy.

"Do you think, Mother, that perhaps—"

"Can't you talk about something else for a while, Spencer?" Charles spoke up curtly.

Catherine's fingers gripped her serving fork.

"I'll see, Spencer," she said, clearly. "Later we'll talk about it."

"If he has it, I want it," Marian insisted.

"Will you change the subject?"

Charles's outbreak wrapped a heavy silence about the children. Catherine's spoon clicked in the bowl of salad dressing. How ghastly, she thought. It's our dissension, using them. Spencer had ducked his head; his nostrils dilated, his eyes moved unhappily from her face to his father's.

"Let's see, school opens on Wednesday, doesn't it?" She sought for safe words with which to rescue them. "You have to-morrow. Miss Kelly is going shopping for you. A coat for Marian—"

"Is she going to select clothes for them?" asked Charles, accusingly.

"Oh, she can do that. I've given her a price limit. The only difficult thing is shopping within that limit."

"I never had a bought coat, did I, Muvver?" Marian broke in. "Only coats you sewed for me."

"You're getting to be such a big girl." What possessed the children, anyway! Catherine heard Charles grunt faintly as if some huge dissatisfaction was confirmed. "And now—"

"You have more important things to do than mere sewing for the children."

"Yes." Catherine was flint, sending off sparks. "And I have money to bridge the difference in price."

Silence again, murky, uncomfortable. Finally the ordeal of dinner was done with. Charles offered, with detectable ostentation, to read to Marian. Spencer pulled his chair around until the back cut him off in a corner with his book on radio-practice. Catherine, after consultation with Mrs. O'Lay, withdrew to the study, where she opened her drawer of the desk, and spread out the array of bills. Not all of them were in yet; this was only the second of January, and a holiday at that. But there were enough! She set down figures, added, grimly—how few bills it took to make a hundred dollars!—and all the time, under the external business of reckoning, whirled a tumult of half recognized thoughts. Unendurable, that dissension should be tangled enough to catch the children in its meshes. Since Christmas day she had held herself remote, ice-enclosed. She had felt Charles try to reach her, felt his fingers slip, chilled, from her impenetrable surface, until he chose this method. As if he brandished the tender body of a child as his weapon, threatening to bruise it against her hard aloofness. Her hands dropped idly on the tormenting bills, and she let herself fully into that whirling tumult. Whatever happened, she must prevent another hour like that at dinner. If they must be opposed, she and Charles, it must be in themselves, not with the children as buffers or weapons. When they had gone to bed, she would go in to Charles.

Could she say, I know you are in love with Stella Partridge? Did she know it? If she said that, he might think that this trip, her going away, was revenge, or jealousy. Well, wasn't it? She could hear his voice, dramatizing the fairy story he read, so that Marian broke in occasionally with faint "Oh's!" or delighted giggles. Why had she decided that she must go? Defense, perhaps; not revenge. She felt again that strong, twisted cable of her own integrity. He wanted her submissive, docile, violating herself. He might say that she had driven him away, had failed him. But Stella—that had begun months ago. She could pick up threads of evidence, all down the days since summer. Then he might deny it, being secretly bland and pleased that she revealed herself as jealous, like a beggar at a door where she had once dwelt. Perhaps there was little to the affair. She had a brief, strange fancy—he had swung slightly in his orbit, so that the side toward her was cold, dead, like the dark face of the moon—and the light, the awareness of her—all of that was turned away, out of possibility of any incidence, any impingement from her.

No. She would tell him only that she wanted to go away for a few weeks. That she would arrange everything so that his life would be quite as always. That she hoped—faint hope!—that he might find some small pleasure in this degree of success she had achieved.

If I pretend that I have noticed nothing, she thought at last, then it may be in the end that there was little to notice. If I can cling to my love, it may be like that old man of the sea, changing into horrible shapes under my hands, but changing back, if I have courage to hang on, into its true shape.

"Time for bed-ne-go," came Charles's voice down the hall.

"Please, can I finish this chapter, Daddy?" Spencer begged.

"Better put your book mark right there, son, and run along."

He had read himself into a better humor, thought Catherine. She brushed the bills into the drawer. Her check would be larger this month.

"Come along, chickens." She stood at the doorway; her glance at Charles gathered him clearly—the line of lower eyelid, the angle of his chin. Marian slid down from his knee, sighing.

"Daddy read me a lovely story, all about a fairy prince."

She bent to kiss Marian good night, with a final pat to the blankets.

"I'll dream about a fairy prince, Muvver," came the child's voice, muffled as she snuggled out of reach of the cold wind.

Spencer's arms shot up about her throat, tugging her down where he could whisper.

"Moth-er, do you think I could have a radio receiving set?"

Catherine smiled.

"Well—" she hesitated. "You have a birthday before long. In March. I'll have to find out more about them. Could you wait?"

"Oh, Moth-er!" His hug was exuberant. "Moth-er darling!"

Catherine closed his door, and poised an instant in the hall, priming her courage. "Now!" she said, under her breath.

Before she had moved, however, the doorbell clattered, smudging her flame of determination.

Charles came briskly through the hall.

"Oh, you there?" But he went on to the door.

CHAPTER III

It was the Thomases, Mrs. Thomas explaining wordily that they had spent the day in town, luncheon, matinee, dinner, and thought they would just drop in for a time, before the ten-thirty train home.

More than an hour to their train time. To Catherine, let down so suddenly from her peak of resolution, the evening was garbled, like a column in a newspaper struck off from pied type, with words and phrases at random making sense, and all the rest unintelligible. Mrs. Thomas was full of holiday vivacity; the plumes on her black hat quivered in every filament. Those plumes bothered Catherine; she had seen them before, perhaps not at that angle, or perhaps not on that hat. No, they were generic plumes; eternal symbol of the academic wife and her best hat, her prodigious effort at respectable attire.

Mr. Thomas wanted to talk shop, if Charles would permit him. One leg crossed over his knee jerked absently in rhythm as he spoke. A student of his was working on psychological tests for poetic creation, an analysis of the poetic type of thought processes. Against their talk, like trills and grace notes against the base chords, rippled Mrs. Thomas in little anecdotes of Percy, of Clara, of Dorothy, of Walter.

"Walter wanted Spencer to come out for a few days this vacation. Be so nice for him to get into the country. But Percy had a little sore throat, and of course with children you never know what that may mean. I told him perhaps between semesters—the children always have a few days then."

"That's very kind of you." Catherine heard the determined phrases Charles set forth: "The poetic mind is never intellectual. Always purely emotional, intuitive, governed by associative processes." She felt that her smile was a mawkish simper. "To think of adding another child to your household."

"I'll tell Walter, then, that perhaps in February."

And presently, Mr. Thomas, blinking behind his glasses, turned his gentle smile toward Catherine.

"We hear great things of you, Mrs. Hammond."

"Oh, yes." Mrs. Thomas nodded. Catherine felt the quick stiffening of attention, and thought, here's what they came in for. What is it? She flung out her hand to ward off danger, but unsuspectingly Mr. Thomas hurled his bomb.

"Dr. Roberts tells us you've been appointed field investigator. He is particularly enthusiastic about it. You deserve congratulations."

"But, dear Mrs. Hammond, are you really going? I said to Mr. Thomas I couldn't believe it unless you told me yourself."

Catherine rushed pell-mell into words. She must stir up enough dust to hide Charles's face, to keep him silent.

"It isn't really settled. Dr. Roberts asked me to go, but I haven't agreed, as yet. Interesting, of course, fascinating." She saw, breathlessly, the little glance of triumph Mrs. Thomas sent her husband.

"I said I didn't see how a mother could leave her family."

"Only for a short time, of course. Don't you think we all need some kind of respite?"

"Well, I remember the doctor sent me to Atlantic City, after Dorothy's birth." And Mrs. Thomas related with gusto her homesickness, her dire imaginings each hour of absence. "You never know what might happen! Even now, I can't help wondering if they are covered warmly enough, although Mrs. Bates promised to stay till we came home."

Inconsequential, drifting bits of conversation—the minutes until they should go were thin wires, drawing Catherine to the brink of the whirlpool. Charles was laboriously talkative, and she heard the rushing of his winds of grievance.

They were going!

"You'll send Spencer out, then, some day. He could come with Mr. Thomas. For a week-end, say. Walter would be so pleased."

And then, as they stood in the hall, Mr. Thomas dropped another bomb.

"You haven't decided, I suppose, about that western position, Hammond? Your husband was talking it over with me at luncheon one day," he added to Catherine. "There's something gratifying in the idea of controlling a department and the entire policy, I think."

It was Charles's turn now to hurry into words, vague, temporizing words.

Catherine returned to the living room and sat down. She had a queer illusion that if she moved too quickly, she might break; she was brittle, tight. Charles came back to the doorway, his chin thrust out. Why, it was funny, ridiculous—caught out, each of them. This must be a dream. It was too absurd for reality. She began to laugh. She didn't wish to laugh, but she was helpless, as if some monstrous jest seized her and shook her. Was it she, laughing, or the jest, outside her, shaking her? She couldn't stop.

"Evidently you are amused." Charles strode past her. She wanted to deny that, to explain that it wasn't she laughing. But she couldn't stop that gasping ribald sound. "Catherine!" he stood above her, enormous, magnified by the tears in her eyes. "Catherine!"

Abruptly the monstrous jest dropped her, limp, and the laughter had burst through the thin partition into sobs. She twisted away from him, flinging an arm up to shield her face, her body pressed against the chair, seeking something hard, immovable, to check its convulsive racking. She knew that Charles bent over her. She wanted to scream at him to go away, to leave her alone, but she doubled her first against her lips. She struggled back heavily to the narrow, tortuous path of control. For days she had walked too near the edge for safety. She could breathe now. If she could lie there, quiet, for a time—but Charles was waiting. Her hands dropped to her lap, she relaxed, emptily, and slowly she turned her face. Charles watched her; alarm, and a sort of scorn on his face. He thought she had chosen that as a weapon—feminine hysterics.

"Well?" His gruffness was a shield over his alarm, she knew.

"I am sorry." Her voice had the faint quiver of spent tears. "I really didn't intend—but it suddenly looked—ridiculous."

"I don't see what's funny." Charles sat down stiffly. "In my hearing of my wife's plans from outsiders."

Catherine drew a long breath. She was back on that narrow path, now.

"And my hearing of yours?" she asked.

"I told you about that offer several months ago." Charles was dignified. "You seemed so little interested."

"Let's not quibble!" Catherine exclaimed. "I can't bear it. It's bad enough—I was coming in to talk with you, when they rang. I hadn't known"—she stared a moment; that was, after all, the dreadful sign-post, indicating their diverging roads—"that you considered that offer seriously."

"Exactly. But you will admit I had spoken of it?"

Ah, he wouldn't take that as parallel. His silence there was to be her fault, too. Only his cold, dead side toward me—Catherine had again that phantasy that he had swung in his orbit. If I go under now, it's for all time.

He must swing back to find me as I am, now. Pride poured through her, hardening in the mold of her intention.

"I hadn't spoken of this field work," she said, clearly, "because I had to think it out first. Dr. Roberts offered me the opportunity a week ago. I did not suppose he took my assent for granted. Although he knows I couldn't refuse it unless the work meant nothing to me."

"But what is it? You—"

Catherine explained. She was clear, hard, swift.

"You have evidently made up your mind to go."

She nodded.

"I can arrange things here so that the children will be cared for. And the house will run, just as when I am in town. It's only for a month."

Charles got slowly to his feet, his mouth obdurate.

"Charles, won't you talk it over with me?"

"I have nothing to say. You seem to lay aside your obligations lightly. But if you are content—"

"Not lightly." She shut her eyes against his face. One hand opened in a piteous little gesture of entreaty. If he should, even now, beg her to stay, wanting her, she would turn to water. "It has been difficult to decide." She lifted her eyelids heavily. "You must see that it is a distinct advance."

"A feather in your cap." Charles was sardonic. "And you must have feathers."

At that she rose, faint color coming into her white face.

"Yes, I think I must. I'm sorry you don't like me—in feathers." Her eyelids burned. "You would prefer, I suppose, dingy ostrich plumes that you had bought, years ago—like Mrs. Thomas's."

"Mrs. Thomas may be a fool, but she's a good woman."

"Oh!" Catherine set her lips against the echoing surge of laughter that rolled up. She wouldn't let go again; she wouldn't!

"I mean she finds her feathers in her husband's cap! Thomas is going ahead in great strides. Ask any of the men in college. And why? Because she is back of him, interested. A man has to feel there is some one interested in what he's doing."

"And a woman doesn't?"

"You see! I say something, trying to explain my position, and at once you twist it into a comment on yourself."

Catherine retreated a step. Her glance winged about the quiet, pleasant room. That little table—they had found it in a Third Avenue store. "It smells like mahogany," Charles had insisted. She could see it in the kitchen, newspapers spread under its spindle legs, and Charles scraping away at the old paint. Their house, built piece by piece. They had never had money enough for more than one chair at a time. And they had loved the building. Now—her glance included Charles, lowering, defensive, unhappy.

"But I am concerned," she said, "as much as ever. You should know that."

"No! You aren't. I come home from class, and you aren't here. I come home at night, from a committee meeting, and you've gone to sleep because you need to be fresh for your own work. This isn't complaining. I just want you to see how you've changed. Why, take this matter of the Buxton professorship. When I spoke of it, the one thing it meant to you was that you might have to leave New York. That's all you could see in it. I haven't been able to discuss it with you, although it might seem important."

Perhaps all that was true. Catherine felt a trickle of doubt through the solid wall of her intention. She had been tired—had she seemed indifferent, absorbed? In a wave of heat the trickle was consumed. She wanted to cry out, "It's not with me that difference lies. It is in you! You wish to blame me, for your turning away—to Stella Partridge. You think I don't know about that!"

He moved uneasily, fidgetting with the painted silk shade of the table lamp.

"All right," she said brusquely. "We'll leave it at that. I am self-absorbed. Selfish."

"I expected you would tire of it long before now," said Charles. "Long hours in an office, at someone's beck and call. When you might be perfectly free to do as you please. I swear I don't see what you get out of it."

"You don't see, do you?" Catherine's eyes were suddenly piteous. "You don't see at all."

"It's evident enough that you can't swing the two jobs, home and office. You're worn out all the time. Irritable."

"Oh!" Catherine's hand pressed against her breast. Something extraordinary in his ingenuous construction of a case against her.

"Now if you could earn more than I do, then I might stay home, give up my work. But you don't. You barely swing the additional expenses you incur. Sometimes I think I'll accept the Buxton offer, just to take you—and the children—out of this city."

Catherine's heart, under her cold fingers, stood still for a long moment and then broke into violent, irregular beating.

"You would have to be sure"—she wondered if he could hear her words—"that I would go!"

At that she hurried out of the room. She undressed in clumsy haste, and crawled into bed, where she shivered, unable to relax, unable to stop the trampling of heavy thoughts through her mind. Charles came in, and went with elaborate unconcern about the business of going to bed. Her mind was a sling-shot, drawn tight to hurl at him innumerable bits of sentences, clattering stones from the ruck thrown off from what they had said. But she held them in, to rattle against her own brain. When he had turned off the light and was at last quiet in his own bed, the dark rose between them heavy, thick. She was aware, in a kind of torment, of his faintest motion.

I must sleep, she thought. If I could shut off these thoughts! She twisted one arm up under her face, her mouth pressed hard on the cold flesh.

Quite suddenly relief came, like a warm rush of air, blowing her empty of battering thoughts. She had a vague sense of something under the cluttered feelings, something hard, clear, shapely, a self distinct from love and hate and jealousy and fear. She drifted just over the edge of consciousness. She was lost in a vast, dark labyrinth, through which she stumbled, hands extended in search of passageways; on and on she labored. Had she touched that wall before? Was she going in blind circles, with no egress? She was running, desperately—sleep closed around her.

CHAPTER IV

Dr. Roberts came gravely around the desk, shook Catherine's hand, and returned to his chair.

"I must have been somewhat in doubt about your consent," he said, "since I am so delighted. You must see Dr. Waterbury to-day."

"Just when do you think I should start?" Catherine sat erect, hard, bright triumph in her eyes. "Of course, there are various adjustments in my household to make."

"The end of the month. You'll have this work in shape by that time." Dr. Roberts jumped to his feet. "I'll make that appointment with Waterbury myself. This is a good one on Smithson! He counted on your being merely half-hearted about the work." He went briskly out.

Catherine's fingers moved idly among the pens and pencils on the tray. Behind her the winter sun made pale blotches on the floor. I've done it, she thought. It's only the beginning! If I hang on, things may work out. A flashing picture of Charles at breakfast, dignified, reticent. Even that! She wondered a little at herself. It's because I've found something beside feelings to live by, perhaps, and so I can endure feelings. I can wait.

She brushed all that away, as with a quick gesture she pulled open the drawer and lifted out the pile of notes.

Margaret telephoned. Would Catherine lunch that day with Amy and her? At Amy's luncheon club. Catherine made a note of the address. At quarter to one, sharp. Upstairs. We'll meet you there.

They would be interested in her news. Approvingly interested. Discomfiting, how eagerly you ran to lap up little crumbs of approval. Get approval out of yourself, Henrietta had told her. Childish of her to crave it outside herself. As if, some way, she had to make up for Charles, to throw something into the other side of the scale along with her own conviction.

She wanted Margaret's advice about shopping, too. New clothes. She would have to look her part.

It was one o'clock when Catherine hurried along the side street, looking anxiously for the number Margaret had given her. The interview with the President had delayed her; it had left her in a state of pleasurable excitation, like the humming of many tiny insects. Across Madison Avenue. She came to a group of old gray buildings, houses, with excrescenses of recent date on the ground floor,—a cleaning establishment—funny how you always saw clothes you liked in cleaners' windows!—an interior decorator's, with heavy tapestry draped over an amazing gilt chair. There, the entrance was just between those shops. Didn't look much like a club. She climbed the stairs cautiously; a door above her opened, and two women came past her, sending her expectant glances, their voices sharp and bright against the confusion of sound into which she climbed. She stopped at the door, keenly self-conscious, as if the pattern of voices was complete, and her entrance might break through the warp. The pattern broke as she looked about the room, large and low, with separate nodules of women. Margaret's bright head shot up from the group near the fireplace, and Margaret swung across the room toward her, slim and erect in her green dress. Amy strolled after her; she had removed her squirrel turban, but her dark hair still made a stiff flange about her thin face.

"This is fine! We've saved a table—" and Catherine, following them into the dining room, edging between the little tables, found herself drawn into the pattern of sound.

"I'm sorry I am late." She slipped her coat over the chair. "The President was talking to me"—she had to release some of the tiny, humming insects—"about my trip west." She told them about that trip. It stepped forward out of dream regions into reality as she talked, as they put in questions, sympathetic, approving questions.

"What does the King say?" Margaret smiled at her.

"Oh, he doesn't say much." Catherine laughed. Why, she could joke about him! She felt a hard brilliance carry her along, as if—she sent little glances about the room, at the women near her—something homogeneous about them—unlike the girls at the St. Francis, still more unlike the woman who lunched at the Acadia, or at Huylers—something sufficient, individual—"What kind of a club is this, anyway?"

"We wanted a place downtown here where we could have good food. All the lugs are in the kitchen. Wonderful cook!" Amy leaned across the table, her eyes afire. She could be intense over food, too, then! "A place where one might bring a guest. City Club too crowded, too expensive, too—

too too! for independent women. There were eleven of us, originally. We called it the "Little Leaven," you know. Now there are several hundred. All sorts. Writers, artists, editors. That's a birth control organizer, and the woman with her is an actress. Anybody interesting comes to town, we haul her in to speak in the evening. Men always have comfortable clubs. This is for us."

"Good food, certainly."

"I thought if you were interested, I'd put you up. For membership. The dues aren't high, and now you are downtown, you might like to run in. Always someone here to lunch with, someone of your own kind."

Catherine smiled. Part of her was amused, but part of her shone, as if Amy's intensity, admitting her to the leaven, polished that hard brilliance—

"I'd like it!" she declared. "Lunching has been irksome."

She watched the women again. They seemed less homogeneous, more individual, as she looked.

"Well, I've been thinking about you." Amy was directed at her with astonishing concentration. "Since I met you. What you need is more backing. You feel too much alone."

Catherine felt Margaret's uneasiness, akin to her own faint shrinking from the access of personal probing.

"You need, as I told Margaret the other night, to touch all these other women who have stepped out of their grooves. It's wonderful, what that does for you. It's solidarity feeling, workers go after it in their unions, and women so much lack it. You think you are making a solitary struggle, and you're only part of all this—" Her sudden gesture sent her empty tumbler spinning to the edge of the table. Margaret's quick hand caught it.

"Don't begin an oration, Amy," she said.

"It's true." Catherine was bewildered to find tears in her eyes, and a rush of affection toward Amy—she might be fanatic, but a spark from her overfanned fires could warm you! "Are any of these celebrities married?" she asked, with apparent irrelevance.

"Oh—" Amy shrugged. "I think they have husbands, some of them. Hard to tell. That woman there has just got her divorce, I know."

She had a moment with Margaret later, standing near the fireplace, while Amy rushed off to greet a newcomer.

"She's a funny old dear, isn't she?" Margaret was nonchalant.

"I like her," said Catherine.

Margaret looked up in frank pleasure.

"I hoped you would. She's really fine, if you get her." Her eyes, traveling across to the small figure in the fur coat, one arm raised in emphasis, were tender. "You'd roar if you heard her comments on Charles. She has a certain cosmic attitude toward all men, lumps them. I'm thrilled, Cathy, at your trip. And your salary! You show some pick-up on this job."

"Will you take me shopping for decent clothes?" Catherine regarded her sister wistfully. "I'm going to dress the old thing up for once."

"Will I! I've always wanted to."

CHAPTER V

During the next weeks Catherine lunched frequently at Amy's club. "You were quite right," she told her one day. "I needed perspective. This place and these women make the whole business of my working seem matter of course. As if I'd be a fool not to. That's a more comforting feeling than my old one, that I might be only an egoistic pig."

"That's the trouble with ordinary married women," declared Amy. "They are all shut up in separate cages, until they don't have an idea what is happening outside."

"Marriage isn't a cage, exactly."

"You just aren't entirely out, yet."

"At least there is comfort in finding that other women want the same thing I want, and get it."

But marriage wasn't a cage, she thought, later. She found herself not so much imprisoned as bewildered. It's more like a labyrinth. There are ways out, if you can find them. Out, not of marriage itself, but out of the thing people have made of it—for women.

Catherine knew, when she approached her mother with her plan, that she had need of perspective and assurance. But Mrs. Spencer's comment was brief.

"I suppose," she said, "you must work this out for yourself. Yes, I can stay nights at your house. Alethea will be away all of February."

"Then it's really a good scheme for you, too?" Catherine begged.

"I'm a little too old to sit up with a croupy child."

"Letty's too old for croup." Catherine refused to look at her mother's implication—that her children might be sick, might need her. "Of course, Miss Kelly and Mrs. O'Lay together can manage the household. There won't be any burden for you. I thought you could have Spencer's room, and he could have my bed."

She and Charles seemed to run on tangents which seldom crossed. A young assistant in Charles's department had influenza, and in the handling of his work, Charles came in for an evening class. Frequent committee meetings, clinic affairs, kept him away on other evenings. Catherine would wake, to hear his cautious blunderings in the dark. He assumed that she slept, and she, fumbling for some noncommittal phrase of greeting, often lay quite still, not speaking.

One mild, sunny day toward the end of January, Catherine came up from town on top of a bus. A little windblown and stiff, she hurried across the campus. In the dim tunnel behind the gymnasium she met Stella Partridge.

"Mrs. Hammond!" Stella halted just where the light through glass panels in a door made a charming picture of her pale face and close, dark furs. "It's been so long since we have seen each other, and I wanted to congratulate you on your—it is a promotion, isn't it? Dr. Hammond is so proud of you."

Catherine's first thought was a flash of resentment that she had worn her shabby coat that morning, instead of the elegance Margaret had selected for her. How childish! she rebuked herself, as she said,

"Thank you. It isn't really a promotion. Just a different phase of the work."

"It will be so nice for you, having the change."

She wants to detain me, to talk—Catherine found a myriad tiny buzzing thoughts, just out of reach—to show me that she knows all about it, from Charles.

"I am sure I shall enjoy it." She bent forward, her words suddenly out of her volition. "What a charming hand bag!" Her finger hovered above it; her eyes, swooping up to the cool dark eyes, were derisive.

"Yes, isn't it?" Miss Partridge's smile was tolerant, amused, just a flicker of pointed teeth. But she thrust the bag under her arm. "I hope you have a pleasant trip. You go soon, don't you?"

A truck came booming through the tunnel, and under cover of its din, Catherine nodded and hurried on.

"You knew she had it," she cried out, half aloud. "You knew it!" At the gate she stopped, pretending to adjust her hat. She had known it, but the sight of it, the actual visible contact with it, had sent a sharp wave of nausea through her. How could she have spoken of it! She was aghast—the words had pounced out, she hadn't said them. There, the nausea had passed, and with her head up to the wind which blew along the Avenue, she could go on, across the street, and up the hill toward home. She doesn't love him.

Catherine was sure of that. She wanted to show off—her power. That's all. She has no tenderness in her.

And as Catherine went silently past the door of the study where Charles sat writing, not looking up, pity moved in her. Why, she thought, he will be hurt, out of this, and I can't save him.

Henrietta came in that evening, and Charles emerged, ruffled and absent-eyed, from the study. He was working on a paper he was to deliver before a meeting of psychologists. On clinic practice, he explained in answer to Henrietta's inquiry. "You know"—he slouched down in his chair—"we're going to run you poor old-fashioned doctors right out of business. Once we have these psychological methods established, there won't be much left for you to do."

"Whooping cough a mere instinct, or is it a habit? And croup and measles and broken legs?" Henrietta waved her eyeglasses at him. "If you psychologists knew a little anatomy and materia medica—"

She and Charles squared off for a friendly skirmish on their pet field of contention. Catherine, listening, watching Charles's lazy delight as he parried phrases and thrust out in pointed words, felt a sudden wash of tears too close to her eyes, and a constriction in her throat. He would come out of his tent, genial, casual, for Henrietta, for anyone. But when they were alone—silence, heavy and uncommunicative. How long since they had laughed, at any silly thing?

"Here, help me out!" Henrietta was flushed with amusement. "He's delivering his whole speech on my head! Oh, I mustn't forget to give you Bill's address." She broke off, fumbling in a pocket of her suit. "Here. Chicago office. A note there will reach him. Aren't you proud of her, Charles?" Henrietta stuck her glasses on the bridge of her nose and stared at Charles. "Just pouncing ahead!"

"Of course Catherine has brains." Charles had withdrawn, his foils sheathed. "Always knew that."

"But these Bureaus and Foundations are so conservative. It's splendid to see them forced into recognition of a woman's ability, I think."

"Their men always seem a little—ladylike." Charles was talking at Catherine, through Henrietta. "Perhaps none of them wished to make a tour of the west this time of year. It isn't my idea of a good time, exactly."

"Don't let him josh you, Catherine!" Henrietta flashed out, warmly.

"Aren't they ladylike? Most of their men not creative enough to make a real place for themselves. They crawl into that snug and safe berth—"

"I've thought the few I've met were much like academic men." Henrietta grinned at her thrust. "Haven't you, Cathy?"

"You see," said Catherine, "Charles disapproves of the whole system, the establishment of a bureau."

"Some one accumulates too much money and looks around for a conspicuous benevolence. Ah, a bureau of investigation! Then some little men hurry in, get jobs poking their noses into various things, and draw down neat salaries out of the surplus money. Mrs. Lynch is pleased. Little men are pleased."

"Why isn't it a good way to get rid of the money?" Henrietta spoke cautiously, as if she suspected traps under the smooth surface.

"Oh, it gets rid of it. But it's artificial. Not a response to some demand in society."

"Charles, are you stuck-up, or jealous?" Henrietta glanced shrewdly from him to Catherine.

"This is not personal, I assure you." Charles slipped into his grandiloquent, tolerant manner, as much as to add, "even if you, being a woman, can not understand its being impersonal."

"Um. Aren't universities endowed with some of this surplus cash, too?"

"Only to some extent. There you have an actual need."

"In other words, the shoe is on the other foot, now." Henrietta laughed.

"It's true enough there's an actual need." Catherine sat forward, eagerly. A sharp inner voice said: ridiculous to argue; he is attacking me, not the Bureau. Trying to belittle the thing I'm in, so that I'll have to shrink with it. But the voice was drowned in an uproar of her refusal to shrink, her insistence upon some justification. "Universities and colleges are a need, of course. But the very thing I'm working on, and Dr. Roberts, too, is the great gap between the human need and the pitiful offering on the part of the colleges. Why won't it do some good, if we can show up that gap?"

"What will happen? You'll write a brochure, which won't be read by any of the people concerned. Change comes from within, slowly, like growth of a child."

"In other words, Catherine, your job is foolishness, and you'd better be home making pies. You are too transparent, Charles. Don't you listen to him!" Henrietta jumped to her feet. "I must run along. Pies are fleeting, too. If you're interested in a thing, that's all that counts."

Catherine rose, slowly. She wished Henrietta wouldn't go. Her blunt indifference to undercurrents had a steadying effect.

"Of course," Catherine spoke hurriedly. She wanted to get to the bottom of this before Henry went. If there was a bottom. "Your interest depends upon your valuation of what you are doing, doesn't it?"

"Somewhat." Henrietta paused. "But you know, you can knock a hole in the value of anything, if you try. I can shoot a doubt straight through doctoring. Why bother to mend people! Children—they just grow up to make blundering old folks." She looked tired, as if the flesh of her cheeks and chin sagged. "But do I shoot it? Not me. Same with your job, same with Charles's job. May make a dent in the old world."

When she had gone, Catherine looked in at the door of the study. Charles presented a shoulder overintent. He knew she was there. To speak his name was like tugging at a great weight.

"Charles." He turned. The weight increased. "You really feel this work is just empty fiddling?"

"There doesn't seem much use in saying what I *think*"—his emphasis pointed out the difference—"since it is taken as limited and personal."

Catherine retreated to her own room, before hasty, intemperate words escaped her. There was a cruel enough abyss between them now; no use to fill it with wreckage.

CHAPTER VI

The following morning, when Dr. Roberts came in with time tables and maps to help complete the itinerary, Catherine responded with apathy to the folders. She heard that doubt gnawing away, a mouse behind the wainscoting. Finally, as Dr. Roberts opened a new map, she let the mouse out.

"What," she asked, "exactly, do you think we are going to accomplish? With the whole thing. Trip, book, all of it."

Dr. Roberts spread the thin map crackling on the desk, and pressed his forefinger into Ohio. Then he lifted his head, and his eyes, shrewdly penetrating, studied her face.

"So—" he said. "It has lost its savor."

"Do you think we can change things, by criticism, or suggestion? Won't all these schools go on in their own way?"

Dr. Roberts sat on the edge of the table, one neat toe pushed against the floor to balance himself, one swinging.

"I'm glad this came up now, instead of somewhere in Ohio," he said. "I suppose we all have hours of wondering what it amounts to, all these mahogany desks and busy people." He brought his fist down emphatically. "But I tell you, something must come of studies like this! Institutions have gone on long enough, nosing along with blind snouts in old ruts. The day has come when intellect, intelligence can step in and say, 'here, that's the wrong path. You're going that way only because it is an old path. Here's the better way.' Conscious, intelligent control. That's the coming idea."

"But can a blind snout open its eyes?" Catherine was intent, serious. "Can you change things? That way?"

"See what Flexner's study of medical schools did for them! Even Smithson's few papers on sanitation have had an ordinance or two as a result. Where does all that agitation about child labor in the South come from, if not from investigation?"

"You see—" Catherine looked down at the pink blotch of Ohio, under the firm, square forefinger. "I must believe in what I'm doing. I can't just do it to earn a living."

"Naturally. I understand that."

"The work I did during the war was obviously of use. The plans for reeducation were fairly snatched out of our hands before the ink was dry on them."

"Yes. An immediate need like that is, as you say, obvious. Easy to believe in. Like baking bread for hungry people."

"I carried over that belief to the Bureau as a whole, I think. Then—I suppose from criticism that I heard—I wondered whether we fooled ourselves."

"I think not, Mrs. Hammond. Perhaps our report won't revolutionize the whole educational system of several states overnight. You don't expect that. But it may affect even a single man, and that's something." He stroked his beard, watching her a little anxiously. "There is just one criticism which has bothered me," he added. "That concerns policy. After all"—his wave indicated the Bureau, established, respectable, heavily done in mahogany—"biting the hand that feeds us, you know. We may be tied too firmly to the social forces that make this possible. I don't know. What I offer myself for consolation is this: there's no such thing as complete freedom. If we can clear away any of the debris and old pitfalls in education, we may at least leave the next generation less obstructed. We are no more limited in policy than churches or colleges. We don't have to lick the hand that feeds us, at any rate."

"Well—" Catherine smiled. "I won't be doubtful, then. I want to be enthusiastic."

And as Dr. Roberts returned to the study of the maps and time tables, she thought: he may be right, and Charles may be right. Each of them thinks from his own center. From his own desires. So do I. And I want this work to have a meaning. To be significant. To *matter*. I believe it does. I *will* believe in it.

CHAPTER VII

Saturday afternoon Catherine stood in front of the long mirror in her bedroom, with Margaret squatting on her heels beside her, pinning in place a band of bright embroidery.

"Too bad there isn't time to send it back." Margaret dropped to the floor, gazing up at her sister. "But that will do, I think. It's very smart, Cathy."

"Can we pack it so that it won't crush?" Catherine brushed her fingers over the warm brown duvetyn. "I scarcely recognize myself."

"It's the way you should look all the time. Take it off and I'll put a stitch in where that pin is." Margaret scrambled to her feet. "I did want you to have that beaver coat, though."

"I've got to pay for these sometime!" Catherine slipped out of the dress. "You beguiled me into awful extravagance."

"Just because I made you buy with a near eye instead of a far eye." Margaret sewed busily. "The middle-class married eye is a far eye, Cathy. It never sees clothes as they are. It sees how they'll look three years hence, and then five years, made over. No wonder you look dubby. Can't ever get style that way." She snapped her thread, and folded the dress over tissue paper. "There, that'll ride. Taking just your steamer trunk?"

"And a bag." Catherine pulled her nasturtium silk kimono over her shoulders. "Too many stops for a large trunk. It's good of you to spend your Saturday here. I'd sent off everyone, so that I could get ready in peace. But there are endless things to see to."

"You're a handsome thing in that rag, too." Margaret rose from the half full trunk. "Wish I'd found an evening dress that color."

"That would have been nice and inconspicuous! And I may not need one. I'll stick this black one in." There was a faint glow on Catherine's cheeks; her dark hair swept in a long curve from brow to heavy coil at the nape of her smooth neck.

"Where are the children?" Margaret seized the black dress and folded it dexterously.

"At the opera—'Hansel and Gretel.' Mother took them. Miss Kelly has Letty in the park."

"Won't they love it!" Margaret whistled the gay little dance melody from the opera. "Do they mind your going?"

"Marian thinks it will be rather fun to have Gram here. Spencer wants to go with me."

"The lamb! There, those are properly packed. You be careful when you take them out. Now, shoes. No, put that blouse in your handbag."

"I declare—" Catherine laughed as Margaret moved competently through the piles. "It's like a trousseau—my second."

"That would please the King, I'm sure." Margaret held off a bronze slipper, turning it critically. "Is he as sulky as he acts, Cathy? He said, 'I don't demand external evidence to make me proud of my wife!'" She imitated the dignified resentment of his tone.

"He's frightfully busy with papers and things." Catherine bent over her traveling bag. In her throat a soft pulse beat disturbingly. To-night—she thought. Oh, I can't leave him—obdurate, silent. I must break through.

"Um." Margaret nodded. Then, suddenly, "I told Mother I thought she had no business siding with him."

Catherine faced her, alarmed.

"And she as much as said she thought you were endangering your home and future happiness. Poor mother! She can't step out of her generation, I suppose. For all she is such a brick."

"Don't put anything into her head, for goodness' sake! She's going to be here while I'm gone. She's fond of Charles."

"The only trouble with Charles," declared Margaret, her arms akimbo on her slim hips, "is that he is a man!"

"You sound like Amy."

"No, I don't. I know he can't help it. You're to blame, partly. You spoiled him rotten for years. He can't get over it in a jiffy. Has that woman got her claws in him? I suppose he's wide open to a vamp."

Catherine's color receded in the swift tautening of her body. Margaret need not trample in. "I don't know," she said, stiffly.

"Excuse me, old thing." Margaret flung her arm over Catherine's shoulders, and rubbed her warm cheek against her sister's. "Rude of me, I know. We'll change the subject."

"I didn't mean to be sniffy." Catherine softened. "I really don't know. I was shocked that you—"

"Um. What are my eyes for, little Red Riding Hood? Anyway, it's a darned skilful move of yours, this trip."

Down the hall clumped Mrs. O'Lay. Catherine hurried into her old serge dress, Margaret locked and strapped the little trunk, and Catherine closed the traveling bag. "Have to finish that to-morrow."

Miss Kelly came, with Letty. Margaret carried the child off into the dining room for her supper, while Catherine sat down with Miss Kelly for a final discussion of the weeks she would be gone. "Eve made out this mailing list—" she finished, "and bought enough postal cards to last. If you would send me one every night—" She gazed at the sandy-fringed, calm blue eyes, at the firm, homely mouth. "I'm sure they will be happy and well, with you."

"I think so, Mrs. Hammond." Not a quaver of uneasiness in her voice.

You might suppose I went off every week, thought Catherine.

Letty was in bed, Margaret had gone, and Miss Kelly, before Mrs. Spencer and the children arrived. Catherine listened to their delighted rehearsing of the story. Marian tried to hum one of the songs; Catherine couldn't recall the exact melody. And under the outer pressure ran the slow, warm flood of waiting, waiting until Charles should come in. What she could say or do she did not know. But anything, anything!

"Will I serve up the soup, Mrs. Hammond?" Mrs. O'Lay was reproachful. "It's half after six."

"Mr. Hammond should be in any minute."

The telephone shrilled into her waiting.

"That you, Catherine? I'm at the dentist's. Got a devil of a toothache. Don't wait for me. He's out at dinner, but he's coming in to see to the tooth. No, it's that upper tooth, where the filling was loose."

They dined without Charles.

"Poor fellow!" Mrs. Spencer was gently sympathetic. "There's nothing so upsetting as the toothache."

Some truth in that, thought Catherine, as she sat in Charles's chair and served. A special dinner, too. If the tooth still ached when he came home— The intangible hope which had grown in her through the day was too fragile to withstand such disaster. Perhaps—was he at the dentist's? Was there an aching tooth? She glanced up in a flurry of guilt at a question from her mother. How despicable of her, dropping into suspicion. Spencer was watching her. He was too sensitized, too immediately aware of moods. It would be good for him, perhaps, to live without her for a time. She brushed away the under-thoughts, and held herself resolutely above the surface of their talk.

Marian wanted to play Hansel and Gretel. "But Gram is too nice to be the witch, isn't she, Muvver? And we must have a witch."

"Miss Kelly could be witch," said Spencer.

"She's too nice, too!"

"She could pretend not to be." Spencer peered at Catherine, and suddenly giggled.

"That isn't funny," protested Marian.

"When your mother was a little girl," began Mrs. Spencer, "I took her to see Uncle Tom's Cabin." The children listened, entranced, to the account of Catherine's impersonation of Little Eva. Catherine, amused, went back to Spencer's giggle. He hadn't accepted Miss Kelly, as Marian had. His laugh was a secret declaration of his withholding of himself. But he no longer protested outwardly.

"And just then, I went out of the kitchen door," said Mrs. Spencer, "and saw Catherine in the loft window of the barn. She had on one of my best white sheets, and she was leaning forward, way out of the window, and waving her arms."

"Oh, Muvver!" Marian sighed in delight.

"I said, 'What are you doing!'"

"You tell us what you said, Muvver," begged Marian, her eyes darkly shining. "Please."

"I said"—Catherine laughed—"that I was going to fly to Heaven."

"Did you think you were, Mother?" asked Spencer.

"Perhaps. I was playing Little Eva so hard that I expected the angels to pick me up, you know."

"An' then, Gram?"

"I called to the hired man. He was in the barn. And he ran upstairs up the ladder and caught your mother by the sheet. So she didn't jump out."

"Would you really of jumped, Mother?" Spencer, in his eagerness, came around to Catherine's chair.

"I don't know. I was a silly little girl, wasn't I?"

"Oh, Spencer was silly to-day," cried Marian. "He wanted to come home right in the middle of the play. He said you were going away to-day, and Gram had to take right hold of his arm."

A wave of color rushed up to Spencer's hair, and his nostrils trembled.

"Wasn't that silly?"

"I did think so, Mother." He gulped. "I got mixed up. If you think so, it feels true, doesn't it?"

"We told him it wasn't to-day. But he kept thinking so."

Catherine remembered the dash he had made through the hall to her bedroom, his halt at the door, his long stare at her. Poor boy!

"You better sit down, son," she said. "Here comes dessert."

Later, when she bade them good night, his arms tightened about her neck.

"You said to-morrow," he whispered, "and I thought maybe it was to-morrow. Because to-morrow is to-day, always, when it gets here."

"We can write letters to each other," said Catherine, rubbing her cheek softly against his hair. "Won't that be fun? We never wrote to each other."

"With my own name on the envelope?"

"Yes, sir." Catherine felt him relax into pleased contemplation of envelopes with his own name.

"It's queer Charles doesn't come." Mrs. Spencer laid aside her magazine as Catherine entered the living room. "Do you know what dentist he goes to?"

"Dr. Reeves, I think. He had to wait until the doctor came in from dinner."

"Oh, yes." Mrs. Spencer ruffled her fingers through the pages. "Alethea went on Thursday," she said. "I'll be glad to move in here. It's rather queer, staying alone."

"I am glad you want to come." Catherine was grateful. "It relieves me of any anxiety. Things should run smoothly."

"Spencer was quite pitiful." Mrs. Spencer looked like an inquisitive little bird. "He's rather hard to manage. Notional. Marian seems more normal."

"She is more phlegmatic than Spencer." Catherine refused to take up that word, "pitiful," and its implications.

"They're both sweet children. They act well-bred in public. It's a pleasure to take them out. Even when Spencer was so distressed, he didn't make himself conspicuous. And when I promised him you'd really be here, he settled down again."

Catherine again rejected the distress. She wouldn't argue with her mother about going away. Too late, now.

"Miss Kelly is very good with them, I think," she said. "She gives them better training than I ever did. I suppose she sees them more impersonally. Even Letty—"

"I don't think anyone trains children better than their mother." Mrs. Spencer was indignant. "You always did very well. Miss Kelly does seem competent, of course."

A sharp ring at the bell brought Catherine to her feet. Perhaps Charles had forgotten his key. But as she hurried down the hall, she heard a shrill guffaw from Sam, and the elevator slid rapidly out of sight as she opened the door.

"Why, Flora! Come in."

Flora, hastening to drag a lugubrious expression over the wide grin Sam had evidently provoked, shook her head, the stiff purple flowers on her large hat rattling like hail.

"No'm, I ain't coming in," she said. "I came to ask a favor of you, Mis' Hammond. You well, and the children?"

"Yes, we're all well." Catherine recalled the dejected, bruised Flora she had last seen. Bruises and dejection had vanished; Flora was resplendent in a spotted yellow polo coat, a brilliantly striped scarf displayed over one shoulder, and—Catherine almost laughed aloud—arctics, flapping about plump white silk-stockinged legs. But she was uneasy; the olive-whites of her eyes shone, and her gold tooth flashed.

"Mis' Hammond, you knows what I done told you, about that worthless puhfessional man." She thrust her hands deep into her pockets, trying to swagger a little. "You recollects? I don' want to bother you, but he's the worstest man. He's tryin' to ruin my character."

"I thought you had him put in prison."

"Yessum. But he's bailed out. An' the case is postponed, while he works against me. He's provin' that I was bad, and let my li'l girl run wild. They shut her up." Flora scrambled for a handkerchief, and rubbed vigorously at her eyes. "My lawyer fr'en, he says if I can get proof about my character, then that man won't stand no trial. He tole me to get a proof from you, Mis' Hammond. You know I worked hard, don't you?"

"What kind of proof, Flora? There, don't cry. Of course I'll help you."

"My lawyer fr'en, he says you should write it out about me. A kinda paper, all about how I done work for you. With your name and where you lives on it. Then you don' have to come to court, you just writes it down on a paper."

"Come in, Flora, and I'll write something for you."

"No'm, I'se going to stand right here."

"Wait, then."

Catherine wrote a brief, emphatic statement. She had employed Flora Lopez for three years, and always found her reliable, competent, hard working. What do I really know about her, she thought, her pen poised at the end of that sentence. Character—she saw again that neat, respectable flat, eloquent of Flora's ambition, and the little boy. She is a self-respecting woman, who has supported herself and her children.

"Just Flora, that former maid of mine," she told her mother. "Wants a recommendation."

"There you are." She handed the sheet to Flora.

"But Mis' Hammond, my lawyer fr'en, he say you have to get a notary seal onto it, or it ain't good in court." She stared at the writing. "You could mebbe send it by mail to me. I moved to a new place. Folks in that house were too nosy. I'm at—"

"I'm going away to-morrow, for a month." Catherine hesitated. "I tell you, we'll go find a notary to-night. There are several along the Avenue, if it isn't too late."

Her mother agreed, rather doubtfully, to wait until she returned, unless Charles came in the meantime.

"I don't think you ought to go out with that colored woman this time of night," she insisted.

But Catherine, hurrying into coat and hat, was off. The notary in the tobacco shop at the corner had gone home. After a cold, slipping walk on sleeted streets to Broadway and down, Catherine found another shop, and a man who could put a seal to her oath.

Flora folded the paper. She refused to put it in her pocket.

"I got to get it safe to my lawyer fr'en," she insisted. "I is obliged to you, Mis' Hammond." She turned her homely, dark face passionately toward Catherine, her wide mouth moving grotesquely as she spoke. "Mos' folks is cruel mean to you if your luck is bad! Women are the mostest mean. Sayin' I neglects my chile—all 'count of my being a good worker. You got somebody to work for you now?"

"Mrs. O'Lay, the janitor's wife. You remember her? She can't cook as you could. Mr. Hammond doesn't eat a meal without wishing you were back."

"I—I jus' couldn't come back, Mis' Hammond. I'se obliged to you, but—"

"Are you working somewhere?"

"Washings, at home. I ain't making so much money. But my lawyer fr'en, he ain't charging me but half rates."

"Do you need money?" Catherine's hand moved toward her pocket book.

"I'se too much obliged, Mis' Hammond, to need it." She looked away, and suddenly darted out across the street, her arctics flapping, her dirty yellow coat flopping about her awkward flight.

Catherine went home, stepping gingerly over the glare of ice. A taxi rattled and skidded to a stop at the door just as she reached the apartment house, and her mother came out.

"Here, you'll slip." Catherine seized her arm, and engineered her passage. "Has Charles come home?"

"Yes, poor boy. He's had an awful time. Tell the driver to go very slowly!" Mrs. Spencer disappeared in the cab.

CHAPTER VIII

"'At Flora, she coming back to wuk for you-all?" Sam made friendly inquiry as he stopped the elevator at Catherine's floor.

"No."

"She say she got grand job for some elegant folks. Sma't worker, Flora is."

Poor Flora—Catherine unlocked the door quietly—lying to Sam, to save her face some way, of course.

If Charles is miserable—hope thrust out a new tendril, waveringly, in a blurred picture of herself ministering to him, pretending tenderly that nothing ever had been wrong.

"Hello." She smiled as he turned from the window, draped in a melancholy air of pain nobly borne. "You have had a horrid time, haven't you?"

"Just a jumpy tooth." He sat down, reaching for the paper. "Your mother was worried about you. Said you went off with a darky hours ago."

"She didn't seem worried. I met her at the door." Catherine went out to the hall closet with her wraps. Her fingers brushed the sleeve of his heavy coat. If I can pretend, she thought.

"It was only Flora," she said as she returned. "She wanted a statement from me, evidence as to her character. That man, you remember, her puhfessional gentleman? He seems to have a scheme to save himself at her expense. We went out to hunt up a notary."

"You committed yourself legally to some defense of her?"

"Yes, indeed. Poor Flora!"

"Unwise, wasn't it? How do you know what she'll do with such a paper?"

"It seemed little enough to do for her. They want to prove she neglected her children."

"Didn't she?"

Catherine wondered; did he mean that implied comparison? At least he wouldn't drag it out, openly, if she ignored it.

"Have you had any dinner?"

"Can't eat with a nerve howling like a fiend."

"Come along, poor boy. I'll find you something."

"Don't bother."

"Come on, Charles." Catherine went into the kitchen. "Here's a wonderful roast beef," she called back, and Charles came reluctantly. "You sit there—" she pushed the chair near the shining white table. "Coffee, or cocoa?"

"Cocoa, if it isn't too much trouble. I'd like to sleep. Had a cup of coffee."

"Did the dentist keep you all this time in his torture chamber?" Catherine moved swiftly from ice-chest to stove. If I can invoke our midnight lunches, all down the past, she thought—I can't go away, without trying to reach him. It is like death.

"No," said Charles. "I haven't been there all the evening."

Catherine stirred the foaming cocoa. Let's pretend, she wanted to cry out; let's pretend!

"I thought probably you would be asleep. Since you start off to-morrow."

"I wanted to see you." Catherine poured the cocoa and set it before him. She stood there, one hand spread delicately, the fingers pressed against the oilcloth. "And you—didn't want to see me, did you!" She was supplicating, provocative, leaning above him.

"I had to stop with some manuscript, at Miss Partridge's." Charles buttered a slice of bread deliberately, and forked a slice of pink meat to his place. "Is there any Worcestershire?"

"And she gave you coffee?" Catherine moved hastily away from the table, and felt blindly along the cupboard shelf for the bottle of sauce.

"Yes." Charles was blandly engrossed in his lunch.

He's as much as telling me that he chose to go to her, when he wished comfort. Catherine set the Worcestershire beside his plate. I won't hear him.

But what a burlesque, my serving him, when I can't, through any outer humility, reach him.

"Want more sugar?" She asked, casually.

"No. This is fine." His upward glance was puzzled, uneasy.

Ah, I have no pride, no decency! she cried to herself. Her heart was beating in suffocating rhythm; her fingers lifted, undirected, aching for the touch of that stubborn, beloved head—the prominent temples, the hollow above the cheekbones, the old intimate brushing across his eyes, down to cup his strong, obdurate chin.

"Charles," she whispered, and swayed backward from his sudden violent start, which clattered the carving knife to the floor.

"Damn!" he clapped his hand to his jaw. "Oh, damn!"

"What is it?"

"That tooth. Hell, I've yanked that filling out." He was on his feet, his face contorted under his hand. "Get me some iodine. He said iodine would stop it."

The tooth was treated. Charles, a little sheepishly, admitted that the pain was less.

"Guess I'll crawl right into bed, before it jumps again. If I can get to sleep—"

Catherine filled a hot-water bag and slipped it under his cheek.

"That feels fine." He looked up at her. "Thanks."

Catherine bent quickly and brushed her lips on his forehead.

"Good night," she said steadily. "Go right to sleep." She lay wakeful for a long time.

"When I come back," she thought, at last— She twisted restlessly. "That tooth—I was a little mad, and it destroyed my frenzy. I ought to be glad, and I'm not."

The hours on Sunday between breakfast and time for her train were telescoped into a band of pressure. Directions to Mrs. O'Lay; final arrangements for her mother; engrossing details devouring the few hours.

The taxi was announced. Letty burst into wails because she couldn't go; she had been discovered busily emptying her bureau drawers into an old suitcase. Catherine, distracted, kissed her mother and hurried away, hearing the determined shrieks until the elevator reached the ground floor. Charles, Spencer, and Marian climbed into the taxi after her.

"You look lovely," said Marian, over and over, stroking the soft fur at the throat of her jacket. "You look just lovely."

Spencer snuggled close against her, without a word. Charles, after a businesslike inquiry into the state of her tickets, was silent. And Catherine's one clear thought was: it is lucky that I can't escape now—like a moving stairway, and I've stepped squarely on it. I couldn't, to-day, furnish the energy, the motive power, to go and leave them.

PART V
IMPASSE

CHAPTER I

Catherine moved slowly up the covered stairway from the Randolph Street station, sniffing at the strange smell of Chicago. What did make it so different from New York? Smoke, blown whirling back in the sharp east wind over the grinding of ice along the lake shore, something more composite than that, which, if she could but decipher, would give her the essential difference between the cities. She snatched at her hat, as she reached the gusty platform. There was Bill, lounging against the paper stand! As she edged through the home-bound crowd, he saw her, with a sharp lifting of his negligent, withdrawn look, and started toward her.

"Catherine!" He drew her out of the crowd, into a little corner protected by the booth.

"What a horrid place I made you wait!" Pleasure shimmered over Catherine, like sun in shallow water. "Have you had to stand here long? Oh, it is nice to see you!" The strange city, the unknown, hurrying people, walled them about in deepened intimacy.

"Fine." Bill smiled down at her. "You look as if you had been eating up this west, and liked its taste."

"I have. I do." Soft, clear brilliance in her eyes, in her smile. "Let's go somewhere, so I can tell you about it. I want to talk and talk."

"There's a place just north of here. Would you like to walk? A little place I found. Wonderful dinners. Or if you want to celebrate, we can go to some huge hotel."

"I don't care. Let's try your little place."

They walked swiftly along the Avenue, the lake wind whipping against them, Bill answering Catherine's random questions about the gaunt, dark buildings they passed, about his work.

"I'm chattering," she thought. "I don't care!"

"Here we are." Bill's hand under her elbow guided her into the doorway of a small white building.

"Wall papers," read Catherine from the hall sign, but Bill steered her to an opposite door.

"Oh, I do like it." She nodded at Bill's fleet, anxious query.

A long, irregular room, with scattered tables, dull gray enamel, shining in the soft orange light of small lamps, and a great brick fireplace where logs burned.

"Sit here, where you can watch the fire without scorching." Bill chose a table in a small alcove. "Now tell us all about it. Have you been made president of one of these colleges? Or endowed? You look amazingly triumphant."

"Do I strut?" Catherine laughed softly, slipping out of her coat, drawing off her gloves.

"Not quite. But—you could, couldn't you?"

"I've had a wonderful time, Bill. Incredibly wonderful!"

"And you haven't been lonely, or homesick? How long since you left New York?"

"More than two weeks. I've finished Illinois. That's why I'm here to-night. I go on to Ohio at midnight. Homesick? Should I be ashamed not to be? The first day or so, I felt guilty. And I woke up at night, thinking I heard Spencer cry out in his sleep, or Letty. Now I just sleep like a baby—or a spinster."

"Henrietta wrote me that they are all O.K. Had a note this morning."

"She wrote me, too. Nice old thing, to drop in on them. I do miss them of course. But—" She looked up, a wistful shadow across her eyes. "Bill, I had forgotten how much time there really was in a day. When you could go straight ahead, just doing the things you had planned. Doing one job. You said I'd have two jobs, didn't you? These last weeks I've had one. And I love it! Not forever, of course. But for this month. I feel like a *person*. Sometimes, almost like a personage! People have been very kind, and interested."

She was silent as Bill turned to consult with the waitress; for a moment her eyes lingered on his head, dark and gaunt against the firelight, and then looked away at the groups of diners. Early yet, Bill had said.

"Well?" Bill watched her. "What a charming gown—like an Indian summer."

"Margaret selected it." Catherine stretched one arm along the table, the loose sleeve of golden brown velvet falling softly away from the firm ivory of her wrist. "I was doubtful about the color."

"You needn't be."

"She bullied me into all sorts of lugs." Catherine laughed. "And I've been glad of it." She hovered delightedly over the tray of hors-d'œuvres. "Like a flower garden!"

"A woman runs this place," remarked Bill with apparent irrelevance.

"Down in a little southern Illinois town, the wife of one of the college faculty wants to start a tea room. She told me all about it. Her husband doesn't want her to. She says she supposes it isn't very high brow. You know, Bill"—Catherine clasped her hands at the edge of the table—"It's happening everywhere. Women are just busting out. That's been what they've wanted to know about me. How I manage it. It's pitiful, their eagerness. Even their husbands. I went out to dinner one night, and the thing the college president wanted to know was all about how I managed. How many people it took to fill my place, and all the rest. I expected to be told in so many words that I ought to be home with my children."

"And you haven't?"

"Indirectly, sometimes. But even the most righteous mothers crave information. How do I manage! It's extraordinary. It may have gone to my head. Like strong drink. I know I'm talking too much. But, Bill, you've boiled me over, all this brew, and I have to talk!"

"I like it."

"You see—" Catherine glanced up doubtfully. "I can't write to Charles. It sounds too much like crowing." She fingered her soup spoon. She wanted to talk about Charles, too. Bill would understand. Those brief, impersonal notes of his: he was well, he was working on his book, he was busy with semester finals, the children were well, yours, Charles.

"You never saw Charles's mother, did you?" asked Bill.

"No." Catherine waited. Bill was never random in his associations.

"He's told you about her, of course?"

"Lots of times. She was devoted to him, wasn't she? You knew her?"

"We lived next door for years, you know. She died just as Charles went to college. His father had died years earlier. Just enough income for comfort, and just Charles. I think"—he grinned a little—"that you'll have to train Charles as long as she did, before he can fully appreciate your career."

"But that was years ago."

"Yes. But—I think I can tell you this, without violation—Charles told me once, talking of you before I had met you, that to him you were the perfect woman, like his mother. Which meant—tender, loving, and devoted."

Catherine's spoon clicked against the soup plate. Her eyelids were suddenly heavy, weighted with memories. Charles had said that to her, years ago. A cold finger touched her heart, binding it, and she knew, through all the brimming delight of the past days, how she had hidden away the troubling thought of Charles.

"I don't mean that she spoiled him grossly," Bill was saying. "She was too New England, too much what we used to call a gentlewoman for that. Charles was simply the center of her life; his welfare, his desires, his future—those things set the radius of her circle. She had nothing else, you see. Except the idea"—the corners of Bill's mouth rose in his slow smile—"that since Charles was a man, he was a superior being. Did women really think that, Catherine? Or was that a concession they knew they could easily afford to make?"

"But Charles doesn't think men are superior." Catherine's smile was uncertain, begging for assurance. "Why, those early experiments of his, the brochures he published, were directed against that very superstition."

"Yes. Intellectually he has come a long way since those early days. But that matters so much less than we like to think."

Catherine waited while the waitress served the next course. Bill's words had evoked a thought clearly from the churning within her; she held it until the waitress had gone, and then spoke,

"You mean, exactly, that he wishes my radius to be his desires, his welfare, his future?"

"That's his old pattern. Bound to hang on, Catherine. Because it is so flattering, so pleasant. Isn't it what we all wish, anyway? Someone living within our limits?"

"Perhaps men wish it."

"You think women don't?"

"Do they?" Catherine shook her head. "I don't want Charles to have nothing but me in his life. Aren't women hardier? Since they've never had that—it is a sort of human sacrifice, isn't it? Men are like vines! Did you know vines wouldn't grow well, some of them, unless you sacrifice to them? Bones and flesh. 'If you have an old hen,' said the nursery man, when I asked him about our Actinidia in Maine, 'bury her close to the roots. Then the vine will shoot up.' And it did!"

"You would make over the old saying about sturdy oaks, wouldn't you?"

"Don't make fun of me. Perhaps I can discover something which will change the world!" She stared intently at Bill. "You—" she hesitated. "You live without that human sacrifice, Bill. You aren't an Actinidia."

"And so, perhaps, I know why men wish it." Bill pushed to one side his untouched salad. "Without any question now of its fairness or justice to women like Henrietta, or you. In the first place, it is convenient, practically so; smooths down all the details of living. But especially, it drops a painted screen between man and the distressing futility of his life. A man with a family and a regular wife, old style, doesn't often have to face his own emptiness. He feels important. He hurries around at his work, and if doubt pricks a hole in that screen, the picture painted there is intricate enough to hide the hole. He has something to keep his machinery in action. If by day his little ego is deflated, there is, to change my figure, free air at home to blow him full again."

"You sound as if you thought all wives were adoring and humble," said Catherine.

"Some of them used to be." Bill grinned at her, and lifted his hand abruptly in a signal to the waitress. "This is supposed to be a party," he apologized, "and not a lecture by me. Tell me more about what you've been doing."

Catherine's talk was fragmentary. Something—what Bill had said, or perhaps simply his being Bill with all the old associations close around him—had blown the froth away from the past two weeks; she had thought that she had become almost a different Catherine, bright, hard, full of enthusiasm and interest, absorbed in her rôle of Bureau-representative. She saw now that her inner self still stood with feet entangled in perplexity and doubt.

"Bill"—she broke into her own recital—"if a man doesn't have free air at home, does he look for it somewhere else?"

"He may." Bill's quick upward glance was disturbed. He knew, then, about Charles and Stella. Henrietta would have told him. "Or"—lightly—"he runs along on a flat tire."

Catherine was silent, her mind skipping along with the absurd figure. Stella Partridge was, after all, too busy pumping her own ego hard to perform that task long for any man. She might flatter him, and cajole—

"Do the children write to you?"

Catherine reached into the pocket of her coat.

"I've been moving too fast the last few days to have letters. I expect a lot to-morrow in Ohio." She spread the sheet on the table. "Here's the latest. Letty made the crosses."

> "Dere Mother I will be glad when you come home again
> because I do not like to sleep in Daddys and your room
> so well. Walter is coming to see me for a day and maybe
> I am going home with him we are being good I love You
> From your loving Son Spencer Hammond Good-by."

"Nice kid." Bill looked up. "Let's see, he is just nine, isn't he?"

"Going on ten." Catherine refolded the letter. She loved the little smudge from an inky thumb in the margin.

"What shall we do now? You have several hours left." Bill set down his coffee cup. "Music? Theater? We can probably find seats for something."

"I'd rather—" Catherine paused. "Is it too stormy for a walk? I never get out of doors any more. This morning, from a window in the building at the University, I had a glimpse of the lake. Could we go there? I'd like to see how much like the ocean it is."

"It's windy, of course."

"I'd like that." A picture of herself, buffeted by winds over a stretch of water—perhaps that would blow away the melancholy cobwebs, would whip her again into froth.

Bill summoned a taxi, and in silence they rode through the long streets, south toward the park, their shoulders brushing as the machine bumped over frozen slush.

Bill slumped forward, his hands linked about his knees, his shoulders an arc of weariness. The long streets seemed drawn past the windows of the cab, on either side a sliding strip of unfamiliar shapes. It's as if a spring had broken in him, thought Catherine, a secret spring which had kept him running. Perhaps Henrietta was right, and he is sick.

"It's a long way, isn't it?" She had a plaintive moment of loneliness. Bill was the one familiar thing in the strange city, and he had retreated almost beyond communication. "I didn't know it was so far."

"We're almost there." Bill straightened his shoulders, and peered out at the sliding street. "In the Fifties. I thought you'd like Jackson Park. More space there."

A moment later he thrust open the door.

"Here!" he called to the driver. "We'll get out here."

CHAPTER II

"There's your lake." Bill slipped his hand firmly under her arm, and they bent slightly forward into the dark rushing wind. At their feet a steady crunching, a restless churning as of china waves; beyond, a stretch of black hidden action under a sky black and infinitely remote, with sharp white stars. "This wind has broken up the shore ice."

Along the sloping beach rose vague suggestions of grotesqueries; piles thrusting tortured heads with ice-hair above the frozen surface, driftwood caught between great blocks of dirty ice.

"It's like Doré's Inferno." Catherine shivered. "You remember? That frozen hell, with awful heads sticking up in the ice?"

"Let's walk along. You're cold." Buffeted, they went along the deserted drive, passing regularly from shadow into the burst of light under the yellow globes that hung above them. "I like that black sky," said Bill. "In New York we never have that."

"No." Catherine glanced westward, through bare limbs of trees. "See, there's the city glare, back there." She was warm again, her blood tingling under the dark rush of the wind; the black hidden movement of the water, the cold vasty black of the sky were exciting, like a shouted challenge.

"Here is shelter from the wind." Bill drew her into an angle made by the porch of a small summer pavilion. "You can put your head out to see the lake, without being knocked flat."

The wind racketed in the loose boards nailed along the lake side of the porch. Catherine leaned back, laughing, out of reach of the gusts. She could just catch the dim outline of Bill's face, his strong, aquiline profile.

"Bill!" She felt suddenly that in the dark, windy night there was nothing else human except Bill and herself; she wanted to burrow into his silence, his withdrawal. Her fingers brushed his arm in soft demand.

"Great, isn't it?" His voice was low and warm, walking under the rush of the wind. "Blows the nonsense clear out of you." He moved slightly so that his shoulder sheltered her. "Warm enough?"

"I shouldn't like to be here alone." She couldn't see his face distinctly—shadowy eye sockets, dark mouth. "I'd feel too little! You keep me life-size."

Silence, warm and comforting, like a secret place within the noise of the wind rattling at the boards, churning up the ice cakes.

"I can't pry into him." Catherine's feeling broke into splinters of thought. "It wouldn't be fair. He'd hate it. Digging under to see his roots. Something passionless and fine in this—no strife—as if he accepted me—whole. Dear Bill."

"Well?" He was smiling at her, she knew. "You have a train to catch, haven't you?"

They stood together in the downtown station. Bill had collected her luggage from the check-room, had brought a bunch of violets for her from the little florist's counter.

"It's Valentine's Day, you know." He watched gravely as she fastened them against the soft beaver of her collar. "I'm starting East to-morrow," he said. "I'll see your family before you do, won't I?"

"You can give them my love first hand. Tell them I'm coming soon."

"I'll tell them you are so triumphant and successful that they will be fortunate to have you again."

Catherine laughed softly. A local train was announced, draining off the waiting people, leaving them almost alone in the station.

"You know," she said, quietly, "you puff me up, Bill. Not when you say ridiculous things like that, but all the time." Under his seeking, hungry eyes, she flushed. "And I am grateful."

A scurry to the platform, as the through express rolled in. Bill, relinquishing her bags to the porter, seized her hand in a hard clasp, and stood, bareheaded, below her on the platform shouting, "Good luck!" as she was carried with increasing rush away.

CHAPTER III

Catherine, braced against the shivers and jounces of the old Ford taxi, wondered inertly what it would feel like to live in such a town, in one of those two-story frame houses, with a corrugated iron garage in the rear, and grayish lace curtains at the windows, with smoke-blackened sparrows scrapping in the front yard, and drifting, curling feathers of soot in the dingy air. I could plan a town like this with a ruler, she thought. A straight line for the business street, a few parallel lines, a few right-angled lines: dots for churches, one of each kind; for moving-picture theaters; for schools; small squares for yards and houses. Factories along the railroad, pouring up the blanket of smoke under which the town lay. Was that the soul of the town, that close-hanging smoke, with its drifting feathers of soot? And then, out at the edge, where the frame houses were far apart, scattered, a handful of college buildings, in medieval isolation. When she had said "Hope College" to the driver, he had shrieked to a baggage master, "Hi, Chuck! Where's Hope Collidge, d'yuh know?"

"Out past the lunatic asylum. You know, down the car track."

Hope College, typical of the small denominational institutions offering a normal certificate. So Dr. Roberts had classified it.

That must be the lunatic asylum, that group of brick buildings with prison windows. They were well out of town, now, the cab skidding and jerking over deep ruts. Gray, flat, interminable fields under a flat gray sky. It's like a dream, thought Catherine, a funny, burlesque of a dream, with me rattling along.

"This it, lady?" The taxi shivered in all its bolts as it halted, and the driver poked his head in at the door. There was a driveway winding between two rows of small blotched poplar trunks, and back from the road two square brick buildings, scrawled over with black network of old vines.

"I don't know."

"Guess it must be." He slammed the door and whirred up the driveway.

Just as Catherine climbed the steps, still moving vaguely in a dream burlesque, a clangor of bells burst out, followed by the clamp of feet, the sound of voices released. She opened the heavy door, and stepped into the hall. The sense of dream vanished; this was real enough. Opposite the door rose the central stairs of the building, twisting up in a dimly lighted well. Up and down them climbed young people, girls, a few boys. Shabby, gaudy, flippant, serious—Catherine watched them, with a sharp resurgence of all her shining belief, her keen, exciting delight in the thing she had come for.

She marched into an office at the left of the hall. A girl sitting at a small table, her smooth, pale-yellow head bent over a book, looked up.

"Is this the Dean's office?" Catherine smiled at her; something like Letty in the yellow hair, although the face was rather strained and thin. "I'm Mrs. Hammond, from the Lynch Bureau."

"She'll be right in." The girl rose and opened the door into the adjoining office, as if in uncertainty. "She hasn't come down from class yet. If you'll sit down—"

"Yes. Do you happen to know whether there is any mail for me here?"

"I'll see." The girl had an awkward, half-suspicious way of staring. "Mrs. Charles Hammond?" she asked.

Catherine sat down on a hard straight chair near the window; the girl's eyes were inquisitive, over the edge of her book. Catherine shuffled the envelopes hastily. Nothing from home. Strange—she had given them this address, and for this date. A bulky envelope from Dr. Roberts, a thin one from Henrietta. She tore open the flap of the latter, and let the round, jerky writing leap at her. Every one was well. Henrietta thought she might be interested in some hospital gossip. Stella Partridge had been doing some work for Dr. Beck, the psychiatrist, and had told several of the other doctors that she thought a medical man should be in charge of the clinic rather than a mere Ph. Doctor. "She says Beck has asked her to help him with a book, but I have a strong doubt. Has Charles found her out, do you suppose?"

Catherine folded the latter, and tried to poke with it into its envelope the swirl of feeling it evoked. For a brisk little woman had darted into the office and at a word from the girl was darting now at her.

"Mrs. Hammond? I'm Dean Snow. Come right in!" The pressure of her palm against Catherine's was like a firmly stuffed pincushion. "Has anyone else with a cold been in, Martha?"

Catherine, passing ahead of the Dean into her office, caught the friendly softening in the voice of the girl as she answered,

"No'm, not this morning. The plumber came, and I sent him over to the dormitory. He says that pipe is rusted and ought to come out. I told him he'd have to see you first."

"That's right, Martha. And you got those letters off?"

"Yes'm."

"Good."

She followed Catherine, closing the door.

"Just have a chair, Mrs. Hammond." She whisked herself into place beside the old roll-top desk, her rotating office chair creaking as she settled down on its springs. A little cubby-hole of an office, with a sort of film of long use over the gray walls and painted floor, over the crammed pigeon holes of the desk, over the huge framed photographs—the "Acropolis," the "Porch of the Maidens," the "Sistine Madonna," and, above the desk, a faded group photograph of gentle faces above enormous puffed sleeves; in the corner a small hat-tree, from which a rusty umbrella dangled.

"You teach, Miss Snow, in addition to being Dean?"

"Oh, yes. Latin and Greek. It's a great relief from plumbers and colds." She had a plump, white face, with gray bangs over her forehead, sharp blue eyes, and full pink lips held firmly together. She has humor, thought Catherine, and common sense, but she's intolerant. "So you're making an investigation of us, are you?" The Dean rubbed at a streak of chalk-dust on the sleeve of her tight dress. "What do you expect us to do after you point out our shortcomings?"

She thinks I am dressy and interfering. Catherine held her hands motionless against her desire to fidget. She's just the kind of sensible woman I can't get on with.

"The Bureau wants to make a constructive study," she said. "Not a criticism."

"We need just one constructive thing." Miss Snow smiled. "Money. We're poor. Small endowment fund. The Baptists around here seem poorer each year. Now I haven't had a secretary for five years. The students help me out, and I deduct the hours from their tuition. If we had money we could do much more. We get fine young people. The godless younger generation doesn't come here. We wouldn't admit them if they wanted to come. Our girls and boys know how to work. They are in earnest. But you don't want to give us money, do you? No, you want to change things. Mrs. Hammond—" She leaned forward, her plump fist coming down whack on her knee. "I've been here almost forty years, as student, teacher, officer. Our President, Dr.

Whitmore, has been here as long as that. Don't you think we know how to run a college?"

Catherine hunted for phrases, gracious, illuminating, with which to justify her mission. So many of these little colleges through the state, such diversity of aim, changes in educational ideas—

"You see," she finished appealingly, "that's our idea. That there should be a clear, definite program in the training of young teachers, and that enough is known about educational needs now to make such a program feasible."

"I've watched young people go out of here for many years now, and I know it doesn't make much difference what they've been taught. If they have the fear of God, if they are earnest and faithful, they succeed. If not—none of your modern folderols will save them. Give them the mental discipline of mathematics and the classics, and they can teach children reading and writing all right. I've seen too many fads in education to take them seriously. First it was natural science that was to make the world over, and we had to raise a fund for a laboratory. Then—oh, there's no use listing them. But I ask you, Mrs. Hammond, what's happened to Rousseau, or Froebel, or that woman a year or so ago, that foreigner, Monty somebody, who had a new scheme? Gone. You have to cling to the eternal verities. Fads pass."

The building quivered under the violent clangor of bells and the sound of hurrying feet. Miss Snow pulled open a drawer and lifted out a shabby, yellow-edged volume. "Here's one thing that stands. Ovid." She tucked it under her arm and rose. "I have a class now. Would you care to visit it?"

In the late afternoon Catherine stood in the hall, bidding Miss Snow farewell.

"It's been interesting, and I appreciate the time you have given me, out of your very busy day," she said.

"I've enjoyed it." Miss Snow shook hands vigorously. "I enjoy talking. It airs my ideas even if it doesn't change them much. I wish you could stay to hear the Glee Club practice to-night. We're real proud of their singing."

"I have to take that very early train." Catherine descended the steps and climbed into the waiting taxi—the same one which had brought her. "The Commercial House," she said.

The early February twilight lay over the fields, as if the smoke had settled more closely on the earth. She leaned back, letting the day float past her, in unselected, haphazard bits. All that zeal and honest industry poured into medieval patterns. The very best of the old patterns, no doubt, with that stern righteousness, that obligation in them. Something infinitely pitiful, touching, in those young things she had watched, awkward, serious, patient, most of them.

"Of course, most of our girls teach only a few years, and then marry," Miss Snow had said. She couldn't have had more finality if she had said, "and then die!"

Luncheon, a hurried half hour in a chilly, bare dining hall, with grace helping the creamed codfish grow cold. The other faculty members, serious and threadbare, like farm horses, thought Catherine, with bare spots chafed by the harness of inadequate salary, of monotony. As untouched by any modern thought as if centuries of time separated them. And each year, young people turned into that hopper.

If I can put that feeling down on paper, she thought, it should move even this mountain of age and tradition. To-morrow, my day will be different; the large colleges are somewhat awake. But there are hundreds of these.

At the desk of the hotel she asked hopefully for mail. Perhaps she had given this address to Charles and Miss Kelly, and not the college. The clerk poked through a pile of letters and shook his bald, red head. Three days without a word, for Henrietta's letter had been written days ago. After a moment of hesitation—amusing, how old habits of economy hung on!—she wrote out a telegram.

"Night letter?" The clerk counted the words.

"No. I want it to go the quickest possible way. I want an answer before that morning train."

In the bare little hotel room, she sat down under the light, her writing pad balanced on her knee. A note to Dr. Roberts.

"There seems no limit to the things we may accomplish," she wrote, "when I see, at first hand, what the catalogue discrepancies really mean, in flesh and blood and buildings."

Suppose something was wrong, at home? She stared about at the dingy, painted walls, with faint zigzags of cracks, and fear prickled through the enthusiasm which enclosed her. This was the first time that letters had failed to meet her. In two hours, or three, she should have an answer to her message. "Please wire me at once, care Commercial House. No word from you here." She picked up her pen again. No use to worry; letters miscarried, and she would hear soon.

She opened Henrietta's letter, to reread the comment on Stella Partridge. Something behind that, she thought. That woman doesn't make incautious remarks. Her mind fumbled with the news, as if it were a loose bit out of an intricate mechanism; if she could fit it into place, she could see how the whole affair ran. That was one of Charles's lowest boiling points, that contention about medical men and psychologists. Perhaps Partridge had been too greedy, and laid those smooth hands of hers on something Charles particularly wanted for himself, for his own job. Whatever it is—Catherine rose suddenly, piling her letters and portfolio on the corner of the dresser—whatever it is, I mean to know about it, when I go home again. I am through fumbling along.

Her room had grown chilly. A wind rattled at the loose sash of the window. She looked out at the angle of street; a hardware store across the way mirrored its enormous window light in shining pans and kettles. The air seemed full of whirling bits of mica. She pushed the window up and leaned out; sharp and wet on her face, the mica was snow, driven along on the wind.

Only an hour since she had telegraphed. She would go down to dinner. Something insidious in the way the soft fingers of worry pried between thoughts, pushed down deeper than thought.

She stopped at the desk.

"If a message comes for Mrs. Hammond, please send it in to the dining room."

"Guess we're going to have a blizzard, aren't we?" The clerk rubbed an inky forefinger thoughtfully over his red baldness. "Coming along from Chicago and the west on this wind."

More pushing of those soft fingers: delay of trains, wires down, who knows when I may hear!

"It may not be a bad storm," said Catherine, and went resolutely in to dinner. But she heard the clerk's, "You can't tell when you're going to get trouble."

In the dining room, a few traveling men scattered about at tables sending glances of incurious speculation after her as she chose a seat; a middle-aged waitress whose streaked purplish hair shrieked aloud her effort to keep youth enough to win tips, and whose heavy, laborious tread spoke more loudly of aching, fallen arches. Catherine started at the twin bottles of vinegar and yellowish oil in the center of the table. Letty's just gone to bed, she thought. Mrs. O'Lay is serving dinner. I shouldn't care to be a traveling saleswoman. The hotel drives my job into some remote limbo. I'll go to bed early. To-morrow, at the University, it will be different. Such a cordial note from that history professor's wife, asking me to stay with them. It was nice of Dr. Roberts to write personally to them.

Good steak, at least. Fair coffee. Finally, as the waitress set a triangle of pie before her, she saw the clerk in the doorway, his eyes focusing on her. He came slowly toward her. It's come, thought Catherine. He ought not to button that alpaca coat; absurd, the way it creases over his fat stomach.

"They just telephoned this from the station," he said, laying a sheet of paper beside her plate. The elaborate scrolled heading, Commercial House, wriggled under her eyes, settled flatly away as she read the penciled words.

> Spencer hurt coasting wired you this morning can you come
>
> CHARLES

"Hope it's nothing serious, ma'am."

Those soft fingers of worry had unsheathed their claws; they tore at her, deep in the unheeded, rhythmic working of her body. She could not breathe, nor see, nor speak. Spencer!

"Nothing serious," he repeated, and suddenly her heart was clattering against her ribs. She could lift her eyes from that paper. Why, he had a kindly face, that bald clerk; his flat nostrils had widened a little, in avid human sniffing at disaster, but his eyes were sympathetic.

"It's my little boy." She could breathe now. "It says he is hurt. Why—" she thrust back her chair in a violent motion, and wavered as she stood up. "There was a telegram this morning. I should have known this morning!"

"That's too bad, Ma'am. It never came here."

"I'll have to get a train." Catherine was hurrying out of the dining room, the clerk at her heels. "When can I?"

"It don't say how bad he's hurt." She felt his hand close about her arm. "You sit down here, and I'll 'phone to the station for you." He drew her into the enclosure behind his counter, and pushed her gently into an old leather chair. "Little fellows stand an awful lot of knocking around. I've got three, so I ought to know. Now, take it easy. Where you want to go? New York City?"

Grateful tears in Catherine's eyes made prismatic edges around his solid figure. As she watched him thumbing a railroad folder, her panic lifted slightly. Perhaps—oh, perhaps Spencer wasn't badly hurt. Charles would be frightened, would want her.

"Um. That's too bad. You just missed a good train." He turned to the telephone. "Gimme the station. Yea-uh. That's right."

Henrietta would be there.

"When's the next through train east, Chuck? Huh? No, the next one." He spit his words out of the corner of his mouth toward the receiver. "Any word of that out of Chicago yet? Well, say, I got a lady here got to get to New York on it. Got to, I said. You got any berths here? Well, you could wire for one, couldn't you? What you hired for?"

He hung up the earpiece.

"He says there's trouble west of here. Snow. That seven o'clock just went through, late. He's gonna let me know about the midnight."

"I'd better go to the station."

"What for? You stay here where it's comfortable. You go up to your room and I'll let you know. I'm on till midnight."

"Just go up and wait?" Catherine was piteous.

"Yes, ma'am. I'll take care of you. Now don't you go worrying. I always tell my wife she'd have the grass growing over all of us if worry could do it. That's the woman of it, I suppose."

"You're very kind." Catherine was reluctant to leave him. He was a sort of bulwark between her and the rush of dark fear. "I ought to wire them—"

"Sure. Here, write it out. It stands in reason he needn't be hurt much, and still he'd want his mother."

Catherine's pencil wobbled in her stiff fingers. Spencer would want her. All day he had wanted her. Hours between them—

"Will take first train." She looked up, her lip quivering. "I wouldn't have time for an answer, would I?"

"You ought not to, if that train's anywhere near on time, and if there's a berth left on it." The clerk turned away, to fish cigars out of his counter for a man who stood waiting, one hand plying a busy toothpick.

"D'yuh hear anything about the blizzard down Chicago way?" the man asked. "Say it's put kinks in the train service."

"You always hear worse than happens." The clerk's glance at Catherine was anxious. But she signed her name to the message and wrote out the address.

CHAPTER V

The midnight express for New York, coming through three hours late, did not stop. The clerk came up to Catherine's door to tell her.

"They ain't an empty berth on her," he said. "Took off several coaches to lighten her for the drifts."

"What am I going to do?" Catherine asked.

"There's a local in the morning. You could get something out of Pittsburgh, if you got that far."

The rest of the night, the next day, the next night, all were to Catherine grotesquely unreal, as if life had been transposed to a different key, where all familiar things were flatted into dissonance and harsh strangeness. All night the scrape of snow-plows and shovels, futile against the snow; the snow which seemed the wind itself turned to dry, drifting, impenetrable barriers. The local, dragged by two locomotives, hours late, like a moving snowdrift itself. The hours in that train, with nothing but snow darkening the windows, hiding the world, driving through the aisles with the opening of the doors. Pittsburgh, late in the afternoon, and no word from Charles. She beat helplessly against the gruff taciturnity of the ticket agent; he had stood up all day confronting cross, belated travelers. There was a train in an hour, making connections at Philadelphia. Night on that train, in a crowded day coach, malodorous and noisy. She felt as if she dragged the train herself, down through strange valleys, where blast furnaces sent up red shrieks of flame, through dim, sleeping towns.

Philadelphia at two, the next morning. A narrow strip of platform across which the wind whirled. Another crowded day coach. Where were these people going, that colored boy, asleep, his feet stuck out into the aisle in their ragged socks, his shoes clasped under one arm—that man and woman, slumping peacefully against each other, mouths drooping wide?

As Catherine stepped down to the platform in the New York station, the huge dim roofs of the train shed spun dangerously about her. A porter loped beside her, pawing at her bag, but she walked away from him, her eyes wide like a somnambulist. She made her way to a telephone booth, and then, when she had lifted her hand to drop in the nickel, stopped abruptly.

If she telephoned, and something dreadful came over the wire, buzzing into her head, it would transfix her there, unable to move, held forever behind that close, dirty glass door. She pushed violently against the door, freed herself, and fled out to the street. She passed on the steps a woman crawling on her knees, one arm moving in sluggish circles, scrubbing. After she had found a taxi and was whirring away through the dark street, the motion of that weary arm continued before her eyes. How dark the city was, and still, as if she had come into it just at the turn of the tide, before the morning life moved in. "Dark o' the moon"—she heard Spencer's voice chanting—"pulls the ole water away from the earth."

When she stepped out of the cab she did not even glance at the house. She paid the driver, picked up her bag, and went into the dim, tiled hall. She was empty, capable of precise, brisk movement. All her fear, her pressure of anxiety, her physical weariness, were held in solution, waiting the moment which would crystallize them. She stood at the elevator shaft, her finger on the button. The car was beneath her, the dust-nap of its top at her feet. The bell shrilled, but nothing else stirred. The man is asleep, she thought, dispassionately, and without haste she began to climb the stairs to the fifth floor.

At the door she stopped again, staring a moment at the small card, Hammond. She had no key. If she rang, she would waken everyone. But she must, in some way, enter. She knocked, softly. Her face, turned up to the dark painted grain of the metal door, grew imploring.

There was her door, and she couldn't open it, couldn't know what was behind it! Like a dreadful nightmare. She pounded with her knuckles. Then, softly, the door opened, and Charles, his bathrobe trailing, his eyes sleep-swollen, was blinking at her. She seemed a dream to him, too!

"Why, Catherine—you? How'd you get here, this time of day?" He whispered, and then he closed the door with a caution alarming in its quietness.

"Spencer! Tell me—" Catherine's nostrils quivered at a strange smell in the dark hall, an odor of antiseptics, of drugs.

"Thought you'd never come." Charles muttered. "Ghastly, your not being here."

"Is he here?" Catherine started to pass Charles, but he caught her, held her a moment. Catherine felt in the pressure of his arms, in his harsh kiss, the thwarted rage, helplessness, distress—she knew she had those to meet, later. Now— "Tell me, please!" she begged. "Spencer."

"He's better." Charles released her. "Sleeping now. Mustn't disturb him." He led the way to the living room, past closed, dark doors. "We'd better go into the kitchen."

Catherine stumbled into a chair.

"He was hurt, coasting. He and Walter Thomas. Right in front of the house. Miss Kelly was just coming out with the other children, to take them all to the park. He and Walter—coasted around the corner, into a truck. Hurt his head. Miss Kelly carried him in here herself." Charles was leaning against the table, his face away from Catherine, his mouth twisting wryly. Catherine touched his hand. "When I got home, Henrietta was here, and another surgeon. His head—" Catherine swung up to a sharp peak of agony—Spencer? She saw, unbearably, that fine, sensitive, growing life of his, smeared over. "They didn't dare move him. Unconscious. Stitches in his temple. They think now he's all right." He grew suddenly voluble, shrill. "You can't tell about such things at once. Have to wait. Might injure his brain. But he's been conscious, perfectly clear-headed, normal. Got a good nurse. Just keep him quiet, flat on his back. Children are tough— Oh, Catherine—"

A door was opening somewhere, an inch at a time. Catherine strained forward, too heavy with pain to rise. She felt Charles's uneasy start, felt the hours of anxiety behind the sharp gripping of his hand under hers. Feet shuffled toward them. Her mother appeared at the door, her blue eyes blinking under the frill of her lace cap, a perceptible quaver in the old hand which held together the folds of her gray bathrobe.

"Thank Heaven you've come, Catherine!" She scuffed across the linoleum and pecked softly at Catherine's cheek. "Poor little Spencer—he asked for you."

"Oh!" Catherine was on her feet, but Charles held her fingers restrainingly.

"Last night, mother means. The nurse said she'd call me the instant he woke. He's really sleeping now. Not unconscious."

Catherine stood between them for a moment of silence. "It stands to reason he might not be hurt bad, and yet want his mother." Who said that? Some one had said it to her.

"We looked for you yesterday," said Mrs. Spencer.

"Blizzards. I couldn't get a train." Catherine felt a bond between them, excluding her, accusing her. Charles stared at her, his eyes sunken, the lines about his mouth deepened; her mother—a thin, wrinkled film seemed drawn over her face, dimming her color. "I came the instant I could. I sat up on a local." She clasped her hands against her breast, against the heavy, pounding ache.

"You must be tired to pieces, poor child." Her mother patted her arm. "Don't feel so bad, Cathy. It might have happened if you'd been right here. And it's turning out so much better than—"

"But I wasn't here," said Catherine, quietly. And then, "What about Walter?" She could see that sled sweeping around the corner. "Was he hurt?"

"Shaken up and bruised. Spencer was steering."

A rustle at the door, a strange face staring at her, crisp and cold above white linen.

"Yes?" Charles stepped forward intently.

"The little boy is awake."

"This is Mrs. Hammond, Miss Pert. She may go in?"

She was a culprit, a stranger, trembling, unable to move.

"You'd better take off your hat and coat, Mrs. Hammond. And don't excite him. He's drowsy."

The dim, shaded light; a little still mound under the counterpane; under the smooth white turban of bandages, Spencer's gray eyes, moving softly with her flight from the door to his bed. On her knees beside him, her fingers closing about his hand. Quiet, not to excite him. How limp and small his hand felt!

"Hello, Moth-er!" He sighed, and his eyelids shut down again.

CHAPTER VI

The next two weeks life was a shadow show outside that room where Spencer lay. "He must be kept flat and motionless," the surgeon said, with Dr. Henrietta nodding assent. "Even as he feels stronger." Catherine was concentrated entirely upon that. Everything reduced itself to terms of Spencer. Books that she might read to him, games she might devise, stories she could tell—anything to keep him content until it was safe for him to lift that bandaged, wounded head. Always there was the terror lest some sign of injury might show itself, some quirk in his mind, some change in personality, some flush to indicate fever and infection. "We think he has, miraculously, escaped any bad effects," said Henrietta, "but we can't be absolutely sure for a few days." At night, when he slept, Catherine would leave Charles in the house, and slip out for a quick walk in the cold March darkness. But terrifying images pursued her—sudden blackness shutting down over that shining, golden reality that was Spencer to her—and she would hasten back, unassuaged of her terror until she stood again at the door of his room.

When her trunk came, she had rummaged through it, selecting all the material of her work, and sending it to Dr. Roberts with a brief note. "My son has been injured and I can do nothing more with this. If you can send someone else to finish the work, please do so. I can not even think of it for the present."

There would come a day, she knew, when she could think again, a day when she would face the lurking shadows of her guilt, would determine what it meant. Not now. Not until Spencer was well.

Charles was waiting, too, she knew. He was subdued, considerate, concerned lest she overtax herself. But he seemed one of the shadows in the outer world.

Then Spencer lost his angelic patience, and began to fret humanly about lying flat in bed.

"A few more days, Spencer." Henrietta smiled at him. "Then this crack in your head will be healed enough."

"But I feel all right now."

Fear, retreating, dragged away the distortion it had given, and gradually the shadows about Catherine grew three-dimensional again. Henrietta warned her: "You'll have a frightful slump, Catherine, unless you let yourself down easily, after this strain."

"I don't feel tired, not at all."

"That's the trouble. And you are. Rest more. Spencer doesn't need you every second now. Let Charles sleep here to-night."

Catherine shook her head.

"I sleep fairly well here, because I know I shall wake if Spencer stirs. Anywhere else I should lie awake, listening."

"But he's safe now. I'm sure of that. The only danger, after the first, was infection. And that's past. Two more days and I'll let him up. I don't want you down." Henrietta paused, her fingers running along the black ribbon of her glasses. "When are you going back to work?" she flung out.

A subtle change in Catherine's face, like the quick drawing of shades at all the windows of a house.

"I don't know." She moved away from Henrietta, to glance in at Spencer.

"Um." Henrietta shrugged. "Well, I'll be in early to-morrow."

That was the first shadow to take real form. When *was* she going back to work? And behind the shades drawn against Henrietta moved a sharp curiosity. What had Dr. Roberts done about the investigation? There had been a note from him, tossed into a drawer. A note of sympathy. Had he said anything about the work? But as she made a faint motion to go in search of the note, Spencer called her.

Another shadow to grow more real was Miss Kelly. She had managed Letty with amazing competence, keeping her quiet and amused. She had come earlier in the morning than usual, to dress Marian and walk with her to school. But she was worried, shying away when she met Catherine in the hall, and her pale blue eyes stared with some entreaty in them. The day that Spencer first sat up, Charles carried him into the living room to the armchair, and Catherine tucked a rug about his feet and left him there, to look out of the window. As she went back to the bedroom, she heard a choking, muffled sound, and there in the hall stood Miss Kelly, her hands over her face.

"What is it?" she asked gently, touching the woman's shoulder. Then, as she looked at the swollen, reddened eyes, she knew. "He's quite well again," she said. "Don't cry."

"I—I hadn't left him a second," Miss Kelly whispered. "Just to help Letty down the steps."

"I know. I haven't thought you were careless."

"I thought I'd go crazy. He's never coasted in the street. The other boy thought of it."

"It was an accident, Miss Kelly. You mustn't blame yourself."

The entreaty faded under the flush of gratitude. Miss Kelly turned and hurried back to Letty's room, her square shoes clumping solidly.

CHAPTER VII

Saturday afternoon. Spencer was dressed, even to his shoes. Catherine had suggested moccasins, but Spencer held out for shoes. "Then I'll be sure, Mother, that I'm really up!" The terrifying pallor had left his face. The bandages were gone, too; just the pink, wrinkled mouth-like scar spoke audibly of the past weeks.

"You'll have to part your hair in the middle, Spencer," Dr. Henrietta had told him, "until this bald spot grows out." And Spencer had retorted, promptly, "I wouldn't be that sissy!"

Catherine moved one of her red checkers, smiled a little, wondering where he had picked up that idea, and glanced away from Spencer and checker board, out of the window. The bare trees of Morningside pricked up through gray mist; the distant roofs were vague. What a horrid day! It seemed too raw and cold for Spencer's first trip outdoors. But he really was well again. Monday he could go out. It was true, Henrietta's prophecy. She was being let down with a thud. There seemed no place where she could take hold of ordinary life again.

Spencer giggled.

"I jumped three of your men, Mother, and you never saw I could."

"Why, so you did." Catherine looked at her dismantled forces. She couldn't even keep her mind on those disks of wood. "There." She moved.

"Oh, Moth-er!" Spencer was gathering in the last of the red checkers. "You're a punk player. You're a dumb-bell!"

"What a name! Where did you find that word?" Catherine watched him; he was teasing her—that funny little quirk in his eyebrows.

"Oh, the fellers say it." Suddenly he swept the checkers into a heap. "I'm sick of checkers."

"Want to read a while?"

"I'm sick of reading. Staying in the house just wears me out, Mother."

The doorbell broke the quiet of the house, and Catherine, with a relieved, "Now we'll see what's coming!" went out to the door. Her mother, perhaps, or Margaret.

"Hello, Catherine." It was Bill, shifting a large package that he might extend his hand. She hadn't seen him since that night in Chicago. She had an impression of herself that night, confident, radiant, but vague and blurred, as if Bill showed her a faded photograph he had kept for years. "Henry said she thought I might call on Spencer," he was saying.

Catherine was grateful for the lack of inquiry. He would know that she had dropped everything in a heap, and that all the ends were tangled and confused. But knowing, he would ask her nothing, would not even indicate his knowledge.

"I've brought something for him." He jerked the arm which held the package.

"Spencer's in here." Catherine led the way to the living room. "Here's a caller for you," she announced.

"Hello, Mr. Bill!" Spencer lunged forward in his chair, but Bill set the box promptly before him.

"This table is just what we need. I thought you might help me with this radio." Bill shook himself out of his overcoat. And Catherine, with a smile at the sudden lifting of Spencer's clouds of ennui, left them.

There were things to be done. She might as well shake off her lethargy and attack them. She heard Spencer's eager voice, Bill's deliberate tones, pronouncing strange phrases—amperes, tuning up, wave lengths. The laundry. Prosaic, distasteful enough. If she began with that, she might find a shred of old habit which would start her wheels running.

She carried the bundles to her room, where she sorted the linen into piles on her bed. She had no list; she remembered Mrs. O'Lay at the door, last Monday, "The laundry boy's here, Mis' Hammond. Should I now just scramble together what I can put my hands on?" and her own indifferent answer. Five sheets. That seemed reasonable. And bath towels—that one was going. Catherine held it up to the light, poked her fingers through the shredded fabric, and tossed it to the floor. We need more of everything, she thought. Sheets—she stared at the neat white squares. If she unfolded them, probably she would find more shreds. Well, she wouldn't look! They cost so much, sheets and towels, and you had so little fun for your money. She stowed away the piles in the linen drawers. Then she opened the bundle of clothing, unironed, tight, wrinkled lumps. Mrs. O'Lay would iron them. Little undergarments, small strings of stockings. At least she didn't have to mend them; Miss Kelly was keeping them in order. She shook out a pajama coat; a jagged hole in the front whence a button had departed forcibly. She would have to mend Charles up. She chuckled; before she had gone away she had bought new socks for Charles, hiding those she had not found time to darn. He would never notice.

She was rolling a pair of socks into a neat ball, turning the ribbed cuff down to hold the ball, when she stopped. One finger flicked absently at a bit of gray lint. What was she going to do? She was sorting those clothes quite as if Mrs. O'Lay and Miss Kelly were fixtures. And she wasn't sure she had money enough to pay Miss Kelly for even one more week.

She piled away the clothing, dodging her thoughts. But when she had finished her task, she stood at the window, looking out at the court windows, and one by one her thoughts overtook her and assaulted her.

Of course I'm going back to the Bureau, the very day Spencer goes to school again. There's no new reason why I shouldn't. Isn't there? What about this feeling—that Spencer was a warning to me—a sign? That's what mother meant. Her hand lifted to her forehead, smoothed back her hair. That's not decent thinking, she went on. Absurd. Superstitious. Spencer might have been hurt even if I had been at his heels. Walter was hurt. Accidents—like a bony, threatening finger shaken at her!

"Moth-er!" Spencer's voice summoned her. Mr. Bill was going now, but he left the radio for Spencer to examine, and a book about it.

"An' he's going to see the superintendent about wires to catch things on, and we can't rig it truly until he gets a wire." Spencer clasped the book under one arm, and drew the black box nearer him along the table. "It's the most inturusting thing I ever saw, Mother." His eyes were bright with pleasure.

"I'm sorry," said Bill, "that we can't install it to-night. But perhaps to-morrow—"

Catherine went to the door with Bill.

"It was good of you to come in," she said. "He's had a dull time."

Bill had his hand on the knob.

"I've been out of town again for a week," he said. "Henry kept me posted."

Then he was going, but Catherine caught at his arm.

"Bill"—in a sharp whisper—"do you think it was my fault? Do you?"

"Catherine!" He was laughing at her, comfortingly. "What rot!"

"Is it?" She sighed.

"You're tired." His hand enclosed hers warmly for a moment. "Henry says you've been wonderful, but not wise—"

There was a clatter outside the door, a firm, "Now wait one second, Letty!" Bill pulled the door open; Letty, her pointed face framed in a red hood, Marian, pulling her tarn off her tousled dark hair, Miss Kelly behind them.

"Oh, Mr. Bill!" Marian hugged his arm, and Letty clambered onto her go-duck that she might reach his hand, with a lusty, "'Lo, Bill!"

"Come back and play with us, Mr. Bill," Marian cajoled him, her head on one side.

But Bill, grinning at her, eluding Letty's grasp, stepped into the elevator and was gone.

"'S'at Marian?" Spencer was shouting. "Oh, Marian, you come see what I got." Marian darted ahead. As Catherine, with Letty's damp mittened hand in hers, came to the door of the children's room, she heard Spencer determinedly, "No, you can't touch it! It's too delicut. Mr. Bill told me it was too delicut. You keep your hands off it! It's just lent to me."

"Who said I wanted to touch your ole radium?"

"It isn't radium, Marian. Radio. And you were touching it."

"Marian, dear, come take your wraps off." Miss Kelly had stowed Letty's go-duck in the hall closet, and followed Catherine. "You musn't bother Spencer."

"He's well now, isn't he?" She lagged into the bedroom.

Catherine sat on one of the cots, watching. She had scarcely seen her two daughters since she had come back. She had known they were well, she had heard Miss Kelly often sidetracking them with, "No, your mamma is busy and you mustn't disturb her. Poor little Spencer needs her and you don't." Miss Kelly had lifted Letty into a chair and was unbuttoning the red coat when Letty set up a strident wail, and stiffened into a ramrod which slid out from under Miss Kelly's fingers.

"Want my Muvver!" she shrieked. "Not you!" She flung herself on the edge of the bed beside Catherine, with gyrations of her red-gaitered plump legs. Catherine, laughing, dragged her up beside her. Letty snuggled against her, peering up with her blandishing smile.

"All right, old lady." Catherine tugged off the tiny rubbers, stripped down the knit leggings, noticing absently the promptness with which

Marian carried her own cloak and tarn to the closet and hung them away. Why, Miss Kelly had taught her to be orderly, she marveled. Then she saw Letty's expression of sidewise expectancy under long lashes. Miss Kelly was looking at her gravely.

"Letty tired." She drooped into Catherine's enclosing arm like a sleepy kitten.

"That's too bad." Miss Kelly was unruffled. "Then you can't show your mamma your own hook that you can reach."

Letty was quiet. Catherine felt the child's body stiffen a little from its kittenlike relaxation, as if her inner conflict was purely muscular, not thought at all. That's the way children must think, she speculated. With a giggle Letty slid down from the bed, hugged her arms about the pile of scarlet garments, and marched to the closet.

"I screwed a hook into the door, low down," Miss Kelly explained. "Usually Letty doesn't have to be told."

"And you don't allow her to beguile you, do you?" Catherine laughed at the self-righteousness in Letty's strut back to the bed.

"You can't," said Miss Kelly, "or they run all over you."

"What runs over you?" demanded Marian.

"Mice!" Letty's shriek was almost in Catherine's ear, as she plumped down in her mother's lap. "Mice!" and she wiggled in laughter. "Free blind mice."

"Isn't she silly!" But Marian giggled, too. "Who's that?" The hall door sounded on its hinges. "Daddy!" Her rush halted at the door. "Oh, I thought you were my Daddy!"

"Did you, now?" Mrs. O'Lay's red face hung a moment at the door, a genial full moon. "Well, I ain't. But you'd best be glad I ain't, for it's little dinner he'd be getting for you."

Marian stuck a pink triangle of tongue after her as she disappeared, clumping down the hall.

"She's awful fat, isn't she, Muvver?" She scuffled her feet slowly to the edge of the bed. "An' she has a funny smell. I don't know what she smells of, but she does."

"Ashes and floor oil," said Catherine. She hadn't noticed it, consciously. She caught Miss Kelly's surprised, disapproving glance. "We'll have to lengthen that dress, Marian," she concealed her amusement, and her free hand pulled at the edge of the chambray dress. "Can't pull it over your knees, can we?"

"I have let out the tucks in four dresses," said Miss Kelly. This was ground she knew. "But Marian is growing very fast."

Catherine's arm went around Marian's waist, and pulled her down at her side.

"Short dresses are the style, aren't they?" She hugged them both, Letty against her breast, Marian against her shoulder. Firm, warm, slim things, her daughters, growing very fast.

"What are you folks doing?" Spencer stood in the doorway, his eyes mournful. "I'm all alone."

"You've got your ole radium," declared Marian promptly, "and you're not sick any longer, even if I can see that cut, and our Muvver can stay with us now."

"Us now!" chanted Letty.

"Oh, you've sorted the laundry, Mrs. Hammond?" Miss Kelly turned from the opened drawer.

"Yes. I left a pile of clothes on a chair in Spencer's room—they need buttons."

"I thought I'd just lay out clean underwear for morning. Perhaps that shirt is with the pile." She went past Spencer, who drew aside with a touch of petulance.

"Suppose we all go into the living room." Catherine brushed Letty and Marian to their feet. "Daddy will be here soon, and we'll all have dinner together for the first time. Yes, Letty, too. It's a special occasion. Spencer's first full-dress day."

"Should I wash for dinner now, Muvver?" Marian still clung to her mother's arm. Catherine, looking down at the brown eyes, was disturbed. Marian was jealous of Spencer. She resented—oh, well, probably that was natural enough. Her legs outgrew her dresses, and her personality was growing as rapidly, shooting up, not wholly caught in civilized patterns.

"Can you keep your hands clean until dinner? Perhaps you might wait until Daddy has come. Run along, children. I want to speak to Miss Kelly a moment."

"What about, Muvver?"

"Business." Catherine was firm, and Marian's mood shifted quickly.

"Show Letty your ole radium," she said, dragging Letty after her, and Spencer pursued them in haste.

"You needn't stay for Letty's supper," said Catherine, as Miss Kelly returned. "You've been very kind to give me so many additional hours. And you certainly deserve to-morrow. It is several weeks, isn't it, since you've had Sunday?"

"That's all right, Mrs. Hammond." Miss Kelly laid the retrieved shirt on the dresser. "Of course, if you don't need me to-morrow." She looked at Catherine warily, her sandy lashes blinking, her nose still reddened from the afternoon. "You will want me next week?"

"Of course." Catherine frowned, a kind of panic whirring in her.

"I wondered. I didn't know. Something your mother said. I knew you needed some one for the children only if you were working."

"You must have misunderstood mother." The whirring deepened into fear, like wings, beating to escape the nets spread to catch her. They all expected her to abandon everything, to step back into the old harness. "Of course, I have made no plans, until Spencer was well. But next week"—she spoke out boldly, denying her own doubts—"next week I shall—" she did not finish that sentence. "At any rate, Miss Kelly, I should tell you in advance. I've just been admiring the way you are training the children. You are quite remarkable with them."

CHAPTER VIII

When Charles came in, Marian flew to meet him, flinging her arms about him as far as they would go, with little squeals of delight.

"Daddy, hello; we're going to have a party. Letty, too. Spencer can sit up at the table."

"I should say I could," broke in Spencer, indignantly.

He looks tired—Catherine smiled at him over Letty's yellow head. Sallow, discouraged. His glance withdrew quickly from hers, stopped at Spencer.

"How's the boy? Fine?"

"Daddy!" Marian pulled at his sleeve. "I thought of something. Let me whisper it."

And Catherine, while Letty slipped from her lap in an endeavor to learn what Marian was whispering, thought: it's a breaking off place, to-night. The interim is over.

"You'd better ask mother." Charles ruffled Marian's cropped head.

"No! A secret, Daddy!"

"Well. Ask Mrs. O'Lay, then."

"Tell Letty!" She pounded on his knee.

"Here, you!" He glanced again at Catherine, and his grin was suddenly like Spencer's. "That's no way to learn a secret. You wait."

Catherine's heart began to beat quickly. He is wretched about something, she thought. Bothered. But he wants to pretend. Marian whisked back, jumping about it. "It's all right! She says sure!"

"Then you wait at the door. Don't let them guess," and he stalked off, leaving Marian solemn in her delight, stationed at the door.

"Chwismas!" shouted Letty. But Marian shooed her out of the hall when Daddy returned.

Dinner had caught the slight tingling mood of a special occasion. Charles was deliberately jolly, and the children responded in expansive delight. Excitement moved pleasantly into Catherine, too, in spite of her sober, concealed thoughts. That other dinner, ages ago, with the children responsive then to the contention between her and Charles. The friendly enclosure of the room, with Letty at her left, Charles across from her, the other two—and Mrs. O'Lay waddling in and out. Above all, Spencer, safely clear of that dark threat.

"Well, it's the first time we've had a jolly dinner party for a long time, eh, Cathy?"

Ah, that was the thing she feared, ironically, under the bright surface, that Charles was building again; not a trap, exactly, nor a prison, but a net, a snare. This was to be proof, this scene, that they must have her, wholly. That her life dwelt only within such walls as these. That her desires, even, were held here. Her eyes were bright and troubled.

The secret came. Ice cream and chocolate sauce.

"Now it's a real party," sighed Marian, contentedly. "And I thought it up."

The telephone rang. Charles sprang to his feet, dropping his napkin as he hurried out.

"Why," asked Spencer, "does Daddy always have to hustle when the 'phone rings?"

"Because he has important business, because he's a man," said Marian, promptly.

"It might be for me." Spencer was hopeful.

"No!" Marian derided him. "Folks don't telephone little boys."

Astonishing. Catherine looked at Marian's calm profile. Where did she pick up her perfect feminine attitude? Instinct, or a parroting of some one, Miss Kelly, or her grandmother?

"Catherine!" Charles was calling. "Some one wants you."

"Now! It wasn't Daddy at all." Spencer was triumphant.

"Move along into the living room," said Catherine, rising. "Mrs. O'Lay is waiting to clear the table."

Then, as she sat down at the desk, she had a hasty, random thought. Stella Partridge hadn't called for Charles once these past weeks. Perhaps that hint of Henrietta's—Margaret's voice cut in.

"Hello! You back?" Catherine settled herself comfortably.

"Just in. Everything all right? I've been talking with Henrietta."

"Yes. Really all right. Spencer had a party to-night, his first dinner with the family."

"Could I see him to-morrow?"

"Of course. Where have you been, anyway? Mother was vague."

"Trip for the firm. To their factories in Boston and Pittsburgh. Cathy, what a shame your tour was interrupted! When do you go back?"

"You mean west again?" A little shock tingled through Catherine, quite as if, while she looked at a group of familiar thoughts, an outside hand shifted the spotlight, and at once a different color lay upon them, changing them.

"You hadn't finished the work, had you?"

"No." That was all Catherine could say.

"Well, Spencer's all right, isn't he?"

"Yes," heavily from Catherine. Silence for a moment. Then Margaret, forcefully:

"I'd like to come right out to-night. Don't be a fool, Cathy! I know just what's happened to you, old dear! Don't you let it! But Amy's waiting for me, and I'm starved."

Catherine stared at the round black mouthpiece. If she could hold that light Margaret threw over things—in which nothing looked the same. But she couldn't talk.

"I'll expect you to-morrow, then?" she asked.

"Yes. Early."

Charles was telling the children the story of the bantam hen he had owned when he was a little boy. Letty was curled up on his knees, Marian sat on the arm of his chair, his arm about her, Spencer had drawn his chair close.

"And I used to carry her around in the pocket of my coat, with just her head sticking out, and her bright shiny eyes and her yellow bill."

"Yellow bill?" murmured Letty.

"Just how big was she, Daddy?" Marian asked.

"I'd like a hen like that," said Spencer.

"Some day maybe we can live in a decent place, where we can have hens."

"And a dog, Father?"

"No, a kitty. A little gray soft kitty." Marian looked anxiously at her father. "I'd much rather have a kitty, Daddy."

"We might have both"—and as Letty opened her mouth wide and pink for a protest—"yes, and Letty could have a kitty or a dog or a pet hen. Well, my bantam's name was Mitty. One day—"

Catherine stepped softly away from the door. She could get Letty's bath ready. And she must transfer bedclothes. Spencer was to move into his own room again, and she had forgotten to ask Mrs. O'Lay to arrange the beds.

When she went in for Letty, the story had gone on to a dog. Mr. Bill's dog. He lived next door, Charles was explaining, and he was bigger than I was. His dog was shaggy.

Letty, protesting, came, full of incoherencies about dogs and kittens and chickens.

"Muvver, to-day Letty wants li'l dog an' li'l kitty an' li'l shickey."

"Not to-day. To-day's over. Now you are a fish." And Letty swam vigorously. Catherine stood beside her cot, looking down at her, fragrant, pink, beatific. A decent place to live in—with live things around them instead of city streets. A tiny, distant alarm clanged in her mind. That was what Charles had said, when he spoke of the offer at Buxton. Was he thinking about that, still? What *was* he thinking about!

Spencer had his bath, refusing her assistance with firm dignity. He was silent, standing at the door of his own room, a thin, pajamaed figure, looking at his own cot.

"You don't need me now at night, do you?" Catherine turned down the covers. "Here, hop in before you are chilly."

"I liked that other bed," said Spencer. "It's much softer."

"Nonsense!" Catherine laughed at him, tucked him in, kissed his cheek softly, not looking at the pink, wrinkled scar. "Same kind of springs. And you're well now."

"Will you be gone in the morning, Mother?"

His question halted her at the door.

"No, Spencer. What made you ask that?"

"I wanted to know."

She snapped off the light and closed his door.

Then Marian was bathed; scrubbing and spluttering, she repeated with funny little imitations of Charles's phrases, the stories about Mitty Bantam and Mr. Bill's dog.

Catherine opened the window to let the steam out of the bathroom, while she hung up limp towels and scrubbed out the tub and restored things to shining order. Her sleeve slipped down on her wet wrist, and she shoved it back impatiently. She'd like a drowsy, warm bath herself, and sleep, dreamless, heavy. But Charles was waiting for her. The interim was over. Pushing her hair away from her forehead with her habitual gesture, she went into the living room.

Charles looked up from his paper, smoke wreathing his face.

"This has been fine," he said, warmly. "Comfortable home evening."

Catherine sat down, brushing drops of water from her skirt.

"Hasn't it?" he urged.

"Well—" She was staring at her hands, blanched, wrinkled at the finger tips, by their long soaking. "If home is the bathroom!" Under her lowered eyelids she saw Charles watching her, guardedly. He set down his pipe with a click.

"If you feel that way!"

"Horrid of me to say it, wasn't it?" Catherine relaxed, her hands limp-wristed along the chair.

"I suppose you are tired. Awful strain, these last weeks."

"Perhaps I am." Catherine twisted sidewise in her chair and smiled at him. "But you look tired, too, poor boy. What have you been doing? I—why, I haven't seen you since I came back."

"You certainly haven't. But I didn't mind. Spencer—well, thank God, that's over!"

"Yes." Catherine discovered that she was so recently out from the distorting shadow of fear for Spencer that as yet she could not talk about it, as if words might have black magic to recall the fear.

"Damned lucky escape." Charles rammed tobacco into the pipe bowl with his thumb. He was thrusting out words in bravado, without looking at Catherine. He, too, had lived in that fear! He sucked vigorously, drawing the match flame down into the pipe. "What are you going to do now?"

The muscles of wrists and fingers leaped into tight contraction, and her hands doubled into fists against the chair.

"I haven't thought, until to-day." Then, suddenly,—better pour out everything. "Nothing has changed, has it, now that Spencer is well?"

"You plan to go back to the Bureau?"

"You mean that you think I should give it up?" Catherine stared at the hard, jutting line of his jaw, at his eyes, feverish, sunken. "Charles, you can't mean you blame me for Spencer's accident?"

"No." He spoke sharply, denying himself. "It might have happened anyway. I know that."

"Oh!" A long, escaping sigh. "If you had blamed me—I couldn't have endured it." And then, "It's hard, not to blame myself."

"That's just it." Charles moved forward, eagerly. "It's frightening. I thought you might feel, well, that you couldn't risk it. Leaving them. I want to be fair, Catherine."

"If you had been away, on a business trip"—Catherine was motionless except for the slow movement of her lips—"and this had happened, I should have sent for you. Would you have blamed yourself? Or given up your work? Oh, yes, I know you'll say that's different. It isn't so different. It wouldn't be, if you didn't make it so."

"Oh, my work." He settled back into his chair. "I've got to tell you things about that. I don't know how interested you are. You've been engrossed." He paused, but Catherine did not speak. "It does concern you! And it's a frightful mess." His eyes were haggard, angry, and his shoulders sagged in the chair with a curious, weary dejection, unlike their usual squared confidence. "I haven't told you. They didn't put me in as head of the clinic. The committee recognized the value of my work in organizing the clinic"—he was quoting, sneeringly—"but preferred to install a medical psychiatrist. You know it was decided last year, unofficially, that I was to be appointed the instant the funds were clear."

"What happened? Who is the head?" Pity extricated Catherine from her own floundering. She knew, swiftly, what had happened, as she remembered a sentence in that letter from Henrietta.

"A Dr. Beck. What happened? The usual thing. The doctors in the town stirred up the usual brawl. This was a medical clinic. No layman could manage it. Any fool with a year of anatomy could do better than a specialist. If you can cut off a leg or an appendix, you know instinctively everything about mental disorders or feeble-mindedness or anything else that touches psychology."

"But you had discussed that with the committee, and they—"

"They agreed with me last year. But they say they didn't realize popular opinion. There was underhanded play going on before I heard about it, and the thing was settled. I don't know just how. It's that feeling—doctors are all wise, established powers, mystic, and we scientists are new. If a man can cure the measles, he knows more about paranoia than I know!"

Catherine clasped her hands, pulses tingling in her finger tips.

"What has happened to Miss Partridge?" she asked.

A dull, brick-glow mounted in Charles's face—anger, or humiliation.

"Has she been ousted, too?" insisted Catherine.

"Dr. Beck has made her his assistant."

"But she's not a physician." Catherine lifted one hand to her throat, pressing it against the sharp ache there. Poor Charles, he had been pounded. If he would only tell her!

"No. But she's shrewd enough to see where her bread will be nicely buttered. She makes an excellent office girl. She—" He was defiant, aggressive. "You didn't ever like her. You'll probably be delighted to hear that she saw which way the wind blew, and even added some puffs of her own. Queering me. Flopping over the instant she saw her own advantage."

That little squirrel smile! And the faint, distinct, metallic ring in her clear voice! Catherine saw her in the dusk of that passageway behind the gymnasium, holding the brown leather bag. I'm soft, she thought, to have no pleasure out of this.

"Well?" demanded Charles. "You see where it leaves me. All this time wasted."

"At least you have the material for your book." Catherine was dispassionately consoling. "And you have that almost done."

"But I haven't. It's clinic material. I can't publish it now. It belongs to them."

"Charles!"

"Exactly. She did part of the work, Miss Partridge. She wants that for Dr. Beck. The committee wants the rest, for its clinic as at present established."

"That's outrageous."

"I could put out a book from my own notes. But it wouldn't mean anything. No authority behind it. No, I'm done with them. Done."

"At least"—Catherine felt slowly for words—"you have your university work. That's the main thing. That hasn't been touched."

"Hasn't it, though?" Charles was grim. "When I've spent all this time, on the score of a great contribution I was about to make!"

"Does it hang up your promotion?" Catherine cried out.

"It does. I heard that this morning, indirectly."

Catherine pulled herself to her feet and stood beside him, hesitantly brushing his hair, moving her finger down to the deep crease between his eyes.

"See here," she said, lightly. "You aren't so done for as all that. You know it."

He thrust his arm violently around her, drew her down to the arm of the chair, his head pressing into her shoulder.

"And you weren't here!" he cried. "There was no one—"

"Poor boy." Her hand touched his head, softly, sensitive to the crispness of his heavy hair.

"You haven't cared what happened to me." His words came muffled.

"Oh, haven't I?" Her fingers crept down to his cheek. "Perhaps I have."

"Haven't shown it much." He lifted his face from her shoulder.

In the instant before she bent to kiss him, there was a scurry of thoughts through her mind—leaves lifted in a puff of wind: He is contrite about Stella Partridge. He can't say that he is. He thinks I don't know about her. No use in airing that. He is through, and unhappy, and I love him.

"Let's not talk any more to-night," she said. "Lots of days coming to talk in. Spencer is well, and we are here, together."

CHAPTER IX

A square, rimmed in solid black, of something full of distant, colorless clarity. Not quite colorless, since an intense turquoise-blue seemed to move far behind it, like a wave. Catherine stared. She had come awake so suddenly that she could only see that square at first, without knowledge of it. Then, as suddenly, she knew. It was the sky, over the black rim of the opposite wall of the court, with window edges for its frame. Almost morning. What a strange dream, digging, trying to push the spade down through roots of dead grass, while someone kept saying, "Make it larger. That won't hold her." Had Spencer called out? Fully awake, she lifted herself on an elbow. The house was quiet. She could see dimly between her and the window the dark mound of Charles's head on his pillow.

That queer dream. As she lay down again, she had it, in a swift flash of association. The Actinidia vine! Bury an old hen at its roots, she had told Bill. She was digging, for herself. Oh, grotesque!

And yet, before she had slept, she had not thought of herself. She had worked patiently, tenderly, to restore Charles. She could hear him, humble, "You mean that, Cathy? You think this isn't a horrible failure? I couldn't prevent it, could I? After all—" and gradually she had drawn him clear of his forlorn dejection.

The patch of sky grew opaque, white. Morning.

There is no wall between us now, she thought. That is down. Love—tenderness—strength—sweet, fiery, ecstasy—all that he wished. Surely he would, in turn—lift her—into her whole self.

CHAPTER X

Charles had taken the children out for a Sunday afternoon walk. They wanted Catherine, too.

"The air will do you good, if you *are* tired," urged Charles.

"But Margaret is coming in." Catherine stretched lazily in her chair. "And I don't want to budge."

Charles had gone, resignation in his voice as he corralled the children out of the door. Catherine closed her eyes. She was eager to see Margaret, and yet a little afraid. She was too like an old scrap bag crammed with thoughts and feelings, tangled, unsorted; and Margaret would want to shake out the bag, sweeping away the jumble of contents.

Charles had said, that morning, "Queer, how down I felt yesterday. That pork roast Friday night was too heavy. Tell Mrs. O'Lay, will you, to go easy on the pork." And then, hastily, "Talking things out with you cleared the air, too. I can see I'd had an exaggerated line on them. I have a plan I want to talk over, some time soon."

Charles, restored, could call his malady pork! At the same time—Catherine rose hastily as the bell clattered. At the same time, she thought, walking down the hall, there had been gratitude, hidden, unspoken, and release in the feeling between them. That feeling was the air itself, intangible, invisible, but holding all these other things of shape or solidity. Charles was himself again, confident, assured, almost boisterous.

Margaret pounced at her, shook her gently, hugged her, marched her back to the living room.

"Fine! Everyone else is out. Now I can bully you." She dragged off her gloves. "You look as if you needed it, too," she said. She leaned forward abruptly and touched Catherine's hand. "Spencer! Oh, it has been awful, I know," and surprisingly her eyes grew brilliant with tears. "But he's honestly not hurt, is he? Henrietta swore he wasn't."

"Honestly all right," said Catherine.

"I wanted to come back, but Henry wired me I couldn't do a thing. So I stuck to the job." She moved restlessly. "And Henry swears there's no danger of any future complication. I worried about that. Spencer's not the sort I want changed by any knock on his head."

"No." Catherine shivered. "They all say there is absolutely no danger."

"Well." Margaret was silent a moment.

She had to say that, to be rid of it, thought Catherine.

"But I know what you've been up to." Margaret's tears were gone. "Wallowing in sentimental regrets. Listening to mother suggests that you must surely see your duty now. And the King, too! Just when I was so proud of you, and using you for an example of what a woman really could do, could amount to, and everything." She laughed. "Don't be a renegade, Cathy."

"Pity to spoil your example, huh?"

"Exactly. Have you seen your boss since you came back? I thought not. Cathy, go and see him. Dress up and go down to your office. Drag yourself out of your home, sweet home, long enough to remember how you felt. If you'll promise that, I won't say another word. Psychological and moral effect, that's all."

"I don't want to see him until I make up my mind."

"It isn't your mind you are making up. It's"—Margaret waved her hand—"it's your sentiment tank. Oh, I know. I have a soft heart, myself, Catherine."

"There's another thing." Margaret had turned her upside down, as she had feared, and she was hunting feverishly in the scattered contents of her scrap-bag self. "Charles." Reticence obscured her. "He's been disappointed about that clinic. He does need—"

"Anybody," declared Margaret with quick violence, "anybody needs somebody else loving 'em, smoothing 'em down, setting 'em up, brushing off the dust. I know! But you can do that anyway. That just goes on—"

"I wonder. You're a hard-boiled spinster, Margaret. What do you know about it?"

"I know a little thing or two about love. You do it all the time, through and around whatever else you are doing. Not from nine to five exclusively." She settled back, a grimace on her lips, as the door rattled open and Letty's piping was heard. "Didn't stay long, did he? You promise me you'll go down to the Bureau. Quick! Or I'll fight with the King like a—"

"Yes, I'll go down." Catherine laughed. "I'd have to anyway."

And Margaret, smiling at her, ran out to meet Spencer.

CHAPTER XI

Catherine sat at the dining room table, staring down at the straggling columns of figures on the sheet of yellow paper. Her mouth was sullen, mutinous. Mrs. O'Lay came through the hall, her broom swishing behind her. She had been redding up the study, and Catherine had moved her bookkeeping into the dining room. Well, there it was. Appalling totals. Bills and bills and bills. She ran her fingers across the ragged edges of her checkbook stub. No hope there. Then her hand crept past the bills to a long white envelope, bearing the Bureau inscription in one corner. Her check in full for the month, as if she had stayed in Ohio and finished the job. Charles's eyebrows, lifted inquiringly when Miss Kelly had appeared that morning, seemed to arch across her name on that envelope. She had only to take out that slip of paper, scrawl her name and "on deposit" across the back, and she was committed. Last night—Charles clinging to her hand—"It's wonderful, Cathy, having things right again. Don't spoil them." And she cravenly had kept silence.

She looked again at the final figures in her check book. Tiny, impotent sum. Her mind busily added to them the figures of the check. But she couldn't take it, unless she meant to go on. Dr. Roberts intended it as an indication of her permanence, a check for the full month, when she had worked only half of it. Her fingers rested on the slip. The bills, the paltry little balance, worked on her in a sort of desperate fever.

I'd have to give up Mrs. O'Lay, too, she thought, to even things. There'll be doctors' bills. That surgeon. Everything's overdrawn. Have to tell Miss Kelly.

She saw herself vividly walking that treadmill. Poor Charles; he had expected some release, financially, from the clinic and his book. Wonderful, having things right—don't spoil them.

She rose quickly, bunching together the devastating bits of paper. She had to see Dr. Roberts, at least. No use trying to think. Her mind was a jellyfish. Perhaps if she saw him, and talked with him, something with a backbone would rise up to rout the jellyfish.

"I may not be in for luncheon," she told Mrs. O'Lay. "But you can manage."

"Sure, you look elegant." Mrs. O'Lay replaced the cover on her kettle of soup. "An' a breath of air will do your heart good."

It did, Catherine discovered. She had been housed too long. Clear, bright, gusty, with bits of paper swirling along the stone wall of the Drive, and sharp white wave edges rushing across the river. Too cold for the top of the bus. She watched the river through the window, and then the shops on the side streets. She was empty, except for bits of external things touching her eyes. Straw hats in the windows, and bright feathers; why, spring would come, soon.

The elevator boy grinned at her widely, ducking his bullet head.

"How'do. Ain't seen you round here for quite some time."

That old thrill of belonging to the building—that woman in furs stepping off at the dentist's floor was eying her curiously—the thrill of expanding into part of this complicated, intricate, impersonal life.

Her office again, long, narrow, caging the sunlight between its shelved walls, and the stenographer rising in a little flurry. "I'll call Dr. Roberts. He was expecting you, I think."

Catherine looked out of her window. No one in the fitting room opposite; she could see the sweep of draped fabrics.

"Mrs. Hammond! I am delighted to see you."

Dr. Roberts bustled toward her, his bearded face cordial, his gestures animated, fidgety. "I wondered how soon you would be in. I should have called you soon. Your little boy has recovered?"

"Yes." Catherine sat down.

"Such a pity. Poor little chap. And calling you back. I must tell you how admirable your investigation is. We've had several letters from people whom you met. You handled them admirably, interested them without antagonizing them. Well, you are ready now to finish the tour?"

"You have sent no one else?" Catherine was cold. That jellyfish in her head was a flabby lump left by the tide.

"No. I want you to go back." His eyes, small, keen, searched hers.

She sighed faintly.

"I can't do it." She was startled at the finality in her own words. "I can't go away, Dr. Roberts. Not—again."

He showed no surprise.

"Your letters," he suggested. "They sounded enthusiastic."

"It was fascinating." There was pain in the folding down of her long eyelids. "But I can't go away. I—" she smiled briefly. "I've lost my nerve. I can't risk what might happen."

"The children, you mean?"

"Yes."

"Um. A pity. Accidents happen, anyway. But of course you have thought of that." He drummed busily with his fingers along the desk.

Catherine straightened her shoulders. She could think clearly now; evidently the jellyfish had existed just for that one decision.

"I had hoped there wouldn't be a chance for me to go away again. I thought you might have sent someone else, and that you'd want me here in the office. You see—the glimpse I had of the real colleges gives enormous vitality to all these catalogues. I'd like to go on, if I could do it right here."

When had she thought that? Astonishing, the way ideas burst out from some deep level, and you recognized them as authentic.

"A pity." Dr. Roberts clasped his hands, twisting his fingers in and out. Here's the church, and here's the steeple, thought Catherine, as if she played the finger game for Letty. "I was afraid of it. But if you will come back, handle the work here—I like the way you write up the material." He clapped one palm on the desk. "Let me think it over. I suppose I might finish the trip myself. I am free now—those meetings have come off."

"There's this check." Catherine took it out of her handbag. "For a month, at the new rate."

"I think that will be satisfactory. It's gone into the budget, your salary, I mean. I don't think the President will suggest cutting it. Not if I make the trip myself. Let me think it over. No, the check is yours."

Just after twelve, by the jeweler's sidewalk clock. She could reach home for luncheon. But she didn't want to! She turned out of the entrance and moved along, graceful, deliberate, toward the cross street and Amy's club.

The housekeeper nodded to her. There were women in a group near the fire, one or two heads turning toward her; no one there who knew her. She sat alone at a small yellow table in a corner of the dining room. She was earlier than her usual hour. That was why she saw none of the women she had talked with. She did recognize several of the faces. Bits of gossip collected about them, highly colored pieces of personal comment, which Amy had thrown off in her intense, throaty voice. That woman who was just seating herself, dropping her heavy, squirrel-lined great coat over her chair, was a successful physician; makes thirty thousand at least. Has to have a young thing adoring her—yes, there's the present young thing, with a sleek bobbed head like a child's, and round, serious eyes. Secretary, housekeeper, chauffeur, slave! Catherine could hear Amy's satiric list. And the two women at the table beyond. Catherine bent over her salad, while the women in the room retreated to some great distance, carrying the bits of gossip like cockleburrs stuck to their garments. It's funny, thought Catherine. I never saw it before. But it is always how they love—how they live—not what they think. Even when Amy talks about them. Even these women.

Her thoughts ran on, clearly. She had wished to lunch there, because she needed something to orient herself, to deliver her out of the smother of her life and all its subtle, intimate pressures of love. She wanted to see women in terms of some cold, dignified, outer achievement. And instead, her mind clattered about them with tales of their lovers, their husbands, their emotional bondage.

Well, was that her fault, her own prepossession? Or Amy's? From Amy had come these irritating recollections. Or was it that women were like that, summed up in personal emotions? She drew on her gloves and left the club rooms.

She would walk up the Avenue and across Central Park. They were having lunch at home, now, Charles, the children. Sometimes in walking her feet seemed to tread thoughts into smoothness; or the swinging rhythm of her body shook some inner clarity up through confused images where she could see it, could lay hold of it.

What was she trying to think about, anyway? Women? Herself? Herself and Charles. And the children.

Men had personal lives, too. But didn't they make them, or try to make them, comfortable, assured, sustaining, so that they could leave them? Find them when they came back? And women having had nothing else, still centered there? She stopped in a block of traffic, looking about with eyes strained and vague.

Petulant, smug faces above elegant furs. Hard streaks of carmine for lips. Faces with broad peasant foreheads, with beak noses. Faces—

The rush carried her across the street. Letty and Marian, her daughters, growing up.

If I knuckle under now, she thought, what of them? She could feel them pressing against her, Letty's silky head under her throat, Marian's firm, slim body against her arm. What I do can't matter very much, directly, to them. They have to live, themselves. She was humble, feeling their individualness, their growth as a curious progression of miracles in which she was merely an incidental tool. Women devote themselves to their families, so that their daughters may grow up and devote themselves to their families, so that—Catherine laughed. Some one has to break through that circle, she thought.

She entered the Park, walking more slowly along the winding path. If she had only sons—the thought of Spencer stood up like a straight candle flame in her murky drifting—that would be different. There was her own mother. Catherine could see her, being wheeled along the beach at Atlantic City, with her friend, Alethea, on a little holiday to recover from the shock of Spencer's accident. How does she manage it, that poise of hers, that sufficiency?

The walk had come to a cluster of animal houses. Catherine looked about her, and on a sudden whim went past the attendant into the monkey house. The warm, acid, heavy odor affronted her. She didn't want to be here. Years ago she had come in, before she married. She turned to go, and met the melancholy flat stare of a small gray monkey. The animal clung to the bars of the cage with one hand, the long, naked fingers moving restlessly, and looked at Catherine, while the fingers of the other hand dug pensively into the fur of her breast. Catherine felt her heart pause; she had a sensation of white excitement, as if she hung poised over an abyss of infinite knowledge, comprehension. A second monkey swung chattering across the cage and dropped from the bar, grabbing at the tail of the monkey that stared, and the moment was gone. Catherine went hastily out into the clear, sweet air. I hate them, she muttered, and hurried away across the brown, dead stretches of park. But she could not escape the vivid recollection of that earlier visit, years ago. She had seen then a female monkey nursing her young, and the pathos of the close-set unwinking eyes over the tiny furry thing had made the curve of long monkey arm a symbol of protective mother instinct.

They're too like us. That's why I hate them. And then, fiercely, men have climbed out of that. Some ways. But they want to keep us monkey women. Loving our mate and children. Nothing else.

She came presently to a stretch of water at the other side of the park, and stopped a moment on the shore. Blue, quiet, with long black reflections of trees from the opposite bank.

My mind has made itself up, she thought. Her pallor and sullenness had given place to an intense vitality in her wide, dark eyes, in the curve of her mouth. It isn't selfishness, nor egoism, this hankering of mine. It's more than that. I'll tell Charles—she laughed softly, out of the wholeness of her release from doubt—I'll tell him that I can't be a monkey woman. He'll help me. He must help me.

CHAPTER XII

She waited until the children were asleep and the house was quiet. Then she knocked at the study door, behind which Charles sat, working on a lecture. She scarcely waited for his "Come" but went in swiftly, closing the door.

"Most through work?" She drew a small chair near his desk. "Why, you aren't working." His desk was orderly, bare.

"Not just now." Charles leaned back. "I—" he hesitated. "You look stunning in that get-up," he finished.

"Yes?" Catherine's smile lingered. "It's not the get-up. It's me, inside."

"Handsome wife." Charles touched her fingers, spreading them wide between his own fingers, crumpling them together in a sudden violent squeeze. Then he leaned back again. "Just been thinking about you," he said.

"Yes? So've I." Vivacity in Catherine's voice, her gesture, a vivacity which had true life from deep inner light, not an external manner. "I wanted to talk to you."

"I've been wanting to talk things over with you." Charles looked away from her somberly. "For some time."

"It's about next year," continued Charles slowly, and Catherine thought, I'll leave the monkeys out, at first. "Our plans, you know."

Something arrested Catherine at the edge of speech, something like the damp finger of air from a cellar.

"I should have brought it up before you went downtown," he was saying. "You were down this morning, weren't you?"

She nodded.

"I didn't realize you were going. And anyway, to-day sort of brought matters to a head."

"Yes?"

"Well, it's my job. I went in to see the Head, to-day." Charles faced her, his eyes deprecating. "You gave me nerve to do that, Cathy. I'd been knocked so confoundedly hard—but I felt better to-day. That's you." Catherine's hands clung together in her lap. "I wanted to have exact data on where I stood. The trouble is, this place is too big. I mean the institution, not my own job. There are too many men eager for a foothold. The Chief was rather fine about it—about my work, especially. Praised it. You know. But he said I'd stepped somewhat out of rank, going abroad. Two men are ahead of me, in line for promotion. Can't have too many professors. Isn't room. All that guff, you know what it is." Charles brought his fist down on the desk. "I should like to get to a place where I can march ahead as fast as I can go. I talked over the whole situation with him, including the Buxton offer." His eyes were suddenly wary, inquisitive. "You remember that, of course? And he agreed with me."

"He advised you to leave the University?" Catherine heard her own voice, like a thin wire.

"He agreed that the chance for advancement, for future accomplishment, lay there rather than here."

"And you wish to go?"

"I had another letter to-day from the president there. It's a remarkable place, Cathy. Small, but endowed to the neck. A few of those small colleges are, you know. I'd have the entire department in my hands, with freedom to work out anything I liked. They want a strong department. Want a good man to build it up." His wariness, his searching of her face had dropped away in a rush of genuine enthusiasm. His words ran on, building the picture, his work, his opportunity. Then he switched, suddenly. "And the place is fine, too. Pretty little town, college community. Wonderful place for the children. The other night, as I told them about my childhood, I felt we had no right to imprison them here. It isn't decent. Shut up in a city, when they are just growing up. Do you think so? All this awful struggle to stretch our income, too. That would be over. More salary, almost twice as much. Living conditions infinitely better. Pleasant people to live near."

"When you got your appointment at the University here, you thought it was perfect. The institution, the city. Do you remember how you felt?"

"It did seem so, didn't it? But you have to watch a thing work out."

"You are sure you are judging Buxton fairly, and not in the light of what's happened in the clinic?"

"I've been thinking about it for months. I spoke about it in the fall—" He stopped suddenly, and Catherine saw the phantom that he had evoked:

his own voice, harsh, "I think I'll take that Buxton offer, just to get you out of town," and her own answer, thrown back as she fled, "You'd have to be sure I would go!"

"I can't decide it alone," he went on hastily. "I'm just trying to show you how it looks to me."

"But you have decided." Her effort to keep her voice steady flattened all its intonations. "Decided that it is much the best thing for your career, much the best for the children."

"I can't drag you off unless you wish to go. I hoped you would like it, too. It—well, it is something of an honor, you know. The way they keep after me. There's a large appropriation for a laboratory. I'd have very little teaching. They seem to have some idea of a creative department."

Catherine was silent. There was something shaking and ludicrous, in the way that courageous light of afternoon had been snuffed out. Why, she had thought she stood at last in a clear road, where she could be sure of direction, and here she was only at the core of the labyrinth again, knocked blindly into an angle of blind wall.

"Catherine!" he cried out against her silence. "If it wasn't for this damned idea of yours, you'd care what happened to me!"

Whirling about in the lane of her labyrinth, shutting her eyes to its maze. "I do care, Charles. That's the trouble."

"After all, it's not just me. It's the children and you, isn't it?" He fiddled with the blotter, shoved it along the desk. "I think it will be infinitely better for you, too." His chin was obdurate. "New York is no place. Overstimulates you. At a place like Buxton, life is more normal. There's a woman's Faculty Club," he added, triumphantly.

Catherine laughed.

"Teas?" she said, "or literary afternoons?"

"They're fine women. Cathy, don't laugh. I hoped you would like it."

"Like it?" She flung out her hands, sensitive, empty palms upwards. "I've just been there! I know what it is like. But I know"—she was sober again—"why, there's nothing for me to do but say yes, is there? I can't say that Buxton offers me no opportunity, except to be a monkey woman, can I?"

"What?"

"Nothing." She doubled a fist against her mouth, and stared at him.

"You've been so sweet these last days." Charles reached for her hand, held it between both of his. "Things were ghastly mixed up, and then we seemed straight again, you and I. You know everything's been wrong since you first took that damned office job. I can't stand it! Our yapping at each other. I hoped you would want to throw it over. I do care about your being happy. Cathy, if you believe, honestly, that it's more important that you should stay here, I'll try to see it that way."

Her hand was reluctant, cold, in the warm, steady pressure of his.

"I can't believe it, alone." The labyrinth shut her in, black, enclosing. "You'd have to believe it, yourself. And you don't."

"It's different, considering the children, too, as well as you and me. What you do, in an office, takes you away from me. What I do, Cathy, that is yours, too, isn't it?"

His fingers crept up about her wrist; beneath them her life beat in heavy, slow rhythm.

"It knocks the stuffing fairly out of everything, if I think you don't care."

"Yes. It does that for me, too." Catherine smiled at him in a flicker of mockery. She caught a faint slackening of his fingers. Stella Partridge! But she knew, even in the impulse to have that out, to insist upon it as part of the winter, that it was better left untouched. Intangible, incomplete, a kind of subtle aberration, it would dissolve more quickly unexpressed.

"I'd be a beast to say I wouldn't go. A perverted, selfish wife. Wouldn't I? I can't be that. I'm too soft. Charles, I do desire for you every chance—"

"You're not soft. You're really fine. You—" He jumped to his feet. "And when we get out there, you'll see. You'll like it! Lots of things for you to do. You will be happy, Cathy. I'll make you happy."

Catherine, leaning back in her chair, lifted her face to look up at him. She heard in his voice the shouting down of fear; he had been worried, then. He had not been sure.

CHAPTER XIII

Catherine sat on the window sill, looking down at the shadows which slanted across the tree tops of Morningside. In the distance roofs still glittered in the afternoon sunlight. Beneath her the spring leaves were delicate and small, keeping their own fine shape, not yet making green masses. A little easterly breeze touched her warm cheek, and she thought, leaning from the window, that she sniffed in it the faint piquancy of Balm of Gilead buds. The last trunk was banging down the hall, its thuds like muttered profanities.

She turned back to the dismantled rooms. How queer they looked, small, dingy, worn. Mrs. O'Lay, in the kitchen, was assuring Charles: "Sure and you needn't worry yourself about that, Mr. Hammond. I'll clear out every stick. Them little things I've saved for myself. I can make use of them."

She was cramming things into the dumbwaiter. Catherine could hear the rustling of waste paper.

Catherine stood up, cautiously. She was stiff, almost dizzy, as if she had bent so long over packing boxes and trunks that her head couldn't without penalty be held upright. Well, it was done. Incredible and astonishing, that the disorder and confusion had come to an end.

"All ready, dear?" Charles stood in the doorway, buttoning his coat, patting his tie into place. "About time we got off."

"Be sure there is nothing left." Catherine went slowly through the rooms, listening to the walls return her footsteps emptily.

In the kitchen Mrs. O'Lay poked among the salvage, bundles, piles, an old black hat of Catherine's mounted rakishly on a box of breakfast food, a dingy cotton duck of Letty's, limp from loss of stuffing.

"I'll finish up here, Mis' Hammond." The broad red face was creased into downward wrinkles. "Sure, an' I hate to see the end of you," she said. "It's fine for you you got a tenant to come in right away, but we'll miss you."

"Taxi, Catherine!" shouted Charles.

"Good-by, God love you!" Mrs. O'Lay waved her out of the apartment onto the elevator.

"Well, we certainly got things off in great style, eh?" Charles beside her in the cab, the bags stowed at their feet, had his erect, briskly managing air. "Everything done, and time for dinner before your train."

Catherine was sunk in a lethargy of weariness; dimly she still sorted, packed, gave directions.

"You know, I forgot about the gas deposit." She emerged frantically from her lethargy. "Five dollars!"

"I'll see to it. Where's the receipt?"

"Let's see—in that envelope. I'll mail it to you. It was good of mother to take the children until train time, wasn't it?" Catherine sighed.

"I tell you, it was a lucky thing we got the apartment off our hands before fall." Charles patted her knee cheerfully. "Awful job, if we'd had to pack up at the end of the summer."

"Awful job any time!"

"Oh, well, a week in Maine will make you forget it all. Especially with the rent off our chests."

"You'll surely come in three weeks?"

"Positively. That finishes up everything. And I'll have to get away then if I'm to have any vacation. Say, be sure to tell old Baker he's got to take me down to the ledges for some real fishing. I haven't fished for two years, except for flounders."

"And Buxton the first of August?"

"Be hot there in August, won't it? Well, I'll have to go then. But I can find a house for us, and sort of learn the ropes before you blow in."

"I wonder—" Catherine's brows met in a deep wrinkle. "I can't remember which trunk I put the blankets in, and the linen. Hope they aren't labeled Buxton!"

"Oh, you got them where they belong. Don't fuss, I tell you. You let me drop you at the Gilberts' now, and I'll go on to the station. I can check these things, and that will give you a few minutes to rest."

"I don't care where you drop me." Catherine laughed. "All my poor mind does is to hunt for things in those trunks and boxes."

"You might as well stop worrying. They're settled."

Catherine stood at the entrance to the hotel, watching the taxi jerk its way along with the traffic. Charles's hand lay on the opened window, a resolute, capable fist. Every one was going home. Home from work. Shop girls in gay tweeds, already faded across the shoulders; sallow, small men in baggy trousers, with bits of lint sticking to them, from the lofts where they sewed—perhaps on more gay tweed suits, or beaded silk dresses for the trade. Moist, pale faces, with a startled, worn expression, as if the warmth of the day surprised and exhausted the city dwellers. And in Maine—a sharp visual image of pointed firs reflected in clear water, with a luminous twilight sky behind dark branches.

"Ought to be glad I'm going," she thought. "Instead of spending the summer here, with these people. And the children—I couldn't keep them here. Could I!"

Henrietta's maid admitted her to the quiet, orderly living room. Dr. Gilbert was in her office. She would be free soon. Catherine sat down at the window, looking idly out at the great steel framework which shadowed the room. How long ago she had looked down into pits of water and uncouth shapes of cranes! New Year's Day. And Henry had said, "You'd be a fool not to go."

The methodical arrangement of the room was restful, sane, after the hurly-burly of the last week. Distressing that confusion could so fray the edges of yourself. She closed her eyes, relaxing into a kind of blankness.

She opened them presently, to find Henrietta in the doorway, staring through her eyeglasses, her mouth firm and compassionate.

"Hello!" Catherine moved hastily erect. "Don't turn that professional stare on me. I won't have it."

"Hoped you were asleep." Henrietta came in. "Bill hasn't shown up yet. Perhaps we'd better go down to the dining room. Your train is so beastly early. Where's Charles?"

"Checking the trunks. He'll be in soon."

As they waited for the elevator, Catherine turned suddenly upon Henrietta.

"You know, Henry, I appreciate your not telling me what you think. I suppose you're disgusted, and you haven't said a word. Not since I told you we were going."

"Not disgusted." Henrietta thrust her eyeglasses between the buttons of her jacket. "I've been rather cut up about it. But it's your affair. I don't see that you could do anything else. Not now, at any rate."

"Perhaps some women could. I can't."

"Women can't alone." Henrietta sounded violent. "Not without men helping them. Being willing to help them. So long as their own affairs come first—"

The door of the elevator swung open.

"When Mr. Gilbert comes in, tell him we are at dinner. And Mr. Hammond, too."

"Yes, ma'am."

Henrietta nodded to the waiter, who led them into an alcove off the main dining room.

"Quiet in here." Henrietta settled herself briskly. Catherine was thinking: Henrietta manages her life so that things, mere things, never get in her way—laundry, or food, or packing. "I wanted to see you make a go of it," said Henrietta. "You're so darned intelligent. It's the children, I know. If it weren't for them, you could stay here. If you would. Probably Charles would pull you along by a heartstring even then. Now, Bill— But I'll let him speak for himself. He has some news."

"Perhaps"—Catherine did not glance up—"perhaps, Henry, I've just been knocked flat at the end of the first round. Who knows? I may get my wind back—in Buxton."

"What can you do in a country town?"

Catherine did not answer; Charles was coming toward them, buoyant, touched with excitement, and behind him, Bill. Charles tucked the checks into her purse.

"I'll mail these others to the Dean," he said. "Great place we're going to. The Dean himself has offered to see to our chattels. Going to store them in some building on the campus until we come. Real human beings in Buxton!"

Catherine looked silently at Bill, as he took her hand for a brief moment. She hadn't seen him for weeks; he had been out of town again. His glance was grave, a little pleased.

"Tell them your news, Bill."

"Oh"—he shook out his napkin—"I'm off to South America next week, to build a bridge."

Henrietta explained. Huge engineering project, throwing a link across mountains, a road for commerce. Difficult enough to interest even a clam like Bill.

Catherine listened rather vaguely; Bill was moving his knife, his salt, his roll, to illustrate. Saves hundreds of miles in shipping, you see, if the thing can be done. A straight line from the interior.

"How long will it take?"

"Can't tell exactly until I see the ground. Perhaps a year. Or longer."

Catherine flung her glance at Henrietta, and found her watching Bill, her blue eyes calmly reflective. Not a trace of dispute, not a faint echo of bitterness, although Henrietta was looking less at Bill than back into whatever secret, intimate hour of decision lay behind the present announcement. This was what Henrietta had meant. That Bill would go alone if he wished, not for an instant expecting Henrietta to drop her life and follow.

"And you're just staying here?" Charles was naïve, surprised.

"Naturally." Henrietta grinned at him. "I can't move my practice. It's a long time, but perhaps one of us can wriggle in a vacation."

"Well!" Charles leaned back. "If my wife—" he broke off, suspiciously.

"Henrietta might reasonably object to being deserted," said Bill quietly. "But she's good enough to see why I wish to go."

Charles paused an instant over that, and then with a shrug came out on clear, safe ground with a question about the work. Catherine listened. She was tired. Her thoughts crawled obscurely, undirected, in a fog of weariness. Charles would pull her along by a heartstring, Henrietta said. Probably. She lacked that cold singleness which Henrietta kept. But Bill never tried to pull Henry by a heartstring. He hid away from her.

"You're not eating a thing, Cathy," said Henrietta. "Too much packing, I suppose. I hope you'll loaf for a while. Do you have the same woman who took us for peddlars?"

"I think so." Catherine stared out of her fog.

"Amelia will have the house opened and ready. Catherine can loaf all summer." Charles was hearty, assured. "It's been a hard winter, some ways."

The talk went on, with coffee and cheese, and Catherine drifted again in her fog. Perhaps one person always hides away. Bill had said something about that, once. In every combination of people, one hides. But if you hide away, then you shouldn't sulk. Play fair.

Dinner was over. Time to go. Henrietta, regretfully, explained that she couldn't go to the station. A case. Bill would walk over.

"I shall miss you, Cathy." They stood at the entrance of the hotel. "And the children. Bill gone, too. I'll have to work like fury."

"You must come out to Buxton when we're settled. Take a week off." Charles glanced at his watch, edged toward the street.

"I may." Henrietta's lips, firm and cool, touched Catherine's. "Good-by."

"We'd better walk fast," said Charles. "I have to get the bags out of the parcel room."

"Want a taxi?" Bill lifted his hand, but Catherine refused.

"It's only three blocks. Let's walk."

At the corner entrance of Grand Central, Charles darted ahead, with a hasty, "Meet you at the clock. You find Mother Spencer and the kids."

Catherine drew a long breath and looked up at Bill.

"South America," she said. "Mountains. And you are really keen about it?"

"It sounds good, don't you think?" He pushed open the heavy door for her. "Too bad we can't have dinner on some mountain peak." He smiled down at her. "What would they give us? Hot tamales, or are those Mexican?"

"South America—and Buxton," said Catherine.

"There is Spencer." Bill took her arm and swung her out of the path of a laden porter. "And the others."

"I hope it will be wonderful, Bill. And I'm not done for, not yet." Catherine could see the children, Letty with round eyes and her doll hugged under one arm, Marian jiggling on her toes with delight.

"I hope that you—" What he would have said, Catherine did not know, for Marian had seen them and hurled herself upon her mother with a burst of staccato excitement. But Catherine had met, for a clear instant, in a lifting of Bill's somber impersonality, a kind of dogged, sympathetic challenge.

"Oh, Mother!" Spencer had his fingers around her arm. "I began to think you weren't coming!"

"Margaret's here somewhere." Mrs. Spencer clung to Letty's hand. "Buying you magazines, I think. Where is Charles?"

"Here's the King." Margaret came up with him. "Hello, Mr. Bill."

"The guard will have to let me through the gate," announced Charles severely, "to settle these bags for you."

"Oh, Cathy!" Margaret whisked to Catherine's side. "We're coming up to see you in Maine, Amy and I. In our own car! Want us?"

"I shall probably stop in Buxton on my way back from George's," said Mrs. Spencer, as she pushed Letty and Marian toward the gate. "I wish you weren't going so far"—she sighed—"but as I've said, I think it's just the place for you all."

Charles was impressing the guard, successfully, so that he did step through, Spencer beside him tugging at a handbag. A flurry of good-bys, and Catherine, with Letty and Marian clinging to her hands, followed him upon the platform. She turned for a last glimpse. Margaret, her bright hair flying, was waving at them; Mrs. Spencer dabbed softly at her cheeks with her handkerchief; Bill—no, Bill had turned away. There, he was waving, too. Marian waggled her handkerchief. Charles called behind her, "Come along, Cathy, your coach is halfway down the track."